AMIAH'S VISIONS
A Paranormal Romance

WENDA S PARSONS

*

**This novel is
dedicated to GOD.
It is also dedicated to
my mother Roslis,
my younger sister Wanda
my father William
and all my amazing
readers.**

*

CONTENTS

Introduction & Useful terms.

1. Amiah and the Amiah Riders.
2. Riding into the unknown.
3. Spying for R135.
4. One crazy night.
5. For the love of Landon.
6. Invisible.
7. Never alone.
8. The Onai twins.
9. Party with a purpose.
10. Party theatrics.
11. The alien shaman.
12. Mystery cosmos.
13. Sexy visions.
14. Trust no one.
15. Fallen rider.
16. Wait and see.
17. Ex-lovers.
18. Drop it.
19. Hidden passions.
20. A higher power.

Connect with the author/Other books.

INTRODUCTION

AMIAH'S VISIONS
A Paranormal Romance novel.

In the year 2224 onward.

Amiah Lily seems to have it all good.

She is young, beautiful and powerfully gifted in psychic and paranormal abilities. Amiah is the leader of the highly successful, all-female paranormal robotcycle club. The Amiah Riders. In addition, she sees visions that have made her very wealthy and resides in a dazzling mansion.

But, when her wildly irresistible lover, Landon, gets locked up for life for a murder he did not commit, slowly Amiah's world begins to fall apart...

Will Amiah's visions be able to help bring the passionate and thrilling love that she shared with Landon back? Or are their sexy times doomed to remain in the past sweet memories of her visions?

Meanwhile from afar, the handsome Onai twins admire and are in awe of Amiah and her visions. Marcel Onai and Chima Onai are the joint leaders of the all-male paranormal robotcycle club. The Chi-Marcels.

The Onai twins have secret seductive plans for Amiah which have nothing to do with her estranged lover Landon.

USEFUL TERMS

Virtual - (in the year 2224) means something that is computer generated and can be physically interacted with. E.g. a virtual mansion, a virtual table, a virtual chair.

Robotcycle – a futuristic robot bike.

Amiah Riders – the name of Amiah Lily's all-female paranormal robotcycle club.

Chi-Marcels – the name of the Onai twins all-male paranormal robotcycle club.

Jelitoonaa – a popular word meaning cool or awesome.

Clairaudient – the psychic ability to hear what others who are not clairaudient cannot hear.

Clairvoyance – the psychic ability to see what is not seen by others who are not clairvoyant.

Telekinesis – the psychic ability to affect and interact with physical objects without physically touching them.

Remote viewing – the ability to view locations and people at any distance away from you.

Telepathy – the transference of thoughts and ideas from a person's mind to any other mind/s.

Virtual sound borders – futuristic technology that prevents sound from being heard outside the virtual sound border.

V.I.S. – virtual invisible sound border.

DISCLAIMER

This is an adult paranormal romance fiction novel. Unless otherwise indicated, all the names, characters, businesses, places, events and incidents in this book are either the product of the author's imagination or written in a fictitious manner. Any resemblance to actual persons, living or dead, or any actual events is purely coincidental. This novel is not a substitute for professional advice and should not be relied upon to make decisions of any kind. Any action a person takes upon the fictitious writing contained in this book is strictly at the person's own risk, own responsibility and neither the author nor the publisher shall be held liable or responsible to any person or entity with respect to any loss or damages.

AMIAH AND THE AMIAH RIDERS

It started, as it so often did, by a soothing ringing noise at either side of Amiah Lily's ears. This gentle ringing immediately alerted Amiah Lily to an incoming appearance of images including pictures of scenes, locations and people. The ringing noise wasn't anything like the one described as tinnitus by modern medical professionals, but more like the on/off ringing of a virtual mobile ringtone. Amiah Lily watched the scene play out in front of her, the same way a small virtual screen would perhaps hover in front of her eyes. She saw herself dressed in a light pink shirt and black jeans wearing low brown heels laughing hysterically, uncontrollably and unrestrained. The other people in the relatively large hall, stood staring accusatorily at the tall woman in the white business suit, who now seemed to be 'frozen' in the middle of the stage. Their faces were a combined mix of sudden perplexed dismay and horror.

No sounds played throughout this scene.

Then, without warning, the scene stopped playing abruptly in front of Amiah Lily. She calmly sent instructional thoughts telepathically to female members of her highly skilled paranormal robotcycle club, the Amiah Riders.

It was time for R134 to commence.

*****

"Is everyone ready?!" shouted a short muscular woman wearing a fitted black jumpsuit that covered every inch of her body except for two small holes by her nostrils. A virtual helmet was also worn by every rider which immediately appeared on the rider when the robotcycle began to move. The virtual helmet could be turned off in numerous ways by the rider, e.g by sensors on the side of each virtual helmet, or via the robotcycle functions.

The rest of the 15 female members present from the Amiah Robotcycle Club all had on similarly designed black jumpsuits, virtual helmets and rode on pre-programmed robotcycles. The programming was done by Melissa Cantim. She was the expert in robot technology in the Amiah Riders.

Some of the riders did acrobatics in a high-spirited manner by occasionally standing on one leg while holding onto the handlebars, sitting backwards with their arms flailed or laying back and using their feet to rest on the handlebars. All the while their robotcycles automatically manoeuvred through the forest area of Brink forest. Ditches were avoided, by each robotcycle swiftly increasing speed forward and lifting up by the front of the robotcycle to 'jump' over any ditch in the way.

"Woo hoo! Jelitoonaa!" an enthusiastic rider named Jan sang quietly to herself as her robotcycle jumped over yet another deep ditch on it's way to their destination. The word 'Jelitoonaa' is a popular word meaning 'Cool, awesome.'

The view around the Amiah Riders grew foggier as they approached Brink Mansion for R134 (134th Rescue mission). Brink Mansion was home to the wealthy owner of the famous refugee charity 'Brinkers El' run by the prominent Mrs Elaine Brinkers. Established since 2200. However, in the large hall 460 miles away, Amiah Lily shifted position uncomfortably on her virtual chair. She coldly listened to Mrs Brinkers continue to deliver her speech on 'Love and seeing the best in others.'. Although very costly, advanced virtual technology developments had allowed everything virtual to be physically interacted with from 2060 onwards. The choice of hall for Mrs Brinkers charity speech, gave no indication of her great wealth. Only the virtual chairs, the designer clothes and jewellery did.

At the north edge of Brink Forest, Jan remote viewed the large, impressive mansion, home to the Brinker family from a short distance away. She confirmed viewed that Mrs Brinkers had been very careless and cheap when organising her security defences for her mansion property. The Brink Mansion security breach would probably be one of the easiest rescues that Jan had ever had the privilege to work on. Jan smirked to herself.

"I know Jan. Total cheapskate, using the oldie words." said Petrina, after also remote viewing Brink Mansion to check the precise locations of security cameras, passcodes, security guards and alarm systems.

"Do we even need these jumpsuits Jan? There's only one man there watching the security screens and he's on his virtual mobile and…" Candice paused and searched the security guard's mind telepathically as far as her psychic skills would enable her. "…and he hates his job and doesn't give a f***"

"Those cameras can be bent out of shape in seconds." an Amiah robotcycle rider said to another member at the back of the group of robotcyclists.

"I've already got every passcode." said a different rider situated in the middle.

"Amiah Lily says the 'jumpsuits stay on'." replied Jan confidently at the front of the group of riders.

"Amiah Lily says, Amiah Lily says," whined a teenage girl on a robotcycle next to Petrina.

The other Amiah Riders ignored her.

The teenage girl's name was Saraina who was still in close training with Amiah Lily herself. Jan read Saraina's mind and saw that the teenager felt nervous to be out with them on her first rescue mission which would be judged by the head of the club Amiah.

Jan got down from her robotcycle and dusted off some random twigs and leaves from her adventurous ride through Brink forest to get to Brink Mansion. She walked over to the robotcycle that Saraina sat on, and quickly noticed how Saraina had gripped the handlebars tightly with sweaty palms. Saraina looked up suspiciously as Jan opened her mouth to speak.

At the same time as Jan was about to say her first word, a long brown heavy branch cracked in half above them, dropping down sharply to the brown soil ground below. It landed upright partly buried in the soft soil ground directly in between where Jan stood and where Saraina sat on her robotcycle. Jan walked around the odd new addition to the scenery of Brink forest, faced Saraina and said, "You've been trained by the best paranormal psychic robotcyclist in history, you've got this, ok?"

Saraina grimaced at being singled out in front of everyone but managed to nod her head in agreement with Jan. Jan winked at Saraina and smiled before walking back to the front of the Amiah Riders.

"Virtual helmets off. Let's do this. I've got to get back to my girls at home." Jan said self-assuredly.

Everywhere outside and inside Brink mansion, each security camera was bent out of shape by the telekinesis powers of members of the Amiah Riders. The alarm system's codes were deactivated using additional psychic skills such as clairvoyance. After walking quickly unseen through the front garden area, past a spectacular musical fountain to reach to the front entry doors, 15 Amiah Riders entered into Brink mansion silently. The front entry doors had been easily opened by Jan's telekinesis. Their steps made little to no noise as the women wore no shoes but had black material with grips under their feet. They knew precisely where they were going in the mansion, having remote viewed the entire property for months beforehand and 10 minutes prior.

Saraina ran silently through the foyer and turned right to continue running up the stairs. She performed an excited twirl at the top of the stairs and allowed herself to smile. There wasn't any other person in her way so far, so there was no need to use her miniature laser gun cleverly concealed under a hairpin at the back of her thick curly blond hair. She turned right and ran straight past the large bathroom to the children's bedroom door. She crouched down on the sophisticated mosaic tiles floor and deftly placed a small blue square by the door. Stepping back from the door a few paces, Saraina watched as a virtual sound border spread around the entire outside of the children's bedroom. Saraina again smiled to herself and turned to go back the same way she had come.

"They're all out by the pool drinking and smoking. Put the V.I.S borders up." Jan ordered five of the Amiah riders. Each of the eight Amiah members crouched down from different sides of the back of the mansion and outside by the corners of the pool area to place virtual invisible sound borders all around the area. The Brink Mansion staff socialising by the pool would not be able to hear any sounds from outside these virtual invisible sound borders, therefore making the R134 even more easier for the Amiah Riders.

"They're up!" an Amiah member shouted exaggeratedly knowing that no member of the Brink Mansion staff would be able to hear her.

"Good. Let's go rescue." Jan replied running towards the front of the mansion again, with eight of the Amiah riders beside her.

They met up with the other 5 Amiah riders in the basement of Brink Mansion. One by one the Amiah members came into the large poorly ventilated, damp, dark, cold and smelly place which was filled with terrified people of all ages. There were about 100 people in total who appeared in need of desperate help. Some of the Amiah Riders quickly administered first aid to those who required medical attention, whilst others gave food and water in the form of tiny pills for the people to swallow. Water and food could be minimised into small capsules, so the Amiah Riders had brought these with them. These food and drink capsules were attached in small pockets on their clothing.

"This is what makes that bitch so bad. She couldn't even give them water and food pills." Jan mumbled to herself while watching a mother put a food pill on her skinny daughter's tongue for her to swallow.

"I hate people like her." another member of the Amiah Riders agreed.

Virtual blankets were given to all the people in the basement and after it was deemed safe for everyone to be able to walk out of Brink Mansion, the Amiah riders led the 100 people out to safety. The 100 people found in the large basement had been kept prisoners in Brink Mansion for at least 2 months. There was a lot of noise when the rescued people came out of the basement. Shouting, screaming, wailing and crying in different languages.

"Can someone view the pool area before we leave!" Jan shouted out to be heard above all the noise of the rescued people.

"No-one is coming for us. The only security guy is sleeping. The party is still going on by the pool." an Amiah rider replied confidently.

"Ok, let's leave this place." Jan responded. She began to communicate everything that had occurred to Amiah Lily telepathically.

Back in the large hall, Mrs Elaine Brinkers had nearly finished her speech on the topic of 'Love and seeing the best in others.'. Amiah Lily stared at Mrs Brinkers with an expertly hidden disgust behind a curious and interested facial expression. She received the telepathic message from Jan and felt her heart race with anticipation of what she knew was about to happen next. And then it happened, just like in her vision she had seen earlier.

Suddenly, robot police stomped onto the stage where Mrs Brinkers was about to close her speech and surrounded the stage. Next, a virtual screen at the back of the stage displayed images of the rescued prisoners at the front of Brink Mansion being looked after by robot paramedics. Some of the people (shown in the image on the virtual screen) were shouting about how they had been kept prisoner in the basement for months after they had joined the Brinkers charity to help them start a 'new life'. Mrs Elaine Brinkers wearing a white business suit now seemed to be 'frozen' in the middle of the stage. The faces of the people in the audience watching were a combined mix of sudden perplexed dismay and horror. Other people in the relatively large hall stood up staring at Mrs Brinkers accusatorily. Amiah Lily dressed in a light pink shirt and black jeans wearing low brown heels started to laugh hysterically, uncontrollably and unrestrained.

Later that evening...

Amiah Lily lay awake in her cream coloured 4 corners post canopy virtual bed. Somehow she couldn't stop her thoughts from racing about the days events. She didn't understand it. She was used to rescue missions being 100% successful and today was no different, so why did she sense that something was amiss. Her mind flashbacked to all the major scenes from earlier on in the day. She saw herself talking with the Amiah Riders about their mission to rescue the prisoners from the basement of Brink Mansion. She saw herself getting ready to ride her robotcycle to the charity venue with two other Amiah riders riding behind and ahead of her. And finally, she saw herself laughing overjoyed as Mrs Brinkers was finally arrested in front of the audience and the millions of viewers watching on virtual screen devices around the world.

So, why couldn't she sleep? Hadn't everything turned out exactly as she had predicted and planned? Amiah wondered.

Amiah Lily turned over again reluctantly onto her left side and squeezed her eyes more tightly shut to try and fall asleep. After 2 more hours at 3:30am, Amiah was still wide awake. She sighed and hugged herself, then outstretched both arms out at either side on her bed. She heard the familiar ringing sound indicating a vision was about to come to her and sat up straight in her virtual bed, clutching the virtual cream coloured duvet around her protectively.

The vision which played out like a movie in front of Amiah's eyes showed an oval shaped green shadow (the size of a virtual house) moving through the night sky and landing over her home. Amiah's home was a beautiful lush virtual mansion where she and all her Amiah Riders resided. To the outside world, the virtual mansion was the home of the Amiah Private Beauty Training Institute. This was just a cover business to prevent the real reason why so many women lived in one mansion together ever being found out. All the Amiah Riders were to act as hairdressers or beauticians whenever there was an outsider visiting the property for whatever reason. In reality, the Amiah Riders were one of the best paranormal robotcycle clubs in the world and their identities and location was also one of the best kept secrets.

But, what did this huge green oval shaped shadow represent? Amiah pondered.

She stretched her arms out again at either side in tired angry frustration. There was a government official coming to visit her home tomorrow afternoon and she wanted to appear as well adjusted and 'normal' as possible. The government official was going to ask her questions again about her ex-boyfriend Landon as a new appeal had started for his release from a high security virtual prison.

Amiah blinked her eyes rapidly to stop any tears from flowing. Placing both hands over her breasts she squeezed them softly while closing her eyes shut tightly.

Landon, she thought.

Amiah felt a rush of love and warmth fill her entire being and forgot about the oval shaped green shadow vision. She tilted her head back softly. Her beautiful thick black afro hair gently brushing against the delicate cream material at the back of the 4 poster cream-coloured canopy virtual bed. She stretched, parted her smooth brown legs gently and bent them both at the knees. Slowly and sensually arching her back, she reached her hand downwards to in between her legs and touched herself thinking of Landon's strong, dark, muscular firm body all the while. Soon Amiah Lily fell fast asleep.

At 7am, Amiah Lily was seated around a virtual grey marble circular table in her conference room with all 17 of her Amiah riders seated around the table. The women were of all different ages ranging from age 18 (Saraina) and age 91, a woman called Frieda. A variety of different human races also were equally present in the Amiah riders. Metallic robot staff in the shape but not the visual appearance of humans, stood in the four corners of the conference room ready to follow any orders given by humans they were pre-programmed to serve.

The Amiah Riders sat in complete silence waiting for Amiah Lily to speak. Some had virtual cups of tea or coffee in front of them. They were all in awe of Amiah Lily's unsurpassed paranormal gifts and knew to clear their minds of anything they did not desire to be telepathically read, while close by her. The Amiah Riders did not know that Amiah Lily could also read their minds from any distance too.

The highly skilled paranormal robotcycle club had been formed by Amiah Lily 3 years ago. Her leadership skills had started with training her friend Jan from college who Amiah noticed had some level of psychic and telepathic ability, nearly as strong as hers. Amiah trained Jan and taught her how to harness her gifts to their fullest extent. Together, they had 'joined forces' at Snaresbeed College. They jointly used their psychic gifts to do everything from passing exams/tests, taking whatever items from local stores, sharing secrets at a cost by reading peoples minds and then selling the information found (anonymously of course)… The list went on and on. There wasn't any psychic ability that was off limits for Amiah and Jan. Although, Amiah Lily was much faster, more accurate and had exceptional blocking skills. Amiah could block the powers of other psychics and paranormally gifted people much easier than Jan.

After completing Snaresbeed college with A* in every subject, Amiah started her first job as Assistant Manager at Kote Robotcycle store and fell head over heels in love with the latest recently developed robot technology…

…The Robotcycle.

Amiah purchased a brand new black and gold robotcycle the very same day she started work at the Kote Robotcycle store. In the year 2218, Robotcycles were an upgrade from the Motorbikes of 2018. Robotcycles are similar to Motorbikes but they are robots so therefore do not require much human control to operate it. A destination is pre-set by speaking to the robotcycle or pressing an option on a small virtual screen at the front of the robotcycle. That was all. Simple. The Robotcycle could be slowed down or stopped simply by the rider telling it to do so or tapping on the virtual screen situated at the front. There were no loud engine noises as there was no engine. The robotcycle voice sensors are able to easily interpret the sounds of the instructions given by the rider in any language or dialect. After work, Amiah rode her new robotcycle for over 8 hours until she was so hungry she was forced to get off her robotcycle to find food to eat.

Her flatmate Jan also soon got into riding robotcycles. Jan stole her first robotcycle when remote viewing at a shopping centre late one Friday night. She went out to get a jumper she liked and saw a standard black robotcycle parked outside the shopping centre in the car park. Her remote viewing showed that the security at the shopping centre was non-existent and that the owner of the robotcycle had left it there and was working miles away. From her training with Amiah Lily at Snaresbeed College, Jan knew what to do next. She telepathically scanned every mind within a mile radius surrounding the robotcycle target, to search for any links connected to the robotcycle. She found none except an old lady who was angry that the robotcycle was blocking her car. So, therefore this is how Jan obtained her first robotcycle, and just like Amiah she absolutely loved riding it.

The more roads and new places Amiah was able to travel to and experience with her new robotcycle, the more different kinds of people she met. Being an outgoing, extrovert personality Amiah made new friends everywhere she went. She would happily start up conversations with anyone and anybody. She felt secure knowing she could read peoples minds and remote view beforehand whenever she was offered to stay overnight or go back to a new friends house for a movie and dinner. Amiah made new friends and had many sexual encounters. She loved the new freedom that riding robotcycles had given her and very quickly built up a collection of over 30 different robotcycles, mostly received as gifts from past lovers.

One stormy evening back in 2221, Amiah had a vision which came at exactly the same time as lightning had struck the tree in her back garden breaking it into two halves. She was in her bedroom in a 4 bedroom virtual house with a large garage containing her 30 robotcycles. The vision showed every single robotcycle she owned with an unknown female rider sitting on each robotcycle. This new vision flashed in front of Amiah's eyes a total of 10 times before stopping abruptly at the exact same time the rain finished pouring outside her house. Instantly Amiah felt intense excitement like she hadn't experienced before. Not even with her many male lovers she had been with in the past. This was a nearly indescribable thrill. A mix of mystery, connection, danger, thrill, passion and the unknown all combined together was one way to make sense of her emotions. Amiah had to find these women and start a robotcycle club and she had to find them fast.

Amiah's brilliant memory recalled each woman's face that sat on each one of her robotcycles and was able to remote view and locate 10 of the women. A further 7 women came to her using their own psychic abilities. Amiah Lily was ecstatic to discover that every single one of the women had some level of psychic ability which would make her newly formed robotcycle club even more powerful and unique. Sadly, the remaining 13 women could not be traced, no matter how hard Amiah and her newly created Amiah Riders tried to use their psychic gifts to find them.

The highly skilled paranormal robotcycle club, the Amiah Riders formed in 2221. Their club message is Rescue & revenge, loyalty, protection, love. Over the following 3 years, the Amiah Riders undertook anonymous rescue missions and protection assignments which made them millions of pounds. Using their paranormal talents, each task was successful and the more they used their psychic abilities the stronger these abilities became. They moved to a secret location in a psychically protected exquisitely designed virtual mansion where they all live and work today in the year 2224 under the fake business name of

Amiah Private Beauty Training Institute.

"Today's business for the Amiah Private Beauty Training Institute is," Amiah Lily paused with dramatic effect and then continued speaking to the Amiah Riders seated on virtual chairs. "...is that we... are going to make sure that this government official understands without any doubt or exception we are a private beauty training institute. Now, I've already checked his credentials and the government is still very silly. Mr. Runton has no paranormal ability whatsoever so there is no need to use your blocking skills around him. I understand that blocking others psychic abilities can cause pain to some of you so I'm happy to say that you won't have to do that this morning." Amiah said.

"Thank God for that!" an Amiah Rider exclaimed out loud.

There was an awkward silence.

"Sorry Amiah, it's just that the last time I had to block Matthew Jada's psychic abilities during R103 I had a migraine for over 5 hours. I'll never forget it." the Amiah Rider, a middle aged woman with short brown hair replied defensively.

"You had a migraine for 2 hours, 33 minutes and 21 seconds Lucy." Amiah corrected Lucy with a frown on her face.

Lucy blushed and sat back in her virtual chair embarrassed.

None of the other Amiah Riders looked at Lucy. They were worried that their thoughts were being telepathically read too. The women did not fear Amiah Lily but they greatly respected her and her awe-inspiring psychic gifts and knowledge of the paranormal. Their respect for her and their robotcycle club was more out of admiration, friendship and love rather than fear or intimidation.

"There will be a training class this Saturday afternoon to practice psychic blocking skills and you can attend Lucy. 4pm. You are free on that day and you don't start your new engineer job until Sunday morning at 7am." Amiah said with ease.

"Yes boss." Lucy replied sitting up straighter in her virtual chair and taking more interest again.

"Lucy has a point though Amiah. It's very hard for us to block when we feel pain doing it. I just wish that we could all be like you. You can block other paranormally gifted people no problem. No problem at all." Jan said hopefully searching her friends mind for an answer.

"I can only teach you what I know from how it works for me. One day you'll all get it." Amiah said.

The Amiah Riders glanced at each other and some of the younger women laughed.

"Never say never." Amiah said looking at the younger women laughing.

The young women laughed a little longer and then straightened up in their virtual seats ready to listen to Amiah again.

"Ok. So the students for their free beauty treatments are arriving 30 mins before the official and Marie will take him to the main beauty training room where he can observe our 'work' before a robot will take him to this conference room. Feel free to read his mind and remote view anything you can while he is here. Tonight we ride!" Amiah finished speaking with a flourish.

"Yeah!"

"Tonight we ride!"

"We going to ride baby!"

"Let's ride down Petejill way!"

"Marvellous!"

"Ready!"

"Jelitoonaa!!"

"Riding, we riding, riding, we riding!"

Amiah smiled happily listening to the enthusiastic shouts of her Amiah Riders expressing their exuberant excitement to be out riding together wherever they felt like going. The world was their oyster.

A vision appeared briefly in front of Amiah's eyes. She hadn't paid attention to the ringing sound because of all the shouting happening around the grey marble circular table. Amiah saw the government official at the front entrance to her mansion.

"Quiet down everyone! He's here early. Saraina and Misty go to the front entrance and welcome him. The rest of you get ready in your positions. Tonight we ride!" Amiah said and waved at a robot to come over and clear the table's contents, in order for it to be ready for when the government official would enter after viewing the main beauty training room.

One hour passed by and the visit from the government official seemed to be going smoothly from Amiah Lily's perspective until he sat down in the conference room to talk with her. Then the mood of the visit changed. The government official whose name was Mr Joseph Rantcun began to badger Amiah with many unrelated questions to her beauty business. Instead, Mr Rantcun asked her repeated questions about her ex-boyfriend Landon.

Amiah felt tension grow inside her. The tension was not because she did not foresee the questions that Mr Rantcun was going to ask. The tension she felt was her hidden anger that Landon was still locked up in a high security virtual prison with no chance of release. She already knew the appeal would not work. Landon was in prison for life. Landon was in prison for the murder of a high-ranking politician. Both Landon and Amiah knew they were innocent. Someone had set them up in the most cruel and unforgiveable way. Amiah had eventually been acquitted of all charges, yet it was plainly obvious that the government still considered Amiah to somehow be involved in the crime.

Amiah Lily was too smart for Mr. Rantcun and answered all his questions exactly the same as she had in court one year ago when she was acquitted of all criminal charges.

Mr Rantcun stared quizzically at Amiah Lily as if trying to look deep into her soul for the answers he wanted to hear, the answers that would confirm that she had just as much guilty blood on her hands as her ex-lover Landon. Amiah Lily sat on her dark orange virtual chair and stared innocently back into Mr Joseph Rantcun's cold blue eyes.

Mr Rantcun's cheeks flushed pink and he quickly stood up and reached out his left hand to shake Amiah's hand who was still seated. Amiah ignored the gesture and placed a virtual glass of water from the table into Mr Rantcun's left hand. Mr Rantcun's fingers wrapped around the cup and he obediently drank from it.

He's real thirsty and not just for water, Amiah Lily thought to herself.

"Well, thank you Mr…what's your name again?" Amiah lied to the government official. She fully well knew his name and she also knew that he had been sweating so much in her presence that he would readily accept the glass of water she kindly offered him.

"Rantcun. Mr Joseph Rantcun." Mr Rantcun replied putting down the now empty virtual glass on the grey virtual marble circular table.

Amiah Lily stood up from her virtual chair.

"Mr Joseph Rantcun. It has been an absolute pleasure to show you around my Private Beauty Training institute this morning. I hope you will consider the release of Mr Landon Ross and I assert that I truly believe that he would never commit such a horrendous crime. Unfortunately I have other appointments to attend to today as I am sure you can certainly appreciate. I wish our wonderful government all the very best in solving this crime and bringing the real killer to justice. Now, I really must get on Mr Rantcun as I have important business to attend to." Amiah Lily said gesturing to a waiting robot member of staff to her right.

The 7 foot tall robot in the shape of a female human wearing a metallic pink mini dress walked over to where Mr Rantcun stood with Amiah Lily.

Mr Rantcun eyed the robot suspiciously up and down.

Amiah Lily waved bye at Mr Rantcun and watched as the female robot member of staff led Mr Rantcun away out of the conference room to walk the short distance out of the mansion to exit her property. Amiah viewed the government official leaving her property via remote viewing with a combination of boredom and inner frustration.

The appeal was not going to succeed.

Amiah felt her body tense up at the thought of Landon

spending his entire life in a high security virtual prison. He didn't deserve to have his life wasted like this. He didn't deserve to never be able to enjoy life again. He didn't deserve to never ride with her on robotcycles naked together again basking in the warm summer nights.

As Amiah's memory flashbacked to romantic, passion filled nights and days with Landon, she also couldn't help but remember the horror of the night before he had been arrested. It was a stormy winter evening and they were laying together on her 4 poster cream coloured canopy virtual bed. Both distraughtly aware that something very bad was about to happen.

Before Landon Ross was arrested the next day at his robotcycle store, he and Amiah Lily had been receiving frequent frightening visions of white fog surrounding the two of them. White fog which moved around them like ghostly pale cloud swirls with sparkling silver lighting striking in between both of them continuously. Amiah read the vision as there would be something powerful and evil separating the two of them very soon. She tried to remote view all the possible enemies from Landon's past and her own past in a vain attempt to find out clues over what was going to happen next. She found nothing. Landon was quiet, kept to himself, his robotcycles, his woman…

Amiah blinked her eyes rapidly to stop tears from forming as more memories came back to her of her last night with Landon.

They had made passionate love like they had done hundreds of times before except this time they clung to each other with a desperate loving intensity that surprised them both.

"Promise me." Landon had said, his eyes glazed with burning love and desire.

Amiah had looked deep into his brown eyes which showed so much love for her and nodded. She would do anything he said.

"Promise me you'll be happy and find someone who loves you as much as I do. Promise me you won't be alone." Landon said loosening his hold on Amiah for the first time that night.

Amiah loosened her hold a bit more too.

"Wha... what Landon?" Amiah replied.

Then it came to her intuitively what Landon was implying. He wanted her to meet a new man! He wanted her to find a new lover to ride naked together on robotcycles on warm summer nights with. He wanted to give up on them. Throw their love away over a few scary visions which even she wasn't sure she was interpreting properly. Landon tightened his loving embrace again on Amiah and Amiah responded by holding him even tighter too. When Landon repeated the words "Promise me." in his sexy deep voice, Amiah could only nod again in stunned confused relenting agreement.

This is how Landon Ross became Amiah Lily's ex-boyfriend.

Yet, Amiah had not dated any other man since Landon had been imprisoned around one year ago. Despite the Amiah Riders efforts to try and get her interested in new often wealthy robotcycle riders who wanted to meet up and take a ride with her, Amiah declined their invites over and over.

Amiah was in love.

She loved Landon Ross, and if he wanted her to play the label of ex-girlfriend to keep him feeling like he was somehow saving her from a lifetime of misery then she would honour her promise. She would speak of him as her ex-boyfriend just for him, for them. But, no-one on this unfair, unjust, cruel Earth could get her to love any man the way she still loved him.

RIDING INTO THE UNKNOWN

At 9pm, most of the Amiah Riders were getting ready to go out on their robotcycles for a night ride with Amiah. The robotcycles were stored in a huge virtual garage which contained over 100 bikes. It also contained the black jumpsuits and black socks with grips that 15 of the Amiah Riders had worn the day before during the R134 mission. Tonight however, they would not be wearing the black jumpsuits, but each rider wore whatever they wanted to wear. There was no need for anonymity unless they were going on a rescue or protection mission. Tonight the Amiah Riders would ride for the pure unbridled exhilaration of riding their robotcycles. Free and fast, energetic and confident, wild and with supernatural talent.

"Nights like this? I looove them. During the day. Just ain't the same." an Amiah Rider called Petra said while walking towards her robotcycle at the back of the large garage.

Petra had long blonde and red hair and wore a red off the shoulder jumpsuit that accentuated her tall thin frame.

"Tell me about it." another Amiah rider called Louise replied.

"We can just spend the whole day riding." Petra continued.

"I know." Louise agreed.

Petra finally reached to her white and red robotcycle at the back of the garage and walked around it, peering closely at different parts of her robotcycle. Louise had simply just got onto hers quickly in one swift move. She touched the small virtual screen at the front of her robotcycle and began to view past robotcycle rides stored into her robotcycle's memory.

"Freson Country lanes, up near the mountainside, rivers... I see you Amiah. What a ride!" Louise exclaimed.

"Something's wrong with my bike." Petra said squinting both her blue eyes continuing to peer closely at her white and red robotcycle.

"Down again the country lane, over...what a ride!" Louise carried on watching her replay of a previous group ride with the Amiah Riders.

Petra closed her eyes and connected with her robotcycle using her remote viewing skills. She first visualised a calendar next to her bike and then highlighted in her mind's eyes 8 hours prior on the calendar. She saw her robotcycle after the last time she had rode it around 10 hours ago. She saw her robotcycle self-clean itself robotically. Petra didn't have time to view the whole 8 hours of her bike's recent history, so she skipped some parts in her mind's eye.

Petra raised her eyebrows high and opened her eyes in amazement before closing them again. She had seen an oval shaped green shadow sitting on her robotcycle weaving in and out of the bike like a seal jumping in and out of water at a virtual zoo show.

"Amiah needs to see this shit." Petra said out loud to herself opening her blue eyes wide.

Lousie's ears perked up.

"See what shit?" Louise answered.

"There was some green egg-shaped shadow thing jumping up and down on my bike." Petra explained.

"Shut up. No way!" Louise said rolling her eyes.

"It's true. View it for yourself." Petra said.

Louise looked over at Petra's white & red robotcycle and tuned into it's energy and memories.

"I don't' see it." Louise said after a few minutes.

"Try looking at precisely 4 hrs 28mins ago." Petra answered.

"I don't see...hold on...ewww." Louise said.

"I told you." Petra said.

"Set the self-cleaner on your bike. That green thing could have given it an STD." Louise joked.

"Ha, ha, ha. You'd better check your own bike sweetie." Petra retorted back.

"It's an orb Petra." Lousie replied dismissively.

"Orb?" Petra raised her eyebrows.

"An orb could be someone who knows you from the spirit world or psychic energy." Louise said sounding bored.

"Jumping up and down like that! Amiah needs to hear about this." Petra said refusing to take on her friend's laid-back attitude.

Louise looked at Petra squarely in the eyes and shook her head.

"Now isn't the right time to bother Amiah Lily. Especially not over some orb bullshit." Louise grumbled.

Petra sighed.

"If it happens again I'll tell her." Petra agreed reluctantly.

"Hey look she's starting up!" Louise said happily getting back onto her robotcycle.

Petra also got back up on her robotcycle and set it to the destination that Amiah had just telepathically communicated to all 17 riders. The riders virtual helmets activated as soon as the robotcycles began to move.

Tonight's night ride was a daredevil route called Gruten Rivers. Gruten Rivers was a visually stunning and extremely challenging robotcycle route. Messy and dirty too, as the robotcycles were riding through muddy and wet grounds. Nevertheless, the robotcycles were still able to operate perfectly to an excellent standard but they got very dirty as an obvious result of riding through these kinds of terrains. The terrain included hilly, marshy, forestry ground and many rocky streams for the robotcycles to jump over.

As Amiah Lily's silver and gold robotcycle jumped over a rocky stream and went down a hilly slope area of the Gruten Rivers route, her thoughts flashbacked to Landon again. She remembered riding with him naked on his robotcycle along this route, one hot summer's night when they were dating. Landon had been sexily naked too. After the ride they had made love by the rocks near a beautiful flowing stream. No-one saw them during their sexy ride and sexy encounter. Amiah Lily had made sure that there would be no-one on that route during their 'date night' by remote viewing the Gruten Rivers route beforehand.

Amiah's happy recall of good times faded when a vision appeared in front of her of Landon looking unhappy in a virtual prison cell. The vision was transparent and therefore did not alter the view in front of her robotcycle.

Landon, she thought.

Everything kept reminding her of him. Landon's memory was in every nook and cranny of the Gruten Rivers route. Landon's memory was in her cream coloured 4 poster canopy virtual bed at night. Landon's memory was in every part of the virtual mansion she owned. Landon's memory was on her robotcycle. Landon's memory was in her, filling her up with a love she found too overwhelming and intensely passionate to leave in the past.

Landon, she thought.

Amiah Lily felt her heart racing fast and her mind began to spin with ideas of how to rescue Landon from the high security virtual prison. She considered all her options during her ride back to her mansion.

Once back at her mansion (sometimes referred to by the Amiah Riders as the Amiah Mansion) Amiah Lily stood around talking with her Amiah Riders about the route they had just rode on.

"Wow! That was Jelitoonaa! When next do we ride?" Jan exclaimed.

"Loved it Amiah! Never rode that route before. Where to next?" Saraina said enthusiastically.

"Aweeesome. Good choice Amiah!" another Amiah Rider said happily.

"Self-cleaning time for my bike I think." Louise said with a grin walking around her robotcycle and looking at the mud and grass left on her bike. "Love Gruten Rivers!"

"Did you see the skulk of foxes that came out to look at our robotcycles?" an Amiah Rider said to another Amiah Rider.

"A full moon was out. How romantic." said Jan.

"Yeah, when do we go back Amiah?" asked Saraina.

"We ride again tomorrow night at 10." Amiah said grinning all around at her Amiah Riders. She could read their minds and was happy to hear their true thoughts about the Gruten Rivers route. The Amiah Riders loved being out on robotcycles with her. She sensed their love, appreciation, admiration and respect for her and Amiah felt elated. Intertwined with her elation over her Amiah Riders was elation for the new plan she had formulated during her ride back from Gruten Rivers. Her new plan to rescue the love of her life, Landon Ross.

"Ok! All of you are jelitoonaa riders. I am very impressed. I only see excellence in my riders permanently" Amiah said with pride in her voice. "Self-clean all robotcycles and there's food back in the dining room." Amiah finished addressing the Amiah Riders with a grin.

In the dining room, Amiah and the Amiah Riders sat on a virtual shining silver dining room table that could seat 32 people. Amiah looked around at the 17 Amiah Riders seated and then her gaze fell on all the empty seats. 13 Amiah Riders were missing. They were yet to be found despite Amiah's attempts to trace the women in her visions. She was 100% sure the women she saw on robotcycles that appeared sometimes in her visions, were meant to be part of her riders. Her riders were incomplete.

Amiah grimaced.

The other seat that was empty was situated on her right hand side at the top of the virtual dining room table. This seat used to belong to Landon but now it was empty. Just like her love life had been empty for a year.

Amiah felt her body tense up and before she could control herself, words came spilling out of her mouth in front of all the Amiah Riders present.

"Landon should be here!" Amiah shouted out in frustration glancing sideways at the empty seat next to her.

The Amiah Riders fell silent immediately.

"Listen up everyone. R135 is commencing at the end of this week. We ride to free Landon on Saturday night. I want everyone to come up with ways we can break into the Duneway (Duneway high security virtual prison) and on Friday we'll all ride with the best idea. Got it?" Amiah said determinedly.

The Amiah Riders began whooping and shouting out their ideas on how to get into Duneway using their paranormal abilities and clever thinking.

"I'll remote view Duneway all week and find out every dumb security system in the place."

"Free Landon!"

"Not guilty!"

"I can get in Duneway today for you Amiah." Saraina said leaning forward in her virtual seat and looking across over to where Amiah sat.

Amiah looked down the virtual dining room table to where she could see Saraina's eager anticipation on her face.

"I already know where every security system is in Duneway

virtual prison, but they have paranormal security staff which will be our main problem." Saraina continued.

"Yes I am aware of them too." Amiah replied. "Then we will have to use our blocking psychic skills."

Some of the Amiah Riders groaned at the thought of using their psychic blocking skills which often brought on painful headaches or migraines during the length of time that the skill was in use.

"It wouldn't be for too long." Amiah said to try and calm her riders.

"Amiah we're not as gifted as you. We feel pain when we block other psychics." Petra said with a shrug.

"You all must train more on a one-to-one basis with me. One day you will all be able to block paranormal people with no pain. I can see it in your futures." Amiah replied assertively. "Getting back to R135, I welcome all ideas on how to safely rescue Landon from Duneway and I don't want to hear any more problems. Only solutions." Amiah said in a firm tone which signalled to everyone that she didn't want to hear another word about any more problems with R135.

The Amiah Riders fell silent again apart from eating noises and shuffling of virtual cutlery while eating.

Robot staff entered the dining room with more virtual plates of food for the hungry riders. By the time everyone had finished eating, the virtual dining room table was almost bare. The long robotcycle ride along the Gruten rivers route had worked up a big appetite in all the women. All the women except Amiah. Amiah had hardly eaten a thing. She hurriedly handed her near full virtual plate of food back to a robot member of staff to take away to the trash. She did this, to ensure her long-time friend Jan wouldn't notice that she hadn't eaten much.

Amiah figured that Jan would worry about her if she had noticed, but luckily she could see that Jan was animatedly talking about that night's ride with three other Amiah Riders seated nearby. Amiah took a deep breath in, held it for a few seconds and then breathed out. She had never felt tension like it. The sharp tension was a mix of her anger about Landon's imprisonment and annoyance over the irritating promise she had been forced to make. Not forgetting the passionate nights she had been painfully deprived of for nearly a year. Amiah was not happy with her non-existent love life, but she refused to play the part of ex-girlfriend and meet someone else. No matter what Landon had suggested in an emotional sex after-thought.

Amiah turned to the person sitting closest to her to talk, until she heard a soothing ringing noise by both her ears. She relaxed back into her virtual seat ready to watch whatever visual scene played out in front of her brown eyes. She hoped it would be about Landon and would be some kind of help to R135.

The vision started with a high-pitched whistling sound that only Amiah could hear. Next she saw a large oval shaped green shadow flying fast around her mansion jumping in and out of the building in different places.

Amiah cocked her head to the side briefly and then focused back fully on the vision in front of her.

The Amiah Riders were used to seeing Amiah appearing to watch 'visions' that they could not see or hear. Seeing visions on request or at random was one of the most outstanding paranormal talents that Amiah Lily possessed. Of course, some of the riders could see visions also, especially during remote viewing but Amiah's visions were more frequent, detailed, foretelling and clear. Everyone is psychic and everyone can train their psychic abilities. However, just like in any field of work, there are always some people who stand out more than others.

Take, Albert Einstein for example. He wasn't the only theoretical physicist out there during his time but, he was one of the best. Even in the year 2224, Albert Einstein was still acknowledged as one of the greatest physicists of all time. Amiah Lily was similarly alike in her field of psychics and paranormal phenomena. She possessed outstanding paranormal and psychic talent. Yet, like most remarkably gifted people in any field, her exceptional skills could not always prevent her human trials and suffering. All the psychic and paranormal gifts in the universe had not prevented her heartbreak over Landon Ross.

Amiah watched her latest vision of the big oval shaped green shadow moving fast all over the outside of her mansion, weaving in and out of the property and diving up and down in her pool area, with curiosity.

Why is this being shown to me and is it a past or present vision? Amiah thought.

She searched the energy of the vision for more information.

Amiah's eyes lit up in excitement after reading the energy of the vision. This crazy new event was happening right now, this present moment at her mansion, in her pool. Swiftly, Amiah called five robots to her by pressing a sensor on the virtual dining room table.

"We have a level 8 security threat. All defences on standby." Amiah instructed to the five robots standing next to her.

The vision immediately ended in front of Amiah's enlivened eyes. She stood up to address the Amiah Riders and spoke to them.

"Listen everyone! We are on level 8 security threat detected as of 1:20am. Robot staff have put all defence systems on standby. The threat is unknown." Amiah hesitated before proceeding. "There is a very interesting enormous green oval shaped shadow...don't laugh... moving fast above also jumping in and out of my mansion and the extended area of my property. Yes, I thought it was funny at first too. I cannot read anymore into it's energy. It's not a block. It's something I've... I've not perceived before. I don't know yet how safe or unsafe it is so we are at level 8 until I find out. Every defence is on standby." Amiah said confidently.

Lousie and Petra exchanged knowing glances.

Amiah intuitively observed the intention behind their exchange.

"Petra. What can you tell the rest of us about the green oval shaped shadow and it's passion for jumping, ducking and diving. Anything?" Amiah said narrowing her eyes at Petra inquisitively.

Petra gulped before speaking.

"I didn't think anything of it. It was just before we went out on the night ride Gruten Rivers route. I could tell there was something wrong with my bike. Not in a faulty way, but it was like the energy around the bike was…off…sick…I can't describe it." Petra said.

"Go on." Amiah encouraged.

"Yeah, well anyway I remote viewed into my robotcycle's recent history to see if could find out why I sensed something weird about it. Then, I saw the same green oval shaped shadow acting the same crazy way you described but my one was smaller. It sat on my bike about 4 hours and a half before we left, dipping, jumping and diving into it like some kind of fish." Petra said.

"We just thought it was an orb, someone from the spirit world." Louise explained quickly.

"No, we didn't" Petra said without thinking.

Louise kicked Petra's ankle hard under the virtual dining room table.

"Stop it!" Petra exclaimed before she could edit her words in front of Amiah Lily.

Amiah Lily sighed. She read both their minds telepathically as they were speaking. She saw that they hadn't wanted to bother her with something that could be nothing important.

"This is not an orb." Amiah confirmed.

"How can you tell?" Louise asked.

"With an orb, if you are psychic developed to a high level, you would be able to identify anything that you would recognise using these senses. If a psychic who is well-developed cannot sense what it is, it's not an orb." Amiah replied.

"So, what is it then?" Petra said, feeling relieved that Amiah didn't take the fact that no-one had forewarned her about this green shadow thing before, too seriously.

"Anything that we do not recognise is unknown until it chooses to be known." Amiah stated matter-of-factly.

Just then, two robot members of staff entered into the virtual dining room.

"The unknown potential threat has been contained within the pool area using a virtual laser dome. It has not tried to leave this area for 10 minutes. We are waiting to see if it is strong enough to penetrate the virtual laser dome which we've activated to protect your mansion and it's grounds." said a short metallic robot in a pre-programmed English human accent.

The robot's appearance was a metallic version of a short male human wearing dark blue jeans and a black t-shirt. There were robots available to buy everywhere in 2224. Amiah Lily preferred the metallic style robots in the shape of humans rather than the realistic human style robots. She wanted to be clear whenever she looked at one of her robot members of staff, that it was plainly obvious that it was a robot and she was a human. Many people of her generation felt suspicious of robots so the metallic version of robots in the shape of humans were the most popular type of robots to buy for businesses, companies, events, etc… Every time there was a small robot rebellion reported on the virtual screen news, people grew more distrustful of the widespread use of robots. They had not been completely banned as of present day 2224, but the realistic human style robots were gradually becoming less and less popular.

For now, however the metallic style robots were of important use to Amiah.

"Thank you. Connect all the virtual security cameras of the pool area to the virtual screen in this dining room also please. Thank you." Amiah said to the robot who had just spoken to her.

"Yes Miss Amiah Lily." the short metallic style robot replied.

Amiah turned her head to address the Amiah Riders who all remained in the dining room. Some were seated, others were standing up talking to each other and some seemed to be communicating with people in spirit that only they (and Amiah Lily) could see.

"Can you all look at these images for any signs as to what this unknown green oval shaped shadow is? Look with your mind's eye and try and see 1. Whereabouts the threat is? and 2. What the threat is all about?" said Amiah Lily to the Amiah Riders clearly.

Some of the Amiah Riders sat back down on their virtual seats. Others chose to continue standing and watch the virtual screen located at the front of the room from a distance.

The large virtual screen now showed images of every angle of the pool area. The dining room grew quiet as everyone watched the images for clues to find out where precisely the green oval shaped shadow was. In addition, they were all trying to sense intuitive messages as to who the unknown security threat was.

"I can see it." Amiah said after a few minutes. "Can anyone else?"

"Nah." an Amiah Rider said.

"Not yet." another Amiah Rider said.

"No sorry Amiah."

"Where is the thing?" asked Jan.

A further 10 minutes passed by until finally someone spoke up.

"Is it the energy I sense in the centre of your swimming pool, Amiah?" Petra asked curiously.

"Yes it is. Remote view it's past history quickly while you can still sense it." Amiah replied. "Thanks Petra."

"No worries." Petra answered.

"Anybody else?" Amiah inquired.

There was another 10 minutes silence before someone spoke up again.

"It's not from here. It's come from the sky, maybe another planet. I don't know." Saraina said non-committedly.

"Yes, I've been waiting for one of you to make that observation." Amiah said. "When something is unknown and the energy is unlike anything we've experienced, there is a possibility that it originated from outside our planet."

"Ah yes! Why didn't I think of that before?" Jan exclaimed.

Petra gave Louise a smug satisfactory look.

"Could it be an alien orb?" Louise questioned out loud.

"It could be anything associated with an unknown alien energy." Amiah replied.

Louise returned Petra's smug satisfactory look back at her.

Everyone in the virtual dining room watched the images on the virtual screen more closely to see if they too could sense the unknown energy. As psychic and paranormal abilities vary, it was expected that not everyone would be able to sense, see or hear the unknown energy. There were a few yawns from some of the Amiah Riders and Amiah noticed that a few of them were struggling to keep their eyes open. They were exhausted from the night ride of the Grutens Rivers route and now from the additional unexpected drama of the unknown security threat. Amiah didn't see any point of the riders who could not sense the unknown energy to stay viewing the virtual screen. It would be better for them to sleep and wake up with energy to help defend the mansion if necessary. Amiah decided to tell them to leave the dining room.

"Hey, is that eyes closing at the back there?" Amiah asked in a friendly, kind tone.

Petra nudged Louise with a sharp elbow jab in Louise's arm. Louise elbowed her back with the same sharpness. Both women stood up at the same time as if they were about to fight or say something nasty to each other. A rider standing nearby did an acrobatic pose in between them by leaning backwards, placing one slender leg in the air and moving swiftly into a shoulder stand before flipping backwards to stand in between Petra and Louise again.

Petra rolled her eyes and sat back down.

Louise turned to speak to Amiah.

"I'm fine, I can stay with..." Louise began saying.

"All of you can go now, it's ok. If there is any trouble the alarm security defence will alert us. Don't worry. Continue to think of ideas for R135. Petra and Saraina, can I speak to you both before you leave?" Amiah said.

When the majority of the Amiah Riders had left the dining room, Amiah spoke to Petra and Saraina while still looking at the images on the virtual screen.

"So, it's just us three that can sense this thing so far." observed Amiah.

"It's in the centre of your pool Amiah." said Saraina.

"Yeah, it is." Petra joined in.

"Is this the first time?" Saraina asked.

"First time what?" Amiah said.

"First time that you've had an unknown possible alien threat in your swimming pool." Saraina asked a bit more nervously this time.

"What do you...Yes, it is." Amiah confirmed. She had faintly heard some kind of sounds from the unknown energy replying to her telepathic communication, but Saraina's voice had distracted her.

"Is it trying to say something to us?" Petra had also heard some faint sounds when she tuned into the energy in the centre of the pool.

"You heard that too." Amiah said turning her head right to glance at Petra.

"Heard what?" Sariana replied. She didn't hear anything apart from the voices of the people speaking in the dining room and the occasional metallic movement of the robots in the room.

"Your clairaudience has captured the unknown energy Petra. Jelitoonaa. Now no more talking, just keep trying to use all of your skills to communicate with it." said Amiah. "Saraina you're doing great, keep it up." Amiah encouraged the youngest member of the Amiah Riders.

There was silence for the next 10 minutes as the remaining 2 riders and Amiah used every psychic and paranormal ability to attempt to communicate with the unknown energy, potential security threat. Each woman's face showed no sign of stress or strain when doing so. They appeared relaxed albeit tired. It was usually the psychic skill of blocking, either your own psychic gifts or other peoples paranormal and psychic powers that led to pain and distress. The three women were at ease. Other things bothered them in life but not using their psychic talents. Psychic and paranormal gifts added to life not detracted from life. Well, as long as they were used with good intentions...

"Ok, what did you hear?" Amiah asked Petra and Saraina. "Saraina, you go first."

"I heard nothing." Saraina blushed in embarrassment.

"Not a thing." Petra shrugged her shoulders.

"Don't worry." Amiah answered reassuredly. "I didn't hear anything either."

Petra and Saraina both raised their eyebrows in surprise at the same time.

"I didn't hear anything…" Amiah continued. "But…I did see a vision of what is to happen. It's leaving soon. It will break through the virtual laser dome in less than a minute. Keep tuning into it's energy! I wish all my riders could see this! Watch!"

Sure enough in just under 60 seconds, Amiah watched her vision that she had just seen, play out in real life on the virtual screen. She narrowed her eyes and could see the green oval shaped shadow move fast out of the centre of her pool and directly upwards towards the virtual laser dome. Easily penetrating through one of her main security defences, the green oval shaped shadow thing continued to move fast through the dark night sky and upwards. Then, Amiah's viewing of the unknown energy went blurry. She rubbed her eyes out of habit when you perhaps think something could be in your eyes. Although, there wasn't a thing wrong with her vision.

Amiah's ability to view the green oval shaped shadow was so strong that her vision of what was happening around her in real life disappeared. It was as if she was actually there close up somehow, paranormally viewing the unknown energy with a front row virtual seat. She saw the green oval shaped shadow and blackness around it. Then, just as she had seen in her vision, a bright green planet came into her view. Amiah's mouth dropped open in amazement as she viewed the large oval shaped green shadow fly into the bright green planet and out of her viewing.

Gradually, Amiah returned back to her present day reality and she could see the virtual screen again in front of her and her two Amiah Riders, Petra and Saraina next to her in her dining room.

"So Jelitoonaa! Amiah, wow! Our first alien visit!" Saraina

laughed excitedly. She hadn't seen nowhere as much detail as Amiah had been able to view, but both herself and Petra had witnessed the dramatic opening of the virtual laser dome sparkle red. It was as if something had triggered it to go from an invisible virtual laser dome into action. A wide circle had opened up for 10 seconds, closed again before returning back to its prior invisible appearance.

"Awesome." Petra said calmly. She expected to see more action and was a little deflated.

"What did you see Amiah?" asked Saraina.

"You are correct. It's an alien!" Amiah laughed, throwing both her arms up in the air dramatically.

"Wait till I tell Louise. I should never have listened to her going on about... it's nothing but an orb." Petra smirked.

"It's a large green oval shaped alien that can change it's size. It comes from a bright green planet 1,000,000 times the size of Earth. It's left our planet now. It will return again at some point and... I think it has come to where we are for it's own purpose and reasons." Amiah explained.

Some of Amiah's knowledge came from reading her own intuitive feelings and not solely from the visions she had viewed.

Amiah called over four robots that were standing nearby awaiting instructions.

"Bring the security threat level back down to 3 and de-activate the virtual laser dome." Amiah instructed the robots.

The robots did as commanded and the security threat level at Amiah mansion was reduced to level 3. Amiah turned back to face Petra and Saraina.

"It will come back and when it does... this time we will be ready for it." Amiah asserted.

"Of course." Petra agreed with a wink.

"It can night ride with us!" Saraina said excitedly.

Amiah and Petra smiled at each other knowingly and then at Saraina who smiled back innocently. The two older women in their mid-twenties were both thinking of the high possibility of fighting to defend themselves against the unknown alien potential threat.

Saraina was thinking of making friends with them.

SPYING FOR R135

"This is going to be impossible." Louise said to Petra.

The two women were waiting for the virtual garage main door to open so they could ride their robotcycles close by Duneway virtual high security prison. They intended to find out more about the virtual prison in order to help rescue Amiah Lily's ex-boyfriend Landon Ross successfully. Both women possessed some level of remote viewing skills and they were already aware of the exact location where Landon's prison cell was situated within Duneway.

The paranormal security guards were the biggest problem. It was difficult for Louise and Petra to read their minds from a distance while also utilising their blocking skills. Utilising blocking skills was vitally important so that the psychic security would not sense their paranormal interference. Amiah Lily and some of the Amiah Riders, could effectively scan read the minds of everyone at Duneway virtual prison, but only Amiah could block other paranormally gifted people without pain.

The Amiah Riders required more practice.

Louise and Petra had been the first riders at that morning's meeting to volunteer to ride nearby Duneway virtual prison. Their task entailed trying to work out how clever the paranormal security staff actually were. The question that needed to be answered was whether or not, the psychic security staff needed to be blocked at all or was there another way?

Petra first arrived at the Duneway virtual shopping centre. She tapped the side of her virtual helmet to deactivate it before stepping off her robotcycle. She looked around the parking area of the shopping centre. It wasn't that busy today as predicted, only a couple dozen hover cars, robotcycles and a few of the old-fashioned motorbikes. Petra tuned into Louise's energy to find out how far she was from her and to telepathically communicate for her to hurry up.

Louise heard Petra's voice talking quietly in her mind and rolled her eyes. She was only five minutes behind Petra. Petra could wait that length of time surely. She wondered if she should use her blocking skills to shut up Petra's whining voice in her head.

"Where did you go?" Petra asked, tuning out of Louise's energy.

Louise felt Petra's psychic interference in her mind instantly leave her.

"Don't do that again." said Louise after tapping on the sensor to deactivate her virtual helmet.

"Don't do what again?" Petra asked as innocently as she could.

Louise glared at her and was about to say something sarcastic back to Petra when Amiah Lily's voice was heard loud and clear inside the minds of both women.

"Oh come on, stick to the plan. I can hear you both." Amiah Lily's voice said telepathically to Petra and Louise.

"Sorry Amiah." Petra and Louise said simultaneously.

There was a short awkward silence that followed. Both women were double contemplating their thoughts and words again, now that they had been starkly reminded of the fact that Amiah Lily could tap into their minds at any time.

"Let's do this." Louise said quietly.

"Ok." Petra replied.

The Duneway virtual shopping centre consisted of 250 shops with 50 cafes and restaurants. Although fairly large, it was not the most popular virtual shopping centre in Duneway, which is exactly why it was chosen by the women to practice their blocking skills. There was always a chance that a random person could also have psychic skills and read into what they were thinking. One of the ways that this was avoided in public was by constantly thinking about anything apart from the real reason you were there. It was kind of like building an entire fantasy identity in your mind. This increased the chances that anyone, say a random stranger for instance who just happened to be using a psychic skill such as telepathy, would not in effect read any true, correct or factual information about you or your intentions.

Therefore, Louise and Petra were now in auto-pilot fantasy world mode. Their minds raced with all different made-up stories, that would deter a psychic mind reader from knowing their true intentions.

For the Duneway virtual prison rescue mission however, the auto-pilot fantasy world mode was too risky. It would be a high pressure, dangerous, life-threatening situation and one slip up in any of the Amiah Riders thoughts could lead to them being killed or captured. Especially since over three quarters of the security guards were professionally trained in paranormal and psychic skills.

Blocking, when done properly was a much more reliable yet painful technique for psychics to use. Amiah Lily was a rare exception to the rule. She could block other psychics/paranormally gifted people and didn't feel no pain whatsoever.

Petra and Louise got into a virtual lift to get to the top floor of Duneway virtual shopping centre. When they arrived at the top floor, they exited the virtual lift and walked past 20 half-empty shops to get to a cafe called Jelitoonaa Café. There were many Jelitoonaa cafes around the world and they were popular. This Jelitoonaa café today was empty apart from a team of robot staff. The café appeared very similar to how Petra predicted it would be by using her remote viewing skills earlier, while riding on her robotcycle.

Louise ordered two coffees, chocolate chip cookies and strawberry yoghurts.

"Nice selection." Petra replied in a dry tone.

"The strawberry ones are my favourite. What's yours?" Louise asked.

"I've always liked peach yoghurts with almonds." said Petra

"So, tell me more about the new office you're working in. I want to know more." said Louise

"It's an office for the executives only. There's not much work to do really. I think business will pick up in the winter when people want to buy more indoor virtual heated duvets." said Petra.

"Well, I hope it all goes well for you. I have a few friends interested. Do you want me to give you their names and contact details now or later?" asked Louise.

"Now, please. All 30 of them, if you don't mind." replied Petra.

Louise held herself back from replying sarcastically to Petra and began to conjure up 30 fake names, addresses and telephone numbers.

In the meantime, Petra tuned into the energy field of Duneway virtual high security prison and remote viewed the entire prison until she found Landon's virtual prison cell. She could see that he wasn't there but didn't react to this discovery. Instead, she moved swiftly onto remote viewing a nearby clothes shop. This would confuse any random psychic from knowing her true intentions. It would just seem like she was looking around the neighbourhood which did not equate to any crime being committed.

In 2224, it was possible that any psychic or paranormally skilled person could view high security virtual places all the time, but professional security psychics were trained to read into the intent behind every viewing. If a security psychic sensed any dangerous intent or criminal intent, they would use other paranormal skills to find out more detail about the individual or group. Brief viewings of virtual high security places by random psychics couldn't be avoided, but telepathic warnings were sent by professional paranormal security to people deemed suspicious.

Next, it was Louise's turn to try and block the paranormal security staff while she used her telekinesis powers to open the virtual door of Landon's prison cell. She had only blocked her psychic ability from being detected for 30 seconds before discovering that Landon was no longer in the same virtual prison cell. Without showing any kind of reaction to this new discovery, Louise stopped viewing Landon's virtual cell and stopped blocking.

Louise felt an ache in her forehead during the short 30 seconds of blocking and took a long gulp of the coffee in front of her. She listened to Petra speak for a few minutes and then joined in with her talking about a topic completely unrelated to R135, the Landon rescue mission.

Petra was back remote viewing Duneway virtual prison again. This time she tried very fast to view all the virtual prison cells in the area where Landon had originally been. There were too many and feeling anxious about being caught by one of the paranormal security staff, Petra soon gave up for the time being.

Their fake conversation over coffee, (pretend) jobs, cookies and strawberry yoghurts would continue to confuse any random psychics or even security psychics that were listening in to their energy or reading their minds.

On Louise's turn to use her psychic powers to help with R135, she took another long gulp of coffee. Getting straight to work, she focused on blocking her paranormal skills and used her intuition to guide her to a different virtual prison cell where she found Landon laying on a virtual bed with his arms folded over his chest. Quickly, Louise used telekinesis to open his virtual prison cell door. Landon's virtual prison cell door flew open.

All of a sudden, Louise felt a sharp pain in the middle of her forehead which made her instantly stop using her paranormal abilities. Louise kicked Petra's ankle under the café table hoping that Petra would realise there was a problem that she could not openly express.

Petra kicked Lousie's ankle back, hoping that Louise would realise that she knew there was a problem that Louise couldn't at this time express.

Petra used her intuition very fast to find Landon's new virtual prison cell and blocked her psychic abilities. No sooner had she done so, she felt a dull and persistent ache in her forehead. She viewed Landon standing by an open door of his virtual prison cell. She watched him step outside and glance left and right. He seemed about to run when a robot member of the virtual prison staff, appeared up from a small square shape on the floor. The robot security grabbed Landon's arm and pushed him aggressively back into his virtual prison cell.

Sensing trouble, Petra exited her psychic viewing and stopped blocking immediately. It was getting way too risky, and her head hurt badly. She wanted to consider all this new information and started to mention about leaving the café to Louise to get back for a dental appointment that afternoon.

"Yes I also need to get back for an appointment with the vet about my yellow Labradors but let me just get some more of the chocolate cookies. Is that ok?" said Louise.

Petra got up from her seat. She had to get out of there before she blew both their covers. There was trouble for Landon at Duneway virtual prison and maybe the two of them had just made it worse. Her thoughts wanted to race to process what just happened, but she couldn't do that here in the virtual shopping centre where any random psychic could listen in.

Petra waved goodbye to Louise and headed towards the café exit doors.

"Maybe next time I'll get more cookies. I'm coming!" Louise sang out happily.

In the car park, Louise and Petra got on their robotcycles, and rode all the way back to Amiah Mansion focusing on enjoying the ride and temporarily forgetting everything else.

ONE CRAZY NIGHT

"Landon." Amiah Lily's distraught voice was heard clearly in the minds of Louise and Petra.

Petra and Louise glanced nervously at each other, as they stood waiting outside the virtual conference room to speak to Amiah Lily about what they had discovered during the trip to Duneway virtual shopping centre. This didn't sound like the usual confident telepathic words of instruction Amiah Lily would send to their minds, and the two riders wondered if they were even supposed to hear it.

Louise started to sweat down her back, on her face and hands. Was she to blame for the trouble Landon was now in at Duneway virtual prison? she pondered. She had been the one to open his virtual prison cell door which led to him being caught by that robot and shoved viciously back into his cell. Louise further considered whether or not Amiah Lily would hate her, for causing more problems for Landon.

But isn't Landon, Amiah's ex-boyfriend? Louise thought, so, she should be a little more easier on me then surely?

Louise's thoughts raced anxiously as she walked into the virtual conference room and took a seat opposite Amiah Lily, next to Petra.

"Relax Louise. It's not your fault." Amiah said in a dreamy, calm tone of voice.

Louise wiped the sweat off her forehead with the back of her hand. The back of her hand was just as sweaty so it didn't make much difference.

A robot passed Louise a handful of tissues.

"Thank you." Louise said after hesitating. She thought

robots were not meant to have real human emotions. It must have been pre-programmed to hand out tissues when people sweat, Louise concluded out of curiosity.

"It's pre-programmed." Amiah Lily answered before Louise could query it aloud.

Louise smiled and felt herself relaxing more.

"If it's anyone's fault, it is the judge and jury and the lying ass witnesses." Amiah stated clearly, still in a dreamy calm voice.

Louise and Petra relaxed more and Petra called a robot over to her to bring her some water to drink.

"Do you want something to drink Amiah?" Louise asked.

There was a strange pause where it felt like the room was spinning for Louise and Petra. After a minute it stopped, and Amiah Lily's voice was heard telepathically inside the two women's minds.

"Practice more!" Amiah Lily's voice angrily and telepathically boomed out in the minds of Louise and Petra.

"Yes I will definitely practice more Amiah, I'm so so sorry." cried Louise

Amiah Lily's facial expression remained dreamy and very calm.

It would have been surprising to anyone unfamiliar with the psychic skill of telepathy to picture that such an angry loud voice was coming out of a woman who visually appeared serene, gentle and passive.

Petra shook her head in disbelief at the way the morning's psychic practice had turned so dangerously wrong. She glared at Louise.

What was Louise thinking? Petra thought, did she think that by opening Landon's virtual prison cell door, that he would just come running out into the sunshine as easy as anything, jump on a robotcycle and reach safely back at Amiah Mansion?

Petra wondered if maybe she should stop hanging around her (Louise).

"Both of you must practice blocking skills more." Amiah Lily continued calmly.

"We will." Louise and Petra answered in unison.

"Ok. Leave me alone for the rest of the day. I will see you both at the end of the week in here for the briefing for R135. In the meantime, you have around 5 days to practice your blocking skills. All the Amiah Riders will be blocking the paranormal security staff on that night and I hope that both of you won't let me down. Keep practicing. You may go." Amiah Lily finished in a dreamy, gentle voice.

Louise and Petra quickly got up and left the virtual conference room. Both were disappointed that their attempt to impress Amiah by volunteering to gather more information about Duneway virtual prison had failed. Failed as in Grade F. They did not impress Amiah Lily. In fact, Landon would now be watched more closely by all the paranormal security staff and the robot staff. R135 would now be extremely more difficult and it was a direct result of the inexperienced psychic and paranormal skills of two of the Amiah Riders.

Amiah Lily sat back on her virtual dark orange coloured chair and called a robot member of staff over to her. The robot brought her a virtual silver tray with a virtual bottle of Recathri very strong rum, alongside a long slender virtual glass. The robot placed the virtual silver tray on the sparkling virtual grey marble circular table in front of her. It then proceeded to pour from the virtual bottle of Recathri very strong rum, into the clear long thin virtual glass. Then the robot left the virtual conference room.

Amiah picked up the virtual wine glass full of rum and squeezed it tight until the virtual glass smashed into little pieces over her right brown hand, the virtual silver tray and on the virtual table.

Luckily in the year 2224, the modern advanced design of virtual wine glasses, ensured the users safety in the event that they were broken accidently. The advanced design of virtual wine glasses made the virtual glass properties become as soft as virtual plastic if there was a breakage in the virtual glass design. When these new advanced designs first came out earlier in

2224, most people had wondered why the inventors hadn't just simply made it so the virtual glasses did not so easily break at all, in the first place.

Amiah took hold of the virtual bottle of Recathri very strong rum and drank straight from the virtual bottle. She drank as much as she could and then paused to catch her breath, drank as much as she could again, then paused to catch her breath. Her wobbling right hand just about managed to place the virtual bottle of Recathri very strong rum down again.

Amiah heard a distinct soothing ringing tone around both her ears, which sometimes preceded an incoming vision. Next, Amiah saw a visual scene of Landon's virtual prison cell with Landon laying on his bed in just his grey boxer shorts. The bed sheets were messily crumpled in an untidy heap near his feet at the edge of his prison bed. Landon was asleep.

Amiah watched the vision with dreamy lovesick eyes. She saw Landon Ross's lean muscular body turn onto his left side while still fast asleep. Memories flooded her mind about the nights he had slept next to her in her 4 poster cream-coloured virtual canopy bed in her bedroom. Although, he didn't wear any boxer shorts in her memories...

The vision playing out in front of Amiah's eyes abruptly ended. Amiah felt a scream of frustration cry out from deep within her soul.

Was that vision sent to torment me? she thought.

Amiah again reached for the virtual bottle of Recathri very strong rum and took a long swig of it's sweet, sensuous, addictive liquid.

After Amiah's fourth swig from the virtual bottle of Recathri very strong rum, she deliberately knocked over the near empty virtual bottle onto the floor. The virtual bottle bounced gently on the carpeted flooring. Changing her mind, Amiah went to retrieve the fallen virtual bottle to drink the small amount of rum she could see still moving about inside. She was stopped in her tracks however, by yet another vision. This vision had no warning ringing tone and just appeared suddenly.

In Amiah's latest vision, she saw the green oval shaped shadow flying fast through the air with a whistling noise and other noises that she could not clearly name. She blinked and raised her eyebrows tiredly, as if this vision was the only thing keeping her awake at this moment.

Where is that virtual bottle? Amiah thought.

She drunkenly tried to walk around the vision to get to the fallen virtual bottle of Recathri very strong rum.

Trying to avoid the vision did not work. Amiah's vision just moved along with her. Soon, Amiah gave up trying to avoid looking at the vision and sat down on a seat close by her. She sleepily gazed with dreamy dazed eyes at the vision playing out like a small movie in front of her brown eyes.

This time in her vision, the green oval shaped shadow was on top of Duneway virtual high security prison. Amiah raised tired eyebrows again, trying to stay awake to see if there was any information she could use for R135. A few more minutes passed by and all the green oval shaped shadow was doing was laying sideways on the roof of Duneway virtual prison.

Is this another vision to torment me? Amiah thought.

She figured that it must be all the Recathri strong rum she drank, and it was messing with her brain.

The vision was there even when Amiah closed her eyes sleepily a few times. After ten minutes of seeing the same scene of the green oval shaped shadow (probable alien) laying sideways on the roof of Duneway virtual high security prison, Amiah vomited and fell into a deep sleep.

Amiah slept for 4 hours and when she awoke, she found herself laying in her pink silk pyjamas on her 4 poster cream coloured virtual canopy bed. She wondered if it was an Amiah Rider who had got her changed or a robot. It didn't matter. She felt a lot better. The sleep had helped her rest from all the preparation towards R135 and the emotional energy it was taking from her.

Why are my riders no good at blocking? Amiah grumbled to herself in her mind.

AMIAH'S VISIONS

She didn't get any pain when using her psychic and paranormal blocking skills.

So, what are the Amiah Riders doing wrong? Amiah mused.

Amiah looked at the virtual clock in the shape of a robotcycle on her wall opposite her bed. The time was 6:30pm. She couldn't wait any longer. They would commence R135 tonight. If her riders had issues with blocking they would just have to take painkillers beforehand, Amiah figured. She telepathically communicated to all the Amiah Riders that they would be briefed in 10 minutes and they would rescue Landon tonight. R135 would commence much sooner than previously expected.

*****

In the virtual conference room for the R135 briefing, not one Amiah Rider questioned Amiah's quick decision to ride to Duneway virtual high security prison that night. They all knew that Amiah was in love and were ready for the adventure of a rescue mission with a purpose very close to Amiah's heart. The suggestion of taking painkillers an hour before, to help with blocking the paranormal and psychic security staff, was also met with approval. Why hadn't anyone thought of this obvious solution before? Some of the Amiah Riders reasoned. If you have a headache you take a painkiller. You don't have to stop the work you're doing, do you?

The briefing lasted just 30 minutes and soon Amiah Lily and all the Amiah Riders were in the virtual garage getting on their individual robotcycles, waiting to ride for R135. Landon Ross would be rescued tonight. At least, this was the plan.

The Amiah Riders rode on their robotcycles for the long 3 hour journey to Duneway virtual high security prison, on the west side closest to where Landon's virtual prison cell was. Some virtual security cameras had been deactivated throughout their ride using telekinesis and remote viewing. Replacement virtual images were sent to the Duneway security teams so that they would not suspect that their virtual cameras were not working.

Amiah had been blocking other psychics and paranormally gifted people since she left Amiah Mansion. The other Amiah

Riders had taken their painkillers and began to block too as they all entered Duneway virtual prison from different entry points.

There were no security staff (paranormal, psychic or robot) at each entry point the Amiah riders entered. All the robot security staff in the west side area of Duneway, had been deactivated by telekinesis. Amiah could see the paranormal security staff were in the north side of the virtual prison. She sighed a huge sigh of relief. Maybe she had been overthinking how hard it would be to rescue Landon this entire time, she thought.

Amiah Lily and five other Amiah Riders, were the first to reach Landon's virtual prison cell door. The other Amiah Riders were close by on their way too. Amiah stepped over yet another fallen robot laying in a heap on the floor and looked at the virtual security cameras hidden within the walls. They were all off.

Amiah smiled. She remote viewed what the paranormal and psychic security staff were doing in other areas of the virtual prison. They were oblivious as to what was going on in the west side of the virtual prison. It appeared the robot security had been left alone to manage the west side of Duneway virtual high security prison at this present time.

Amiah glanced around quickly feeling suspicious. This was too easy. She was just about to use telekinesis to open Landon's virtual prison door when Jan cried out in pain. Then, Melissa, Louise, Petra and Saraina (who were all with Amiah), held their foreheads and made pained expressions on their face.

Immediately, Amiah turned back down the way she had come and started running. The Amiah Riders ran after her. Quickly (while running) Amiah telepathically communicated to the Amiah Riders the word "Run.". She didn't say a single word more. Their cover was blown. Time was up.

Now that the Amiah Riders were no longer blocking the psychic and paranormal security staff, there was a high risk that one of the security team would psychically sense that something was up. There was a risk that Amiah Lily and the Amiah Riders would be discovered in the west side of Duneway virtual high security prison.

Although she was full of high hopes during the briefing earlier that evening, Amiah Lily had spent five minutes informing the Amiah Riders of what to do in the event of a serious emergency. In the potentially very dangerous event that they were unable to block the paranormal and psychic security staff for the length of time required for R135, the Amiah Riders were instructed to run. Get the hell out of Duneway virtual prison and don't look back! These were Amiah's exact words, and then everyone was further instructed to return to Amiah Mansion on their robotcycles.

However, just because an Amiah Rider stopped using their blocking skills for whatever reason, this did not indicate a definite life-threatening situation on rescue missions. It was always 50/50. A kind of high risk/extremely dangerous half and half chance of getting caught. Paranormal or psychic security would still have to possess the accurate intuition, paranormal skills or psychic perception to sense that there were intruders in their premises. As with any type of skill, errors could still be made.

Psychic or paranormal security staff would have to intelligently interpret any signs, symbols or messages from the spirit world to be able to work out more information. This is where psychics and paranormal security may not be as effective as the world in 2224 assumed. A lot of signs, messages, symbols were either misread, not read properly at all or other factors blocked their reliability. Other factors such as alcohol, drug use, illnesses, stress, an unhealthy diet and for those who believe in a higher power such as God, could interfere with psychic skills.

No matter how skilled a psychic or paranormally gifted person was, there was always the possibility that someone, something, a supernatural being maybe, was out there in the universe with greater control. This supernatural being would be infinitely more skilled and stronger than any living thing, e.g. God. This supernatural spirit would always be powerful enough to intervene. Well, as long as it wanted to…

As the final Amiah Rider parked their robotcycle safely back in the virtual garage at Amiah Mansion, Amiah Lily remote viewed Duneway virtual high security prison. She smiled to herself as she watched the robot staff, psychics and paranormal staff continue their regular routines with no idea of the amount of chaos that had occurred over 3 hours ago. They hadn't been discovered so far. There was still the risk that a psychically trained security member of staff would be able to find out what had occurred in the west side of Duneway virtual prison but this was a risk they would have to take. The identities of Amiah and all the Amiah Riders were shielded by black jumpsuits that covered their bodies completely with only small holes by the nostril area. So, at least if any member of the Duneway security team did find out, they would still not be identified.

"My God, Amiah! I'm so sorry, I couldn't take it anymore." an Amiah Rider with long ginger hair exclaimed loudly.

"The painkiller idea doesn't work long enough." another Amiah Rider stated in dismay.

"I've never felt the pain this bad before." Jan whined.

"We'll just have to take higher doses." Saraina said.

Louise giggled.

"I don't think the pain is physical. It's like something out of this world is causing it." Louise replied.

"Like our new alien friend." Petra suggested.

Some of the Amiah Riders laughed.

"Could we not ask the alien to return and give us a cure for the blocking headaches?" Melissa joked back.

"Alien security would be just as crap as the Duneway psychic team, trust me." Jan said.

"Not if it's trained by us. I can be a paranormal alien trainer. You all can pay me. You are welcome." said Louise taking a courtesy in front of some of the Amiah Riders.

The Amiah Riders all laughed at her in a friendly manner.

Amiah calmly listened to the friendly chatter around her in the virtual garage with mixed emotions. She was relieved that her Amiah Riders were all back safely and no longer in any pain but sadly acknowledged to herself that this was their very first failed rescue mission. She decided not to interrupt or remind them all that even though they had escaped, this was still a failed mission. Landon remained a prisoner.

Landon! Amiah screamed silently in her mind and she was sure she heard Landon's voice speak back telepathically to her saying clearly the single word "Help."

"Amiah, we nearly freed him." Saraina said softly, standing next to Amiah looking up at her while still seated on her robotcycle.

Amiah didn't reply but half-smiled at Saraina's innocent encouragement.

Saraina sensed that Amiah wasn't happy and looked down at her robotcycle embarrassed for having said anything at all.

Amiah walked confidently in the direction of the centre of the virtual garage. Some of the Amiah Riders were busy activating the self-clean function on their robotcycles or chatting about that evening's failed rescue mission. Amiah sent a loud telepathic message to every Amiah Rider in the virtual garage.

"We will ride again tomorrow night to free Landon. Be here at 7pm on your robotcycles in full black jumpsuit gear. Take extra painkillers beforehand. We were very close to success in our mission and I think it our duty to try again. We owe it to Landon. You all remember how he donated some of the more advanced robotcycles that many of you have the honour of riding on today." Amiah paused to take a deep breath in before continuing. "One to one training slots for blocking skills start at 11am tomorrow morning. I will train you all again starting in alphabetical order so... Antoinette will be first and Zara last. I believe the pain you experience during blocking can be controlled with more practice and effort. None of you are in any pain now so always remember that any pain you experience cannot last."

"That's because we stopped blocking!" Lucy said out loud.

Petra kicked Lucy at her ankle.

"It's true!" Lucy exclaimed kicking Petra back on her right ankle.

Amiah's eyes narrowed. She was trying to sound as optimistic as she could under the circumstances. The circumstances being the harsh reality that it was the Amiah Riders very first failed rescue mission. Also, Amiah knew that if it was not her fault in any way, then it was her riders.

Still, Amiah wanted to keep the women happy and not start critiquing them too obviously. In most ways she loved her Amiah Riders and was extremely proud of the paranormal robotcycle club she had formed. However, Landon in prison suffering, asking for help, not making love with her, not riding with her, was messing with her view of her riders, Amiah reasoned. She wondered if this was why she felt like she was holding back from cursing all the women in the garage out?

Amiah relaxed her eyes and ignored Lucy before finishing her address to the Amiah Riders with another telepathic message to all of them.

"I love my psychic girls. Best robotcyclists in the universe. Jelitoonaa, skilled, smart, gifted, talented, beautiful and unsurpassed psychic riders. You can do it! All of you can. I have faith in us. Antoinette, 11am. I'm off to bed. Landon is trying to talk to me telepathically."

Landon wasn't trying to talk to Amiah telepathically. Amiah had heard one word and no more came through since then. Before Landon was imprisoned both of them had decided upon a few rules. One rule was that the less they tried to talk telepathically to each other, the less chance that any of the paranormal/psychic security guards would discover their communication. In fact, the word "Help" had been the first time Amiah had heard Landon's voice in her head for months. This only made Amiah even more mixed up in her emotions. She wanted to lash out at someone, something, anyone for the pain she and Landon were unfairly going through. However, it made no sense to lash out at her riders in a moment of madness.

No sense at all, she thought sadly.

AMIAH'S VISIONS

"Amiah, why hasn't our training worked so far though. I've had 3 one to one sessions this year already." Lucy exclaimed again slurring her words.

"Lucy my lovely, you just have to practice more often. You're drowsy and fighting sleep. Get some rest and I will see you first before Antoinette at 10:30am." Amiah spoke out loud to Lucy looking at her eyes.

Amiah read the energy around Lucy and saw that Lucy's mind was very sensitive to the type of painkiller she had taken. This particular painkiller was interfering with her moods and if Lucy didn't sleep it off soon, the whining would carry on. Probably for hours, Amiah presumed. Yet, Amiah sensed a danger around Lucy also and walked towards her quickly to gain more information about it and to see if there was anything else she could do to help.

At the same time Amiah reached over to where Lucy was standing, Lucy collapsed to the floor.

"Is she alright Amiah?" Saraina quickly kneeled down next to Lucy with concern on her face.

"She's sleeping, vital signs are good." Amiah replied calmly.

"You knew something was going to happen, that's why you rushed over here." Saraina asked with a look of admiration in her eyes.

"If you have an overly sensitive head to painkilling medication you can sometimes feel very drowsy. Poor Lucy has probably been fighting sleep since she left Duneway virtual prison. I'll get a robot to take her to one of the bedrooms. The robot medical staff will watch over her as she sleeps it off." Amiah replied confidently and serenely.

"Did anyone else feel drowsy?!" Saraina shouted loud enough so all the other Amiah Riders present in the virtual garage could easily hear her.

"Nah" Petra replied shouting at Saraina from the opposite end of the garage.

"No!" Louise shouted from the back of the garage.

The other Amiah Riders nearby confirmed "No" or shook

their heads.

Amiah smiled at Saraina. She was impressed how Saraina had taken the initiative and enquired of the other Amiah Riders experience with taking painkillers to prevent blocking pain. Amiah was equally happy that it was only one of her riders that could not use the painkiller option for blocking relief. Well, at least not the same painkiller that had got her so drowsy tonight during R135…

"Tomorrow we ride! Goodnight my queens!" Amiah telepathically communicated to the remaining Amiah Riders who responded with shouts, claps, whistles and excited squeals.

Saraina watched curiously as a medically trained robot member of staff lifted Lucy and placed her gently on a hover mat.

"Lucy is fine. She really is just sleeping." Amiah reassured Saraina.

Saraina looked at Amiah with worry in her eyes which Amiah knew was unnecessary. She was about to read into Saraina's energy to see if there was anything wrong with her too but stopped herself in her tracks.

Landon. Amiah thought passionately to herself. She wanted to be alone. She needed to be alone. She needed him. The Amiah Riders issues would have to wait till tomorrow. With that thought, Amiah half-smiled at Saraina and looked at Jan who understood what she meant by that look. Jan walked over to Saraina and put her arm over her shoulders.

"It's ok. Amiah knows what she's doing. If she says Lucy needs sleep, then that's all Lucy needs right now. There's no need to worry. Trust Amiah, ok?" Jan said kindly to Saraina.

Amiah walked out of the garage and headed back into her mansion. She made her way through her courtyard, into the porch area and then onto the foyer. Turning left, Amiah walked a few minutes to get to the dining room. In the dining room, she briefly picked up a few of the ham and lettuce sandwiches that were left on the virtual table.

Why is there no hot food this evening? Amiah grumbled in

her mind.

She made a mental note to talk to the head robot in charge of food prep tomorrow morning.

Next, Amiah walked into the virtual lift and exited on the 4th floor to go to her bedroom. Munching a few bites of her sandwich as she walked down an exquisitely decorated wide corridor, she heard a distinct soothing ringing tone by both her ears. She hadn't yet reached her bedroom and sat down in the stunning corridor to watch her latest vision and eat her sandwiches.

Amiah called over a robot standing nearby and instructed it to get her two gold virtual cushions (to sit on), a virtual glass of water, hot chilli crisps and a virtual glass of Recathri very strong rum. Amiah didn't know what she was about to see and something told her that it would add more drama to this already very dramatic night.

The tall 7-foot metallic robot quickly came back and kneeled down with a long virtual tray containing the items Amiah had requested.

"Leave it there thank you." Amiah said raising one eyebrow quizzically at the robot. She could tell the robot wanted to sit down next to her just like a human did.

As Amiah predicted, the tall metallic robot in the shape of a human female clearly hesitated before standing up reluctantly and shrugging its silver metal shoulders.

Amiah rolled her sparkling brown eyes and focused again on the vision in front of her. Pale green coloured mist continued to conceal something behind it, that had not yet been revealed in the vision. Amiah wondered what it was. Her intuition wasn't giving her any clues. Only her assumption alerted her that it was almost certainly a vision that would probably ignite more theatricals before she could finally sleep. Before she could finally sleep and dream about Landon.

After five minutes of Amiah watching her vision while finishing eating her sandwiches, the pale green mist cleared.

Amiah's brown eyes zoned into the oval shaped green shadow immediately. She almost choked on a final piece of bread that hadn't had a chance to be chewed properly in her mouth.

The unknown threat alien thing was back.

Amiah glanced quickly at the Recathri very strong rum on the virtual tray that the strange acting robot had placed next to her on the silk red carpeted floor. All she wanted to do was lay down and passionately touch herself while thinking of her lover, or ex-lover as Landon had insisted she be called.

Now, I have another problem to deal with, Amiah thought.

Amiah watched the oval shaped green shadow moving fast in the dark night sky and then raised one eyebrow watching it dip in and out of her virtual garage. Amiah turned her face to the right where the tall metallic robot stood some distance away awaiting her next command. The robot looked back at Amiah with bright silver eyes. It was ready for action whereas Amiah wanted to sleep. Amiah opened her mouth to speak to the robot but before she could she heard a strange male voice next to her left ear.

"Talk with me. You can hear me. Talk with me. Alone." said the unknown deep male voice next to Amiah's left ear.

The robot stood facing in Amiah's direction still waiting for further instructions.

"It's ok. False alarm." Amiah said smiling at the robot.

The robot returned to it's original position of facing forward.

"Who are you?" Amiah telepathically communicated to the unfamiliar male voice that she had just heard.

"I think you know." the strange deep male voice replied.

"Are you this oval shaped green shadow in front of me? That I can see right now in my vision." Amiah said calmly out loud.

"Yes. Talk with me." the voice had changed to a high pitched female voice and was heard near Amiah's right ear.

Amiah got up to walk back outside to her virtual garage. She felt no fear whatsoever. Even her sleepiness was gone. Suddenly, excited energy filled her entire being. She walked past some of her Amiah Riders in various areas of her mansion and used her blocking skills so they would not know where she was going. There was no need to worry them or get them excited until she knew exactly what they were dealing with or about to deal with.

Passing by the virtual dining room on her way out of her mansion, Amiah picked up a virtual bottle of Recathri very strong rum and two virtual glasses. She figured this to be a friendly, 'welcome to planet Earth' gesture that could put the alien at ease. Smiling to herself and feeling overconfident and powerful, Amiah walked assertively towards the garage and waited for the virtual doors to open.

When the virtual doors opened, Amiah stepped inside and walked into the centre of the garage, just as if she was about to give instructions to her Amiah Riders. This time however, she communicated to the alien that she could not yet see or sense.

"I'm here." Amiah said telepathically, visualising the oval shaped green shadow in her mind's eye.

Amiah waited and repeated her telepathic communication 5 more times.

There was no answer.

Amiah looked at her virtual bottle of Recathri very strong rum in her left hand and the two virtual glasses in her right hand and tears came into her eyes. She blinked them away and repeated her message again.

"I'm here."

Suddenly, an unknown male high-pitched voice shouted from directly behind Amiah Lily.

"I'm here." it said.

Amiah turned sharply around, dropped one of the virtual glasses and gasped.

FOR THE LOVE OF LANDON

Amiah gasped as she saw a teenage version of Landon standing in front of her. Then she gasped again as she watched Landon's body fly up towards the ceiling of the virtual garage and change shape. It was the alien again, back in its original form of an oval shaped green shadow. Amiah narrowed her eyes. She was not scared.

The alien changed shape and form around 50 times while Amiah stood still carefully observing it's actions. She saw the alien change into a younger version of herself, change into her black and gold robotcycle, change into a bright cluster of colours, other coloured oval shapes and many other forms. Amiah felt like the alien was either trying to impress her or showing off. Still, she was not frightened in the least.

Seeing as this alien liked to play games, Amiah sat down on the ground and poured herself a virtual glass of Recathri very strong rum. She knew how to play her own games. She had already made sure she was blocking this alien with her paranormal blocking skills. Whether or not it was working however remained to be seen...

When the alien landed again on the ground after flying up and down numerous times, Amiah telepathically communicated with it.

"Have a drink with me. I have Recathri very strong rum." Amiah communicated in her mind to the alien.

The alien changed into a bright cluster of sparkling colours and appeared to have a heartbeat and looked as if it was breathing. The colours were too bright for Amiah to look at, so she looked away while extending her right hand with her virtual glass of Recathri rum and offered it to the alien.

The alien placed itself next to Amiah. A small compartment type of door opened on it's left side and a long gold sparkling tongue slithering out. Amiah put the virtual glass of very strong rum on the gold tongue instinctively. The alien sucked it inside itself in one fast slurp.

Amiah smiled. To somebody else perhaps, this whole scenario would sound ridiculous but Amiah was used to the weird and wonderful. Aliens should be treated the same as everyone else. There was no evidence to prove they were any smarter or any less intelligent than humans. Amiah believed in equality between all beings. The more time she spent around this alien, the more questions she had and now would be a good time to start asking them.

"What's your name? Where do you come from? I'm Amiah. This is planet Earth. Welcome to Earth!" Amiah said out loud.

"My name is Recathri. I am from planet … There is no way to pronounce our planet's name in your English language on Earth." Recathri replied in the sound of an elderly woman's tired voice.

Amiah smiled again.

"Recathri! Nice to meet you! Why Earth and why now?" Amiah said unable to hide her amusement. The alien wanted her to believe it's name was the same as the very strong rum she had just handed it. Amiah knew it was lying or maybe it got drunk faster than humans. The alien did not seem inebriated.

"I call myself Recathri as there is no name in your English language on Earth, close to my real name back home." Recathri explained.

"Right." Amiah nodded. "So why are you here and why all these theatrics? Is there a reason?"

"Theatrics no. I am showing you who I am. My planet wants to learn from your planet. Call it in your English language, research. I came to research Earth first and you are someone I can trust." Recathri answered in a high-pitched female voice.

Amiah thought to herself for a while before replying. She didn't sense any danger around the alien that had named itself after the Recathri very strong rum.

No danger so far, she thought.

"Of course you can trust me! I'm happy you picked Amiah Mansion for your research. I will introduce you to the rest of my riders tomorrow. We are a paranormal/psychic female robotcycle club. We stand by values of rescue & revenge, loyalty, protection and love." Amiah replied.

"I know." Recathri answered and changed shape into a teenage version of Landon Ross.

Amiah turned her head away and then quickly looked back again, her eyes widening.

"Don't play with me like that. If you know how to free Landon, that's fine but stop pretending to be him. You will never ever be him!" Amiah shouted at the Recathri alien.

Recathri alien changed shape again into a 6 foot tall thin green oval shape.

"Listen, if you can change into any shape, be a robotcycle." Amiah suggested, holding herself back from getting too angry.

The Recathri alien changed into a glowing gold robotcycle and began to speed around the garage performing all kinds of stunts and theatrics.

Amiah watched with a slight smirk on her face.

This is better, she thought, soon this alien will become one of the Amiah Riders.

When the Recathri alien in the form of a glowing gold robotcycle stopped racing around the garage, it parked itself in front of Amiah. Amiah instantly jumped on top of the robotcycle in front of her. As she did she noticed that her body had disappeared.

"Where am I?" Amiah asked curiously to the Recathri but intuitively she felt very safe.

"Anything that touches me without my permission, sometimes gets turned what you call... invisible." the Recathri alien replied in a deep male voice. "Do you still want to ride?"

"Let's go!" Amiah said with zero fear.

Next, the Recathri alien in the shape of a glowing gold robotcycle took Amiah on one of the most thrilling rides so far in her life. They rode through the hilly, marshy, forestry terrain of Gruten Rivers with the Recathri flying in the air at different times.

"Be careful that air security doesn't catch you!" Amiah laughed excitedly.

"Only you can see this robotcycle. No-one else will be able to see it." Recathri alien replied in a deep male voice.

"Keep that voice." Amiah happily answered.

Suddenly, Amiah heard a soothing ringing tone by both of her ears. A vision was coming through.

The Recathri alien continued to ride through the air, sometimes through the hilly terrain below and at other times weaving in and out of the forestry parts. Amiah sighed and calmed her excitement to focus on the information that was about to be shown in the upcoming vision.

The vision played out like a movie in front of Amiah's brown eyes. Amiah saw Landon laying in bed with a handful of pills in his right hand and an old-fashioned glass of water in the other hand. Amiah watched in dismay as Landon put his head back and dropped each white pill one by one into his mouth. Landon then used his right hand to drink some of the water from the glass he held in his left hand. Landon then fell back on his prison bed and closed his eyes.

Landon! No! Amiah desperately tried to communicate telepathically with Landon.

She had temporarily forgot the risk this entailed considering all the paranormal security staff present at Duneway high security virtual prison. Not to mention the robot staff. Who knew if the robot staff were now able to use psychic and paranormal skills just like humans? The thrill of the ride with the Recathri alien gold robotcycle thing quickly waned and Amiah knew what she had to do next.

"Recathri, go to Duneway high security virtual prison. I have a friend who needs our help." Amiah instructed the Recathri alien in the same confident tone that she would use to instruct any of her Amiah Riders.

"Ok." the Recathri alien replied.

The glowing gold robotcycle flew into the air and flew very fast. So fast that the world below became a blur for a few minutes. When Amiah could see below her again, she was in Landon's prison cell sitting on the Recathri alien's glowing gold robotcycle form.

Amiah jumped off the alien robotcycle and rushed over to Landon who lay seemingly lifeless on his bed. She checked his vital signs and scanned his energy. He was ok but very weak and in a deep sleep from the pills he had taken. Amiah identified the white pills as sleeping pills. She reached to hold his hand and the Recathri alien spoke to her telepathically.

"You cannot touch him in your invisible state. It is very dangerous." the Recathri alien warned Amiah.

Amiah reached for Landon's hand, squeezed it and placed it on her face tenderly. Glancing back at the Recathri alien, she answered it.

"And you cannot speak to me telepathically here in this prison. That is very dangerous." Amiah whispered quietly in the direction of the gold glowing Recathri alien robotcycle.

Amiah used her psychic blocking skills and remote viewed the entire prison to check for any signs that anyone knew she was there. There were no signs that any of the paranormal staff or robot staff knew of Amiah's presence in Landon's cell.

"I hope you're right and they can't see your robotcycle with your glowing gold self." Amiah whispered sarcastically to the Recathri alien.

The glowing gold robotcycle turned invisible and whispered back in a voice heard by Amiah's left ear.

"They cannot see whatever form I am in. Only people I choose can. You are safe." the now invisible Recathri alien robotcycle form replied.

Amiah ignored the Recathri and stared lovingly at Landon in his deep sleep. She dreamt of this moment where she could be so close as to be able to physically reach out and touch him again. Now, this moment was here and she didn't want to waste it.

Amiah laid down on top of Landon's sleeping body, hugged him and kissed him passionately. She hugged him even though he could not hug her back and she kissed him even though he could not return her kiss.

Thirty minutes passed by and Amiah forgot the Recathri alien was in the prison cell with her. She reached down to caress Landon's dick, slowly moving her hand up and down the length of it until it became hard in her hands. Landon moaned out loud. Amiah smiled. She thought that would do the trick. Slowly taking off his grey boxer shorts, she grabbed hold of his erection, opened her legs and straddled Landon's love member.

Amiah made love to Landon, riding him with an intense passionate urgency that she hadn't felt in a long time. Landon moved with the same sexual energy as Amiah but he remained with his eyes closed. Landon was sleep-sexing. Making love in his sleep. He moved his dick in and out of Amiah and then raised the top half of his body up to hold Amiah tightly.

Eventually, the two lovers climaxed together. Landon came inside of Amiah, loudly groaning in ecstasy. Amiah screamed her orgasm out in her mind. Both their hearts were pounding, and they were breathing fast in unison. They held onto each other lovingly for five minutes before Amiah heard a piercing ringing tone by her left ear.

Opening her brown eyes quickly, Amiah frowned to see that Landon still had his eyes closed. Landon fell back on his bed and began snoring. Amiah felt like shaking him to wake him up but the vision in front of her eyes caught her attention immediately.

Amiah saw robot security staff running quickly to Landon's prison cell. They were 5 minutes away, Amiah estimated. Amiah jumped off Landon and intuitively jumped on top of where she remembered she last saw the Recathri alien's robotcycle form. Feeling the robotcycle beneath her, although she couldn't see it, she whispered to the Recathri alien.

"Ride back to Amiah Mansion now!" Amiah instructed the Recathri alien assertively.

Amiah held onto the glowing gold robotcycle (the current form of the Recathri alien) as everything around her became blurry and misty. The alien robotcycle flew up into the air and sped along the dark night sky.

Amiah felt extremely happy and extremely in love. She enjoyed the thrill of the night ride back to Amiah Mansion. Finally, after a 30 minute ride she could see below her. Amiah was back in her virtual garage and her invisibility had gone. She hugged herself warmly while rotating both her shoulders around in circles.

She could barely believe what had just happened. She had made love to Landon. Landon Ross, the love of her life. He had held her tightly and rocked her world just like he had done so many times before he was imprisoned. They had embraced during their lovemaking and there was no way he could think she was going to look for a new man after what they had just shared together. She was Landon's girl. Landon was her man. Together forever.

"Amiah, you should not have done that. I warned you not to touch him while invisible. I cannot make you invisible again." the Recathri alien said angrily in a deep male voice.

The Recathri alien was in an oval shaped green shadow again and located on the ceiling of the virtual garage.

Amiah looked up at where the voice had come from and grinned happily back at the Recathri alien.

"You worry too much. On this planet Earth we humans try to live our lives with no fear." Amiah bragged to the Recathri.

She didn't want the alien to spoil her high, her happiness and her joy at what had just happened with Landon. There wasn't anything that could go wrong as the deed had already been done. It was over. She had got away with it.

What is the Recathri's problem? Amiah thought.

"Remember not to tell anyone that I am here researching

your planet." the Recathri alien said in a high-pitched female voice.

"Eww... go back to the other voice, please!" Amiah replied staring upwards. "And, by the way I will tell my riders in my club. The Amiah Riders. They know how to keep a secret and all of them I guarantee you are 100% trustworthy."

There was a long pause and the silence hung in the air like an unspoken heavy weight.

"Ok, so I will now allow the Amiah Riders to see me also." the Recathri alien conceded finally, speaking in it's deep male voice.

"Ok! So, where are you going to go first?" Amiah said feeling a little bored now.

She had other sexier things on her mind. Sexier things that were much more exciting than questioning an over-anxious alien, who was only showing off around her to help with its dull research.

"Duneway high security virtual prison." the Recathri alien replied.

Amiah's smile dropped.

"Why?" Amiah asked raising her eyebrows, while anxiously looking up at the Recathri alien for answers.

Landon was at Duneway. She didn't want anything the alien did around there to get Landon in any kind of trouble.

"Is this worry I see expressed by your human facial expression?" the Recathri alien responded.

"No. It's anxiety. Look it up." Amiah retorted back and looked away from the ceiling.

"Ok. See you later or is it jelitoonaa!" the Recathri alien said and disappeared.

As soon as the Recathri alien disappeared, Amiah walked out of the virtual garage and made her way through the virtual courtyard, porch, foyer and into the virtual lift to get to her bedroom. Yawning a few times as she walked along. She did not pass any of her Amiah Riders on her way back to her room, only a few robots who turned their heads to watch her but did not interfere.

When Amiah reached her bedroom, she danced all the way towards her 4 poster cream coloured virtual canopy bed and threw herself backwards on top of it. Then she touched herself slow and tenderly using her hands to caress her succulent breasts first, before moving downwards to her love box.

Amiah then caressed her body faster and faster before releasing an orgasm of total bliss and ecstatic surrender. Amiah soon fell into a beautiful sleep with her eyes shut and a wide smile on her lovely brown face.

*****

The next day, early in the morning around 7am, Amiah telepathically spoke to all the Amiah Riders during breakfast. She informed them about the Recathri alien and her adventurous night ride with the alien in it's temporary form of a glowing gold robotcycle. She told them how she had been able to visit Landon and hug him in her invisible state. Amiah didn't tell them that she had made love with him.

"You only hugged him!" Jan laughed.

Some of the other Amiah Riders giggled along with her.

Amiah felt her brown cheeks grow warm.

"Yes, he was sleeping, and I didn't want to wake him up." Amiah replied out loud. She quickly moved onto the next topic. "Here's the virtual security cameras recording of the Recathri alien and I in the garage talking. Take a look at the screen when you've finished eating. It will be here to view over again as many times as you wish. There is only thing that was important to this alien that named itself after our Recathri very strong rum here on Earth. This is, that we all keep the alien's presence here on our beautiful planet a secret."

"We can't tell anyone. Not even my husband or kids." said one of the Amiah Riders frowning.

"Definitely not Jason!" Lucy said out loud to the woman who had just spoken. "Don't forget what happened the last time you trusted my brother with a secret about my surprise holiday getaway. Ok, I won't say it." Lucy finished talking quickly.

"Try and keep this Recathri alien a secret as I think we will definitely see it again one day in the future. When it returns, I am going to try and bargain with it, so that we can all get to experience invisibility." Amiah said happily to her Amiah Riders. "And, of course I want all of you to get to ride it in the form of the glowing gold flying robotcycle! That part is even better than being invisible, trust me!"

"It's a shame you don't have footage of you flying through the air on that glowing robotcycle!" Petra exclaimed. She watched curiously with her eyes lighting up in amazement at the images being shown on the virtual screen located at the front of the room.

The virtual screen displayed the security footage of last night's encounter between Amiah Lily and the Recathri alien in its various forms. The Amiah Riders watched with keen interest and listened carefully to all that was said. After the first showing had finished, some of the Amiah Riders wanted to watch the security footage over again. Saraina was one of them. She was very excited about the return of the unknown oval shaped green shadow.

"Jelitoonaa! Did you see when the Recathri changed into the glowing gold robotcycle?! That was the best part! I wish I was there to see this. When will the alien be back? Call me next time Amiah?" Saraina exclaimed enthusiastically.

Amiah smiled at Saraina's innocent enthusiasm.

"Ok, if anyone can sense any new information about the Recathri alien then let me know. I am about to start the one-to-one blocking training beginning early. I'll start with you Antoinette in the conference room in 30 minutes." Amiah said happily.

"Yes boss." Antoinette replied.

After 30 minutes had passed by, Amiah and Antoinette sat together in the virtual conference room. Amiah talked to Antoinette.

"Firstly I will assess your level of blocking ability and then afterwards we can talk about what issues arose and how you can improve, ok? You don't have to take any painkillers beforehand as the moment you feel any kind of discomfort just say 'Stop'. Is this alright Antoinette?" Amiah instructed calmly.

Antoinette eyes glanced left and right nervously a couple of times.

Amiah could sense that she was tense to be assessed by her. She decided not to reassure her but to let Antoinette's anxiety fuel her practice session to make her try harder. Amiah continued to speak without waiting for Antoinette's response.

"In precisely 5 minutes all the lights will turn off and a black dome will cover the entire room so that both of us will not be able to see anything with our physical eyes. I will move seat and find another virtual seat to sit on or I may stand anywhere in this room. I will use various psychic and paranormal skills to discover anything about you and you will have to try and sense my psychic energy and block it, ok?" Amiah explained. "I will inform you when we are about to start. Any questions?"

"What will you try to find out about me?" Antoinette asked pretending to be more confident than she felt.

"Anything you don't block." Amiah said.

"Ok." Antoinette replied back.

There was silence in the conference room for a few more minutes before the lights turned off and a black dome covered nearly everything in the room. Amiah and Antoinette were inside this black dome. Then, Amiah spoke again. This time Amiah spoke telepathically to Antoinette and was heard as a voice in Antoinette's mind.

"Start." Amiah instructed calmly.

Thirty seconds of further silence ensued before Antoinette shouted out in pain.

"Stop!" Antoinette shouted.

The black dome disappeared, and the two women were now sitting side by side at the virtual grey marble circular table.

Antoinette held her head back and had her right hand over her forehead.

"I'm sorry Amiah, I couldn't do it. From the moment it went black I had a headache which just got worse the longer time I spent trying to block you." Antoinette said. Her breathing was fast and shallow. Amiah called a medical robot who was standing nearby. The robot came over to the two women with a virtual silver tray with drinks, water and tablets.

"Wait, I think it's gone... yes... it's totally gone now!" Antoinette said with relief.

"Good." Amiah replied with a serious expression on her face.

Antoinette was an exceptional paranormal robotcyclist and had managed to block other psychics during previous rescue missions before. Was it more practice she needed or was it the fact that Antoinette was trying to block her that resulted in her failure during this practice blocking session? Amiah considered to herself.

"I think I maybe the problem Antoinette. I know you have done exceedingly well blocking other psychics during rescue missions in the past so it must be me. I guess I'm too strong a psychic for you." Amiah said resignedly.

Antoinette thought quietly for a moment.

"Let me try again Amiah." Antoinette finally replied.

This was the reaction that Amiah wanted.

"Ok. Starting again in 2 minutes." Amiah replied.

On the second practice session, Antoinette managed to keep blocking for 10 minutes 50 seconds before she shouted out the words "Stop!".

The black dome disappeared for the second time and the lights in the virtual conference room went on. Antoinette drank some water from the virtual glass and held her forehead with her right hand. Amiah waited 5 minutes for Antoinette to compose herself again before speaking.

"Jelitoonaa! I only read your mind for the final 5 minutes of your blocking practice. I will have to be careful around you now!" Amiah said jokingly to Antoinette.

In reality, she wasn't scared if any of her Amiah Riders would be able to block her as she loved and trusted all of them. Besides, she hadn't used her strongest paranormal skills on Antoinette like she did the first time around. This was to try and build

Antoinette's confidence in herself and her blocking abilities.

"Wait till I tell the other girls that I can block Amiah Lily from reading my energy and thoughts for 5 minutes. Have any of the other women been able to do that like ever?" Antoinette said enthusiastically.

"Jan has. When she was younger." Amiah admitted. "I want you to try to remember how you used your blocking skills the first time and the second time. What worked for you? What didn't? What could be improved? Try practicing blocking with other Amiah Riders and I promise you can only get better."

"I will, thanks Amiah." Antoinette drank some more water and picked up two handfuls of chocolate biscuits from the virtual tray.

"Hey, leave me some." Amiah joked.

Antoinette smiled, poked her tongue out in a joking way and got up to walk out of the virtual conference room.

Similar practice sessions with all the Amiah Riders on separate occasions took place for the rest of the morning up to mid-afternoon. Some of the Amiah Riders needed more help than others. The longest practice session was with an Amiah Rider called Melissa.

Melissa Cantim was the programming expert of the club. She could design, build and program robotcycles, advanced virtual technology and anything else that needed programming. The reason why Melissa's practice blocking session took so long, was that after 5 practice attempts Amiah saw an image of Landon in Melissa's mind.

Landon was standing up next to his robotcycle wearing a white tracksuit, which Amiah viewed clearly coming from Melissa's mind. Instantly feeling jealous, Amiah had spied on the emotional energy around the image of Landon in Melissa's mind. Luckily for Melissa, Amiah didn't find any love emotions only some angry emotions attached to the image.

Amiah questioned Melissa in a light-hearted way so as not to get any defences up from Melissa while she was talking with her. She wanted Melissa to continue being open and relaxed so

Amiah could further read her thoughts without her knowing.

"I feel for you Amiah. I know you love him and I'm angry that you are going through so much because of him being in jail. I can see it in your energy and feel it in your voice whenever you speak about him and even sometimes when you don't mention his name. It's not fair and we need to rescue him. Shit Amiah! We've succeeded in every rescue mission so far! Why can't we find a way to get Landon out of Duneway!" Melissa exclaimed.

Amiah was impressed by Melissa's passion about rescuing Landon and her empathy for what she was going through without Landon next to her. She wondered if Melissa and the Recathri alien could work together to create invisible robotcycles that the Amiah Riders could use…

"Amiah are you listening?" Melissa asked

Amiah snapped out of her thoughts of how she could use Melissa's programming talents to help the club and rescue Landon. "Yes, I'm listening. Thank you for your concern but I am fine. I talked with Landon before he went into prison and he would want me to keep riding, look after the Amiah Riders and enjoy my life."

"I know but it must hurt sometimes knowing that he's not here to enjoy life with you." Melissa replied.

"If you want to help Melissa, keep practicing your blocking skills and one day we will try and rescue Landon from Duneway high security virtual prison again." Amiah answered.

There was a short silence between them both for a few minutes. Melissa looked at Amiah with a hopeless 'I wish I could help you' expression. Amiah sat patiently waiting for Melissa to process the information and speak.

"Ok, but if you ever need anyone to talk with, I and all the Amiah Riders are here. We love you, you know this right?" Melissa said finally getting up to leave the virtual conference room after this extra long one-on-one blocking practice session.

"I know. I love all of you too." Amiah smiled. Melissa was lucky that she didn't sense any romantic emotions attached to the image of Landon, that Amiah had psychically read in her mind. Amiah didn't know how she would have reacted if there was a romantic love energy attached to the image of Landon in Melissa's mind. The way she felt right now, she could easily have...

Amiah's trail of thought faded away as she heard a soothing ringing tone by both of her ears. An incoming vision was coming through. Melissa had left the virtual conference room and Amiah was alone again to watch her vision by herself, with the exception of a few robots in various corners of the room. Amiah peered with interest at the misty orange vision that had now appeared in front of her.

In the vision Amiah saw a misty orange colour like orange smoke getting lighter and denser in places. She could not see anything behind the orange mist only more of an orange backdrop. Then, Amiah heard the sounds of babies crying loud by both her ears. Sensing that this vision was very important, Amiah felt confused as to what the babies could signify.

What does babies have to do with a paranormal/psychic female robotcyclist club? Did they need rescuing? Amiah wondered.

Amiah used every psychic and paranormal ability she had, to read more into the strange vision and the sounds of babies. For some reason, she couldn't find out anymore information than what was in front of her. She wondered if someone was blocking her psychic skills from finding out more.

Could it be the Recathri alien? she thought.

The Recathri alien was the only newcomer she had allowed to come into her mansion recently. Why would the Recathri alien block her ability to read her visions though? What benefit would that be for the alien? All these thoughts raced around in Amiah's mind.

After 10 more minutes of not getting anymore information from the vision and listening to babies crying around her, Amiah used one of rarely used paranormal abilities. She cut the vision off from playing in front of her. Sometimes this worked and other times it didn't. On this occasion it worked and the sounds of babies crying loudly stopped along with the misty orange vision.

Amiah breathed a sigh of relief when the vision and crying noises stopped. Maybe she was just tired, it had been a lot of hard work trying to train up her riders to use their blocking skills. Putting the vision and sounds of babies crying to one side of her mind, Amiah got up from the virtual conference room to go and get something to eat.

INVISIBLE

Eight months later...

Amiah rode into her virtual garage on her black and gold robotcycle with the Amiah Riders close behind her. She parked her robotcycle near the front entrance on the left-hand side and stepped off her robotcycle to run to the nearby virtual toilets. She desperately had wanted to pee for over ten minutes ago so had sped back home to Amiah Mansion. This time however, Amiah felt something different coming out from her. It was a gush of clear fluid. Amiah called out for help telepathically to the Amiah Riders.

"My waters have broken! It's happening!" Amiah said excitedly.

"I'll get the midwife robot to be on standby in your bedroom as planned." Jan said to Amiah helping her friend out of the toilet and onto a virtual hover mat to take her to her bedroom.

Amiah Lily was 8 months pregnant with Landon Ross's first child. Her child was conceived during the time she had made love with Landon (in her invisible state) after the Recathri alien had taken her to Duneway high security virtual prison. Amiah felt mixed emotions during her pregnancy. Part of her was of course elated, that she would be having a baby by the man she loved even though he wanted her to find a new man. Another part was very angry that she would be a single mother and Landon would never be around her to look after the child. Her child would not know it's daddy except for regular prison visits.

"Aaaargh!" Amiah exclaimed in pain. "I can't have this baby on this mat. Get me to my bedroom quickly!"

"Don't worry, it's not far, we'll be there soon! Everything's ready for you and our new Amiah Rider." Jan replied.

Saraina, Lucy, Petra and Melissa were also running alongside the virtual hover mat as it made it's way by pre-programming swiftly through Amiah Mansion, to get to Amiah Lily's bedroom. Amiah laid on her back with both her legs bent wearing a low-cut red top. A green virtual blanket covered over the lower half of her body. She had been preparing for the moment of her love child's birth since 6 months ago when she had first found out that she was 2 months pregnant.

Amiah had noticed that she was putting on weight and had been throwing up every morning at the same time for weeks. Jan had joked with her that she might be pregnant and Amiah had laughed for a while until all of a sudden she realized that it could be a real possibility. Landon had never been able to get her pregnant before even though they never used birth control. This is why Amiah did not seriously consider that she was pregnant until Jan suggested it. Then everything fell into place. The morning sickness, the nausea, the non-existent monthly period, the nightly visits from Landon in her dreams telling her he loved her.

With all the psychic and paranormal gifts Amiah Lily had, for some reason she had not been able to foresee a baby was on its way or see any visions of a baby or child. This was highly unusual as when other women around her had been pregnant, Amiah would know intuitively. She was so skilled at sensing a new life in a woman that she had been hired a few times by previous male lovers to find out if women they were having affairs with were pregnant. Each time Amiah would be 100 % accurate. It was like as if she had 'a nose for smelling a new creation', one of her past lovers called Mak had commented.

Yet, Amiah Lily could not sense her own new creation or new life that had been steadily growing inside her womb. She was so oblivious, that she had unknowingly been pregnant for 2 months. There were signs that something was up with her body for 8 weeks, and still she had not realised. Amiah put it down to the fact that she was very busy training up the Amiah Riders to improve their blocking skills and getting on with day-to-day business.

The Amiah Riders had been on 2 more rescue missions during the first 8 weeks of her pregnancy so Amiah had many other important things to keep her mind occupied. Still, where were her foreseeing visions when she needed them? Amiah thought. Her visions were one of her most revealing paranormal gifts and they had let her down. To this present day, laying on her back on her virtual hover mat about to give birth, she still had no intuition about what the baby would look or behave like.

Would the baby look like her or Landon? Would the baby be a boy or a girl? Amiah wondered. She remembered informing the doctors and nurses that she did not want to know the sex of her baby and that she would prefer if they did not tell her. Amiah wanted to encourage her natural psychic abilities to reveal the baby's gender along with more information about her future child. No information about the baby, however, was disclosed to Amiah Lily in any paranormal or psychic way. Feeling upset about this, Amiah had talked it over with Jan after a night ride out on their robotcycles. Their conversation went as follows: -

"You know I always thought that I would get so much insight and intuitive knowledge about a child that I was carrying if I ever got pregnant. I'm getting nothing. Nothing at all." Amiah complained to Jan.

"Not even a dream or vision." Jan replied genuinely surprised.

"Not even a dream or vision." Amiah repeated out loud.

Jan hesitated before speaking again.

"It's probably all the extra hormones messing with your radar." Jan joked.

"No Jan, it's something else. It doesn't make sense. I've known more about ex-boyfriends' mistresses pregnancies than my own. Something is very off. It's like the baby is…" Amiah said

"Nah, it's because this is the first time your body has gone through this pregnancy thing and you're overthinking it. When you relax more, then more insight will come to you." Jan replied confidently.

Amiah laughed. "That sounds like something I would say."

"Well, I did learn from the best." Jan smiled. She put an arm around Amiah's shoulders and squeezed her in a half hug. "Just take it easy more. You probably need more rest. You have to rest for two when you are two."

"I am tired but not from this baby. I'm tired from the ride. Let's go eat!" Amiah said.

Returning back to the present moment, Amiah laid on her back on her 4 poster cream coloured virtual canopy bed with her legs bent at the knees. She screamed out in pain as the head of the baby began to show at the entrance of her lovebox.

"Breathe, breathe, breathe. Blow out through your mouth. I can see the head." the robot midwife said in a pre-programmed voice to sound like Landon.

"Landon!!" Amiah screamed out again and felt the baby leave her body.

Finally, it was over. Wiping sweat from her forehead and slowing down her breathing, Amiah waited to hear the sound of the baby crying. Instead, there was a prolonged silence in her bedroom.

"Well, where is my baby. Boy or girl?" Amiah panted, her breathing quickening again.

"Amiah, I'm so sorry." Jan answered, her voice cracking with emotion.

Amiah felt an instant feeling of pure terror. She thought she was about to have a panic attack but she managed to calm herself before speaking again.

"Just give me my baby. I don't care what it looks like." Amiah said quickly.

"Amiah, I think you should…" Jan replied.

"Jan! Give me my baby!" Amiah shouted.

"Ok." Jan gulped back tears and placed an invisible heavy object onto Amiah's chest.

Amiah stared at Jan questioningly and then the invisible

heavy object let out one big cry. It was her baby laying on her chest crying loudly.

Her baby was invisible. She had given birth to Landon's invisible love child.

Jan, Saraina and Petra began crying also.

"Everyone get out! Get out!" Amiah shouted.

"Amiah, I..." Jan tried to find the words to console Amiah.

"Get out!" Amiah repeated again telepathically and also vocally very loudly.

Everyone in the bedroom looked at Amiah with shock and sadness. Then, they one by one left her bedroom including the midwife robots and other robot staff.

Amiah let out a bloodcurdling scream which all the Amiah Riders heard even the ones who were far away riding on their robotcycles. Her arms shaking with disbelief, Amiah tightly held onto her invisible baby resting crying softly on her chest. Next, she used her right hand to where she thought the baby's bottom was, so she could push it upwards to breastfeed it. She managed to get herself in a sitting position and felt a tiny mouth latch onto her left nipple and start suckling. While breastfeeding her invisible child, Amiah began slowly processing what had just happened.

How could this be possible? she raged inwardly.

She could feel that she was breastfeeding a human baby, but she could not see it with her physical eyes. Not even with her psychic or paranormal eyes.

Is this what the Recathri alien had tried to warn me about on that night at Duneway high security virtual prison? she thought, how could the alien be so evil? How do I tell Landon that he will never be able to see his child?

Amiah's mind raced with panicked thoughts.

Amiah looked down again at where she thought her baby was. She could still feel it suckling on milk from her left full breast. She reached her other hand down to feel the baby to see if it was a boy or a girl. It was a baby boy. An invisible baby boy.

Amiah reached her hand back up to lightly feel the features

of her invisible child's face. The invisible baby boy had her nose. Amiah was certain. Amiah had a wide cute nose which she could feel her new little boy had exactly the same shape, only smaller. The ears of her new baby simply felt like tiny ears to Amiah. The baby's hair was soft and wavy. Amiah wished with all her heart that she could see her new baby boy. She telepathically called out to the Recathri alien in her mind.

"Recathri! It's Amiah Lily. I can't see my newborn baby boy. He's been born invisible just like I was invisible when he was conceived with Landon at Duneway virtual prison. You need to come see me now and reverse this shit." Amiah pleaded telepathically to the Recathri alien.

Amiah waited for a response from the Recathri alien. She didn't care if he showed up with the remedy for invisibility or telepathically spoke to her and said what the cure would be. Any way that the Recathri alien wanted to inform her of how she could see her newborn baby boy again was ok with her.

The alien needed to act fast though. This wasn't fair on her or on Landon. After all they had been through with the unfair arrest, the repulsive jail sentence and the failed rescue attempts, this new blow was too much. It was plain cruel. If the Recathri alien did not reverse this invisible disease on her new baby, it would live to regret it.

If it lives long enough that is, Amiah thought angrily.

Amiah felt both her eyes flash brightly with burning rage and anger. She stayed awake holding her invisible baby for the next few hours. Often running her hand gently over it's features to try to sense with her psychic or paranormal abilities more about her baby. Amiah knew that she loved her baby more than anything else in the world. She loved him probably more than Landon and she would do anything to restore him back to being a 'normal' baby that she and other humans could see.

The Recathri alien had still not replied to her telepathic message so in desperation Amiah sent one last message from her mind to the energy around the alien.

"F*** you Recathri!"

Then Amiah fell into a deep sleep.

While Amiah slept, medical robots came into Amiah's bedroom and took her invisible child quietly off her chest. Next, they placed the invisible baby into the colourful four poster virtual cot next to Amiah's four poster cream coloured virtual canopy bed.

As the baby slept in the decorative four poster virtual cot, an oval shaped green shadow hovered over the baby briefly before disappearing. The invisible baby woke up and started crying. The oval shaped green shadow appeared again briefly and hovered directly over where the invisible boy lay. The baby stopped crying immediately.

The Recathri alien disappeared again.

*****

Four years later...

Amiah closely watched her invisible child, Brandon Ross, on his first black and gold mini-robotcycle with amusement and pride. Brandon was the name that Landon had chosen for their invisible baby boy when they had travelled to visit him at Duneway high security virtual prison. Landon's great great grandfather's name was Brandon P. Ross and he lived in a time where there were no robotcycles. There were only the old-fashioned style bikes called motorcycles.

Amiah glanced at the photo of her son's great great great grandfather on a virtual photo placed above the mini-garage area of her son's enormous virtual playroom. In the virtual photo, Brandon P. Ross was standing next to one of the old-fashioned motorcycles wearing the full old style biker gear. The old-fashioned biker gear he wore consisted of black leather gloves, black & navy blue motorcycle jacket, brown ankle motorcycle boots, black motorcycle pants and a luminous green and white helmet. The elder Brandon P Ross stood proudly next to his motorcycle in the photo and looked like an older more serious version of Landon.

Amiah returned her gaze back to Brandon and for what felt

like the millionth time over the past four years, she wondered if her invisible son looked more like her or his father. When Landon had first met his son Brandon (just over 3 and a half years ago) he was just as shocked and angry as Amiah was. Landon had wanted to get some of his paranormal friends to come to Amiah Mansion and try to contact the Recathri alien from the energy left in the garage. Amiah told him that it wasn't worth trying as she and her paranormal bikers had already attempted in numerous different ways to do this already. Nothing worked. The Recathri alien was keeping its distance, and there wasn't a psychic or paranormal skill that could make the alien help them unless it wanted to.

At Duneway high security virtual prison, Amiah had to hide the baby's true invisible appearance under a cleverly designed 'human virtual masked bodysuit' that was safe to cover Brandon's body. This 'human virtual masked bodysuit' was designed by Melissa Cantim. The reasoning behind it was so that no-one would sensationalise the invisibility of the child if Brandon had to go out in public.

The expert design of the 'human virtual masked bodysuit' was so effective at covering up Brandon's real invisibility that one day while out shopping, a male model scout had approached Amiah. The model scout had wanted to take photos of Brandon to enter him into a local toddler modelling competition. Amiah had made up an excuse of course, as there was no way she wanted to bring any unnecessary attention to Brandon. This would only increase the risk that his true invisibility would be discovered.

Landon had believed Amiah straight away about their son's invisible appearance that no-one could see. Both their anger was initially turned towards the Recathri alien who had befriended Amiah and not stopped them from making love on that fateful night. If it was this dangerous for them to touch each other while Amiah was invisible, the Recathri alien should have intervened. It was only fair and it was the humane thing to do. Yet, what did the Recathri alien know about humanity?

Amiah pondered; the alien was on planet Earth (in an unknown location) conducting 'research'.

The Recathri alien had told Amiah that it was sent to Earth to learn about the planet, to learn about humans, to study etc… Why had it not had the foresight, compassion or empathy to warn Amiah of the severe, dangerous and disturbing consequences of making love, while in the alien's induced invisible state? she further pondered.

Landon had told Amiah exactly the same thing that Amiah had thought, the day she had given birth to Brandon. They both thought the Recathri alien was evil.

Whether or not the Recathri alien was evil though, it had to be contacted and communicated with in a very clever way in order to return Brandon back to a 'normal' human appearance. Every day, Amiah and her Amiah Riders tried to contact the Recathri alien using their psychic and paranormal abilities. It soon became very clear that the Recathri alien was ignoring their pleas for help. Oddly, even the security footage of the alien's visit and conversation with Amiah in the virtual garage had been deleted.

Melissa Cantim, the programming expert of the Amiah Riders, could not find a way to restore or retrieve any saved copies of the security footage. It was as if the Recathri alien had managed to somehow get into the mansion and use some kind of unknown skill to delete every trace of the security footage. Who else would want to do that, apart from the alien? This was the thought on everyone's mind the day after Brandon was born and the Amiah Riders searched in vain for the security footage. It was gone. Forever.

"Brandon!" Amiah exclaimed out loud, snapping back into reality frowning, as little Brandon fell off his mini-robotcycle for the fourth time.

A delighted squeal of laughter came from Brandon who was rolling around on the floor saying the words "Robotcycle! Daddy and mummy love robotcycles!"

Amiah giggled along with Brandon and rushed over to pick

him up and hug him. Although invisible, Brandon wore clothes and trainers so that he could be recognised as a little boy.

"Yes Brandon! Mummy and Daddy love robotcycles! You're going to love them too one day when you're older. Mummy and Daddy are going to teach you to be the best robotcyclist this world will ever see. Believe this my handsome, talented, gorgeous little boy." Amiah said affectionately.

"Daddy. I want Daddy." Brandon replied. He released himself from his mother's hug and ran back to sit on his mini-robotcycle in his playroom.

Amiah sighed. "We're going to visit Daddy very soon."

"I want Daddy nooooww!" Brandon turned his mini-robotcycle around and drove fast towards Amiah. He then rode his mini-robotcycle over a pair of Amiah's trainers which were on the floor.

Amiah laughed and faked an angry expression on her face. She then play-chased Brandon around the virtual playroom making funny faces to get him to laugh. Eventually, Brandon burst out laughing after staying silent for a few minutes. After Brandon had stopped laughing, he spoke to his mum in a quiet voice.

"Daddy gone. Mummy sad." Brandon said and jumped off his mini-robotcycle and hugged Amiah's legs.

Amiah blinked back tears from her eyes and knelt down to hold her invisible son again. She used all her psychic gifts to try and sense the energy around Brandon. To try and sense what he could possibly look like or anything that might help to enable her to see him for the first time. Still, nothing. There was just a blurry mist of grey and orange. There were no facial features, no hair or skin colour, no indication of what his destiny was to be coming through in any of her visions so far. No warnings around him and no insight as to when she would see her son with her own eyes. It was too upsetting to think about so Amiah changed the subject.

"Mummy is not sad. Mummy always looks like this when she's... when she's hungry. Yes, I'm hungry and need to eat something. Are you hungry Brandon?" Amiah asked.

"No... Mummy hungry!" Brandon said and raised both arms in the air.

Amiah smiled. "Let's go and get something to eat."

At that moment a robot member of staff came into the virtual playroom carrying a virtual tray of ham & cheese sandwiches and small virtual glasses filled with orange juice. The robot placed the virtual tray down on a small blue virtual table near the centre of the playroom. Then the robot left the playroom.

Amiah grinned again at Brandon. "Let's eat!"

"Yeah!" Brandon exclaimed. He ran over to the virtual blue table and picked up three sandwiches in his left hand. He began to bite into all the sandwiches at the same time.

Amiah blinked back tears again. Landon used to be behave ravenous with food just the same way. Always choosing more food than he could eat.

She further recalled a sexier memory that Landon had often acted 'ravenous' with her body, yet he could never get enough of eating her lovebox...

Amiah looked away from her son and looked down at her body. It had been years since she had made love with Landon. Around 4 years and 8 months. She was sure she was drying up. She couldn't face being with another man like Landon had suggested.

This must be real love, Amiah thought.

A quiet ringing tone suddenly sounded near to Amiah's left ear. Amiah braced herself to focus on the incoming vision but did not sit down. She felt relaxed enough to handle whatever she was shown. Amiah watched the white mist clear gradually in the vision which played out silently in front of her. The white mist in the vision continued on for another ten minutes and Amiah grew bored.

Amiah glanced over at Brandon a few times during the vision. Brandon was still happily eating and drinking at the virtual blue table. Amiah continued to stare at the vision and searched the energy of it, to find out further information. She could sense that it was half and half. This meant that there was half a seriousness to it and half truth to it. It was a scene which had a lot of playfulness around it. Amiah felt her heart race a little faster and her breathing quicken with excitement.

Is this a vision about my son Brandon? she thoughtfully considered, in curious anticipation.

"Mummy are you talking about me?" Brandon said out loud.

The vision that Amiah had been watching and psychically deciphering, abruptly stopped playing in front of her.

Amiah sighed in exasperation. She was so close. She nearly felt like she was certain the vision was going to give her some insight, some clues, something, anything about Brandon.

Brandon, she thought, my invisible loving bright gifted and adorable son.

Did the vision stop because of Brandon's innocent interruption? Amiah pondered, if this was the case, what would have been revealed if Brandon did not speak at that precise point in time?

"Brandon, I didn't speak my gorgeous boy. What did you hear?" Amiah asked Brandon.

"I heard you say you love me mummy." Brandon replied and ran over to his mini-robotcycle and jumped on it. "You love me, food, Daddy and robotcycles!"

"Yes I do, my jelitoonaa son. Yes I do." Amiah replied.

Brandon was already racing around the playroom again on his mini-robotcycle and didn't respond to the reply that his mother Amiah had said back to him.

Amiah watched Brandon again with pride and admiration. Even though Brandon was invisible, he didn't let this hold back his confidence or self-assurance in the world. He was a strong-willed child at the age of 4 and his invisibility did not hinder him. It only affected the emotions of people who would dearly love to be able to see him. It hurt and angered Amiah. It enraged and frustrated Landon.

Part of Landon's frustration was that he felt powerless to do anything to help Amiah find the alien. Landon had some level of psychic ability, but it was nothing like Amiah's. So, if Amiah and her gifted Amiah Riders could not trace the alien's whereabouts, then how could he find a cure for his son's invisibility?

Together, Amiah and Landon had talked about how they could try and make the Recathri alien return to give them a cure for their invisible son. Their conversation had gone horribly wrong somehow. Amiah playbacked the last part of the conversation from 3 years ago in her mind...

"You know what Amiah? I wish you had never made a pact with this alien dude." Landon had said to her when she had visited Duneway high security virtual prison one day, with Brandon.

"Dude. No-one uses that word anymore Landon." Amiah had replied.

Amiah recalled how Landon had held baby Brandon in his arms looking down at him with a blank expression on his face. Amiah had tried to read him but couldn't get past his angry emotions to reveal the hidden feelings underneath. Brandon was wearing the 'human virtual masked bodysuit' which covered up his invisibility in public.

"So tell me what else did you make a pact about? The Amiah Riders?" Landon had suddenly retorted back at her.

Amiah remembered that she had remained calm. She previously had some foresight about this visit to Duneway virtual prison and she knew that Landon would be mad at her. Really, he was mad at the Recathri alien just like her but sometimes if he was overtired, he would just direct his anger at other things. Amiah knew this about him.

"Are you just going to sit there and let dude get one over on you and me? Is that it Amiah? Look at our son, Amiah!" Landon had looked down at the fake yet expertly and realistically designed human covering for his invisible son and frowned.

"Melissa made him look like an Indian baby." Landon had said coldly.

"Like you could have made him look any better as a mask or

in real life." Amiah had snapped back defensively.

Immediately she had regretted her words. In her heart she did not mean what she had just heard coming from her own mouth. It wasn't her speaking, it was the stress of the entire mad situation.

Amiah had been overjoyed when Melissa had come up with the idea to invent a 'human virtual masked bodysuit'. Without Melissa's creative genius, their son would not even be able to walk around in public for fear of being discovered as invisible. There wasn't any point in criticising Melissa's expertise and bringing race into it was just plain stupid. This wasn't the Landon she knew. He hated racism of all kinds.

"Listen, I know this is hard for you. It's hard for me too. It's hard for Melissa and all the Amiah Riders to deal with. We've spent 4 years looking 24 hours a day for the Recathri. We... we've tried everything. Everything." Amiah had said trying to remain calm.

"So, are you just gonna give up?" Landon had replied.

"We never give up, do we?" Amiah remembered half-smiling at him.

Landon hadn't replied and there was an awkward silence between the two for the next ten minutes. They had stared at each other in silence. Each remembering good times that both of them had shared together. They had appeared lost in their own private thoughts.

"A Da-Da. A Da-Da." Baby Brandon had spoke up in the midst of the silence.

"He said Da Da." Landon's voice had cracked with emotion.

Amiah remembered that she had seen a tear freely escape from both of Landon's sexy brown eyes.

Amiah had heard baby Brandon say "Da-Da" before so wasn't surprised.

"Amiah, he said Da-Da." Landon had repeated to her. "Say it again Brandon my boy, Da-Da, Daddy. I'm your Dad."

"Da-Da-Da-Da-Da-Da-Daddy." Baby Brandon had said and let out a long loud giggle.

Landon had begun to talk softly to their baby and repeat the words that he had so longed to hear since Brandon was born. Amiah recalled how she had watched quietly while Landon played with their son. In real life, their invisible son.

The 'human virtual masked bodysuit' was so realistic it fooled everyone she had passed at Duneway virtual prison. Some had even ridiculously commented that the child was the image of her and others had even more crazily stated that the baby was the image of Landon Ross. Amiah acted polite and friendly with all the staff at Duneway, especially the paranormal security guards. Her psychic and paranormal blocking skills reassured her that no-one not even the specially trained psychic staff would be able to see into her mind. Her mindset was too well protected.

In addition, Amiah blocked the words that she and Landon spoke from being heard correctly by anyone else listening. This was another paranormal skill that Amiah Lily possessed, and it was very effective. Anybody listening in to them talk each time she visited Duneway, heard a totally made-up conversation that Amiah Lily had edited in her mind beforehand. All the paranormal/psychic security staff, including the other prisoners had no idea who Amiah Lily really was and what she was capable of. This made it even more fun during visits to see Landon.

After Landon had returned to looking at her with confused anger in his eyes, Amiah spoke.

"Didn't we agree that all our anger would be directed at the Recathri? Not at anyone we know." she said.

"I know that." Landon had replied sorrowfully.

Amiah had paused briefly. "So let us work out together how we can contact it, the thing that's done this."

"You told me that everything you've tried hasn't worked." Landon had stated in exasperation.

"Well, maybe it's time I just talked to the news people about what happened." Amiah had said in desperation with a shrug of her shoulders.

Landon had laughed. "You don't mean that. You know that

our son would not be our son anymore. He would be a research baby prodded and picked out, used and abused."

"Maybe we could refuse that kind of research." Amiah had desperately suggested. She knew she was clutching at a broken straw. She knew that she would never go through with that final resort. It would put Brandon's life, the secrecy of her paranormal gifts and the talents of the Amiah Riders at risk. Amiah just wanted to try and give Landon some hope that it was still possible that one day they would both see their son. Even if that meant giving him false hope.

"Amiah you don't fool me. You would never do that. Stop trying to pacify me. You know there is only one way you can do that... and we can't do it here." Landon had smiled and winked at her.

Amiah remembered the sweet sensation of her body growing warm with love for Landon, as she had smiled tenderly back at him.

"I love you Amiah but you need to look elsewhere. I'm going to be in here till I die." Landon had said dismissively.

Amiah had instantly felt overwhelmed with anger. "What has that got to do with..."

Landon had then reached over and held Amiah's hand tightly. "Do it for me and for our son. He needs a Dad in the outside world. Don't make him grow up without a father like I did. Amiah..."

Amiah had then stood up very quickly. She recalled taking baby Brandon out of Landon's arms in one swift movement. Too angry to speak she had walked away fast from Landon holding baby Brandon close to her chest. She remembered not looking back at him. What was the point?

This isn't Landon, Amiah had thought to herself sadly.

She didn't recognise that person in there. Baby Brandon had cried loudly all the way out of Duneway virtual prison.

"Daddy sad." Brandon unexpectedly said out loud.

Instantly, Amiah snapped back into present day life and out of her daydream. She walked over to where her invisible son sat on his mini-robotcycle.

"Maybe I'll find you a new Daddy. He will be happy. Would you like that?" Amiah said looking at her son where she believed his eyes would be.

"Yes, new Daddy!" Brandon shouted and raised both his arms in the air happily.

Amiah couldn't help but smile at her son's innocent excitement.

NEVER ALONE

Amiah lay in her four-poster cream coloured virtual canopy bed, reached her right arm high in the air and brought it down fast with her right fist clenched tightly. Her fist created a deep indent in her silk cream pillow next to her. Amiah looked across at the indent mark quizzically. She hadn't hit her pillow that hard.

Or did I? she thought.

Amiah turned to face in the other direction and felt her skin growing hot with anger. The Recathri alien was still nowhere to be found and her love child, her adorable son Brandon remained invisible to her. Brandon was invisible to everyone, but it was the fact that both her and Landon could not see their love child that hurt the most. If only she could see Brandon for a few minutes, an hour or even to be blessed with a single day of seeing her son. This would give her the highest joy that she would trade anything for.

Or perhaps, if Landon could be granted this wish of seeing their son for a few minutes, an hour or a single day. This would give her a similar ecstasy. At least Landon would then be able to describe in fine detail to her about if Brandon had her facial features, her hair or if he looked like his Dad.

Amiah brought her left arm high in the air and brought it down again in a tight fist, with an angry thud down on her cream silk pillow. She held back the urge to scream. She didn't want any of the robot staff or an Amiah Rider to hear her and come in to see what was happening. She was the leader, she had to show control and confidence. Just like on her mostly successful rescue missions that she had led in the past with the

Amiah Riders. She led them to victory in 99% of those missions and she would again. Amiah sat up suddenly filled with pride and determination.

"I am Amiah Lily, leader of the Amiah Riders. We are the best paranormal & psychic robotcycle riders in world history. There is nothing that we can't handle." Amiah whispered to herself in between her fast angry breaths.

Amiah rolled over to the side of her bed and put her feet down on the cool virtual grey and white marble floor. The floor had previously been carpeted but as the weather changed her flooring automatically updated. It was summer in England so most of the flooring around Amiah mansion had been swiftly amended by a pre-programmed system created by Melissa Cantim.

Amiah's pink manicured pretty feet found some flat trainers to slip into, and she stood up stretching both arms above her head. She picked up a hairbrush from the dressing table next to the virtual canopy bed and began to brush her long afro hair into a ponytail at the top of her head. Her hair was still soft from the long twist out hairstyle she had worn during the day, so her styling did not take her very long. Amiah sat back down on her bed and tried to slow down her breathing. After a few minutes, her breathing went back to a calmer state.

Amiah reached down to pick up the bottle of Recathri very strong rum off the floor. It was empty. Amiah threw the virtual bottle away from her and heard it smash at a distance. Amiah got up and went into the luxury bathroom attached to her bedroom. She splashed her face multiple times with cold water, looking up into the gold framed virtual mirror in her virtual bathroom at different intervals. Blinking her eyes, each time she looked up.

She saw another bottle of Recathri rum, located at the side of the robotcycle shaped virtual bath, picked it up and threw it away from her. The half-full virtual bottle smashed away from her again, when it hit the side of the virtual bathroom's light gold and white wall.

Amiah had on black leggings and a white off the shoulder top. She wore a white gold necklace with the name Brandon and a love heart shape intertwined around her son's name. She touched this necklace tenderly at first and then squeezed it until her hand began shaking. Releasing her hand quickly from squeezing her son's name on her white gold necklace, Amiah ran out from her bathroom and towards the virtual door of her large bedroom. She had to get out of there. She had to find the Recathri alien and force it to turn her son back to normal. There must be a way.

The time was 5 minutes past midnight and no-one except the robot staff members watched as Amiah ran through the family room, through the foyer, the porch and out into the front courtyard. Once outside, Amiah again felt the strong urge to scream. She wanted to scream out so loud that the Recathri alien would hear and come flying back to the Amiah Mansion and turn her son back to visible.

Amiah had tried this before, a year ago, and it hadn't worked then.

What would make it work this time? Amiah thought sadly.

She turned right to run towards her virtual robotcycle garage. Quickly entering into her garage, she jumped onto her black and gold robotcycle which was ready and waiting near the front entrance. Her robotcycle virtual helmet immediately came into place and Amiah sped off into the dark warm night air.

She had no idea where she was going and didn't care.

"Where are you going?" an unknown male high-pitched voice shrieked by Amiah's left ear.

Amiah ignored the stranger's voice. She was used to hearing random voices and seeing visions and was experienced enough to know that if you ignore them, they can oftentimes go away. Well, at least her voices and visions did. She realised that not everyone's paranormal experiences could be controlled as easily as she usually was able to. This time however, Amiah was slightly curious as to why the voices around her continued to whisper and shriek into her left ear.

"Nooooo. Amiah turn back." an unknown female deep voice shouted in Amiah's ear.

"Where?" a serious tone said into Amiah's ear, neither male nor female.

"Go back." a child's voice whispered.

These unknown voices kept on saying similar words and short sentences near Amiah Lily's left ear and Amiah ignored them. Amiah was too distracted with her own thoughts to even command the voices to stop. Her mind was focused on the Recathri alien, how to find him and pure outrage over not being able to see her son.

Amiah's mind was not absorbing the surroundings of her night ride. She could have rode through the most interesting and stunning terrain and still not have batted an eyelid at the beautiful scenery around her. So intense was her focus on finding a way to get to see Brandon. Soon, the unknown voices speaking near Amiah gave up. Amiah barely noticed when they had stopped.

After hours of riding on her black and gold robotcycle, Amiah's robotcycle stopped on a secluded beach, 276 miles away from Amiah Mansion. Amiah's robotcycle expertly manoeuvred over the sandy beach and stopped. Amiah's virtual helmet disappeared while Amiah remained seated on her robotcycle looking out into the dark blue cool ocean. Her face portrayed a mix of worry and frustration. She quickly remote viewed Brandon in his nursery back at Amiah Mansion. Brandon was asleep with four robot security guards and 3 robot nannies in his room.

Amiah switched her focus to remote view the rest of her mansion and happily viewed that all was well. Amiah sighed to herself, got off her robotcycle and looked around the beach. She wasn't sure which beach she was at, but it seemed to be entirely empty. Then a vision of three words appeared in front of Amiah. The words written in green appeared in capitals and were "Faith virtual beach."

"Faith virtual beach." Amiah read the words out loud to

herself and laughed. "Is anything real anymore?" Amiah shouted out into dark night sky which was lit up by virtual lights in different places on the beach.

Suddenly sounds of two men laughing came from behind Amiah. Amiah assumed they were voices and ignored them but then she sensed human male energy close by her. She immediately turned her body to look at the back of her robotcycle. She was irritated to see two tall mixed race men (of Chinese and African origin) standing at either side of the back of her robotcycle. Quickly scanning their energy for any kind of threat to her safety, Amiah was surprised to find that she could not read them. It was as if she was being blocked by something or someone. The only people who could block her paranormal skills were other paranormally skilled people, which meant that...

Amiah swiftly rode her black and gold robotcycle forward a short distance and then turned it around to face the direction of where the two men were standing. She watched them warily from a distance and they watched her warily back also. Amiah started to block them from seeing into her mind and memories but was it too late?

How long have these men been standing behind me? Amiah thought, and how strong are their psychic skills?

She looked at the men up and down again. They were identical twins, around her age and they were... attractive. Not as handsome as Landon, but still good looking, very good looking. She estimated they were both over 6 feet tall and took care of their appearance. Both had on muscle fit polo shirts in black and drawstring rise pale green shorts. Both had black curly hair and two shining red robotcycles were driving towards them unmanned.

Amiah watched the men each get on separate red robotcycles and ride towards her on them. As they got close to her, Amiah activated her robotcycle virtual helmet, ready to ride away from the men. The men also had their robotcycle virtual helmets on. There was a brief pause before Amiah sped off on her robotcycle all the way down the sandy beach with the twin men riders in tow.

As Amiah rode fast and free down the length of the beach, she looked in her mirrors and saw that the men did not seem to be chasing her but keeping up with her. Their robotcycles were just as fast as Amiah's and they could easily have overtaken her at many different points, but somehow they had chosen not to.

Amiah deliberately rode her robotcycle across areas of the beach where she would have to manoeuvre around rocky areas. She then performed perfect acrobatic stunts on her robotcycle in front of the men. She began to enjoy herself and smiled as she could see the twin riders trying to copy all of the stunts she did so easily, and successfully. They were good but not as good as her Amiah Riders, Amiah concluded.

After 30 minutes of this, Amiah heard ringing in both her ears. She felt her face grow warm.

What am I doing? she thought, I'm out here showing off in front of two men I don't even know, while little Brandon is still invisible, Landon's in jail and the Recathri alien is out there somewhere hiding from it all.

Amiah grimaced and slowed down her black and gold robotcycle. She waited for the vision to appear and temporarily forgot about the twin men riding behind her.

Amiah saw a large green oval shaped shadow flying around Amiah Mansion and dipping in and out of the virtual buildings. Amiah's heart immediately began to race with excitement and hope. The Recathri alien had returned to Amiah Mansion while she was away. She had to get back as soon as possible. Amiah sent telepathic messages to all of her Amiah Riders to try to communicate with the Recathri alien but also sent a strict warning for the Recathri alien to not be allowed to see Brandon.

"Jelitoonaa! Who taught you how to ride like that?" one of the twin men exclaimed.

"Me!" Amiah shouted back at them and sped off back down the sandy beach to head home all the way back to Amiah Mansion.

Her mind focused once more on the Recathri alien and a cure for her son's invisibility, Amiah did not even notice the two men following behind her at a distance, for the entire 4 hour ride home...

THE ONAI TWINS

Amiah arrived back home at Amiah Mansion drenched with sweat. She rode her black and gold robotcycle into her virtual garage and towards the centre. Once in the middle of her garage, she jumped off her robotcycle and used all her paranormal skills to sense where the Recathri alien could be located within Amiah Mansion. A huge grin formed on her face when she sensed that the Recathri alien was in the virtual garage with her.

"You're back! Welcome!" Amiah shouted out loudly. She had previously decided that if the Recathri alien was to ever return, she would use the tact of being nice at first, before fighting.

Give the alien a chance, Amiah thought deviously.

"I never left." a sorrowful male voice spoke from behind Amiah.

Amiah stifled a laugh. The alien didn't fool her.

"Let's get to it, Recathri. My son Brandon is invisible, you know this already. I can't see him. Landon cannot see him. Nobody can see him and you're going to cure him." Amiah answered speaking quickly.

It took every ounce of strength she had within her, to hold her back from threatening the alien.

Amiah figured that it would take one virtual mobile call to the government, that was it. Then the government would be aware of alien presence in the country. This would mean that they would put the world on high alert. Other countries, neighbouring planets with known alien lifeforms would all begin to watch for the new unknown visitors to Earth. If everyone already known in the universe were all watching out for the Recathri alien, this would make it more likely that the alien would be identified. New Alien Identification rules followed that; any alien visiting a planet which they are not a citizen of, must make themselves known to the rulers of that planet. That had been the law since the year 2080, when the first mass alien visitation had been present on the Earth for over 10 years...

The Recathri alien flew around Amiah in the shape of a green coloured deer and then changed into other animal shapes directly in front of Amiah. Amiah watched the alien change shape again and again in front of her but wasn't impressed. After a few minutes, Amiah shouted at the alien.

"Give me the cure for my son now!" Amiah screamed at the Recathri.

The Recathri alien flew up towards the ceiling of the virtual garage in the shape of a large green oval and disappeared. Amiah screamed up at the ceiling in pain.

"Recathriiiiiiii! You biitttchhh!" Amiah yelled before dropping down on her knees on the garage floor.

Amiah burst out crying. She couldn't stop the grief from coming out of her eyes. It had been building there for so many years. Finally, she was able to let out her long held in, painful anguish. Severely triggered by having the answer for her son so close yet so far from her, Amiah kept on crying. Alas again, her best hope for a cure for Brandon was gone. Brandon remained invisible to everyone who loved him.

"Hey, can we come in?" a male voice shouted over at Amiah from the front entrance of the virtual garage.

Amiah looked up, tears still running down her beautiful brown face. For some reason the automatic doors had not closed behind her to prevent anyone walking into the virtual garage. She would have to do a security review soon.

This should not be happening, not now, Amiah thought.

Amiah blinked away some of her tears and recognised the men at the front of the virtual garage, as the twins who had rode with her at the virtual beach.

Did these men follow me all the way home? Amiah thought.

Next, as if suddenly remembering who she was, Amiah stood up and telepathically called four robot security staff to her. They came immediately from standing watching in four different areas of the garage. Two stood by her left and two by her right.

"This is private property, and you are trespassing. Leave now." Amiah shouted at the twin men.

"We overheard and saw the whole thing! We think we can help you." one of the identical twins said enthusiastically.

Amiah's emotional defences went up even higher.

"Anything you heard was not meant for you to hear. You will not be able to leave until you have been assessed by security for a potential risk assessment." Amiah responded confidently.

The virtual front entrance closed behind the twin men who were now walking slowly towards Amiah Lily.

"We know everything. Trust us. We can help you." one of the twins said.

"Who are you?" Amiah said calmly.

Her intuition told her that there was no threat detected with these men, but she wanted to show her authority and continue with the security risk assessment anyway.

"We are the Onai twins. I'm Chima and he is my twin brother Marcel. We run a paranormal biker club called the Chi-Marcels." Chima said.

Both the Onai twins had reached in front of Amiah Lily, and now stood only a small distance away from her and the security robots by each side of her.

"Chima and Marcel. Chi-Marcels. Yes, I've heard of an all-male paranormal robotcycle club." Amiah said feeling intrigued against her better judgement.

"Takedown and distribute, loyalty, protection and love." Marcel said.

"I'm Amiah of the Amiah Riders. Rescue and revenge, loyalty, protection and love." Amiah said.

There was a period of silence as the three leaders of the two best paranormal robotcycle clubs in England looked at each other without saying a word. The silence was eventually broken by Chima.

"So, you're Amiah Lily. Aww, do you want a tissue?" Chima said with a half-smile on his face.

"Here, take this." Marcel said, handing Amiah a white tissue from a pack of tissues.

"Thanks." Amiah took the tissue from Marcel and smiled at him.

"Which twin did the crazy jump stunt at the beach, was it you?" Amiah continued.

"That was me." the Onai twins said in unison.

Amiah laughed and felt herself starting to relax a bit more. When she formed the Amiah Riders, she knew there was an all-male paranormal riders club out there somewhere. However, she had left it up to fate, whether or not they would ever meet each other. Now, fate and destiny had brought the two paranormal robotcycle clubs together at last. Amiah grinned at the Onai twins imagining the two clubs riding together on rescue and takedown missions. Then, like a quick flash back into reality, a vision of Brandon sleeping appeared for a few seconds in front of Amiah's eyes. A fast vision of Brandon with his colourful pyjamas on, but no face or body could be seen.

"You've seen something. What did you see?" Marcel asked.

"Don't act like that's something new to you Marcel." Chima interrupted sarcastically.

Amiah rolled her eyes. She had a quick intuition that there were some family dynamics that were being blocked by both men from her to view into. Amiah wondered if they could intercept her visions, along with knowing when she was viewing one they could not see. It would be very useful to have the Onai twins and the Chi-Marcels around so they could learn from each other. Amiah continued to use all her blocking skills to stop them finding out anything she did not want them to yet know, about the Amiah Riders.

"I saw my invisible son Brandon but you already know this, as you were listening in to my conversation with the Recathri alien." Amiah stated matter of factly.

"It was hard not to hear it!" Chima exclaimed.

"Chima, shut up!" Marcel said firmly glaring at his twin brother.

"It's ok." Amiah shrugged her shoulders.

She really did not have time to explore their family issues. She was more concerned about their level of robotcycle, paranormal and psychic skills and how they could benefit the Amiah Riders.

"We have to get our two clubs together." Marcel said, as if he had just read Amiah's mind.

"Yes, I would like that." Amiah replied. "You know my son needs a cure for his invisibility and that alien you just saw is called Recathri. He refuses to help."

"Tell us something we don't know..." Chima frowned.

"Yes, we know, and we want to help you and the Amiah Riders." Marcel quickly cut into his brother's words.

"Help me how? Can you trace the Recathri alien or do you know how to restore my son back to being visible again." Amiah inquired further.

"We've only just..." Chima started to speak but his brother Marcel interrupted him again.

"I know some people who might be able to help with the search for the Recathri and to help find a way to make the little boy visible again." Marcel explained. He saw the glimmer of hope light up again in Amiah's eyes. "We will help all we can but we can't make promises though. Our track record of successful mission is 100 % and..."

"99.9 %." Chima interrupted smiling at Amiah.

Amiah didn't smile back. She heard Marcel's words repeating back to her in her mind. "Get out of my head." Amiah said.

Chima laughed.

"Sorry Amiah, I didn't know if I would be able to communicate telepathically with you." Marcel said.

Not to be out done, Amiah sent telepathic words into the minds of both Chima and Marcel.

"Sorry, I didn't know if I would be able to communicate

telepathically with you." Amiah said telepathically back to Chima and Marcel.

Chima and Marcel glanced at each other with approval and Chima raised both his eyebrows. Marcel looked back at Amiah.

"Nice and clear. You *are* Amiah Lily." Marcel said with a flirtatious smile.

Amiah felt her cheeks grow warm and was surprised that she looked away shyly before looking back at Marcel.

It really has been too long since I've been with a man, Amiah thought feeling embarrassed.

Chima turned around and started walking fast out towards the front entrance of the garage. Marcel called after him.

"Chima, where are you going?" Marcel shouted at him.

"Takedown at Braxtim Company starts in 50minutes. Time to stop pussy footing around and get back." Chima shouted back over his shoulder.

"Damn!" Marcel exclaimed. "We'll be back!" Marcel finished talking and turned to run after his twin brother.

Both brothers appeared to be arguing as they got on their red robotcycles and sped off out of the Amiah Mansion grounds at high speed.

In the centre of the virtual garage, Amiah stood still with two security robots standing on either side of her. She felt intrigued and slightly amused by the Onai twins. It was "jelitoonaa" to finally meet them and she could foresee many good times were coming up ahead in the future. She hoped that the Chi-Marcels would be able to find a way to help restore visibility back to her invisible son Brandon.

However, even if they didn't, there was something about the identical twin riders that excited and enthralled her. Maybe it was the way they handled their robotcycles, maybe it was the paranormal and psychic skills that bonded her with them. Maybe it was their similar purpose to their missions. The Amiah Riders being about Rescue & Revenge, loyalty, protection and love. The Chi-Marcels being all about Takedown & Distribute, loyalty, protection and love. Whatever the appealing mystery was that the twin men had evoked in Amiah, she wanted to experience more of it.

"You can go robots. Let me know if those men return. Thank you." Amiah said to the robots on her left side first and then repeated the same sentence to the robots on her right side after.

"Ok Amiah." each robot said, before walking away from Amiah back to their original places in various parts of the garage.

Amiah sent a telepathic message to the energy that she remembered had been around the Recathri alien. She knew the alien could hear her. Her telepathic message went as follows: -

"I know you listened in to that whole conversation I just had with the Onai twins. I want you to listen again and listen good. If Chima, Marcel and the Chi-Marcels cannot cure my son Brandon, then you and everyone on that dumb planet you've come from are *dead*."

*****

Marcel and Chima arrived at Braxtim Company headquarters after an hour-long ride from Amiah Mansion. They were met by 17 other men on red robotcycles who had been patiently waiting for the Onai twins to turn up. These men were part of the Chi-Marcels paranormal robotcycle club and they were ready to begin T128. T128 is the Takedown & Distribute mission of Braxtim Company. Marcel and Chima simultaneously telepathically communicated the same message to all the Chi-Marcel riders.

"We're here. Sorry for the delay. Met *the* Amiah Lily of the Amiah Riders last night at one of our virtual beaches and… got caught up. You all know what to do. Let's go!"

At that order, the Chi-Marcels raced down the hilly area of land that was in front of Braxtim company and rode fast towards the main building. Three of the Chi-Marcel riders rode straight through virtual glass security doors which had been deactivated by the telekinesis skills of a Chi-Marcel. Robot security staff began to start firing laser guns at them but the Chi-Marcels had on protective clothing. Therefore, the robot's laser gun weapons had no effect on them.

Some of the Chi-Marcels proceeded to run over the security robot staff while others rounded up the human members of staff and took them away. All around the Braxtim main building, Chi-Marcels were 'at work' riding their robotcycles over robot staff or running around taking human hostages.

So far it had been successful. Chima and Marcel watched the chaotic scenes from a short distance away. They both remote viewed everything that was happening inside the building with admiration and satisfaction.

"Damn, we're good." Marcel said to Chima.

"Best paranormal robotcyclist club known to this planet." Marcel answered with a smirk.

"What do you think she'll say?" Marcel said

"What can she say? It's over. She won't be stealing from those school kids no more." Chima replied.

"Bye bye Ms Braxtim." Marcel said nastily.

The Onai twins watched via their remote viewing skills into Braxtim company buildings. They could see the destruction that the Chi-Marcels had caused. They had smashed up offices, destroyed all the robot security staff and had human hostages in various rooms around the building. They watched as six of the Chi-Marcels entered into a large office where a woman sat on a desk swinging her legs casually back and forth.

Chima scrutinized everything he saw via remote viewing as he listened in.

"You're wasting your time, you know." Ms Braxtim said in a bored sounding voice.

The three Chi-Marcels ignored her and walked directly to the right side corner of the room. Then one of the men cut into the virtual wooden flooring with a glowing red shaped object and pulled out a bundle of paperwork. He flicked through the documents and said the words "Done." He then went over to talk to Ms Braxtim who stared at him coldly.

"You all make me laugh. Pretending to be so righteous when you are all just a bunch of bullies and wankers." Ms Braxtim said grumpily.

Two Chi-Marcels stood at either side of Ms Braxtim but Ms Braxtim was not even attempting to fight them or run away.

The Chi-Marcel holding the paperwork, stood in front of Ms Braxtim and spoke angrily to her.

"20 years of robbing from special needs children's school funds. Bitch!" the man spat at her.

"Bitch." one of the men standing near to Ms Braxtim repeated.

Ms Braxtim began laughing manically and hysterically. She had long dyed blue hair that touched down to her waist. As she laughed, she threw her head forwards and back fast with her body shaking.

"She's high." the Chi-Marcel who held the paperwork said. "Just take her and put her with the others. Clear all the security footage and everyone out."

Two Chi-Marcels held Ms Braxtim by both arms and led her out of the room, as she screamed uncontrollably with laughter at them.

A Chi-Marcel walked to where Ms Braxtim's virtual chair was and cut into the seat. He pulled out a handful of small white pills and showed them to another Chi-Marcel. The other man just shrugged.

"Let's get out of here." he said to him.

The Onai twins sat back on their red robotcycles. The other Chi-Marcel riders would be joining them soon to ride back to the Chi-Marcel mansion.

"Another successful mission." Chima said proudly.

"Bet the Amiah Riders don't roll like we do." Marcel laughed.

"Amiah Riders. The woman can ride..." Chima replied.

"You like her." Marcel said

"You like her." Chima retorted back quickly.

Just then the rest of the Chi-Marcel riders returned to meet with the Onai twins and together they rode away from Braxtim company headquarters. During the journey, Chima and Marcel kept performing stunts next to each other as if they were trying to outdo each other. When they all arrived back to the Chi-Marcel mansion, Chima and Marcel got off their robotcycles and eyed each other in silence. One of the Chi-Marcel riders felt compelled to speak up to break the awkward silence.

"Success! When's the next takedown?" a rider called Jason said

"That bitch is crazy. Braxtim woman. She acted like we weren't even there." another Chi-Marcel rider called Derek exclaimed.

"Drugs." a different rider called Chris replied.

"The robot police have found them. I'm watching the whole thing. Tune in men." Jason said.

The men laughed and smiled watching the police arrive at Braxtim company. First of all, the robot police found the paperwork on the ground in the reception area with a note which said "Evidence of fraud.". Next, they saw all the robot staff laying in broken up heaps on the floor with their laser guns scattered. The robot police also saw all the wrecked offices and equipment. Finally at the back of the building, they saw each human member of staff tied up and asleep in the corridors.

"They won't remember anything. I wiped the recent memories parts of everyone's brain for the length of time that we were there. Can never be brought back, trust me." Derek said confidently.

"Security footage destroyed. It's like we were never there." Chris replied.

"How can the police not know who we are still? We've done this over 100 times." Derek said.

"They don't care. They take the credit for it. Another crime they solved and get paid for, that's all they care about." Chris said.

"That's right. We don't care cos we get paid by the person who sent us to take down Braxtim." Jason chimed in..

"That person, always anonymous… probably he/she is in the police too." Chris wondered out loud.

"Probably." Jason replied.

"Who cares." Chima and Marcel said in unison.

"Jason's right. As long as we get paid and we're stopping evil people." Marcel said.

"We give money back to the communities who were stolen from too. Takedown and distribute." Chima stated.

"Winners." Derek said.

"So, what is this about Amiah Lily? You've finally met her for real this time?" Derek asked Chima.

"For real this time" Marcel questioned.

Chima looked down and then up again.

"Chima told me that he had met Amiah when…" Derek began to say but Chima cut him off.

"It was a mistake. I thought it was her at the time but it wasn't. She looks different from what I imagined." Chima explained.

"You thought she would be more manly looking because she's one of the best female robotyclists?" Derek said with a half-grin.

"No, not really. Just different." Chima said.

"Well, yeah she definitely is different." Marcel said wistfully. "We have to arrange for both our bikers clubs to meet. The sooner the better."

The Onai twins and the Chi-Marcels separated to go and either shower, eat breakfast or sleep. They had been awake all night preparing for T128, making sure that everything would run smoothly. Chima and Marcel chose to go and shower before eating. The twins had bedrooms separate from each other with shower/bathroom attached. As each man showered, they heard ringing noises in their ears similar to the ringing noises that Amiah Lily sometimes heard. They both knew that a vision would appear in front of them soon.

In their separate showers, Chima and Marcel watched the new vision appear, as water streamed over their tall, muscular bodies. This latest vision showed Amiah Lily giving birth to her invisible baby. Marcel looked on with disgust. Chima stared expressionless at the vision.

"What the hell?" Marcel said out loud as he watched.

Chima couldn't find any words to say so he just kept watching.

After the vision ended, both men got out of their separate showers and waited for an automatic drier to dry their skin controlled by female shaped robots.

"Thanks beautiful." Marcel said with a wink at the female robot.

"Anything you desire, big boy." the pre-programmed female robot replied in a sexy voice.

In the other shower, Chima's skin was also being dried by a pre-programmed female robot. He still could not speak after watching the vision of Amiah Lily giving birth. So, Chima did not communicate back after the female robot wished him "Good morning handsome." in a flirtatious voice.

The two men got dressed and met downstairs in the dining room. Some of the Chi-Marcels were already eating breakfast in there. Chima made his food selection quickly, at the 'robot staffed breakfast buffet' and Marcel also made his food selection a few minutes later.

Sitting down at a white oval shaped large virtual table, Chima bit into an avocado and poached egg toast. Marcel took long swigs of his peanut, banana and cinnamon smoothie. A few minutes passed by before either of the men spoke to each other.

"When do you want to meet up with the Amiah Riders? Tonight?" asked Chima

Marcel looked thoughtful and then answered Chima's question.

"Tomorrow. Invite them here for a dinner party." Marcel said grinning.

"Jelitoonaa. Time?" Chima said looking down at his half-eaten poached egg and avocado toast.

"6." Marcel suggested.

"Ok. Are you sending someone over to Amiah Mansion with the invites? I can go." Chima replied.

"Hand deliver invites? Are you in a time warp bro?" Marcel

laughed.

"Shows respect, doesn't it?" Chima answered back sharply.

"And what would you know about that?" Marcel said.

"I'll look into finding some shamans and inquire of the aliens that we know of, to find out if they can help cure Amiah's son." Chima said, ignoring his brother's obvious sarcasm.

"Good. Let me know what you find. I'll get the robot staff to set up the virtual dining room ready for them, prepare the food and drinks, get the virtual guest rooms ready..." Marcel winked at Chima.

"Hmmmm. Ok." Chima sounded less enthusiastic.

."What's up with you? This will be jelitoonaa to meet up with the all-female paranormal robotcycle club?" Marcel replied.

"Nothing." Chima said.

Marcel grimaced. "Let it be nothing. Don't mess this up. Amiah and the Amiah Riders could be very, no, extremely useful to us. We need to look after this connection, if you know what I mean."

Chima didn't reply and stood up to get another avocado and poached egg toast from the breakfast buffet.

"Get me another peanut, banana and cinnamon smoothie!" Marcel shouted after him.

"Get it yourself, I'm going to look for shamans and aliens!" Chima shouted back after picking up another poached egg toast with avocado from the buffet along with a coffee too.

"I'll get it myself." Marcel shouted.

Some of the Chi-Marcels seated around the large white oval shaped virtual table pretended to be talking or eating, so as not to get involved in the brothers conversation. Marcel looked around at them, and observed that not any single one of the Chi-Marcels were looking up at him or Chima.

Chima was different somehow, but Marcel wasn't sure what was up with his brother. Of course, he knew Chima had a temper and a sharp sarcasm similar to his own, but he didn't show it too much around other people. Usually when they were alone together somewhere, Chima liked to point out the many things that he thought Marcel could improve on, to do with the organisation and management of the Chi-Marcels. Marcel also liked to point out to Chima, the many things that Chima could improve upon, to do with the management and organisation of the Chi-Marcels. The Onai twins disagreed over a lot of things, but kept it private as much as they could. This was to display good leadership and promote unity within the Chi-Marcels paranormal robotcycle club.

The Onai twins were only human after all so Marcel figured that a couple of random displays of disagreement would not hurt the club. However, Marcel sensed something was brewing in Chima and he didn't like it. His twin brother behaved sometimes like he had forgotten that they shared exactly the same psychic and paranormal gifts. Therefore, Marcel could read Chima's mind as easily as Chima could read Marcel's mind.

Both men could block each other's psychic skills being used on them at any time. Many times although, this would arouse suspicion in either brother when the other brother started to use their blocking skills. It signalled that there was something that one of the brothers was trying to hide, which had the potential to breed a dangerous distrust.

Chima had been blocking Marcel since they had spotted Amiah Lily alone on one of the virtual beaches they owned. Marcel had blocked him too but more out of a kind of sibling retaliation game of 'you block me and I'll block you back.'. Childish as it may seem, this was what it was like between the Onai twins at times.

Marcel remembered how Chima had blocked him from reading his mind after he came back from a date with a woman he had liked for years. Marcel had been playing a joke on his brother, and remote viewed Chima's date for the entire 4 hours he was away. Chima would never have known that this is what happened, if not for one revealing night out riding with Marcel. When they had stopped riding to take a break, Marcel had made a weird joke about women who loved to undress men by the lake to get them to suck on their boobs. Chima instantly knew the joke was about him and that Marcel had watched his date psychically from afar.

Subsequently, Chima learned that if he wanted privacy with a woman on a date, he would always have to remember to block his psychic twin brother and all other psychics at the same time. Marcel was not going to ruin Chima's sex life with women. It bothered Chima that Marcel would want to watch in the first place. Chima often wondered if his sexcapades were more exciting than his brothers...

Marcel went out on dates and brought women back to the Chi-Marcel virtual mansion, just like Chima did. Yet, Chima didn't once consider remote viewing Marcel on a date. He didn't care what Marcel was up to.

The Onai twins grew up without a human mother or father. They were raised by robots that had escaped from a research facility and were in hiding in a virtual underground bunker in a remote area of a deserted beach. The beach was deserted as there were too many hazards that were a risk to human life. Hybrid mixes of beach creatures such as jellyfish, snakes and turtles combined with alien DNA had created dangerous animals that kept the deserted beach empty of human life. All human life except the Onai twins in their virtual underground bunker with the runaway research robots.

Chima and Marcel had been named by the escaped robots. The name Onai was chosen by Marcel when he and Chima eventually left the virtual underground bunker, to live and work in the City. Adapting to city life and not the underground world the robots had created for them both, was surprisingly easy. Chima and Marcel had been aware of their extra sensory gifts from toddler age. They did not only learn from the robots they could see with their eyes but the spirits around them they could see and hear. So, in a way the Onai twins grew up with humans but not humans they could see with their physical eyes. It was their spiritual eyes that could perceive, see, hear, feel and interact with the spirit world not their physical eyes. Even so, their spiritual eyes were as clear if not much clearer than the vision of their physical eyes.

Chima and Marcel had also remote viewed the areas around them and all the cities, towns, places, countries they wanted to know about. It was simple for the Onai twins. The transition from living hidden lives of secrecy, into living confidently around other humans in a busy city, was smooth and successful. Still, elements of secrecy forever would remain with the Onai twins.

Similar to Amiah Lily, the Onai twins had been obsessed with riding the latest advanced robotcycles. It quickly became the twin's main passion. Soon the men began having visions, which led them to form an all-male paranormal robotcycle club. Chima and Marcel named their newly formed paranormal robotcycle club, the Chi-marcels. The Onai twins found male riders all over the country. They rode up north and down south, up north again and back down south again. Each new vision would inform them of yet another location, for them to discover a Chi-Marcel gifted rider, to join their biker club.

The Chi-Marcel riders were from all different backgrounds and nationalities, but they had many things in common with each other. Firstly, they were all-male, confident and talented robotcycle riders. Secondly, they all had high levels of psychic and paranormal skills. Thirdly, they all agreed to the club's motto which is Takedown & Distribute, loyalty, protection and love. There were 30 men shown to Chima and Marcel in their visions but only 17 men were found. The exact locations of the other 13 men had not yet been revealed to the Onai twins at present.

Nevertheless, both men were confident that the other Chi-Marcels would be found within their lifetimes, and they looked forward to when their club would be complete. The successful record of the Chi-Marcels is known to all who require their paranormal and psychic services. Mostly on a basis of anonymity, they would be contacted and paid privately. Every person the Chi-Marcels had ever worked with, were remote-viewed daily by the fastest viewers in the club as part of their regular security procedures. Any threat to their club's work would therefore be discovered immediately.

Well, any external threat...

PARTY WITH A PURPOSE

Amiah Lily felt the Onai twins strong psychic energy around her in her cream coloured four poster, virtual canopy bed. It was so powerful that she could not sleep for hours, while laying alone thinking of them and everything that had occurred. When Amiah Lily did eventually fall asleep, the Onai twins were there again in her dreams with the same strong psychic and paranormal energy. It was so intense, that Amiah had to scream to force herself awake from the dream whereby the Onai twins were just staring at her from a distance.

Amiah sat up scared and startled by her dream. Sweat dripped down her face, back and chest and her heart thumped so loud she could hear it beating. Reaching for her virtual glass of water on her bedside table, Amiah took several sips to try and regain her composure. To try and calm herself down.

Amiah breathed in and out a few long slow deep breaths. She stretched her legs out which were huddled in the fetal position and brought them back tucked into her chest again. Then, Amiah stretched out her legs and repeated the same sequence four times before getting up out of her virtual bed to use the bathroom.

In her virtual bathroom, Amiah splashed her face with cold water and rubbed her eyes. The Onai twins had a very strong energy around and within them. The only way she could stop their energy interfering with her sleep was to stop thinking about them. Amiah believed that the more she focused on a person or group of people, the more of their energy she could pick up on. Maybe she had been thinking of the Onai twins too much and she should switch her mind to other more important things, Amiah wondered to herself.

Amiah felt a pang of guilt. Really and truly, she should be thinking about Landon or how to cure her invisible son Brandon. Amiah quickly dismissed this thought and rationalised it. It was only because this was the very first time, she had met the leaders of the Chi-Marcel paranormal robotcycle club and she felt curious.

Curiosity, that's it, she thought.

Curiosity was leading her to have the energy of the Onai twins in her thoughts and dreams. Although, she had quickly got them out of her dream life however, by deliberately screaming to wake herself up out of the dream.

As a child, Amiah learned she could usually escape her nightmares and wake herself up out of bad or annoying dreams by screaming. Whatever dream Amiah experienced, all she had to do to come out of it at anytime was to scream in the dream. When Amiah screamed, she would wake up out of any dream state. Even a paralysis dream state. It was a very useful thing for her to do. Amiah had also tried to teach the Amiah Riders how to get out of unwanted or annoying dream states. Some of the Amiah Riders had understood the concept and applied it. Others found Amiah's idea 'unworkable'. Basically, 'unworkable' meant for them, that Amiah's theory on screaming in dreams didn't work.

Suddenly, Amiah heard the sound of heavy footsteps running away from her but no-one else was in the room with her. Amiah grew suspicious. First, she felt a nearly overwhelming strong psychic energy relating to the Onai twins in her thoughts and dreams, and now she heard footsteps running away from her.

Are the Onai twins remote viewing me or trying to psychically gain access to my thoughts and dreams? Amiah considered frowning.

She automatically began blocking the Onai twins instead of thinking about them. She hadn't slept at all the night before and she needed to get some sleep before the dinner with the Chi-Marcels and Amiah Riders tomorrow evening.

There was an old saying Amiah had learned in her school days. It followed that where you focused your attention, energy would flow to it. She wondered who had first come up with that quote, as this was a simple explanation of how some of her paranormal skills worked. All Amiah would do is focus or bring her attention to something and energy from whatever that something was, would flow to Amiah.

"I need to stop thinking so much about those twins." Amiah said out loud to herself.

Amiah came out from her bathroom and got back into her cream coloured four poster canopy virtual bed. Amiah cleared her mind from everything relating to the Onai twins. She didn't think about Chima or Marcel. She didn't think about meeting the Chi-Marcels tomorrow evening. She tried not to think about how Marcel had said he would help her find a cure for Brandon.

If the Onai twins energy was in fact, that powerful, Amiah was not ready to have them in her thoughts or in her dreams too frequently. It wasn't fair on her or her Amiah Riders. The Amiah Riders looked up to her for leadership, training, friendship and clarity. If she was confused by the psychic energy of the Onai twins, mistakes could be made. There was no room for mistakes or errors in rescue missions. It was not only bad for business, but it was also bad for the reputation of Amiah Lily and the Amiah Riders.

Changing her thoughts back to the Amiah Riders, Landon and her invisible son Brandon, Amiah felt the energy of the Onai twins leave her bedroom. In replacement, Landon's energy came through and embraced her with love and passion. Feeling more like herself again, Amiah fell asleep with her legs wrapped tightly around part of her cream-coloured virtual duvet.

In the morning, Amiah showered and got dressed to go downstairs to address the Amiah Riders in a meeting after breakfast. The breakfast room was a new addition to the Amiah Mansion and had been converted from a spare guest room which was not needed. The Amiah Mansion already had plenty of those and did not require any extra. Inside the newly furbished virtual breakfast room was a buffet where Amiah Lily and the Amiah Riders could choose anything they wanted to eat or drink.

"Morning Amiah!" Jan sang out happily.

"Good morning Amiah!" Saraina said smiling.

"Top of the morning to ya!" Petra said also smiling.

"Amiah, jelitoonaa day to you!" Louise chimed in.

Amiah grinned back.

Most of the Amiah Riders greeted Amiah and were talking excitedly and happily with each other around the breakfast buffet or while seated on virtual seats around a yellow circular virtual table. The virtual table changed colours intermittently. Therefore, for five minutes it was a yellow colour, the next five minutes it was a black colour, the next five minutes it was a pink colour, etc…

Amiah chatted with Jan who was sitting next to her. They were discussing the new brief Amiah had received for a rescue mission.

"This would be R270 I believe." Jan said to Amiah.

"R269." Amiah replied biting into her French baguette with cheese and bananas.

"What about the recent rescue mission that we did last Thursday, wasn't that R269?" Jan asked.

"No, Amiah is right. Last week was R268 I'm sure of it." Saraina joined in with the two other women.

"Jan, I have a visual memory of every detail of every mission. It's R269." Amiah said confidently.

"Are the men coming with us from the Chi-Marcels?" Saraina inquired a little louder than she had intended to.

Saraina had spoken up at a time when the breakfast room had been quiet so everybody in the room overheard the question. The other Amiah Riders joined in the conversation which had originally started with Jan and Amiah.

"Why do we need men on a rescue mission? They will mess it up." an Amiah Rider grumbled.

"Man hater. Yes Amiah. Bring the men with us!" Louise exclaimed.

"The Chi-Marcels are sexy as f***." Petra shouted out.

"I'm telling you all. Once you let one man in, they will take over. That's part of their club motto for f***s sake! Takeover & Distribute." another Amiah Rider said.

"It's takedown. Takedown & Distribute." Louise corrected the other rider. "I know Chima and Marcel can takeover, takedown me anytime but unlucky for them… I'm not for distribution." Louise said jokingly.

Amiah's ear perked up and felt hot at the mention of the names of Chima and Marcel. Now, she understood the reason why most of her Amiah Riders were so happy and enthusiastic that morning. They weren't just excited to see her. They weren't excited about the new breakfast room. They probably weren't even that excited about the next new rescue mission. They were excited about meeting all the male riders of the Chi-Marcels this evening and their club leaders, the Onai twins. Amiah felt a little annoyed but then realised that this was only to be expected. There were heterosexual, bisexual and gay women in the Amiah Riders, so it wasn't just that the Chi-Marcels were men. It was due to the Chi-Marcels being equally skilled as robotcyclists, with paranormal and psychic abilities just like the Amiah Riders.

"Ooooh wait till we take them on a night ride through Gruten Rivers." Petra said and waved her hand about fanning her face pretending to be getting hot and bothered.

"I'll take them on a night ride, let me tell you that!" Saraina shouted out louder than she intended.

The entire breakfast room filled with amused and happy laughter and Saraina's face went red with embarrassment.

"It's ok." Amiah said to Saraina. Then, addressing the other Amiah Riders around the table, Amiah continued on and said, "Remember the Chi-Marcels are not our friends yet."

"They can be my …" Petra started to make a joke, but Amiah

interrupted her.

"I was going to save this till the meeting afterwards but seeing as I have all of your attention right now, I might as well say this here. The Chi-Marcels are not our friends until they can prove themselves trustworthy of our love, protection and loyalty. Look at their club motto, Takedown & Distribute. How do we know for sure they will not try and sabotage or takedown us? How do we know for sure that they are friends and not foes? Do we know the Onai twins apart from what we've heard or sensed using our psychic/paranormal skills? You are all aware they have psychic/paranormal skills too but to what extent? This means that they cannot be trusted yet. It will take a few years to observe how they are as people. Don't be fooled. For the protection of our club the Amiah Riders, I am asking you to not get close to any of them until we can ensure the safety of our own." Amiah said seriously.

"I'm already in love with Chima." Jan teased light-heartedly.

"Shut up Jan." Amiah replied fast.

There was laughter in the large virtual breakfast room again.

Amiah sighed inwardly but did not let anyone see her quiet disapproval. Instead, she pretended to laugh along with her Amiah Riders. They were happy. Ecstatic probably.

Why spoil their fun when they all work so hard daily, for the Amiah Riders? Amiah thought.

As the ecstatic laughter quietened down, Amiah stood up and spoke again.

"Listen everyone! Just promise me this one thing, that you will use every paranormal skill you have to find out the true intentions of the Onai twins and the Chi-Marcels at every chance you get. I want you all to be mind reading, remote viewing, listening to spirit guides, deciphering the signs, summoning the ancestors etc... and for those of you who see visions like me, remember what you see and try to connect the dots." Amiah finished talking and sat back down in her virtual seat.

The virtual breakfast room fell quiet. It was like as if the very important issues of the value, protection and safety of their paranormal robotcycle club, had suddenly become starkly apparent.

"We will protect our club Amiah." Jan said.

"I will sort out the Chi-Marcels. They won't fool me." Petra said.

"They don't know who they are dealing with." Louise agreed.

Amiah shook her head vehemently.

"No, they do. This is why we need to be very careful. Blocking skills training in one hour, alphabetical order. Thanks ladies!" Amiah instructed with an air of authority.

There were a few groans heard but overall, most of the Amiah Riders responded in agreement.

"Yeah, let's do this!"

*****

The Amiah Riders were ready. All 17 of them, with Amiah Lily's black and gold robotcycle leading the front of the group. Two Amiah Riders were on either side of Amiah. They were Jan and Saraina who were also ready to go riding on their robotcycles. Amiah telepathically spoke to the Amiah Riders.

"Ok ladies, let's all enjoy tonight! Just remember that the Chi-Marcels are not our friends until we find out more about them and how they operate. Any problems report back to Jan, Saraina or myself. In an emergency, I want everyone out of the Chi-Marcel mansion immediately. We don't want to be caught up in any drama or conflict which has nothing to do with us. I've remote viewed the property and I don't see any threats to our safety so far. So... tonight should be jelitoonaa! Let's ride!"

With that final telepathic statement (spoken by Amiah to all the Amiah Riders), all the robotcycles went off riding towards the north of Amiah Mansion.

Destination: Chi-Marcel mansion. Time estimated for length of journey: 3 hours.

After riding for around 3 hours, Amiah Lily was the first to ride up to the front entrance virtual security gates at the virtual Chi-Marcel mansion. The tall silver virtual security gates opened slowly to allow Amiah and her Amiah Riders entry. They rode up more cautiously now through the front gardens, past the water fountains and large virtual glowing grey statues of robotcycles towards the front entry virtual doors. Outside the front entry virtual doors, a Chi-Marcel rider sitting on top of his red robotcycle was waiting for them.

"Welcome to the Chi-Marcel mansion. I am Derek. I'm here to take you over to the guest virtual garage where your robotcycles can be left safely. The Onai twins, Chima Onai and Marcel Onai will meet you in there. Follow me this way." Derek said to Amiah Lily.

"Thank you." Amiah replied.

Amiah and the Amiah Riders followed Derek on his robotcycle around the right side of the Chi-Marcel mansion towards near the back of the mansion, where two large virtual garages were situated.

"This is the visitors virtual garage." Derek said as the virtual doors disappeared at the front of the visitors garage.

Amiah Lily rode in first on her black and gold robotcycle with Jan and Saraina close behind her. Then the rest of the Amiah Riders rode into the visitors virtual garage. Chima was already in there with his twin brother Marcel. Amiah, Jan and Saraina rode over to them.

Robot staff inside the visitors garage, indicated with their robotic arms, the direction in which the Amiah Riders should park their robotcycles. The Amiah Riders parked their robotcycles where they were shown and got off their bikes. Amiah, Jan and Saraina were directed to a different area to park their robotcycles but Amiah refused.

"We will stay with the Amiah Riders, thank you." Amiah said to the Onai twins.

"Jelitoonaa." Chima said.

"Ok." Marcel said.

Amiah turned her robotcycle around with Jan and Saraina copying her movements. She then rode over to where the rest of her Amiah Riders were parked and parked near to them. Jan and Saraina also parked near to the other Amiah Riders. She was about to say something to them when Marcel began to speak.

"Welcome again to the Chi-Marcel mansion. I am Marcel Onai and this is my brother Chima Onai. We are the leaders of undisputedly the best paranormal, psychic robotcyclist club in history." Marcel announced assertively.

"Best all-male robotcyclist club." Chima quickly filled in. He didn't want there to be a dispute about which was the best robotcyclist club, so early on during their first biker clubs meet up.

"Yes, yes, best all-male robotcyclist club. It is my honour and great pleasure to entertain the best all-female psychic and paranormal robotcyclist club tonight, for dinner at the Chi-Marcel mansion. Come this way, I'm sure you are all very hungry from the long ride up here. The robots have refreshments for you until we get to the main virtual dining room." Marcel explained.

"We are appreciative of your kind invite. We look forward to meeting the rest of the Chi-Marcels and enjoying the pleasure of your company at dinner. Thank you." Amiah replied.

Some of the Amiah Riders took drinks and snacks from the robots, as they walked behind Chima and Marcel who were talking to each other. Once inside the Chi-Marcel mansion, the Onai twins gave them a brief tour of various parts of the virtual mansion as they passed by different rooms.

"Behind this door is our virtual conference room and on the opposite side you can see the virtual door to one of our many virtual guest rooms." Marcel said

"Interesting." Amiah replied.

After a few more minutes walking around different parts of the ground floor of the Chi-Marcel mansion, Chima spoke.

"And here... is the main virtual dining room, especially reserved for very important guests." Chima said.

The virtual security doors to the main virtual dining room disappeared and many of the Amiah Riders gasped at the stunning décor of the main virtual dining room.

Inside the decorative virtual dining room, there were

moving realistic images of robotcycles flying around in the air above a long 'glowing orange' virtual dining room table. The virtual gold hover chairs hovered a distance above the virtual white and silver marble flooring.

There were framed virtual photos of Chima, Marcel and the Chi-Marcels in different locations on their robotcycles, at one side of the virtual dining room. At the head of the virtual dining room was a large virtual screen above a hovering glowing silver stage. The virtual dining room was as richly luxurious as all the other parts of the Chi-Marcel mansion. There were even realistic images on another side of the virtual wall, displaying different scenes from all over the universe. Giving the impression to anyone looking at the virtual walls that they were really in another world all together.

Each dining place is labelled with the name of the rider whose seat it was. Amiah found her virtual hover seat which was located opposite Marcel's dining place, at the centre of the long dining room virtual table. There were empty virtual hover chairs at either side of her. Robot staff came over to take away the virtual hover chairs. Jan and Saraina therefore, sat a short distance from Amiah on the second available virtual seat at either side of Amiah. Amiah sat down on her hovering virtual gold chair and swung her legs briefly.

"This is jelitoonaa!" Saraina exclaimed loudly.

Chima laughed, as he took his hover virtual gold chair out from under the dining room table and sat on it.

"You get used to it." Chima said with a wink at Saraina.

"How much did these cost you?" Jan asked Chima.

"We acquired them from an anonymous giver…probably around £1 million per virtual hover chair, they retail at." Marcel answered before Chima could reply.

"You have a very impressive home Chima." Jan said approvingly.

"It's been our home and base for the Chi-Marcel riders for what is it… 5 years now." Chima replied, glancing at Marcel for his added confirmation that his guess was accurate.

"About that yes." Marcel added.

"The menu has an 'anything you desire' course." Saraina said. "Do you mean that anything on this planet and neighbouring planets that are edible, you can cook for us tonight?"

"Anything in the universe we will cook for you tonight." Marcel said.

Amiah and Jan looked at each other disbelievingly. Not many people enjoyed eating the food from other planets as they often had flavours that did not mix well with human tastebuds. It was likely the Onai twins were just showing off about how well connected they were. Perhaps, trying to show how successful and popular they were.

The Chi-Marcels riders entered the room next and took their places on separate hovering virtual gold seats, on the other side of the long glowing orange virtual table. There was a lot of chatter in the dining room as everyone started talking with each other. It was like as if they had known each other for years. The conversation flowed easily between the two paranormal robotcyclists clubs without any awkward pauses or silences. Amiah and the Onai twins were not talking. Amiah continued to look at her menu and around at all the other riders chatting away in the room. Her mind was elsewhere.

At the thought of eating alien food from other planets, Amiah's mind had wandered off into thinking about the Recathri alien and her son's invisibility. Currently, her son Brandon was being looked after by his grandparents, his four cousins (two adults and two children) at home in Amiah Mansion. There were also robot staff constantly around Brandon to cater to his every request or need.

The Recathri alien hadn't appeared again at Amiah Mansion, no matter how many times she had tried to telepathically communicate with it. Her invisible son Brandon remained unseen by human eyes and his real self also remained hidden from the rest of the world. Brandon could not go out without wearing a 'virtual body suit' and it hurt Amiah to see her son being looked at by passers-by with his fake appearance showing. Amiah wanted the whole world to see her love child with Landon. She was elated that she had finally had his child but saddened by not being able to see the child which was born out of so much love, wild times and passion.

Robot members of staff who had been standing waiting at the sides of the dining room, started to move towards the people sitting at the long glowing orange virtual table. Other robots also entered the room, in order for them to take the food and drink selection choices from each person. Amiah ordered her starters, main, desert and drink selection.

"Thank you." a robot said to Amiah, and then moved on to the next person that was waiting to be served.

Amiah looked up in the air above them at the moving images of robotcycles flying around at varying speeds. Occasionally, the robotcycle images would dip down near to the glowing orange virtual table and then fly back up again. It was an impressive and beautiful sight to behold. Amiah made a mental note in her mind to order some of these flying images of robotcycles for Brandon's playroom. He would love it! Amiah thought happily.

After all the food and drink selection choices had been ordered by everyone in the main dining room, Marcel addressed the room using virtual speaker devices. Virtual speaker devices amplified the voice of the person who was using them. Amiah noticed that everyone seated at the long orange virtual table had a virtual speaker device, fitted into the table directly in front of them. Amiah listened as Marcel began speaking.

"I'd like to welcome the Amiah Riders again to our Chi-Marcel mansion! It's jelitoonaa to be in the presence of the best psychic and paranormal robotcyclists in history!" Marcel stated excitedly.

"That's us!" one of the Chi-Marcel riders shouted back.

"Yeah we are!" an Amiah Rider said using her virtual speaker device.

Marcel grinned around the room.

Chima used his virtual speaker device and spoke to everyone

present in the main dining room.

"Your food and drinks will be with you shortly. Enjoy!" Chima said.

Upon saying that sentence, robot members of staff entered the main virtual dining room again carrying many virtual trays complete with various foods and drinks. The robots efficiently distributed the food choices and drinks to all the people sitting at the glowing orange virtual table. Amiah, the Onai twins, the Amiah Riders and the Chi-Marcels all began to hungrily eat and drink.

15 minutes passed by and the main course was brought out by robot staff. 30 minutes later and dessert was received by everyone. As everyone sat eating dessert, a movie showing the Onai twins and the Chi-Marcels riding on their robotcycles, played on the large virtual screen at the front of the dining room.

Amiah and Jan exchanged smug glances. Both were thinking that the Amiah Riders were just as brilliant robotcyclists as the Chi-Marcels, and couldn't wait for them all to go out on a ride together.

"If you don't have to go back in a hurry, we can go riding tonight. All of us. If you're ready." Marcel said.

Amiah's eyes narrowed. She was blocking everyone in the room from reading her thoughts and also blocking psychics from a long distance away. Marcel seemed to have read her thoughts or maybe it was Jan, Amiah thought to herself. However, Amiah soon relaxed again thinking that it was probably Jan that Marcel had mind-read. Amiah made a mental note in her mind to remember to train Jan more in blocking skills later on that week.

"I don't know what my Amiah Riders have planned for later on. I will ask them." Amiah replied taking a sip of her champagne. At a different occasion, she would have drank the entire contents of the virtual glass down in one go, but she found herself holding back from being too informal.

"Oh come on, you can't come all the way up here and not go out for a ride with our Chi-Marcels!" Chima exclaimed.

"Yes she can. It makes sense to ask her riders first. They could be exhausted from the ride up here and need to rest first. Why don't you all stay overnight in the guest rooms, and we will escort you all back tomorrow morning?" Marcel suggested calmly.

"They don't look tired." Chima replied looking around at the lively conversations that were going on between most of the Amiah Riders and the Chi-Marcels in the main dining room.

Chima was right. The two paranormal robotcycle club members were getting on like a house on fire. There were resounding sounds of laughter and excited, animated conversation that made the virtual dining room noisy with vibrancy. Chima looked at Amiah Lily smugly. Marcel glanced at both of them and then spoke up.

"Chima, it's not only about whether the Amiah Riders are tired. It's about what they want to do next. They're free just like us." Marcel said

"To do whatever we want." Jan said.

"Which is exactly what we do." Amiah chimed in.

"We are happy with the choice you have made in advance. We know you will be back again soon and we will be happy to welcome you back again." Marcel said.

"Thank you." Amiah said in response and stood up.

"Oh-oh did my brother upset you?" Marcel asked.

Chima rolled his eyes.

"No, I'm just going to use the ladies room." Amiah replied.

"Me too." Saraina said.

"Ok. If you forget where it is just ask one of the robots nearby and they will show you." Chima said.

"Thanks but I remember where it is." Amiah said holding back laughter.

Did Chima forget that Amiah can remote view any property? Saraina wondered to herself. Navigating around the Chi-Marcel mansion was as easy as if Amiah had a virtual map held in her hand. Amiah did have a map but it was not in her hand, it was in Amiah's mind.

Amiah and Saraina confidently walked out of the main virtual dining room, turned left and found the ladies room. They used separate toilets. Amiah heard Saraina giggling excitedly from her toilet cubicle.

When the two women had finished, they washed their hands and sat down on soft virtual sofas which were in a waiting area attached a short distance away from the toilet section of the ladies room.

"Something funny you sensed in the toilet Saraina?" Amiah asked with an amused smile.

"Yes! I psychically heard a conversation of the ancestors of the Onai twins in the toilet. They were saying that the spiritual gifts came from them and the Onai twins are taking credit for something that has been passed on generationally. They went on and said that even the robotcycle skills were passed down generationally, from ancestors who used to be awesome motorcyclists back over two hundred years ago. I just thought that was so funny." Saraina giggled again.

"Did you get the ancestors name and date they were alive on Earth?" Amiah inquired.

Saraina's face turned into a serious expression.

"Saraina. Try not to get carried away by what you hear and instead find out the meaning behind the words and who could possibly be saying those words to you. Think of the 'who' and the 'why'. You know that those ancestors could be lying. Not everyone's ancestors tell the truth. Especially if they know that the person listening could misconstrue it to serve their own purposes. Do you hear what I'm saying?" Amiah warned.

"Yes Amiah." Saraina said

"Good." Amiah replied.

"I do have other good news that I can definitely confirm though." Saraina continued.

"Good. What's that?" Amiah asked.

"I've been blocking everyone at the Chi-Marcel mansion since we got here and so far... no headaches, no migraines, no pain in my forehead area...I feel fine." Saraina said happily.

Amiah grinned at Saraina.

"Saraina this is the best news so far tonight! Well done! What do you think helped you to block successfully?" Amiah inquired.

"I don't know. I practiced and practiced all the tips during your blocking training sessions and seems like something I've learned has suddenly clicked in my brain tonight!" Saraina replied.

"Jelitoonaa Saraina! We can talk more about what you are actually doing in your mind to block other psychics when we get back to Amiah Mansion tomorrow. For now, keep doing what you are doing." Amiah said.

"I will." said Saraina.

Amiah heard a soothing ringing tone by her right ear. It was an incoming vision. She wanted to watch it without being disturbed so she spoke to Saraina.

"Saraina go on ahead of me. I'll be back in the dining room in a little while, ok."

"Ok. Bye!" Saraina leapt off the virtual sofa happily and half skipped half walked back to the main dining room.

Amiah settled back onto the virtual sofa to watch her latest vision. When the dark purple mist cleared on the vision playing in front of Amiah's eyes, she could see the black silhouettes of two men. She immediately sensed the energy of the Onai twins.

Next, Amiah saw the black silhouette of a man turn bright red and grow smaller and smaller. Then the other black silhouette shape of a man came close to her and kissed her on the forehead.

The vision then suddenly disappeared.

PARTY THEATRICS

Amiah sat still on the virtual sofa in the waiting area of the ladies room. She blinked her brown eyes a few times and cocked her head to the side briefly. Here she was enjoying herself in the company of two handsome, talented and paranormally gifted men, while Landon was rotting away in jail. Not literally rotting away, but his quality of life was certainly eroding dangerously. Time is precious. Every day, every night without Landon was another day and night that they would never get back. How could she be smiling, laughing and talking with a room full of attractive gifted men, while her love child with Landon Ross could still not be seen with human eyes? Her adorable baby, her only son Brandon Ross, Amiah pondered.

"Brandon!" Amiah whispered.

Amiah immediately focused on her invisible son's energy and connected to him via her remote viewing skills. She began to remote view the location where Brandon was situated. Then she focused in on watching her son. Brandon was awake playing with his two cousins in his playroom while his grandad sat nearby watching a movie on the large virtual screen. Brandon ran around laughing and hiding from his cousins and appeared very happy. Amiah smiled to see Brandon happy and well. He did not seem tired in the slightest. He was an energetic, curious and adventurous child.

If only Landon and I could see him! Amiah mused.

Amiah yearned desperately to see even a glimpse of her love child with Landon. Even if it were only in a dream or a vision that lasted 10 seconds. To have some idea of Brandon's facial features would mean the world to Amiah. Of course, she had tried asking the psychic artists in the Amiah Riders to draw an image of Brandon based on the energy they could all read around him. The images had initially first made both Amiah and Landon feel excited and joyful. Yet, after a few hours of flicking through pages and pages of various images drawn by the psychic artists, something was plainly wrong. All the images drawn were different from each other.

So, whose psychic artistic impression of what Brandon looked like was correct? No-one knew. Amiah had thanked her paranormally gifted artists for trying, but they could see she was disappointed that not any two of the images drawn were alike. Other ideas attempted by the Amiah Riders to find out what Brandon truly looked like failed also.

The Amiah Riders tried using a group spirit communication, dream work, summoning visions, asking the ancestors and other psychic/paranormal skills. To their surprise, nothing worked. It was like as if the Recathri alien itself was somehow blocking every single thing which was done to reveal Brandon's true identity. The questions everyone secretly asked themselves, was whether or not the Recathri alien could be horrifyingly more stronger and more powerful than they were? Could the Recathri alien be even more powerful than any psychic or paranormal human being on planet Earth?

Amiah felt her face grow hot with anger and her hands started to shake. Oh, how she wished she could strangle the Recathri alien right there and then! she angrily thought. The way she felt right now she would have done it instantly before even asking for the cure for invisibility. The Recathri alien deserved to die for what it did to her son. If only she could get it to listen to her and play by her rules, by the Amiah Riders rules. Not by the crazy rules of whatever planet it had come from. There had to be a way for her to see Brandon for the first time and forever onwards. Amiah vowed that she was going to find it.

Amiah recalled that Marcel had promised that he would try and help find the cure for her son's invisibility. She assumed that meant that Chima and the Chi-Marcels would all help too. Didn't they come as a team? Amiah mused.

Amiah thought about Marcel's offer but remembered to continue blocking everyone at the Chi-Marcel mansion from reading her thoughts or energy. She got up from the virtual sofa in the waiting area of the ladies room, and began walking back to the main dining room.

Upon entering the virtual main dining room, Amiah heard music being played loudly. She saw that some of the Amiah Riders and Chi-Marcels were dancing and enjoying themselves. Others were sitting down eating and chatting with each other. She could see the Onai twins, Jan and Saraina were one of the many who remained seated, enjoying their food and drink.

Amiah returned to her hovering virtual seat and sat down. She finished eating her vanilla ice-cream with strawberry jelly and chocolate chips in silence. The Onai twins were talking with each other and not paying attention to her. Amiah looked up at them and felt the room spin fast around her. Was it just her or had the music turned eerie and off key? she thought confused. Everything her eyes could see grew blurrier and blurrier. Amiah knew she was in some kind of trouble, and she telepathically communicated to her Amiah Riders.

"Help me!"

Amiah's upper body fell face first into her leftover vanilla ice-cream and strawberry jelly with a splash and thud.

"Amiah!" one of the Amiah Riders shouted out.

"Amiah! Oh my God!" Jan exclaimed.

"What have you done to her?" Saraina yelled at the Onai twins.

Jan, Saraina and all the Amiah Riders ran over to where Amiah Lily lay collapsed on top of her dessert. Jan and Saraina gently pulled her up off the virtual table and wiped the ice-cream and jelly off her face. There was no need for anyone to check Amiah's vital signs as every Amiah Rider is trained to read the life energy of a person. Reading Amiah's life energy reassured every Amiah Rider that Amiah was alive and well. She had fallen into a deep sleep. The Amiah Riders knew it could be a psychic or visionary sleep whereby Amiah would have important paranormal or psychic information shown to her.

The Onai twins reached by Amiah's side with two medical robots who had a medical hover stretcher floating next to them. They didn't seem surprised at all.

"Overwhelm energy surroundings conflict." Marcel said seriously to his brother Chima.

"Yes, happens." Chima replied.

"There isn't a way you can turn down the energy." Marcel said.

"Not if you're that sensitive and powerful. No." Chima answered.

"Then next time we…" Marcel started to speak but Jan interrupted him.

"Er hello! Amiah needs a guest room to rest now please, thank you." Jan said loudly to the Onai twins.

"She is having one of her psychic dream visions." Saraina explained in a gentle voice. "Amiah Lily can fall asleep suddenly if a vision comes to her which is too strong for her to process while awake and fully conscious."

The Onai twins glanced at each other quickly. They held a different view as to why Amiah Lily had suddenly fell asleep in the middle of eating her dessert. They did not share them with the Amiah Riders at this time as their emotions were obviously high after witnessing Amiah in distress. Instead, the Onai twins helped Jan lift Amiah's body onto the medical hover stretcher and escorted her outside to go with her to the guest room. Two medical robots, Jan and Saraina also followed Amiah Lily on her medical hover stretcher.

The virtual guest rooms were located at the back of the Chi-Marcel mansion and had views that overlooked the awe-inspiring huge robotcycle shaped swimming pools and beautiful gardens. The Onai twins did not go inside the guest room which Amiah, Jan and Saraina all had king size beds to sleep on. They reminded Jan and Saraina that if they needed any further assistance then robots in the room would cater to their every need. Then, the Onai twins wished them well and left to return back to the main virtual dining room.

The virtual guest room had three virtual hover beds separated from each other with virtual borders separating each bed. The virtual borders therefore appeared transparent but could be operated to change colour. So, in effect, no-one would be able to see the bed of someone who had changed their virtual border colour to black for example. They also had the additional feature of sound virtual border control, which also ensured that no outside sounds could be heard from inside the virtual border. This ensured a quiet night sleep even though there were other people in the guest room. Each guest room included virtual screens, gym equipment, bathrooms, virtual sofas, virtual wardrobes full of clothes and shoes for women and 3 robot staff amongst other luxuries.

The medical hover stretcher carrying Amiah Lily floated over the king size bed on the left hand side of the room. The king size bed was located in between two other king size beds. Then the medical hover stretcher disappeared leaving Amiah Lily sleeping peacefully on her king size bed. Jan and Saraina undressed Amiah slowly and carefully.

"Robot bring me pyjama shorts and top size 16 and a wet flannel." Jan shouted over at one of the robots who was standing in a corner.

"Yes Jan." the robot replied and got the items from the virtual wardrobe nearby.

Jan took the items from the robot and together with Saraina changed Amiah into pyjamas. She wiped the sweat off Amiah's face, neck and other areas of her body. It was a hot summer night. The air conditioning worked well in their virtual guest room and Jan could read that Amiah's body temperature was ok.

"I nearly thought I wouldn't be able to read Amiah's life energy as she told me that she had been blocking everyone since we left Amiah Mansion." Saraina said to Jan.

"I don't know exactly how it's turned off. Possibly when she asked us telepathically for help, her blocking immediately stopped. I'm not sure." Jan shrugged.

"So, I guess we are spending the night here." said Saraina.

"Looks like it." Jan replied.

"I wonder what she's dreaming about." Saraina continued.

"Remember what Amiah taught us. She said that if she was to stop blocking for any reason then we are to observe with all our paranormal senses the energy around her. If we sense any unknown or unwanted energy within Amiah's energy then we have to find out who it is and tell them to leave her." Jan said.

"Or... we have to do whatever it takes to remove that energy from Amiah. Whatever it takes. That means anything right?" Saraina asked enthusiastically.

Jan laughed. "Yes Saraina, anything."

"Come on. Let them try." Saraina whispered confidently to herself as she went to use the bathroom near her king size virtual bed.

Meanwhile, Amiah was locked in one of the weirdest paranormal dreams she had experienced in a long time. Numerous images kept flashing in front of her and disappearing. She had nearly panicked thinking that her entire life was flashing in front of her. People had told her that this kind of thing happened just before a person left their physical body to join the spirit world. Amiah tried to use her paranormal senses to get herself out of this strange dream. She screamed out for her ancestors and listened to the voices that were talking around the images for clues on how to escape.

Amiah's body went cold and then hot before going cold again, multiple times. She felt hands touching different parts of her body and dissolving into cool water on her skin. The images that appeared rapidly in front of Amiah's eyes, were too fast for her to remember most of them. It was chaotic but Amiah persisted to search for the meaning of the dream.

Finally, Amiah heard the voice of one of her ancestors from 500 years ago. She could sense strong love and affection coming from a female ancestor, who had passed away at the age of 93.

"You will see Brandon. Power..."

The rest of what Amiah's ancestor said, could not be heard over the sound of loud arguing which overpowered the rest of the sentence. More chaotic flashing scenes followed with the sounds of people arguing about things in an unknown language. All the scenes flashed by Amiah so fast it confused her.

Will I be able to remember all these images and words when I wake up or is the Recathri alien somehow messing with my mind? she thought.

Surely, the Recathri alien is the only enemy I have, that is powerful enough to do unexpected paranormal alien stuff like in this crazy dream, Amiah continued to think angrily.

Suddenly, all the flashing images and words in foreign languages stopped in Amiah's dream and she saw the large green oval shaped shadow at a distance. Amiah wasn't going to let the Recathri alien get away with disrupting her dinner with the Onai twins and the Chi-Marcels. She used her power and entered herself into the midst of the energy she felt around the Recathri alien which she could see. She then read as much information from the Recathri alien using her paranormal mind reading skills. The Recathri alien made a high-pitched sound all the while and wrapped itself around Amiah's image in the dream.

Amiah remained calm and visualised a gold protective shield all around her body. The Recathri alien slid out of the hold it had on Amiah, and surrounded her gold shield trying to enter back inside it. Amiah's image in the dream grinned widely and then she focused on bringing an end to this tormenting dream.

Ten minutes more went by with the Recathri alien still trying to enter into Amiah's gold protective shield all around her. There was no way for the alien to enter inside, so it resorted to making more high pitched squealing noises as Amiah sat smiling smugly at it. Then Amiah focused her attention again on exiting the tormenting dream. She had managed to obtain a lot of information found in the Recathri alien's mind. This was the only good part of the dream. It was time for her to use every bit of strength and paranormal power she had to leave the dream. Her Amiah Riders needed her to be with them. They were alone with the Chi-Marcels. Who knew what was going on? Amiah wondered.

The image of Amiah's face in the dream changed into many different shades of various colours. Dark clouds appeared above her, and lightning struck down on her gold protective shield three times.

It was at that moment that Amiah finally woke up.

"Welcome back." Jan said looking concerned but happy.

Amiah rubbed her eyes and stretched both arms above her head. She sat up in the bed she laid on in her virtual guest room.

"Got him… I mean it, I mean whatever it…it was Recathri." Amiah said calmly.

"I knew it!" Saraina said. "Here. Do you want some water to drink? Jan and I changed your clothes."

Amiah did not answer. She was thinking about all the new information about the Recathri alien, that she had acquired from it's mind (wherever that was located).

How will I manage to translate it into modern day planet Earth English? she thought. What about the Amiah Riders and Brandon? How long did I sleep for? What did I miss? Amiah's mind raced with all these thoughts.

"Give her a few minutes to catch herself." Jan said.

"It's alright." Amiah smiled at both of them assuredly. "I'm fine. How are both of you?"

"We're good." Jan and Saraina said in unison.

Amiah quickly remote viewed her home and the main dining room. Brandon and the other members of her family were ok. The rest of the Amiah Riders were… in different parts of the Chi-Marcel mansion. Many of them were paired with a man from the Chi-Marcel riders. Some had a few Chi-Marcels in their guest rooms and others remained in the main dining room getting more closely acquainted intimately. Amiah shared what she could see about the other Amiah Riders, with Jan and Saraina via connecting her remote viewing skills with theirs.

Jan and Saraina watched the scenes shared with them for five minutes. They all psychically viewed the rest of the

Amiah Riders having fun, laughing, joking, kissing and some getting naked with the men from the Chi-Marcels paranormal robotcycle club.

Saraina giggled. "It was going to happen. We all have so much in common."

"True." Jan agreed.

"Well, I thought maybe they would start off with a brother/sister type of friendship first but…" Amiah raised her eyebrows at the party antics and displays of wild behaviour she could see her Amiah Riders doing. She felt a small twinge of guilt.

Have I been working my Amiah Riders too hard and isolating them for too long with frequent tasks, training, rescue missions and other club duties? No wonder they are all going wild now at the very first dinner with the Chi-Marcels and the Onai… Amiah thought, before pausing.

The Onai twins! Amiah mused after a short while had passed.

Amiah had been so engrossed viewing what her Amiah Riders were getting up to around the Chi-Marcel mansion, that she had forgotten about the Onai twins. Amiah quickly disconnected from viewing the Amiah Riders. This stopped Jan and Saraina viewing also.

"Ohhhh!" Saraina exclaimed a bit too loudly.

Jan and Amiah looked at her.

"Sorry. It was getting juicy." Saraina said truthfully.

Amiah ignored her and immediately got on with connecting to the energy of the Onai twins to find out what they were up to. She used all her paranormal and psychic powers to find them in the Chi-Marcel mansion but could not find them. She focused harder yet still she could not perceive them or their whereabouts. Had the Onai twins left their home? Were they out riding on their robotcycles at night? Or, were they blocking her like she was blocking them? Amiah pondered.

She decided to telepathically try to talk to them. First of all, she called Marcel telepathically.

"Marcel. It's Amiah. I am feeling much better. Where are you?

I want to talk to you and Chima."

"Amiah. Good to hear that you are feeling much better. My brother and I can meet you in the virtual conference room. There are mini hover transportation devices outside each guest room if you don't feel like walking. We will see you soon." Marcel replied telepathically to Amiah.

"I'm going to talk to the Onai twins. They are in the virtual conference room. You don't have to stay and wait for me. Go and have fun!" Amiah said to Jan and Saraina.

"Yes!" Saraina grinned.

"Remember to check the energy of any Chi-Marcel before you get too close, and if they are blocking you, that's a sign that they're probably hiding something, ok?" Amiah warned them both.

"Jelitoonaa." Jan answered enthusiastically.

"Later!" Saraina replied.

Amiah half smiled as she watched two of her Amiah Riders happily leave her to go and have fun with the Chi-Marcel robotcycle riders. Again, she felt another guilty pang that she had indeed been working them too hard. The Amiah Riders were hardworking, dedicated, talented and gifted paranormal robotcycle riders. They deserved a break. Maybe she should start an annual four-week holiday event from business related projects, and also schedule more rides together.

Amiah frowned at this thought. She frequently received requests for her help and the Amiah Riders assistance. There was a backlog of over 200 different potential mission requests that needed to be assessed and/or undertaken. Amiah wished there were more paranormal and/or psychic robotcycle clubs in England. So far, she only knew of her Amiah Riders and the Chi-Marcels. If there were any in other countries, she was not aware of their existence.

If there did in fact happen to be other paranormal robotcycle clubs in other countries, it would make good sense that they were keeping themselves hidden. No robotcycle club would want too much scrutiny as this would make it harder to carry out their missions safely. However, the more people Amiah worked with and the more missions the Amiah Riders went on, eventually the public would learn about them. On that day, Amiah planned to be open about some club secrets but she would never ever be ready at any time, to tell all...

Never, Amiah thought proudly to herself.

Amiah got up from bed and walked into the bathroom to shower. Then she got dressed in a light brown mini skirt and white fitted top with low silver heels to go and meet the Onai twins.

The Onai twins were waiting for Amiah in the virtual conference room which was similar to the main virtual dining room. There were images of robotcycles flying around in the air above them. Although, instead of a long glowing orange virtual table, there was now a circular glowing orange virtual table. Amiah entered through the virtual doors that disappeared after scanning her body up and down. A robot greeted her.

"Miss Amiah Lily, hello again. Follow me." the robot instructed clearly.

Amiah followed the robots to the opposite side of the circular glowing orange virtual table. Already seated were the Onai twins on hovering silver virtual seats. Amiah sat down on a hovering seat and turned to face Marcel sitting next to her.

"Hey, I'm back. Sorry about earlier. I have psychic dreams that can interrupt me at any time. Hope I didn't worry you too much." Amiah clarified in a friendly voice.

The Onai twins smiled at Amiah.

"No worries Amiah." Chima replied.

"You require help with the Recathri alien. Chima and I have been discussing this while you were asleep." Marcel said.

Amiah assumed that the Onai twins remembered her request for help when they talked with her in her garage at Amiah Mansion. She was effectively blocking everyone at the Chi-Marcel mansion from reading her thoughts. She didn't sense that her blocking had been overridden.

"Yes. You remember from the time we spoke in my garage.

My son Brandon was born invisible after the Recathri alien turned me invisible during a demonstration of it's power. While I was invisible, I conceived a baby with my... with my ex-boyfriend Landon in Duneway virtual high security prison." Amiah explained.

"You managed to get into the prison unseen as you and the alien were both invisible to human eyes." Chima said.

"The paranormal security staff could not sense your energy as you were blocking them." Marcel said.

"Correct. Correct." Amiah nodded at them.

"Your ex-boyfriend Landon. Was he affected by the invisibility that the alien put on you?" Chima asked.

Amiah winced slightly at hearing Chima use the words 'ex-boyfriend'.

"No, he's fine. It's just our son was born invisible to human eyes." Amiah continued on.

"What about animal eyes? Have you observed your son... erm..." Marcel inquired.

"Brandon. Brandon Ross." said Amiah.

"Brandon Ross." Chima repeated.

"Have you observed your invisible son around animals such as pets like dogs, cats, or birds outside? To see if the animals can see your son." Marcel asked.

Amiah blushed slightly. She felt embarrassed. She had been so preoccupied, that neither herself, Landon or the Amiah Riders could see Brandon, that she hadn't considered that a pet dog or cat might be able to. Then, Amiah had a follow up thought which she spoke out aloud.

"Who cares if a pet dog or cat can see my invisible son! That's not the point. I can't see him and everyone else who loves him can't see him. Are you here to help me or not?" Amiah said. Her embarrassment releasing sharply through anger instead of being more genuinely expressed.

There was a few minutes silence in the conference room after Amiah's angry response to Marcel's question. During that time, Amiah felt her face and neck grow hot. To make things more complicated she had a brief 30 second vision of Landon sitting on the virtual table in front of her. Landon's face displayed a screwed up irritated angry expression that Amiah knew she too also held back from showing. The Onai twins didn't look bothered or moved by her outburst, they just were not speaking. Amiah decided to fill in the silence.

"Maybe the animals can see my invisible son, maybe they can't. I really don't think that is of relevance for myself and his father right now." Amiah said using every ounce of strength to remain calm and composed. She briefly saw another vision of herself reaching across the table and scratching the eyes of the Onai twins out. This brief vision turned Amiah's inner anger into a mild humour at her unfortunate situation.

"We have many contacts who we think may be able to help you. Your issue is now our issue too. Every resource available to us we will use to restore Brandon to full visibility. With or without the Recathri alien's co-operation. Myself and my brother Chima, on behalf of the Chi-Marcels join with you in your mission for Brandon's visibility." Marcel stated confidently.

"Thank you." replied Amiah. This was more like what Amiah wanted to hear.

"We will set daily tasks for the Chi-Marcels to use their paranormal and psychic skills to contact the Recathri alien. We will contact shamans, other alien contacts, other paranormal and psychic humans… we will support the invisible boy in any way we can. We will also support you and the Amiah Riders to join with you on any missions relating to the return of Brandon's visibility." Chima explained.

"Thank you so much." Amiah responded. Her eyes were filling with tears. The mild humour had turned into grief. Grief from all the memories of the pain she felt realising she had never seen the love child that she and Landon created together. Grief from remembering that Landon had made her promise that she should be his ex-girlfriend and get on with her life without him. Grief from the confusion that she felt as to why this could be happening to her?

Amiah's intentions had always been for good with the Amiah Riders. Her love for Landon was pure, passionate and real.

So, why is one of the worst possible scenarios playing out in front of me concerning little Brandon? Amiah thought. No-one understood fully the depth of pain and anguish she felt, no-one.

"We have already started contacting some of the people and aliens we have mentioned. There is an elderly shaman called Mangia who lives and works in the city under a fake business called Reiki Mangia. We would love for you to accompany us to visit him and allow Shaman Mangia to read your energy to learn more about the Recathri alien." Chima suggested.

Amiah hesitated before answering.

"I have new information which I gathered from the Recathri's mind in the psychic dream I had tonight but it's in the Recathri language. I don't understand and can't speak their language. I previously spoke to the Recathri in English and the Recathri spoke to me in English." Amiah explained.

"Jelitoonaa Amiah. Yes, this new information should greatly assist in finding out more about the Recathri and possibly even the planet that it came from." Marcel said smiling.

"How do I know I can trust the Mangia shaman? Have you got any information about him?" Amiah asked.

Shaman Mangia was new to Amiah. She didn't know him and like everyone she didn't know, she didn't trust him. She didn't trust new people fully at all. This included the Onai twins and the Chi-Marcels. Although, she still appreciated their willingness to help her and Brandon immensely. Trust had to be earned.

"If you take down your blocking defences, I can transfer all the knowledge we have about Shaman Mangia into your mind." Chima said.

"Chima!" Marcel exclaimed. "Sorry Amiah. Chima can be a bit rude sometimes." Marcel glared coldly at his brother.

"How is that rude?" Chima exclaimed back.

Amiah rolled her eyes. Family dynamics. She didn't have time for it.

"My blocking defences are there for my safety and the safety of my Amiah Riders. I am sure you are using your blocking skills too and so are the Chi-Marcels." Amiah retorted back at Chima.

Marcel looked at his brother and smirked.

"What?" Chima said glaring at his brother momentarily.

"Anyway, do you have any information I can read the old-fashioned way for now? On virtual papers or a virtual view tablet perhaps?" Amiah requested sweetly. She still needed to keep the Onai twins and the Chi-Marcels on her side regardless if they were showing signs of obvious discord.

A robot came up to Amiah carrying a single gold virtual A4 size paper. The gold virtual paper had only two words written on it in the colour silver.

SHAMAN MANGIA INFO

Amiah turned the gold single sheet of virtual paper over and over again in her hands. Not able to find anymore words on the single virtual paper, she looked at the Onai twins quizzically.

"Is this a joke?" Amiah questioned.

"Relax. If you relax and use your psychic skills to focus on the words you will know every single thing we know, about Shaman Mangia." Marcel said.

"We knew you would be blocking us, so we transferred the information of Shaman Mangia into this gold virtual sheet of paper. All you have to do is touch it, and focus on the words written on there." Chima explained.

Amiah held the gold virtual sheet of paper with both hands and focused on the words, Shaman Mangia written in silver. Precisely, 60 seconds went by before Amiah lifted her head up again to speak to the Onai twins.

"Thank you." Amiah said.

"You are very welcome Miss Amiah Lily." Marcel said with a smile.

Amiah appeared deep in thought.

"What's wrong?" Marcel inquired.

"Shaman Mangia has a very high number of alien friends doesn't he?" Amiah questioned.

"Yes, this is why we believe he would be very useful in helping contact the Recathri alien to find a cure for Brandon." Marcel replied.

"It's a good thing." Chima agreed.

"He may be able to decipher the Recathri language that you read from it's mind tonight." Marcel said.

Amiah happily smiled at the Onai twins and both Marcel along with his brother Chima smiled back at her.

Inside the privacy of Amiah's mind however, she thought that anyone who had that many alien friends... was probably near enough an alien themselves.

THE ALIEN SHAMAN

Amiah and Jan pulled up on their robotcycles into the parking area of the Resu U Reiki Experience centre. As soon as their robotcycles turned off, their robotcycle virtual helmets disappeared also. Both women got off their robotcycles and waited for the Onai twins to arrive.

"We're here first." Jan said.

"They'll get here soon. Are you still blocking?" Amiah replied.

"Yes for as long as I can. I will empty my mind if I need to stop." said Jan.

Amiah felt another pang of guilt. She had been feeling them a lot lately. Jan had to take a couple of painkillers before they set off to ride to the Resu U Reiki centre. Jan had headaches when she blocked other psychics for too long. The painkillers were to prevent Jan getting those headaches. Amiah felt bad about this. She wondered if she was pushing her Amiah Riders too hard regarding their work...

"Hello Amiah, are you here with me?" Jan inquired. "You look like you're miles away."

Amiah snapped out of her daytime reverie and back into the present day situation.

"Of course I'm here. Look, I can see the Onai twins pulling up over there." Amaih said quickly.

Chima Onai and Marcel Onai had just pulled up on their red robotcycles into the parking area of the Resu U Reiki Experience centre. After getting off their bikes, they waved over at Amiah and Jan.

"Go inside! We'll meet you in there!" Marcel shouted over at the two women.

"He wants us to go inside." Jan said.

"Let's go then." Amiah replied.

Amiah and Jan walked through the busy parking area and made their way to the front entrance of the Resu U Reiki centre. They waited for security robots to scan them to check their identity before entering inside.

The Resu U Reiki Experience centre was located inside a large virtual building with 10 floors. The reception area is extremely busy. Amiah was glad that both Jan and herself were blocking other paranormal and psychic people. The busier a place was, the more likely that there were other people with gifts similar to theirs around. Although, the opposite was also true. It would only take a single psychic in an empty building or within a certain distance away, to be able to read their minds if Amiah and Jan were not using their blocking skills.

The Onai twins entered the centre a few minutes later to join Amiah and Jan.

"Hey! You rode down here faster than us!" Chima said smiling.

"We had the route programmed into our robotcycles before we left." Jan replied smugly.

Amiah and Marcel exchanged quizzical glances. Everyone knew that robotcycles were pre-programmed and would automatically take the rider to any destination he/she wanted.

Are the painkillers causing Jan to say silly things or is it just a slip of the tongue? Amiah thought.

"Well, we're all here now and I'm ready to get to business. Where is he?" Amiah asked.

"Follow us." Chima said.

"Alrighty then!" Jan exclaimed.

The Onai twins led Jan and Amiah through the crowds of people to a virtual lift on the far right hand corner of the large reception area. Then they all got into a virtual lift with eight other people. The other people got out of the lift at different floor levels. Amiah, Jan and the Onai twins stayed inside the virtual lift until they reached the top floor. Floor number 10. At floor number 10, all four of them exited the lift and stepped outside into a long corridor which had numerous virtual doors along each side.

"Behind each of these virtual doors are modern offices with the latest robot technology and workspaces for robots." Chima said.

"Shaman Mangia." Marcel tittered to himself. "Highly spiritual and at the same time highly into science and technology."

"The two are linked." Chima said as the group continued to walk along the corridor on their way to speak to Shaman Mangia.

Hopefully, Shaman Mangia would be able to give them the answers they were looking for. This thought was in each of their minds as they waited outside a green virtual door with images of unrecognised 'faces' coming out from it. The 'faces' with no body would appear randomly on the virtual door. Then the images of 'faces' would hover out a short way from the door before returning back into the green virtual door.

"Nice." Jan said closely peering at the 'faces' near to her on the green virtual door.

The Onai twins began to speak with the images of 'faces' coming in and out of the virtual door.

"I know it was wrong. I'm sorry that happened to you." Chima said sadly to one of the 'faces' coming out of the green virtual door.

"It would have been easier if only they made it easy." Marcel said sorrowfully to another of the 'faces' coming out of the green virtual door.

"The love you had is not wasted. It's in you." Chima said glumly at another of the 'faces'.

"You are enough and that is all that matters." Marcel said in a voice which sounded like on the brink of tears.

"If we could turn back time, we would have held your hand every step of the way." Chima said with hope in his voice.

"Things will get better." Marcel said with the same hopeful voice as Chima.

"Better days are coming." Chima said to another 'face' that had floated a short way out of the green virtual door.

Amiah and Jan observed the scene in front of them in complete silence. Obviously something new was going on between the 'faces' (appearing in and out of the green virtual door) and the Onai twins. Something new that both Amiah and Jan had not seen before. They were not frightened in the slightest. Only curious and observant.

The Onai twins spoke kindly and hopefully to each of the 'faces' floating in and out of the virtual green door for the next 10 minutes. Amiah and Jan patiently observed with interest. Then, Amiah heard Brandon's voice speak loudly next to her right ear.

"Mummy, when are you coming home? I miss you."

Amiah immediately stopped her patient observation of the strange scene in front of her and spoke loudly to get the attention of everyone.

"My son needs me home. How long is this going to take?" Amiah said firmly while at the same time sending a telepathic message of reassurance to her invisible son.

"Brandon. Mummy is at work. Find a toy to play with. I'll be home when I'm finished. Tonight I will be home. Mum loves you." Amiah telepathically communicated to Brandon.

All the 'faces' on the green virtual door turned to stare at Amiah with wide-opened eyes. Chima and Marcel looked at Amiah calmly. Then the green virtual door with all the unknown 'faces' on it disappeared.

"Time to go in." Chima said triumphantly.

"Ladies first." Marcel said.

Amiah and Jan walked into the modern furbished office which incorporated the latest advanced robot technology, with no fear. There were robots everywhere. Not just the standard human style metallic robots that were more frequently seen, but most items in the room had a robotic element to it. Along with the frequency of robot tech in the office, there were hover virtual tables and hover chairs too.

An elderly man whose skin glowed of a variety of interchanging colours, with a long wiry pointed grey beard, sat in the lotus position on a transparent hover virtual chair. It was Shaman Mangia. In front of Shaman Mangia, is a clear hovering circular virtual table. The clear circular virtual table contained virtual papers, virtual portable view tablets, food/drink and robot equipment of varying shapes and sizes. The robot equipment were such that Amiah and Jan had never seen before. The robot equipment on the virtual table were breathing in and out. It also looked like they had a mix of virtual and hover elements included within their outward robotic appearance.

Amiah yawned. She was not here to learn more about the shaman's alien like appearance or about the latest new robot technological advances. Nor was she here to learn about how to communicate with 'faces' on green virtual doors. She was present in this office for one main reason and one main reason only. To find out if Shaman Mangia could help her in any way, find out more about the Recathri alien to cure her son's invisibility.

"I know why you're here Miss Amiah Lily." Shaman Mangia mumbled to himself.

"Hello Shaman Mangia. I've brought two of my friends to see you today. They need some help." Marcel said.

Shaman Mangia stroked his long wiry grey beard gently while looking at the four new visitors into his office. His office smelt of burning sage but none could be seen anywhere.

"Hello Shaman Mangia." Amiah said smiling at him.

"Hello Shaman Mangia." Jan said also smiling at the Shaman.

"Your office is very impressive. I don't think I've ever seen so much variety of advanced robot tech anywhere else in the country." Amiah said.

"Did you bring gifts?" Shaman Mangia said narrowing his eyes at the women.

Amiah looked taken aback. The Onai twins hadn't

mentioned anything about the necessity of bringing gifts to the old man Shaman. Amiah desperately needed this first meet up to go smoothly as she wanted the shaman on her side. Brandon had to be made visible again.

So, if bringing a gift would help me to achieve this goal then why didn't the Onai twins warn me in their virtual gold paper the night before? Amiah thought.

The Onai twins started to laugh.

"He's joking Amiah." Marcel said.

"Ohh ok." Amiah said with a smile. Personally however, she thought that the joke wasn't funny at all. Her invisible son missed his mummy and here she was making small talk with an alien looking like shaman. But, Amiah had to keep up her friendly persona for Brandon's sake...

"Ok. Now that the introductions are done with, let's get down to business. Eat and drink what you like except for Miss Amiah Lily. Miss Amiah come with me." instructed Shaman Mangia.

Shaman Mangia then moved away from the clear circular virtual table on his hover chair where he remained seated in the lotus position. He went through a white misty area which had suddenly appeared out of nowhere. Amiah could not see behind all the dense white mist.

"It's ok. Just follow him through all that white mist." Marcel said.

Amiah giggled. "See you later!" She wasn't scared. Her amusement was returning to her at the sight of all the white mist. The white mist reminded her of how some of her visions started in the past.

"All the best Amiah." Jan said sitting down on a hover chair and picking up a banana to eat.

The Onai twins sat down on hover chairs aswell, but soon started to move around on them to explore other parts of Shaman Mangia's office.

Amiah spoke to Jan telepathically in her mind.

"Jan. Watch the Onai twins and learn more about them. Even

if they are blocking you, just watch them anyway."

Jan heard Amiah's voice in her mind just before she was about to take a second bite out of her peeled banana. Jan threw the quarter eaten banana back down on the clear circular virtual table and swiftly moved (on her hover chair) to catch up with the Onai twins.

Hover chairs were controlled by touching sensors on the chair which showed a map of the seated persons location. A person would touch an area of the room on the map and the hover chair would move into that area. The speed of the hover chair could also be adjusted in the same way.

Amiah walked confidently through the white mist and had memories of her visions that started with white mist. She remembered a beautiful vision of her making love with Landon. This vision had started with white mist in front of her eyes before she saw the two of them naked, indulging in passionate lovemaking.

Amiah felt her heart sink a little.

For at the end of this white mist was not Landon's sexy naked body and hers intertwined, but the alien looking old man (albeit highly gifted) shaman.

MYSTERY COSMOS

The white mist cleared away to reveal a completely different scene from the robot filled office that Amiah had just been in. Amiah now stood in what appeared to be a beautiful park filled with colourful flowers and trees. In the distance, Amiah could see a lake with ducks on it. A short distance in front of her, sat old man Shaman Mangia. Amiah smiled at him. She was more than ready to get this meet up over and done with. As lovely as the scenery around her was, she was Brandon's mum and Brandon wanted her to be home with him.

Shaman Mangia, sat in the lotus position on green grass, in the middle of a circle of old-fashioned shamanic drums. All the drums were playing by themselves. No-one was operating the drums lined up in a circle around Shaman Mangia. Well, no-one that could be seen with physical eyes. The shaman himself had his own shamanic drum in front of him. The shaman's drum was beating by itself to a rhythmic African beat along with the rest of the drums. The drums collectively made booming and vibrant beats that caused Amiah to feel dreamy and relaxed.

"Come and meditate with me Miss Amiah Lily!" Shaman Mangia said telepathically to Amiah.

Amiah frowned. She knew she was effectively blocking other psychics and paranormal people but the Shaman had just communicated with her in her mind.

Is it all the drumming that has lowered my blocking abilities? Amiah thought.

Or was it the dreamy feeling that had enveloped her since hearing the beating shamanic drums? Amiah pondered and then concluded that it didn't really matter which one it was. She was ready to allow the old man shaman access to part of her mind anyway. The shaman had to have some access to Amiah Lily's mind in order to view the information about the Recathri alien.

Everything Amiah had learned about the shaman from the single virtual gold sheet of paper, given to her by the Onai twins seemed trustworthy. Shaman Mangia had a lengthy history and excellent reputation of possessing exceptionally high spiritual, psychic, paranormal and alien communication skills. He had no known links with criminality or any type of ruthless evil-minded organisations. He had recommendations from people Amiah knew and respected. He had even worked with people Amiah had completed successful rescue missions for in the past.

Amiah wanted to believe that the Onai twins were honest and genuine in their interest to help her. So, she would take this risk and trust Shaman Mangia unless she discovered a reason not to. She would continue blocking access to other parts of her brain, and definitely close off the memories she had of the Amiah Riders and Landon. The only part of her mind she would leave open for the shaman to interpret, is the part which held the information about the Recathri alien. With that thought Amiah sat down in the middle of the circle of drums and moved her legs into the lotus position. Only a single large shamanic drum, which was beating by itself playing loud rhythmic sounds, stood in between Shaman Mangia and Amiah.

"Miss Amiah Lily. I am here to help you. What is it that you desire" Shaman Mangia telepathically communicated to Amiah.

Amiah felt her eyelids grow heavy with an overwhelming feeling of sleep approaching. Yet, it wasn't sleep. It was a shamanic drum induced trance. Amiah allowed herself to relax into the deep sleep like trance and listened out for the shaman's further telepathic communication.

"Miss Amiah Lily is here to find a cure for her son Brandon's invisibility. The child Brandon was conceived whilst Miss Amiah Lily was in an invisible state. Miss Amiah Lily is a psychic and paranormally talented woman who teaches others, cares for others and has spent years helping humanity in rescue missions. I call upon all spirits, aliens or/and any other entities that can help restore visibility back to Brandon. Giving thanks and praise to the most High for everything is good and well." Shaman Mangia said.

Amiah heard Shaman Mangia's voice resonate above the booming rhythmic beating sounds of the shamanic drums. The shaman was no longer speaking telepathically to her but is now speaking to other dimensions, the spirit world and alien planets. Amiah's view of the shaman in front of her and the large shamanic drum faded away as her eyelids grew way too heavy for her to keep open. Amiah's eyes shut and her view changed again.

Now, all Amiah could see was a dark black empty space with Shaman Mangia and herself sitting in the lotus position next to each other looking forward into the darkened abyss. Amiah's eyes were opened in this trance induced vision which she shared with the shaman. She could not see anything around her but darkness. It reminded Amiah of her memories of her son's appearance. There weren't any visual memories, just a dark void of nothing to be seen.

Amiah's face grimaced, remembering the fact that even though she possessed probably the best psychic and paranormal talents, she could not see Brandon. Amiah couldn't perceive any of Brandon's visual appearance through any of her psychic or paranormal senses. She was sure it was the Recathri alien blocking her and hopefully today she would find out.

Bright gold sparkles finally appeared a few metres away from where the shaman sat in the lotus position next to Amiah. They formed in clusters together and split into hundreds of small oval shapes. The oval shapes of bright gold sparkles flew above, behind, in front of and at the sides of Amiah and the shaman. Next, words in a language Amiah did not understand were spoken.

"Yes. I understand. Ah... well no it didn't. I get it. I don't get it. Why? Tell me more..." Shaman Mangia communicated in

English back at one of the oval shapes of bright gold sparkles.

Amiah patiently waited for their communication to finish.

Shaman Mangia turned to speak to her. "This is Briddiii, it is a close alien friend of mine. It says that you are very beautiful, and it is searching the galaxy to try to find out information about the Recathri alien and invisibility. It is reading the information from your mind about the Recathri alien as we speak."

"Tell Briddiii thank you." Amiah answered. "Who are all the other oval shaped clusters of gold sparkles? Are they my... or your ancestors in spirit or other spirits or more aliens?"

"A mix of all of those and more." Shaman Mangia replied. "Just ask them to tell you who they are and they will. Don't be afraid."

Amiah grinned to herself. She had zero fear. Therefore, she felt calm and relaxed. The old man shaman obviously did not know her well enough yet.

"Would any of my ancestors in spirit, spirit guides or any other spirits like to talk to me to help me find a cure for my invisible son?" Amiah shouted out.

Shaman Mangia laughed. "They can hear you even when you whisper." he said.

"Amiah! I love watching you!" an oval shaped cluster of gold sparkles said from in front of Amiah.

"Amiah, we're so proud of you!" a different oval shaped cluster of bright gold sparkles said.

"Amiah, I am your great, great, great, great, great, great, great, great grandfather. Lovely to meet you!" another oval shaped cluster of gold sparkles said from behind Amiah.

"You will see Brandon!" a different oval shaped cluster said.

"Hey everyone! I'm happy to hear you!" Amiah replied enthusiastically.

Shaman Mangia began to speak in an unknown language to a group of oval shaped clusters of bright gold sparkles on his left-hand side. Meanwhile, Amiah listened to her spirit ancestors talk to her and replied back to most of them. Overall, Amiah's spirit ancestors (who were present in the trance the shaman had put her in today) were positive and encouraging about her. There was no negativity or pessimism. The spirit ancestors today all had good energy.

Is this because my ancestors are good or is it because Shaman Mangia has requested for only helpful spirits to be present? Amiah considered.

"I don't see that man Landon in your long-term future." one of the oval shaped clusters of gold sparkles blurted out suddenly.

Amiah remained calm. Similar to living human beings, Amiah knew that spirits could make mistakes or lie for their own purposes. She slowly turned to look behind her and then turned her whole body around in the lotus position to face the spirit who had said those words.

"And who are you? Amiah asked gently.

The oval shaped cluster of bright gold sparkles flew away from Amiah, returned back and flew away again.

"Who or what was that?" Amiah inquired from any of her spirit ancestors who were listening.

"Who is that?" one of the oval shaped clusters asked the other clusters of sparkles.

"It's not one of us!" another oval shaped cluster replied.

"It's someone we don't know Amiah, sorry." said a different oval shaped cluster of gold sparkles.

"It's ok. No problem." Amiah calmly replied. She was here to decipher the Recathri information and to find out if anyone knew more ways to help cure Brandon's invisibility. Any other stuff or revelations were not important right now. Besides, she didn't know if that was a deceitful spirit that had somehow managed to sneak into Shaman Mangia's trance with her. Amiah decided not to think anymore about what was said so it wouldn't grow a seed in her mind.

My future with Landon is our private love mystery to unravel. It's nobody else's business. she thought.

The oval shaped clusters of gold sparkles flew faster around the dark abyss for about five minutes.

"What's happening?" Amiah said as she felt her body being lifted up towards the dark space, above and away from Shaman Mangia, moving through all the oval shaped gold sparkle clusters.

"You are safe." Shaman Mangia telepathically communicated to Amiah.

Amiah kept moving upwards into more and more darkness, leaving the shaman and the oval shaped clusters of gold sparkles far behind her. She entered into a purple mist where all she could see with her physical eyes for a while was this mist and nothing else. Next, as Amiah felt her whole body fly upwards, she saw oval shaped planets in the distance of green, yellow and white. Was this where the Recathri alien came from? One of these oval shaped planets? Amiah pondered.

Amiah studied the three new planets and stored their information away in parts of her mind. Why had the Recathri home planet changed to oval? She thought that it had previously been round like the Earth? Or did she remember incorrectly? Would she be able to fly into these planets and see where the Recathri came from? she wondered. She wished she could control the direction in which she was going.

Afterwards, Amiah viewed a large (the size of the Amiah mansion) oval shaped green shadow leave the green planet and fly away from it. It was the Recathri alien. Amiah could sense that revolting energy anywhere. She wondered if the alien could see her or not. She wanted to speak to it so tried to communicate telepathically.

"Recathri! Recathri!" Amiah communicated telepathically with the energy she had stored in her mind that belonged to the Recathri alien.

"Amiah Lily. Give up. I pre-warned you about the danger of touching another human while invisible. You didn't listen. This is your own wrongdoing. There's nothing I can do." the Recathri alien spoke telepathically in English to Amiah.

Amiah felt like someone had slapped her across the face. The Recathri alien blamed her for her invisible son.

Is it insane? she thought.

"How f**king dare you Recathri? I had no idea how powerful your invisibility spell was. Don't turn this around on me! It is your responsibility to not put something so dangerous into my hands knowing that I had no idea of the extreme consequences. You took advantage of my naivety, and you must solve this problem. It's your fault! All your fault!" Amiah shouted telepathically into the Recathri alien's mind.

The oval shaped green shadow changed the direction it was flying in and started to fly towards where Amiah was floating in space.

"Yes come and face me and tell me how to cure my son!" Amiah shouted again telepathically to the Recathri alien.

Unfortunately, to Amiah's dismay, the Recathri alien changed direction just before it reached near enough for Amiah to punch it with her clenched fist. She watched angry and frustrated as the Recathri alien altered its course and flew back into the oval shaped green planet. Amiah wanted to follow it and go into this newly discovered green planet. Instead, she felt unable to steer herself to the left or the right. She found herself reluctantly relying upon wherever the dream like trance was destined to take her.

Amiah looked around to see if she could see planet Earth anywhere. She could not. Just as Amiah had figured, the Recathri alien was from another part of the galaxy that was not yet discovered by humans. Amiah felt a fierce hatred of all three of the oval shaped planets, whose representative had refused to help her cure Brandon.

Didn't they have laws and rules on these planets that would forbid them to cause harm and distress to citizens of other planets? If aliens from these planets had bad intentions, then shouldn't I report everything that I know to the governments of planet Earth? Amiah thought.

Amiah sat in the lotus position floating in space easily. She could feel her heart pounding and her breathing speed up. Then she found herself flying downwards fast through the blackness of space and into purple mist. Amiah could not see through the purple mist. Her body relaxed and her breathing slowed back down to normal. Amiah closed her eyes tight. Hopefully, all of this... her invisible son, the evil alien, Landon in jail and the oval shaped new planets were all just a very bad dream. Her mind began to spin with images that were revolving around too fast for her to recall any of them. Amiah heard voices speaking in unknown languages all around her.

She experienced all of these psychic and paranormal sensations for what seemed to Amiah like a very long time, but actually was only 5 minutes in Earth time. When the images and voices stopped, Amiah opened her eyes again. She was back in the beautiful park sitting in the same lotus position, with the shamanic drum in front of her.

Shaman Mangia was gone.

Amiah took a slow long deep breath in, held it there for 3 seconds and then slowly breathed out. It was real. All of it was real. Otherwise why would she be in this beautiful park sitting in the lotus position with a shamanic drum in front of her waiting for old man Shaman Mangia to return?

Amiah knew she had to turn her frustration at the problems in her life into strength. She had to be strong for herself, Brandon, Landon and the Amiah Riders. All of them needed her guidance, leadership, strength and power to live their lives to their highest potential. Amiah would not let any of them down. She remote viewed the Amiah Mansion while waiting for the shaman to return. Everything appeared fine. She viewed Brandon holding a half-eaten biscuit in one hand and a toy robotcycle in the other. Amiah could see Brandon's grandparents on Landon's side of the family, around her son. Brandon's grandparents were watching Brandon and his cousins in the main virtual living room while talking with each other. They were all ok.

Amiah remote viewed the Amiah Riders who were still back at the Chi-Marcel mansion. The Amiah Riders were out riding with the Chi-Marcels, at one of the beach locations that the Onai twins owned. Amiah watched with admiration at the ways in which her Amiah Riders rode their robotcycles with expertise and talent. She observed the way the Chi-Marcels handled their bikes.

Amiah raised both her eyebrows. She was impressed. The Chi-Marcels seemed just as adept and talented as the Amiah Riders were on their robotcycles. Amiah continued to watch with curiosity and interest. The two paranormal and psychic robotcycle club members performed many intricate and daring stunts while riding along the beach. Next, she viewed two of the Amiah Riders on their robotcycles, jump over a rocky area from opposite sides. While in the air, they stood up on their bikes and somersaulted over to exchange places onto each other's robotcycle. Both women landed professionally on the other side of the rocky area on different robotcycles.

Amiah grinned widely with satisfaction.

Maybe I should add to my club's motto the words 'Unrivalled & unbeaten.' Amiah mused.

"Amiah Lily." a voice said in front of Amiah.

It was the voice of Shaman Mangia.

"Shaman Mangia. I am here waiting for you." Amiah responded telepathically to the shaman who she could not yet see.

"Your ancestors informed me that you prefer to be called Amiah. I am still talking with them. Very interesting family line you have. Very interesting... I'll be five more minutes." Shaman Mangia said.

"Ok." Amiah replied from her mind to the mind of the shaman.

It made sense to Amiah that her ancestors were enthralling the old man shaman. She was a living product of her ancestors brilliance. In effect, her lively, wild, confident, exciting and gifted personality came originally from her ancestors DNA.

Soon, Shaman Mangia returned again to sit in front of the shamanic drum and Amiah Lily. The rhythmic booming of the shamanic drum (including the drums in the circle around them) immediately stopped playing beats. It fell silent, except for the rustle of leaves and branches from the trees. There were no birds singing in the shaman's picturesque park.

"I'm here, Amiah." Shaman Mangia said. "If you may allow me access to parts of you mind, I will transfer in English all the information that you read from the Recathri's mind. I will also transfer new information I have obtained from speaking with the spirits about the cure for Brandon's invisibility."

Amiah felt instantly appreciative and happy.

"Access permitted." Amiah replied smiling.

"Ok. I'm sending them over now." Shaman Mangia said.

"Good. Thank you so much Shaman Mangia. I truly appreciate all you have done to help Brandon. Thank you." Amiah replied.

"No problem, Amiah. Did you receive it?" asked Shaman Mangia.

"Yes thank you. Just a moment ago." said Amiah.

"Good. We have to go back now. Are you ready?" Shaman Mangia said.

"Yes." Amiah replied.

A mixture of purple and white mist descended upon both of them, enveloping them within it so that they could no longer see each other. This time there was a distinct sweet aroma of roses within the mist. Then slowly the white and purple mist cleared away. Amiah and Shaman Mangia were now back in the shaman's robot filled office on separate transparent hover mats. Amiah stepped down off her clear hover mat quickly. She had received the info she wanted and it was time to get back to Brandon.

"Jan!" Amiah shouted telepathically to Jan. "I've got it. Let's make excuses and go back to Amiah Mansion. I will tell the rest of the Amiah Riders to get ready. We ride back home in an hour and a half."

Upon hearing Amiah's voice inside her mind, Jan ran over to Amiah with a fake pained expression on her face.

"Amiah, I am so sorry to cut your meeting short but there's

been a sighting of the Recathri alien at Amiah Mansion. We have to leave immediately!" Jan exclaimed.

Amiah checked all her blocking skills were back up. She had put them back on straight away after receiving the info from Shaman Mangia. Amiah double checked to be sure. She could not sense any energy, psychic, paranormal or alien looking into any parts of her mind. Amiah relaxed a bit more.

"Thank you for letting me know Jan. I will tell the shaman and the Onai twins what's happened." Amiah said.

At that precise moment, the Onai twins and Shaman Mangia walked over to where the two women were standing. Shaman Mangia had a disappointed look on his face, having overheard what Amiah and Jan had said.

"You're leaving already." Shaman Mangia said glumly.

"We have a sighting of the Recathri alien flying above Amiah Mansion. It could be that the alien is finally going to bring a cure for Amiah's son Brandon." Jan said excitedly.

Shaman Mangia observed Jan quizzically. He could tell that something was not quite right.

"We will visit again another time Shaman Mangia. If you ever require help from myself and the Amiah Riders, we will be happy to assist. Just contact me. I have put my contact info in your mind. Now, I'm sorry but we must go now." Amiah stated assertively.

"I will. See you again soon." Shaman Mangia replied and turned to walk away into a white and red mist which had suddenly appeared in one corner of the room. His long wiry grey beard trailing on the floor behind his glowing body of interchanging colours.

Shaman Mangia stood in front of the white and red mist to wave goodbye before disappearing into the mist.

The Onai twins calmly walked with Amiah and Jan to get out of the shaman's office, to walk along the corridor towards the virtual lift. After exiting the Reiki U Resu Experience centre, the Onai twins spoke to Amiah.

"We have loved having the pleasure of your company and the

Amiah Riders at our Chi-Marcel mansion. You are welcome to come back again at any time. We look forward to working with you again." Marcel said.

"We will continue with you on our joint mission to restore visibility back to Brandon. We won't give up. See you back home." said Chima.

"We have enjoyed meeting you, the Chi-Marcels and Shaman Mangia but now we must get back to Amiah Mansion. We won't be stopping at your lovely mansion. Jan and I will ride directly home and the Amiah Riders are shortly leaving to join us there." Amiah said.

Amiah had already communicated telepathically with the Amiah Riders that they were to return as soon as possible to Amiah Mansion. It was time for them all to go. They had lots of new leads about the Recathri alien which needed to be assessed both paranormally and psychically. There was no time to waste.

Amiah and Jan got on their robotcycles and so did the Onai twins. The four riders rode together for 30 minutes of the journey and then separated to ride along different routes home. This is so that they could eventually reach to their separate locations on their robotcycles to different mansions.

Later on, back at Amiah Mansion, Amiah thanked Jan for coming up with a quick excuse to leave Shaman Mangia's office.

"Jelitoonaa Jan. Quick thinking and realistic excuse." Amiah said appreciatively. She couldn't wait to see Brandon again. She had missed him and wanted to hear his voice around her again.

"Yes it was. They had no choice but to believe what I said anyway." Jan replied.

"I'm going to check on Brandon. Then, I will process all the new information about the Recathri alien and call a meeting of the Amiah Riders. Possibly tomorrow." said Amiah.

"Tomorrow will be better as today they'll be exhausted from spending time with the Chi-Marcels." Jan said.

Amiah looked down and then gradually looked up again.

"Jan." Amiah said.

"Yes Amiah." Jan answered.

"Do you think I'm pushing the Amiah Riders too hard?" Amiah looked at a friend with concern in her eyes.

"Nah, don't be silly. We love it! It's not even like it's work to us!" Jan exclaimed.

"Ok." Amiah said.

Her long-time friend would say that. She was the closest person to her apart from Landon. Amiah made a mental note in her mind to ask the other Amiah Riders in one-to-one sessions about their feelings regarding the workload she had given them.

Every day the Amiah Riders trained in robotcycle, psychic, paranormal and blocking skills. They also corresponded with and researched people who sent requests for rescue missions. In addition, they also undertook complex rescue missions. Sometimes there were conflicts and added work involved with these rescue missions which made them harder to solve successfully. During the past four years, up unto present day, the Amiah Riders also worked daily on finding a cure for Brandon's invisibility. This involved intense research using their psychic and paranormal skills.

Jan, however, seemed to be handling all the extra work fine. Despite the sheer intensity of it all. She was the only Amiah Rider who had pets living with her in her room. Jan had three golden labradors that she called 'my girls' collectively. They lived with her in a separate part of Amiah Mansion but were forbidden to freely roam around the mansion. Some of the Amiah Riders had been born with genetic conditions that made their skin break out in itchy rashes, due to an allergic reaction to dogs. They took daily medication for these conditions, but this only reduced their symptoms. It did not stop them. To lessen their chances of experiencing symptoms, it was only fair that Jan's pet labradors were kept away most of the time.

Amiah wondered if she should buy pets for the rest of the Amiah Riders rooms. This could give them some downtime from work. It didn't have to be dogs. Amiah could buy them fish, cats, spiders, snakes, parrots… whatever they requested. Amiah made another mental note to suggest this idea during her regular one to one sessions with each of her Amiah Riders.

I must take care of them. This is my responsibility as club leader. Amiah thought.

Amiah made her way through Amiah Mansion to her son's playroom where she had sensed he was presently located. She walked through the virtual security doors, which always disappeared as soon as she walked towards it. Melissa Cantim had programmed them that way. Melissa Cantim is the programming expert of the Amiah Riders.

"Mummy!" Brandon squealed from his place on his mini-robotcycle.

"Brandon, come here!" Amiah shouted over at her invisible son.

Brandon quickly rode over to Amiah on his mini-robotcycle, got off his bike and fell into the loving, protective hug of his mother. Brandon could not see his mother's eyes as he held onto her. Just as Amiah could not see her son's eyes as she held onto him. Both mother and son's eyes were filled with tears. Both mother and son blinked away those tears so that each other would not know the sadness they both carried within. The hug ended and Brandon spoke.

"Mummy can you see me?" Brandon asked innocently.

Amiah felt like someone had suddenly yanked at her heartstrings. Her heart began to pound loudly. She didn't know what to say. She knew that this day would come eventually. Someone must have told Brandon that he was invisible while she was away. This is exactly the reason why she had tried for so long to keep Brandon away from the public and distant family or friends. This is why she had protected Brandon, by dressing him up in a virtual body suit whenever he had to go outside in public. It was a last minute decision to allow Landon's parents and Landon's nieces and nephews to look after Brandon. Amiah knew there would be a small element of risk involved.

Amiah's heart gradually reduced it's loud thumping intensity. To Amiah's relief, Brandon had sped off again on his mini-robotcycle and was riding around on it around his playroom.

Landon's parents came over to greet Amiah. Two of Brandon's cousins closest to his age were playing together in another part of Brandon's playroom. Amiah stared at them coldly.

"Who told..." Amiah started to say but then caught herself.

These elderly people were Landon's parents. They were one of the precious links she had left of Landon in the world. More importantly, Amiah wanted Brandon to know his father's side of the family. There is the possibility that Brandon would never know his father for longer than a few hours a week in a controlled environment. This wasn't how she had envisioned the love child she created with Landon growing up. This wasn't in her vision at all.

"Amiah darling, how are you and how was Chi-Marcel mansion?" Landon's mother, Mrs Ross, said to Amiah

"Good you're here! Brandon is a handful just like his Dad at that age." Landon's father, Mr. Ross joined in.

Amiah opened her mouth again to say something, but no words came out.

"You look tired, lovie." Mrs Ross said

Mr Ross could sense something was not quite right so he smiled at both of the women, waved and went over to a corner of the room. In the corner of the playroom, Mr Ross fell backwards onto virtual orange and green bean bags dramatically. Mrs Ross watched him and giggled.

"Don't worry lovie, Brandon won't be like his grandfather." Mrs Ross teased.

"That's not the point. Who..." Amiah started to speak again but was interrupted by Mrs Ross.

"Amiah we would love to stay longer with Brandon and can't thank you enough for inviting us to your gorgeous home to spend time with him...but we have to go back home..." Landon's mother explained hurriedly.

Amiah relaxed a bit at the thought of Landon's family leaving Amiah Mansion. She felt some of her composure returning.

"That's absolutely fine Mrs Ross. I completely understand that everyone has their own lives and things going on. Would you like an Amiah Rider to escort you home while the family get into a hover cab." Amiah inquired calmly.

"We've already called a hover cab and it's waiting for us outside." Mrs Ross said. She looked over at Brandon, held Amiah's hand and squeezed it gently. "One day we will all see little Brandon. God works in mysterious ways. His wonders to perform."

Amiah hid her surprise from showing up in her facial expression.

God? Amiah thought to herself.

Amiah couldn't recall Landon's family ever talking about God or religion before.

Is this something new that their family is trying? Amiah mused.

She believed that there indeed was a higher power but she didn't know who or what it's real name was. The concept of there being a God was as much a mystery to her, as psychic/paranormal powers was to a human that did not possess those skills.

Amiah simply nodded in agreement and waited for Landon's family to leave. Amiah had no plans to invite them back anytime soon.

Next time, Brandon would come with her.

SEXY VISIONS

The next day at the Chi-Marcel mansion, the Chi-Marcels were seated on hover chairs facing a hover stage which hovered high over the floor. They were inside the main virtual meeting room. Upon the hover stage addressing the Chi-Marcels were the Onai twins. Chima Onai and Marcel Onai. Marcel pointed at an area of a map located on the virtual screen behind him.

"So, for us to help Amiah and the Amiah Riders find a cure for Brandon's invisibility, we must start here." Marcel explained.

"That's us!" one of the Chi-Marcels shouted out.

"Yes, it is the Chi-Marcel Mansion." Chima confirmed.

Laughter filled the main virtual meeting room until Marcel spoke again.

"It is within our professional scope to use our psychic and paranormal skills to find out where the Recathri alien is and/or find another way to cure little Brandon." Marcel said.

"You do not need to travel anywhere unless you have a definite lead which requires you to do so." Chima explained.

"You want us to work on the..." Jason (a Chi-Marcel rider) began to ask but then hesitated.

Chima looked thoughtful as if trying to answer the question that Jason hadn't finished speaking.

"Well, we were thinking that we should separate our assistance for Amiah and the Amiah Riders into two." Marcel said.

"Two?" Chima inquired curiously, as if he was hearing this for the first time.

Marcel ignored Chima's question.

"We will keep within our club's parameters and do what we

know." Marcel said. "It's gonna be another Takedown mission men!"

There were some exuberant elated shouts and clapping heard from the audience of Chi-Marcels watching and listening to the Onai twins on the hover stage.

Chima remained quiet.

"The first part is the Takedown mission of the Recathri alien and the second part is a new venture called a Restore mission. The full mission name is Restore Brandon's Visibility mission. RBV." Marcel said. "Whichever part we succeed in first does not matter. Both parts of RBV must be successfully achieved before we close the mission. Any questions?"

The room fell silent as all the Chi-Marcels now realised the difficulty and extent to which their psychic and paranormal skills would be tested. None of them had much experience with Takedown and Distribute with aliens in missions. Although, many takedowns which involved humans, often seemed as if the humans could potentially be undercover aliens. The RBV mission would be one of the biggest challenges yet for the Chi-Marcels and this fact had suddenly hit them.

Chima sensed the uncertainty of the Chi-Marcels and spoke up to reassure them.

"Humans are the cleverest species in the galaxy. Don't see the Recathri as an alien. See the Recathri as just another target to takedown. Amiah Lily will send us all the information she has about the Recathri target and we will do what we do best. Takedown the target and distribute everything from it's planet over to us." Chima said smugly.

There were more elated exuberant shouts of agreement and clapping heard from the Chi-Marcels. Marcel smiled gratefully at his twin brother. Chima winked back at him.

"Takedown the target and distribute everything from it's oval shaped green planet over to us." Marcel repeated in approval.

"You got it." Chima grinned at him. Then, addressing the Chi-Marcels, Chima asked them if they had anymore questions before the robots handed them all their work schedules on virtual papers.

"You say we can work from home, but the Amiah Mansion will have the most energy history of the target. It would also have the little boy's energy and aura there, which would help us with RBV. It would make sense for us to work also from Amiah Mansion." Jason suggested.

"We will consider your request and get back to you on that one." Chima answered.

"The women at Amiah Mansion have too many blocking shields up. I don't think we will be able to read anything more than what we already have access to." Derek said to Jason who was seated next to him.

"Derek can you say that out loud please." Marcel said. He had overheard the conversation between Derek and Jason in his mind and wanted them to share it with everyone else.

Derek's face went red but he had been ordered to say what he said, so he did.

"I said…" Derek stuttered. "I said that the Amiah Riders can block our psychic skills and they will only let us sense what they already know. If they already know and have read the target's energy and/or Brandon's aura or energy… surely that information would have been passed onto us. So, what new ideas will there be for us? None." Derek finished with a shrug.

Some of the Chi-Marcels argued other points that would make it necessary to work from the Amiah Mansion and the Chi-Marcel mansion. This debate went on for another 20 minutes. The Onai twins cleverly answering all the questions that were put to them about the reasons why working from the Chi-Marcel mansion was more suitable. When the debate had quietened down, the robots handed out virtual papers with information about the Recathri target and Brandon. The information had been received from Shaman Mangia to be treated in confidence. Marcel reminded the Chi-Marcels again of this.

"The information that you are receiving is private and confidential from Shaman Mangia. After you touch the virtual paper, all the info of the target and Brandon will be sent into your minds. The gold virtual paper will disappear after this happens. Do not tell Amiah or any of the Amiah Riders this information. We will wait until Amiah sends her version which we expect to be sent over this afternoon." Marcel informed.

"Alright Onai's." Jason shouted out from the back row of hover chairs in the main virtual meeting room.

In the main virtual meeting room, there were also virtual tables with hover chairs for people to sit around and discuss matters. However, for the purpose of this meeting, the Onai twins decided to talk to the Chi-Marcels from the hover stage.

"Ok that's it for today's meeting. See everyone at the garage. Today's robotcycle ride is the Mountain Tarantula route." Chima concluded.

Everyone in the main virtual meeting room got up to leave and go over to the virtual garage of Chi-Marcel mansion. The virtual garage is filled with red robotcycles and some black robotcycles in one corner. There were robot members of staff holding refreshments and walking around ready to serve.

The Onai twins and the Chi-Marcels all got on to their robotcycles and sped off in the direction of the Mountain Tarantula route. This route was only a 30 minute ride away. The Onai twins had deliberately purchased the Chi-Marcel mansion in a location where they had many different exciting robot-made, robotcycle routes nearby.

The Mountain Tarantula route is designed and created by specialised robots who have been programmed to come up with original inventive ideas. Some of these specialised robots (otherwise referred to as Creator Robots) were responsible for creating the virtual beaches that the Onai twins owned and various other robotcycle routes.

Mountain Tarantula route is exactly as the name suggests. It is a route which contains mountains and tarantulas (large, hairy, biting spiders). The presence of the tarantulas adds to the danger, thrill and the advanced level of expertise required for the robotcyclists on this route. No protective clothing was allowed to be worn except virtual helmets.

Any robotcyclist attempting to ride along this mountainous terrain and risky route would require 5 years of robotcyclist experience at a very high level. All the Chi-Marcels and the Amiah Riders had this high level of expertise. Although, Amiah Lily and the Onai twins had exceptionally high expertise.

The Onai twins rode in front of the the Chi-Marcels on their red robotcycles. They expertly rode up the sides of mountains and down the slopes of mountains at high speed. They made sure that they handled their robotcycles perfectly and that they would not fall onto the biting tarantulas that roamed freely around. The robots had designed the Mountain Tarantula route to have hundreds of thousands of tarantulas everywhere on the ground. Another way to show that you had expert robotcycle skills on this route, is that no tarantulas end up getting killed by your robotcycle. A rider could not ride over and kill any tarantula on the Mountain Tarantula route otherwise he/she would be immediately disqualified from attempting this route again for the next 5 years.

Usually, the Mountain Tarantula route remained empty except for the Onai twins, Chi-Marcels, Amiah Lily and the Amiah Riders. Other talented young robotcyclist daredevil riders, were also occasionally found riding on their bikes around the Mountain Tarantula route. Robot members of staff could sometimes be seen chasing after them as they would many times enter the route illegally. Not all of these brave young robotcyclists that wanted to attempt the Mountain Tarantula route were there without consent. The riders who did not have permission were in the minority.

The majority of the other young highly skilled robotcyclists, passed the entry requirements for the route. They were not invited to join the paranormal and psychic robotcycle clubs because no high level of psychic or paranormal skills were sensed in any of them so far...

The Onai twins and Amiah Lily both secretly hoped that one day they would find the rest of their respective club members at the Mountain Tarantula route. They knew that a paranormal/psychically talented robotcyclist who is skilled enough to be able to complete the Mountain Tarantula route... would be yet another great asset to their clubs. Finding someone or others, similar in skills and gifts like the Chi-Marcels and the Amiah Riders would be 'jelitoonaa' (awesome).

The Onai twins and the Chi-Marcels continued the challenging route with as much ease and confidence as a ride in the park. In fact, after the Mountain Tarantula route was successfully completed by all, the Chi-Marcels were bored. The Onai twins sensed their boredom.

"Well done men! Successful as always!" Chima encouraged them telepathically.

"Now decision time!" Marcel said telepathically to the Chi-Marcels. "We re-ride the Mountain Tarantula route or we go back and start work on RBV?"

"Ride towards the direction you want to go in next." Chima said.

All of the Chi-Marcel robotcyclists rode in the direction of the exit of the Mountain Tarantula route. This signalled to the Onai twins that their Chi-Marcels were ready to leave and get back to work on their latest mission. Consequently, the Onai twins rode around in front of the Chi-Marcels on their robotcycles, to lead them through the exit to head back home.

On arrival back home at the Chi-Marcel mansion, the Chi-Marcels separated to get something to eat while the Onai twins remained sitting on their red robotcycles. Both men had heard the soothing ringing tone indicating an incoming vision and they didn't want to move until it appeared. Sometimes their visions were lengthy and if there happened to be a hover or virtual seat around, it was good thinking to sit down to watch. Especially after a very long robotcycle group training session. The Onai twins were hungry and thirsty, but the vision could not wait.

The vision soon appeared like a single small virtual screen in front of Chima Onai and Marcel Onai's eyes. Just because they were both watching a vision at the exact same time, did not mean that the vision appearing in front of them both contained the exact same content.

The Onai twins each watched the vision unravelling before them with curious eyes. Unknown to both of them, on this particular occasion, they were both in fact viewing the same vision. They both saw a man and a woman naked together making love in the distance surrounded by a pinkish, greyish mist and nothing else. They could not see the faces of the couple, only their bodies intertwined in passionate lovemaking. The couple having sex began to slowly move forward to the front of the vision. Then the faces became clearer. It was Amiah Lily and one of them. The vision stopped playing in front of the eyes of the twin brothers.

Marcel burst out laughing.

Chima grinned at his brother.

"Do you see what I see?" Marcel sang to his brother happily as he got up off his robotcycle.

"Ah, but if you saw what I just saw..." Chima smiled back, also getting up off his bike.

"What did you see?" Marcel asked suspiciously.

"Nothing." Chima replied vaguely. "What did you see?"

"Nothing." Marcel said with the same vagueness.

"Ok. I'm famished! You coming to get something to eat bro." Chima asked.

"Yeah." Marcel said.

The identical twin brothers walked outside the virtual garage and through the front gardens to enter the Chi-Marcel mansion. They didn't say a word more to each other as they ate in the dining room. Both men recalling the vision of one of them making passionate love with Amiah Lily. Except... one thing bothered both of them... which of the twin brothers was in the vision naked with Amiah's nude sexy body?

*****

Later that afternoon, at Amiah Mansion, Amiah sent over all the information she had about the Recathri alien to the Onai twins via telepathy. The Onai twins sent a message back simply saying the following words. Received with thanks.

Amiah felt pleased that she had now enlisted the psychic and paranormal talents of the Onai twins and the Chi-Marcels. With their support and assistance in what she had agreed would now be referred to as the RBV mission, Amiah was certain they would succeed. It was just a matter of time before the Recathri alien would have no choice but to give the cure for invisibility to her. As soon as Amiah received the cure, she would heal her son and this would be the happiest day of her life.

Amiah went out to the back of her mansion where there was a majestic luxury swimming pool. She was dressed in a gold and yellow bikini and dipped her toes into her swimming pool to check the temperature of the water. It was cool as she had anticipated. The weather on this day is warm and sunny. Originally, Amiah planned to take Brandon out swimming with her but at the last minute he threw up some food she didn't recognise twice on his playroom floor.

Could it be all the junk food that Landon's parents have been feeding him while I was away? Amiah frowned and quickly dismissed this thought.

It had been a few days since she had viewed Mr Ross giving her child crisps, ice-cream, jelly babies, chocolate and assorted sandwiches all at once, simply because Brandon had asked for them.

Amiah smiled at this memory. Even though no-one could see Brandon, he was already a confident, assertive and clever child. Brandon had asked his grandfather for all of the treats and his grandfather hadn't the heart to refuse him. Maybe Mr Ross felt sorry for his grandson and this is why he gave Brandon what he asked for without saying 'no'. He wouldn't have been the first person looking after Brandon to 'agree' with anything Brandon requested. Even robots had been known to make up stories because Brandon had told them to do so.

There was the time a few months ago where Brandon had broken a virtual ornament in the living room and got the robot to 'take the blame'. Brandon had told the robot to say that it broke the virtual ornament, and the robot did as it was told. This led to the robot being dismantled to check for errors in its programming before being rebuilt again. When Amiah had heard of what happened, she had done a remote viewing of the energy in the living room. Amiah could see everything that had occurred in her virtual living room since it was first constructed. She found the date she was interested in and there it was. Her son giving the robot instructions like an adult with the voice of a little kid. The robot (like most people) listened to Brandon and did what he said without question.

A giggle escaped from Amiah's mouth as she jumped into the deep end of her swimming pool. She began to swim lazily on her back up and down the length of her pool. She felt totally relaxed finally, after her hectic few days at the Chi-Marcels mansion and deciphering the information from old man shaman at home.

Shaman Mangia had translated all the information that Amiah had viewed from the Recathri's mind. Now, Amiah had enough knowledge about the Recathri alien to take to the governments of planet Earth. She knew where the Recathri's home planet could be found in the galaxy. She knew what other species on the new alien planet looked like. She knew what the Recathri's ultimate purpose was on planet Earth. It wasn't a very dramatic purpose, but it was enough to get the alien in trouble for not reporting to Earth's authorities of it's presence.

The Recathri alien was illegally trespassing on Earth. It had broken the law by not informing governments of planet Earth of it's intentions. The purpose of the Recathri alien being on Earth was to study and research everything about it. It was to make contact with one intelligent being on Earth and to study the rest. The Recathri had chosen her, Amiah Lily, to be it's single contact. It was very interesting to find out more about the alien and it's home planet but none of the information mentioned the invisibility cure.

Amiah blinked her eyes and then shut them briefly as the cloud moved away to reveal the sun's brightness. When would be the perfect time for her to give all her information about the new planets and the Recathri alien to the governments of planet Earth? The Onai twins and the Chi-Marcels were now also working on the RBV mission along with herself and the Amiah Riders. How long should she wait before using her best weapon so far against the Recathri alien? Amiah pondered.

Amiah swam backstroke up and down the length of her pool for a further hour while considering all her future options in her mind. She felt blissful. With all the help she had, Amiah was sure that it wouldn't be very long before a cure for Brandon's invisibility would happen. Then, Landon and herself would celebrate and be able to see the love child they had created together face to face.

For what seemed like the millionth time, Amiah again imagined what Brandon would look like in his true visual appearance. Would Brandon's face look more like her or more like his Dad, Landon Ross? Would Brandon have thick afro hair like her, loose curly dark brown hair like his Dad or a gorgeous mix of the two of them? Would Brandon smile like her or smile like Landon? What colour were Brandon's eyes? Did Brandon's nostrils flare when he got angry like his Dad? Did Brandon have thick or thin eyebrows? What were Brandon's feet like? Amiah wondered.

When Amiah finally got to see Brandon fully, she knew she would want to check him all over to make sure he was ok. Not being able to see her son physically made it harder to look after him when he was ill. Nevertheless, Amiah wanted to look on the bright side to help her to remain hopeful. It would be just a matter of time before Brandon would be visible to all. Amiah needed to believe this to be true, with all her heart.

Amiah reached the shallow end of her pool and lifted her body up out of the pool to sit at the side. A robot member of staff passed Amiah a gold-coloured towel. Amiah used the gold towel to dry and wrap her long braided hair, leaving some hair hanging outside. Amiah got up and walked over to lay down on one of her hover pool recliners which were also virtual recliners.

Therefore, the recliners hovered and also glowed with sea blue colours, due to their virtual design. All virtual equipment glowed to a certain extent.

Although, no sooner had Amiah laid down on her virtual hover recliner, then a new vision appeared in front of her eyes. There had been no warning ringing tone this time.

Just like the Onai twins had seen in their vision earlier on while seated on their red robotcycles, Amiah saw the same. First, she could see a couple having sex at a distance and then she saw close up. Amiah saw herself and one of the Onai twins naked caressing each other's body and kissing passionately.

Unbeknownst to Amiah, the same vision the Onai twins had seen finished at that point. The Onai twins vision of the same scene went no further. Amiah's vision however, proceeded on with the sexy and raunchy scene. In detail…

Amiah watched in amazement as she saw her hand grab hold of one of the Onai twins limp dick. She then saw herself massage Mr Onai's dick in-between her breasts slowly while straddling him. Amiah could hear Mr Onai moaning in ecstasy and herself saying the words "Ride me again honey."

Amiah felt a rush of warmth fill her cheeks as she curiously watched the sex scene play out in front of her.

Which one of the Onai twins am I straddling like that? Chima or Marcel? Amiah thought. She looked at the size of the dick on the man she was still sitting on and caressing in the vision.

Hmmm, not as big as Landon's. Amiah smiled to herself.

This scene was no way like the way she and Landon would make love. There wasn't enough wild lusty passion. Yes, she could see they were having sex but she knew enough about sex to see that it wasn't the most thrilling sex. Yes, there was passion but not to the level that Landon could make her reach to.

Landon.

Amiah suddenly felt a pang of guilt for enjoying watching the sex scene in the vision. She closed her eyes so she could no longer see the vision and tried to focus on images of Landon in her mind instead.

Landon.

Amiah was surprised to discover that although she could not see the vision with her physical eyes anymore, she was still watching it in her minds eye. In her minds eye, the vision of her having sex with one of the Onai twins played out even more clearly, than if she had her eyes open.

"Ohhhh! Yes baby give it to me." Mr Onai said to Amiah in the vision.

"You want this. Take it." Amiah murmured into the black curly hair of Mr Onai as she lay on top of him gyrating slowly.

In the vision, Mr Onai laughed a deep dirty laugh.

Amiah stood up and opened her eyes wide. Closing her eyes wasn't preventing the vision from being shown to her. Her emotions moved from curiosity to anger.

Is this a ploy by the Onai twins to get me to sleep with them? Have they sent this vision to me to turn me on? Is it all a lie that they are just interested in helping me find the Recathri alien and restoring Brandon's visibility? Amiah's mind raced with these thoughts.

Amiah sat back down on her sea blue hover virtual recliner and got herself into a comfortable position with her legs open wide. Two could play at this game. Amiah focused on the energy of the Amiah in the vision in front of her and got into her aura. Once inside the aura of the Amiah in the vision, Amiah began to control her actions. She had done this only a handful of times before with visions that she didn't like the look of. She would enter the vision and alter it.

This time it worked. Amiah manipulated the Amiah in the vision to lay on her back with her legs wide open and both her arms above her head. This was how Amiah herself was laying on the sea blue hover virtual recliner. She listened to the voices speak in the vision that continued to play out in front of her.

"Come. Take me again. I want you so bad." Amiah's voice in the vision said.

"I know baby." Mr Onai replied sexily.

As Mr Onai moved to lay on top of Amiah in the vision again, Amiah moaned and gyrated her body in anticipation of his dick entering her. Mr Onai positioned his dick near her lovebox and whispered in her ear.

"I'm going to f*** you so... har... hard...I'm going to f***... Amiah baby open up for me." Mr Onai frowned.

"I'm trying honey. I'm trying. Oh, you've gone soft." Amiah heard herself say these words in the vision.

Amiah grinned inwardly. She had deliberately closed off the entrance to her lovebox so that nothing could penetrate it. Similar to people who have vaginismus but utilised differently by Amiah. Amiah knew how to shut her lovebox off at will, at her command, whereas people who suffered with the medical condition called vaginismus have an involuntary reflex.

Amiah gleefully watched Mr Onai try a few more times in the vision to have dick in lovebox intercourse with her, but it did not happen. This was hilarious to Amiah and she held back her laughter while watching herself in the vision hold Mr Onai to comfort him.

"I don't know why this has happened. We can try again later." Amiah heard herself say in the vision.

Amiah (watching the vision) felt a bubble of hysterical laughter fill her belly which she tried to keep down. She was worried that it would interfere with her interception of the aura of Amiah in the vision. The consequences of her laughing out loud were unknown to her and she was going too good now for her to mess this up.

After 10 minutes of watching the Amiah in the vision and Mr Onai cuddling and reassuring each other with tender words, Amiah got ready to do the same 'closing up' thing again. Again, Amiah lay on her back with her legs wide open and made sure she was inside the aura of the Amiah in the vision. Then, as Mr Onai laid on top of her and tried to penetrate her again, she deliberately 'closed up' her lovebox muscles so that she was unable to feel Mr Onai's dick inside of her.

Amiah gulped back her laughter. This was all too much

hilarity for her to keep inside and she sat up quickly and finally let the deep frivolous laughter escape from her mouth.

In the vision playing out in front of Amiah's eyes, both Mr Onai and the Amiah in the vision stopped what they were doing and stared in her direction. Amiah put one hand over her mouth to try and silence her laughing. Then, the vision abruptly stopped playing in front of her eyes.

Free to laugh as loud as she wished, Amiah laughed hysterically. Tears of exuberant mirth formed in her eyes. Amiah blinked away the tears of mirth and held her tummy as she bent left and right in extreme hilarity. It took some time for Amiah's laughing to subside.

When she had finished with her hysterics, Amiah remembered the looks on the faces of Mr Onai and herself in the vision. They both displayed a mixture of shock and relief. The relief was probably that if they did hear Amiah's laugh from a distance, both probably welcomed the interruption. Hearing Amiah laugh distracted the couple in the vision from their awkward sex disaster moment.

Amiah sat up and wiped the tears from her face using her left hand. The Onai twins had no clue who they were dealing with. Whether or not they had sent this vision to her to get her to sleep with them, she didn't know. She had managed to intervene in the vision in the funniest way to her. She felt like calling Landon and telling him about what she had done, but then remembered that Landon wouldn't see it as funny as she did.

Landon would hate the Onai twins, she was sure he would, if he knew. Amiah decided to keep her vision to herself. Not even her Amiah Riders would know what had just happened. Jan would see the funny side like her, but even Jan did not need to know this. Other thoughts that Amiah had were concerning the location of the couple making love.

Where was I and Mr Onai in that vision? Is it a future event vision, a warning vision, a mind transfer vision or another type of vision altogether? Amiah thought.

The location of the couple in the vision was blurry. It didn't appear as if the couple were making love in mid-air. It was a kind of blurred scenery backdrop that Amiah could not gain any information from. The backdrop scenery consisted of a blur of colours that hid the surrounding environment of the couple entirely.

Amiah got up from her sea blue hover virtual recliner to walk around her pool to enter back inside her mansion. She walked past some of the Amiah Riders on the way to her room to take a shower.

"Amiah, it's good you're here, the new leads on the Recathri alien are not…" one of the Amiah Riders began to explain to Amiah.

"They are not consistent appearances at Duneway and the Chi-Marcels reported that they are consistent appearances. Thank you. I know. Be on your guard around the Chi-Marcels. Work closely with them. Trust your intuition and let me know if you sense any wrong-doing. Anything at all." Amiah said finishing off part of what the Amiah Rider was going to say, before she had a chance to say it.

The tall, blonde haired Amiah Rider blushed and nodded at Amiah.

Amiah walked past a few other Amiah Riders who each tried to tell her new updates on the Recathri alien but she answered all of them before they finished their sentences. This was another benefit of her psychic abilities; she often knew what people would say prior to them speaking.

It wasn't always easy to read people though. The Onai twins were proving a challenge. There was nothing Amiah Lily loved more than the exciting risk of a challenge. Although, she wished with all her heart that one of her challenges did not have to involve her innocent loveable son Brandon.

TRUST NO ONE

The soft moans, gasping and breathless raspy voices coming from behind the virtual grey desk in one of the many study rooms at Amiah mansion, were irritating Saraina. Here she was seriously trying to practice her remote viewing and blocking skills and people around her were messing about. It was either Petra or Louise behind the sofa with one of the Chi-Marcel riders called Garcen. Garcen had arrived at Amiah mansion only a few hours ago to 'help' with the search for the Recathri alien. Both Petra and Louse had been seductively flirtatious with him, as soon as he took one step into the decorative virtual study room.

Saraina knew the immediate flirting was not a good sign. She sighed loudly to herself. There was a time and place for everything, and this wasn't the time. Petra and Louse were supposed to be helping her with her training. How could she impress Amiah Lily if she wasn't getting the practical training she required? Saraina wondered sadly.

During a recent group meeting, Amiah had tested everyone's blocking skills and to Saraina's surprise her skills had gone down. To her even greater surprise, it was now Jan, Petra and Louise who could block other psychics and paranormal people for longer periods of time. Feeling embarrassed, Saraina had signed up for further intense blocking and remote viewing training with Amiah. Amiah had kindly declined, partly due to her increased workload with the RBV (Restore Brandon's Visibility) mission and partly for other reasons. Amiah worked closely with the Onai twins and spent all her free time with her son Brandon. One to one training sessions with Amiah therefore had overall ceased to be as frequent as before.

Now, sitting in the exquisitely decorated virtual study room, with creative and inspirational virtual art work all around her L shaped virtual white corner desk, Saraina rolled her eyes. Was this the way women in the Amiah Riders behaved as soon as there were men around? she pondered.

Garcen was not even good looking in her opinion. Since she had first met the Chi-Marcel riders she had started to question whether or not she was even attracted to men at all. Of course, she had blended in with everyone as she thought this was the right thing to do to represent Amiah Lily as part of the Amiah Riders. Yet, she had this inner sense that she had gone into automatic acting mode. She pretended to flirt when it suited her, but her heart wasn't in it. She was not even turned on.

Saraina wondered if she should go over to where she believed her 'badass mentors' were with Garcen and...

Saraina paused mid-thought. And what? Louise and Petra had told her to practice blocking them while they talked with Garcen. She would only find out if she had been successful if Louise and Petra could not read her mind during the time she was blocking. So, Saraina would get a high score if Louise and Petra failed to read her mind. Effectively placing Saraina back into the top leagues of blockers in the Amiah Riders. Remembering this, Saraina held herself back and continued to block. Although, it wasn't as easy to block out the whispers, excited squeals and slippery sliding noises coming from behind the virtual grey desk.

It felt curiously easy on this occasion to block Louise and Petra. Saraina felt no pain whatsoever.

Could this be because the two women are so consumed with lust for Garcen that they aren't even trying to intercept my thoughts? How unprofessional! Saraina thought briefly to herself.

Then, she changed her thinking to how this would benefit her blocking skills reputation with Amiah Lily. Maybe, Amiah would place her in the top league of blockers along with Jan, Louise and Petra. She would be given higher responsibilities and more power within the Amiah Riders. These thoughts stopped Saraina from interrupting the untimely lovemaking she could annoyingly overhear.

She crossed her feet and placed them up on the virtual white L shaped corner desk and leaned back a little in her hover chair. She may as well just keep blocking and relax until her 'naughty' mentors had finished doing whatever they were doing. Saraina closed her eyes and focused a separate part of her mind on something happy. Instant images came into this part of her mind. They were images of her naked with another woman rubbing their bodies together in ecstasy. Saraina began to feel hot and excited. All the passionate sex noises she could hear in the background combined with the vivid images in her mind's eye. She happily watched herself making love with an unknown gorgeous large-busted woman, who had the most dreamy eyes and lips.

Saraina felt a rhythmic beating between her legs and blinked her eyes open quickly. She wasn't about to join the 'badass mentors' by playing with herself during a training session. She quickly glanced over in the direction of the virtual grey desk where Petra, Louise and Garcen were hidden from view. Look how they had brought her down to their level of unprofessionalism. Even if they were not dedicated and proud to be Amiah Riders, she was. She sat up straight on her hover chair and tried to block out the noises around her by focusing on her ears closing tightly.

This idea did not work. Saraina closed her eyes again to go back into the happy place she was at before, but her mood had dulled. Louise and Petra were useless. They were not role models for her or anyone else in the Amiah Riders regardless of their high talents and abilities. Saraina considered telling Amiah Lily of how her training session was rudely disrupted but again hesitated. Amiah had enough serious problems to deal with right now and the actions of her dick-obsessed mentors would only exasperate Amiah's stress levels.

Saraina remembered seeing Amiah drinking from a bottle of Recathri very strong rum, one evening when she had walked past the conference room unnoticed. Well, at least Saraina thought she was unnoticed. She never could tell with Amiah. If Amiah had sensed she was watching from a distance, then she hadn't let on. Amiah had been pouring virtual glass after virtual glass of very strong rum and drinking each one. After watching Amiah throw the empty virtual bottle of Recathri rum on the floor and hearing it smash, Saraina had gotten scared and ran to her bedroom. The energy around Amiah was too powerful on this night and fear had built up in Saraina until she couldn't watch anymore. The next day, neither women said anything about the night before. To this day, Saraina hadn't a clue whether Amiah had known she was watching her or not.

Saraina concluded that Amiah should not be bothered by the silly actions of a few. She would handle the time wasters herself. Exactly how Saraina would do this, she did not yet know.

Finally, Louise, Petra and Garcen got up one by one from behind the grey virtual desk. Each person was fully dressed and were obviously trying to act like nothing had happened. Saraina grimaced to herself.

Do they think I'm completely and utterly stupid? she thought.

She quickly changed her expression of disgust before the threesome turned to look over at her. Now, Saraina's face displayed a blank curiosity. She spoke before any awkwardness could ensue.

"How did I do?" Saraina asked as the threesome sheepishly walked over to her.

"How did you do with wha…" Louise retorted.

Petra nudged her with her elbow.

"You did jelitoonaa! Well done. We could not read anything in your mind at all." Petra said.

"Yes! Yes! It was like a blank canvas." Louise giggled. "Nothing was there."

Saraina held back from responding with a hundred different sarcastic responses, that had suddenly entered her mind.

"Jelitoonaa! I'm so happy! Can you make sure Amiah Lily knows that I passed today's blocking training session with flying colours too, please? Thank you!" Saraina replied.

"Of course!" Garcen answered winking at her.

"She means for us to inform Amiah not you, you dumbf**k." Louise said to Garcen playfully.

"Yeah, you dumbf**k." Petra joined in with Louise.

Garcen just stood there grinning idiotically.

Saraina had her smile fixed on her face, only because she knew the report from Louise and Petra would prove to Amiah that her blocking skills were improving.

"And you know what? I didn't have any headaches at all." Saraina said proudly.

"We'll send a report to Amiah Lily about your outstanding performance during the blocking training session. What else do you have planned for today?" Petra said.

Saraina raised her eyebrows at Petra's question to her. She again resisted the urge to say what was really on her mind about the troublesome three standing in front of her. She wanted to tell them all that they had made it crystal clear that she was not their main interest. She also wanted to tell them all to take long cold showers because their sex stench was decidedly repulsive. Instead, Saraina stood up to leave the study room, waved her hand to signal 'bye' and spoke clearly and firmly.

"Got an appointment with my robotcycle after lunch. Thank you for the training session. Please remember to inform Amiah Lily as soon as possible." Saraina said confidently without smiling.

"Yes, we will!" Petra and Louise said in unison happily.

After Saraina exited the virtual study room, she breathed a sigh of relief. She had never been in such an unprofessional environment in all her time at the Amiah Riders. The Chi-Marcels were lowering the standards and professionalism of some of her colleagues. She would not let this happen to her. For a start, she didn't even feel attracted to any one of the men in the Chi-Marcels. They seemed mostly cocksure and aggressively overconfident of their talents and abilities, in Saraina's opinion.

Saraina recalled being out on a robotcycle ride with the rest of the Amiah Riders and the Chi-Marcels. The Chi-Marcels frequently cut in front of the Amiah Riders and performed stunts while doing so. The other Amiah Riders had laughed about this later on. Saraina just felt like the men were showing off, as their riding ability was no better or more impressive than any of the Amiah Riders. Saraina could blend in and pretend she enjoyed the company of the Chi-Marcels, but her intuitive sense told her there was something disingenuous about them that she disliked.

Saraina walked over to the other side of Amiah Mansion and ate some fruit and biscuits in the dining room. There were a few other riders in there with some men from the Chi-Marcels eating, drinking and talking. She waved over at them and they waved back at her. Saraina did not go over to join them but ate by herself quietly. She left the virtual dining room 1 hour later to go for a ride on her robotcycle.

As Saraina entered the virtual garage to get on her robotcycle parked inside, she felt a few kicks in her tummy area. It was a weird sensation that Saraina had never felt before. It wasn't painful. It was like something had instantly kicked her tummy three times from the inside. Saraina thought that it was probably a spasm which had a medical explanation. She definitely did not have time to research what it could be at the moment. All Saraina desired to do right now, was to forget about this morning by riding far and wide away from Amiah Mansion.

Saraina figured that if she could stay out riding for a long period of time, the Chi-Marcels may have left before she got back for dinner. So, she wouldn't have the chance of accidently bumping into Garcen and remembering all the dirty sounds he had made behind the desk with Petra and Louise.

All the Amiah Riders had a variety of robotcycles to choose from in different colours and of different advanced speeds and other functions. Today, Saraina chose a shining yellow robotcycle with one of the highest speeds. She rode out of the virtual garage at the highest speed, unsure of which route to take or where her destination should be set to. Her main promise to herself was to keep riding forward on her gleaming yellow robotcycle, until Amiah Mansion was left far, far behind her...

*****

"Brandon!" Amiah called out to her invisible son.

"Mummy!" Brandon called back and ran over to hug Amiah's legs.

"Brandon, meet my two new friends. This is Chima Onai and this is Marcel Onai." Amiah explained to her son.

"Chiiimaa. Marceeeelll." Brandon repeated.

"Jelitoonaa Brandon! You got their names right!" Amiah replied.

Inside the large virtual playroom, the Onai twins glanced at each other questioningly. They remained silent as Brandon walked in front of them and behind them, while feeling the material of the jeans the men wore. Chima was the first to break the silence as he crouched down to speak to Brandon at eye level. Even though of course, he could not see Brandon's eyes.

"Hey Brandon, I'm Chima Onai and this is Marcel Onai, my twin brother." Chima indicated with his hand and pointed at Marcel who remained standing.

As if this was his cue to join in, Marcel also crouched down to speak to Brandon at his eye level.

"Brandon, I'm Marcel Onai. This is my identical brother Chima. We run a paranormal robotcycle group similar to your mum's Amiah Riders. Except our group is named after my brother and I. It's called the Chi-Marcels. Do you like robotcycles?" Marcel asked Brandon.

"Robotcycle, robotcycle! Mummy loves robotcycles!" Brandon jumped up and down excitedly.

Chima, Marcel and Amiah all grinned widely. Brandon ran off from them and got onto his mini-robotcycle and sped back over to them again.

"I'm the best rider just like mummy. You can't catch me!" Brandon shouted at the three adults in front of him.

Brandon turned his mini-robotcycle around and sped off in the direction of his other toys. He deftly manoeuvred around the combination of virtual and hover toys that were on the floor and did a few jumps over other smaller objects. Amiah, Chima and Marcel watched Brandon with huge smiles on their faces. It was clear that Brandon was already talented at riding mini-robotcycles and would make a brilliant robotcyclist in the future. Amiah turned to talk to the Onai twins with a look of pure pride and admiration for her invisible son, still visible on her face.

"As you can see, invisibility cannot stop inherited talent and skill from developing at an early age. We are very proud of him already." Amiah said.

"And you have every reason to be Amiah." Marcel replied.

The three of them watched Brandon ride around his virtual playroom for another 30 minutes in silence. Although Amiah watched her invisible son pridefully, the Onai twins both noticed the sadness in her eyes when they looked over at her.

"We will do everything we can to ensure that RBV is a success and find the Recathri alien." Marcel suddenly said, interrupting the silence.

Chima and Amiah both stared at Marcel. It was like as if Chima had stopped both of them in their trail of thought while observing Brandon. Amiah sighed loudly as she snapped out of her reverie. Chima blinked his eyes twice and frowned, as if he also had again 'woken back up' to the seriousness of the task set out in front of them too.

"RBV must succeed. The Recathri alien will give me the cure. I can see it happening in the future. I just don't know how or when." Amiah said.

"I see it happening in the future too." Marcel agreed.

"Ok." Amiah said assertively getting back to business. "Now, you've met my son, you can see that he's invisible and you can imagine how this has hurt and upset my... my ex-boyfriend

Landon and I."

"Ex?" Chima asked

Amiah felt her cheeks grow warm instantly, but she quickly composed herself. Landon had reminded her that he wanted her to refer to him as her ex. Landon didn't believe he would ever be released from Duneway top security virtual prison. He didn't want Amiah to stop her life because of him. But, why did she feel like this was easier for her to say now than at other times? she wondered.

"Erm... that's what I said, my ex-boyfriend Landon. Landon is Brandon's father. He is currently serving life at Duneway high security virtual prison." Amiah explained. Her cheeks returning back to their original brown colour.

"I remember now." Chima said.

"You can speak to him on a virtual video call if you want to introduce who you are to him." Amiah suggested eagerly. "It's safe. I know how to block everyone listening to our conversation so that they will not hear the true words being said. Anyone listening will overhear a fake conversation that I send to their minds."

Amiah figured that maybe she would feel less guilty about her eagerness to describe Landon as her ex, if she knew that Landon liked and approved of the Onai twins. She called a robot member of staff over to her by nodding at one that was standing nearby in the corner of the room. The 7-foot-tall robot designed in a human female form, walked over quickly to where the three were standing.

The female robot stood in front of the Onai twins, in between them both.

"Call Landon Ross at Duneway virtual high security prison." Amiah instructed the female robot.

"Calling Duneway virtual high security prison." answered the female robot.

Instantly a virtual screen appeared on the torso of the female robot. The virtual screen displayed the inside of a small room which had a single clear virtual table, and a single clear virtual chair. There were robot prison staff in all 4 corners of the small room and there was a robot which was not visible who was helping conduct the virtual call. This unseen robot would have the images of Amiah and the Onai twins on it's torso. The female robot in front of the Onai twins, displayed Landon Ross wearing a grey jogging bottom and grey sweatshirt.

"Who?" Landon said with a curious look on his face.

Amiah moved closer to the female robot so she could also be in the virtual video call.

"Landon, it's me Amiah. How are you doing? Thanks for remembering to be ready for this virtual video call. I thought you might be late or forget or something." Amiah said. She quickly observed Landon's appearance and noticed the dark circles around both his eyes.

"I'm Marcel and this is my brother Chima. We are the Onai twins of the Chi-Marcels. We are going to help Amiah with the new project she is working on. We can guarantee that we will succeed." Chima explained.

"Amiah told me about both of you. I didn't expect you to look like…" Landon narrowed his eyebrows.

"They're identical." Amiah filled in before Landon could finish speaking.

Landon ignored Amiah and stared at Marcel first for a while before shifting his gaze to stare at Chima.

Amiah felt her cheeks grow warm again. She knew what Landon was about to say before she intervened. Landon was about to say that he didn't expect the Onai twins to look so strong, muscular and physically attractive. When Amiah had described the Onai twins to Landon, she had mentioned that they were tall and identical but she had deliberately left out how good looking both of the men were. The appearance of the twin men were like something that you would expect to see in a supermodel male fashion show. Amiah also knew the very next thing that Landon was thinking. She knew that Landon was now wondering how long it would take for the Onai twins to try to get close to Amiah… romantically…

Suddenly, the idea to introduce the Onai twins to Landon seemed like the worst idea in the world. Then, Marcel spoke up.

"We saw your robotcycle rides from the Gruten Rivers route and you have our highest respect and admiration Landon." Marcel said with awe evident in his voice.

Landon's eyebrows lifted and then his face relaxed a little.

"The way you did that triple back flip! I will never forget it. Wow!" Chima exclaimed moving his hand to further explain his enthusiasm and point of view.

"And the one where you rode your bike at high speed off the edge of a cliff, performed a double somersault and used a virtual parachute to get back down again…just wow, like jelitoonaa!" Marcel added.

Landon laughed.

"You had to be there. All the factors were against me that night… the wind, the heat…I didn't sleep for a week before with all the practicing day in and day out. You understand me?" Landon said.

"I totally get it. My brother and I have done the same but not that triple back flip. That was out of this world." Marcel continued.

Amiah knew that Marcel was lying. Just a few hours earlier that day, when she had shown recordings of Landon performing stunts on his robotcycle, the Onai twins had asserted that they easily have done all of them many times before. Yet, if the Onai twins were trying to get on the good side of Landon, it seemed to be working. Landon relaxed more into the conversation and began to talk enthusiastically about the many thrilling adventures he had been on with his robotcycle.

Amiah listened to the men talk about their love of riding robotcycles but did not join in. She felt relieved that Landon and the Onai twins seemed to be getting along with each other. Chima and Marcel were helping her in the RBV mission (Restore Brandon's Visibility) and they should know who Brandon's father is. Also, shouldn't Landon know who these men were who she would be working so frequently with? Amiah pondered to herself. Still, Amiah felt a weird sense that something was wrong with this first introduction.

After 30 minutes of the three men talking animatedly about riding robotcycles, Landon spoke to Amiah directly.

"Amiah? You've been quiet. Is everything ok?" Landon asked as if suddenly remembering that Amiah was watching the virtual video call.

"Landon. You and I know that I've done everything you're talking about with the Onai twins. I'm not hearing anything new." Amiah joked back at him.

Landon and the Onai twins laughed.

Amiah smiled at Landon.

"Seriously, she's right." Landon said after he had finished laughing. "There is not a single stunt or route in this country that Amiah hasn't excelled at. She's the best."

Amiah smiled and could see the Onai twins look of admiration and respect as they looked in her direction. Landon spoke the truth but were the Onai twins being fully honest? Amiah wondered.

Perhaps, if Landon would get serious and ask them more personal questions, this could change the mood of the conversation. Luckily for her, Landon said that he had something to do and wouldn't be able to stay on the virtual video call for much longer. Before Amiah could even hint at some of the work they had already completed, to help their invisible son Brandon, Landon had ended the virtual call.

"He went quick!" Marcel exclaimed.

"He's in prison Marcel." Chima said

"Oh yeah." Marcel said.

"They have set time limits for each activity." Amiah explained. "I think they only have a 40-minute time slot for virtual video calls on a Friday."

"Mummy! I heard Daddy!" Brandon shouted out from a short distance away.

Amiah gasped in surprise at herself. She had totally forgotten to give Brandon a few minutes to see his dad on this recent virtual video call. Brandon was the reason that the Onai twins were present today at Amiah Mansion. It was all about finding ways to help restore Brandon's vision. So, why didn't she prioritise Brandon speaking to his dad, on the virtual video call that had just ended? she pondered. Quickly regaining her composure, Amiah shouted back at Brandon.

"What did you hear son?" Amiah shouted over at Brandon.

"I heard Daddy say he loves me." Brandon shouted back and then sped off in the opposite direction on his mini-robotcycle.

Amiah couldn't stop the tears from welling up in her eyes. She turned her face away from the Onai twins so they couldn't see the strong emotional reaction that her invisible son's words had triggered in her.

It was too late.

Marcel had noticed the tears that had filled Amiah's eyes and placed his arm around her shoulder softly.

"We'll find the Recathri alien. I promise you." Marcel said soothingly.

Amiah burst out into uncontrollable tears which fell quietly below her eyes over her smooth brown face. Swiftly, Marcel turned Amiah around and held her sobbing face to his firm, muscular chest in a tender hug. Amiah cried and cried. She cried for all the years she had never been able to see her beloved invisible son. She cried in confusion over Landon insisting she was his ex. She cried over the guilt that she had conceived a child, that would never grow up with his real father. She cried over everything in her once 'jelitoonaa world' that now had been cruelly and unfairly broken apart.

Chima looked on and did nothing.

When Marcel released Amiah from his friendly, comforting hug, Amiah stepped back from him. She lifted her chin slightly higher and faced him squarely in both eyes.

"Right, let's get back to work." Amiah announced confidently.

Her tears and sadness had gone. They were immediately replaced with increased relentless determination, strength and courage. Brandon's visibility would be restored one day. Amiah believed this with her whole heart and soul.

*****

Saraina had not felt so exhausted from a long robotcycle ride in years. As she stumbled through the corridors of Amiah Mansion to get back to her bedroom late in the evening, she had an idea why. She hadn't eaten anything since that morning. No-one had noticed her dizzily walking through the long corridor towards her bedroom. There were no other Amiah Riders around. Only robot members of staff patrolled up and down the mostly empty corridors leading up to her bedroom.

She had felt tired but ok enough to walk, when she first got off her robotcycle. She had managed to say a few words of greeting to other riders in the virtual garage. She passed by a few Amiah Riders in the foyer of the mansion too. It was only when she reached the corridors that the exhaustion had affected her walking. She caught herself from falling down for the third time before finally she entered into her bedroom. Grabbing two bananas from her virtual orange bedside table, she threw herself down onto her virtual double bed.

Hungrily, Saraina ate the two bananas. She called over a robot staff member in her room and ordered it to go and get her dinner from the virtual dining room. She ordered: Grilled Salmon with a soy sauce marinade, garlic flatbread, cucumber yoghurt, coconut rice and orange juice. The robot took Saraina's instructions and left her bedroom.

As soon as the robot left her room, Saraina felt two sharp kicks in her tummy area again. She thought she must still be hungry, so she looked in her fridge for some yoghurts she could eat until dinner. Then, just as she held her tummy while sitting down, she looked up to see a man standing in front of her bed.

Saraina knew it wasn't a vision or an apparition, it was a real human being in her room.

"Hello Saraina." Garcen grinned widely at her with his head tilted.

Every hair on her body wanted to scream at Garcen.

"Get out of my room Garcen!" Saraina yelled. "I'm going to tell Amiah!"

Saraina telepathically tried to communicate with Amiah. It hadn't always worked when she tried this before and right now it felt there was something very strong blocking her. Saraina looked at Garcen in horror.

"You're blocking me calling Amiah, you bastard!" Saraina shouted at him. "Amiah! Amiah!"

"Relax. Amiah's gone out with the Onai's for a night ride. Didn't you get the memo?" Garcen said menacingly. He had straightened his lopsided staring at her and was now holding his head coldly straight. His eyes intensely peering all over her body.

"You men make me sick!" Saraina yelled again. She quickly tried to communicate telepathically with any other Amiah Rider to desperately get help from this nasty man who had broke into her room.

None of the Amiah Riders answered her telepathic calls to them. There seemed to be a very strong block preventing her messages getting through.

Suddenly it hit Saraina like a bucket of ice-cold water in the face. This evil man, Garcen, if that was even his real name, was blocking every telepathic communication from her. Saraina's mind raced with other ideas on how she could escape from what was plainly obvious could happen next. Garcen was going to try and sexually touch her.

Just like as if she had predicted the future, Garcen sat his sweaty, smelly, shirtless body down on her double bed with messy orange bedsheets. Saraina felt frozen to the spot. Garcen acted like what he was doing was completely normal. He knelt in front of her and began to unzip his trousers. Saraina felt like she was going to be sick and she did. She vomited up the bile of the two yellow bananas she had just eaten. When she had finished throwing up, Garcen bent his face down and licked the vomit. It was at this point, Saraina's horror turned into anger. This man was evil and as an Amiah Rider she hated all things evil.

Saraina screamed out to her ancestors in her mind. She

screamed out to her great grandmother, her great-great-great grandfather, her great-great-great aunties and any other ancestors whose spirts were watching over her. She didn't know if it would work, but this was her last hope to save her from what this nasty man was about to try and do to her.

Garcen pushed Saraina's legs open and only then Saraina's screams were answered.

Loud fire alarms began to ring all around Saraina's bedroom and throughout Amiah Mansion. Water sprinklers turned on drenching Saraina and Garcen with water as they both jumped off the bed simultaneously. The main lights switched off and emergency lighting came on. The siren type noise of the fire alarms were persistent and impossible to ignore.

"What the f***?" Garcen shouted. He hurriedly pulled up his trousers and ran out of Saraina's bedroom.

Puddles of water from the water sprinklers were forming on the floor. Before Saraina left her bedroom, she hurriedly looked out of the window to see where the fire could be. She could smell smoke and hear objects crashing from below her. She saw flames of fire coming from out of the windows below.

There was an actual real fire on the ground floor.

There was no time to lose. Saraina had to find a way to get out from the second floor safely before the fire reached any higher. She called on her ancestors again.

"Help me!" Saraina screamed out again to her ancestors in her mind.

All of a sudden, hover ambulances appeared by Saraina's window, and she was told telepathically to open the window and drop herself down into the waiting hover vehicle. Now, Garcen was gone, there was no-one blocking her telepathic communication.

Saraina landed safely in the hover ambulance which transported her to the nearest virtual hospital.

FALLEN RIDER

The grey cremated ashes flew around in different directions downwards from the Bryon Crab cliff edge. The atmosphere and overall mood was somber and serious. The Amiah Riders and the Chi-Marcels sat on their robotcycles watching the whole sad scene take place. Their respective leaders Amiah Lily and the Onai twins paying their respects first, standing behind a virtual red gate on the cliff edge. Silence enveloped everyone. There were no noises coming from the seagulls that flew around in the air above the robotcycle riders. Each rider appeared lost in their own deep thoughts. They were possibly contemplating their own eventual mortality, perhaps remembering memories of Garcen Oxsett or maybe something entirely opposite.

Saraina's thoughts were opposite from the majority of the Chi-Marcel riders. They were also, almost certainly, the reverse of Louise and Petra's thinking at this time too. Saraina thanked her ancestors continuously over and over again in her mind. If she could sing out loud her joy and satisfaction with the outcome of her screams for help, she would happily do so. In Saraina's mind, Garcen brought his own death upon himself. She fully believed that this was Garcen's karma catching up to his evil ways.

At first when Saraina heard the news that Garcen had died in the fire on the ground floor at Amiah Mansion, she had been confused due to all the terror she had experienced the night before. Jan had come to visit her in the virtual hospital and informed her that they would be staying at the Chi-Marcel mansion for a few months. Initially, Saraina wasn't sure if she could truly believe that there would be no threat from Garcen anymore ever again. She wondered if it had all been a terrifying nightmare and none of it was real. Saraina had asked Jan to repeat what she just told her about Garcen dying in the fire. The second time Saraina heard it, her confusion slowly began to turn into relief and happiness.

Of course, Saraina could not show any of her inward happiness to Jan. It would be inappropriate. It would also mean that she would have to tell Jan about everything that happened with Garcen's attempt to rape her just before the fire started. Saraina knew Amiah Lily had been more hopeful and optimistic since she had accepted help from the Onai twins and the Chi-Marcel Riders. If she were to tell everyone that Garcen was a dirty, smelly, sweaty rapist (which would be the truth) then Amiah would never work with the Chi-Marcels again. She was sure of it.

Amiah had shown many times how fiercely protective she was of her and all the other Amiah Riders. Amiah would cut off the Onai twins and the Chi-Marcels immediately for this horrifying betrayal of the trust and respect between the two robotcycle groups. Then, there would be no extra help in the RBV mission to restore Brandon's visibility and Amiah would be down again. Amiah would try and hide it like all good leaders do, but Saraina figured that the loss of the alliance would upset her deeply.

It was for these reasons that Saraina chose to keep what had happened between her and Garcen to herself. She was safe now. Her ancestors had turned up at the last minute and pushed forward the karma she was sure that Garcen had coming to him from a very long time ago.

Luckily, Saraina had not been physically hurt in any way by the fire, but she had fainted in the hover ambulance. The doctors ordered a few tests and she was to remain in hospital until the results came through. In her hospital room, Jan had told her that Brandon had been saved in a very similar way to herself. A hover ambulance had appeared just below the window of his bedroom (attached to Amiah's bedroom), a security robot had then gently lifted Brandon and dropped him safely into the waiting hover vehicle. Brandon survived the fire unscathed to the great relief and delight of Amiah Lily.

No other Amiah Riders or Chi-Marcel riders were hurt in the fire. Similar to Amiah Lily who was out riding on her robotcycle with the Onai twins at the time of the fire, so were most of the club riders. The few robotcyclists who remained at Amiah Mansion, were luckily in areas of the mansion where they could easily run outside as soon as they saw the instant flames appear, seemingly out of nowhere.

One of the Chi-Marcel riders called Ernest, described witnessing the spread of the fire on the ground floor. Jan had described to Saraina, Ernest's statement about what happened the night of the fire...

"I was just swimming up and down the pool, it was very quiet... I think I was the only one left in the mansion. The rest of the men had gone out on their robotcycles with the women. I wanted to stay because... oh it doesn't matter...anyway...what happened was...I looked up and boom! Burning fire! Hot red flames everywhere I could see in front of me. Maybe a virtual computer-generated error had caused the explosion but I did not hear any bang? Anyway...I got the hell out of there, fast, very fast. I mean, I've never moved so fast in my life! I left the pool area via the exit at the back and called the fire people who told me they were already on their way and then I called Chima and Marcel using mind transfer..."

Jan had then looked up at Saraina after reading the statement to her from Ernest. She looked into Saraina's eyes as if she could tell that something was missing from this story. Jan appeared to want to question Saraina more about the mysterious fire, but a doctor had interrupted by entering the hospital room. The doctor began to explain to Saraina that her blood sugar levels were very low and this is why she had fainted in the hover ambulance. While the doctor was explaining Saraina's treatment plan, Jan got an urgent call from Amiah and had to leave.

Snapping out of her reverie and back into the present moment, Saraina held her elated smile inside of her. The treatment plan had worked and her sugar levels were back to normal again. Saraina felt ready to resume work as an Amiah Rider after spending a week in hospital. Here she was however, at the funeral of Garcen and not currently doing the work she loved doing. Nevertheless, Saraina figured that this was all part of her role as an Amiah Rider so she attended to pay her respects to the fallen Chi-Marcel robotcyclist. This would be in line with how she had been trained and within the values of the Amiah Riders. The truth however would remain with her for eternity. The Chi-Marcels could not be trusted and Garcen was a bitter disgrace to robotcyclists everywhere.

Amiah stood next to the Onai twins to show solidarity for the loss of their Chi-Marcel robotcyclist Garcen Oxsett. She had only met Garcen once very briefly at the Chi-Marcel mansion. He had appeared loud, outgoing and full of life just like the rest of the Chi-Marcels and the Amiah Riders. He was a talented robotcyclist and gifted psychic according to the way the Onai twins recalled their memories of him. Garcen's death and the unexpected fire at Amiah Mansion baffled Amiah. Usually, she had warning visions of impending serious life-threatening disasters. This time, Amiah didn't recognise any signs that would have indicated all the disaster that was to occur.

Amiah thanked a higher power in her heart, mind and from the depths of her soul for saving the life of Brandon and her Amiah Riders. A shiver ran through Amiah's body at the thought of losing Brandon or any of her Amiah Riders. It was a terrible unforeseen tragedy that one of the Chi-Marcels lost their life at her mansion. This tragedy must never happen again and the fire at Amiah Mansion continued to be investigated.

No direct cause for the fire had been found so far. Amiah and the Amiah Riders had used their remote viewing psychic skills to view the past and present time of the fire. They didn't see anything that would help the fire investigation. Literally, the flames appeared out of nowhere. Exactly the way it was described in the statement of Ernest, the Chi-Marcel rider.

Amiah was used to occurrences that other people would be scared of, find highly weird, very strange or extremely impossible. She was the best paranormal, psychic robotcyclist in the country, the world and probably the universe. Amiah smiled inwardly at her own self-praise in her thoughts. She had an unmistakeable sense that the Onai twins were good but not as good as her. She did not fully trust them. It was too early for that to happen.

From all the reports about the fire so far, Amiah again wondered what caused the virtual power surge which set the ground floor alight so instantly and deadly. Virtual technology buildings very rarely set on fire. There were a few instances whereby a fire could be caused, and these were nearly impossible to occur. One of the rare instances would be an unlikely serious error in programming. A serious programming error could potentially cause a very high computer-generated power surge, that would heat up all the virtual tech. to such an extreme heat it would set them on fire. Safety features within virtual tech design, normally would shut down the virtual tech before it reached a certain temperature. On the night of the fire, it was assumed that the safety features had failed along with other highly unusual and extremely rare errors.

Melissa Cantim (the technical expert) later confirmed that there had been no errors in the computer-generated virtual tech on that fatal night, and the security features were working normally. So, there seemed to be no technological, logical or rational explanation. Amiah knew the only option left would be a psychic, paranormal or alien interference that had started the fire somehow. She mulled over the idea that the fire was caused by an enemy or enemies of either herself or her Amiah Riders. Her mind raced with names and the psychic/paranormal abilities of anyone she had met previously in her lifetime.

Is there anyone who could be powerful enough to cause the fire and to also be cruel enough to kill a Chi-Marcel rider? Amiah shuddered at the thought.

Amiah looked out over the clear blue ocean below. She narrowed her eyes as she peered at the area of the sea where she had previously seen the ashes of Garcen fall into. Why was Garcen's skeleton remains found in the virtual lift coming down from the second floor of her mansion? Amiah pondered. The second floor was where Saraina had safely escaped the fire via a hover ambulance.

Why didn't Garcen remain on the second floor which would have saved his life? Why did Garcen run towards the flames instead of staying in the upper levels of the mansion? Amiah thought sadly.

Amiah didn't say the words she thought out loud. This wasn't the right time or the right place to talk over what she was receiving from her curious, intuitive mind. No-one with any sense would use the virtual lift during a fire and go down into the burning blaze? For one thing, the temperature in the virtual lift would have been unbearable. None of this added up in Amiah's reasoning.

Amiah shuddered again.

Did Garcen Oxsett deliberately kill himself? she wondered.

Suddenly, Amiah's thoughts were interrupted by the words of Marcel and Chima speaking in unison.

"To the Chi-Marcels and all robotcyclists present here today! Our gifted brother Garcen is gone but will never be forgotten. We ride on!"

The Onai twins joined hands and lifted their joined hands in the air in a signal of unity and power.

Amiah Lily got back on her black and gold robotcycle. Her virtual helmet activated and moved into place. The Onai twins did the same on their red robotcycles. All the robotcyclists (including the Amiah Riders and the Chi-Marcels) turned their robotcycles around to face away from the cliff edge to start riding back to the Chi-Marcel mansion.

The funeral for Garcen Oxsett had ended.

WAIT AND SEE

It was the very next day, after the fire at Amiah Mansion, that the Onai twins had immediately extended an offer of hospitality. They proposed that Amiah Lily and the Amiah Riders could stay with them at the Chi-Marcel mansion. Amiah accepted their offer straight away. Amiah wanted to continue working with the Onai twins and the Chi-Marcels on the RBV mission. She also wanted to restore any 'lost trust' that the Onai twins may have about her, following the unfortunate death of Garcen Oxsett. If Amiah had refused their offer, it would have caused possible distrust to grow between the two paranormal robotcycle clubs. Suspicion over who or what at the Amiah Mansion started the fire, which killed a Chi-Marcel might spiral out of control. Amiah could not let this happen. She desperately needed the help and assistance from the all-male paranormal and psychic robotcyclists club, now more than ever.

It had been over a month since the fire and there were so many questions that remained to be answered. Amiah still did not know for sure if Garcen's death was in fact a suicide. There still was no explanation as to how the virtual technology managed to overheat so dangerously as to set alight. Melissa Cantim could not explain it. No-one could explain it. The only suggestion that had proposed by Melissa was to dismantle all the virtual technology at Amiah Mansion and start over again. Melissa stated that a complete redesign with extra additional safety features, would be one of the best ways to ensure that this tragedy could never occur ever again.

To redesign a new improved virtual technology system for Amiah Mansion, this could take many months or even years. Melissa said that she would begin creating blueprints for the new virtual Amiah Mansion but could not guarantee a completion date.

"It's possible but I'm not sure when it will be possible, if that makes sense?" Melissa had said when discussing the future of Amiah Mansion with Amiah.

Amiah had visions of a brand new virtually glowing mansion which had a new interior design and external appearance. Melissa would succeed at this task. It was just a matter of time. Amiah held back telling Melissa that she had a vision of her success with the redesign of Amiah Mansion, as she did not want this to in any way hinder what was destined to take place eventually anyway. Amiah had discovered over the years that the more you tell people what would happen in the future, the more likely the timeline of those predictions would change or alter. Not that the prediction wouldn't occur. The prediction would just occur at a different time than expected. It was like as if, once someone knew for sure that an event or occurrence was to happen they would behave or do something that would affect the time in which it did.

Amiah remembered back to the past when she had been working in her first robotcycle store when she was younger. Upon a customer's request, Amiah Lily had read the palm of a petite young woman before she chose a robotcycle to buy. Amiah had seen a vision in front of her but pretended she was getting the information from the customer's palm. The vision revealed that the young woman would have a healthy baby boy in the future. The young woman had been very excited, especially at the clear detailed description of the baby's looks and appearance. Later, the petite woman got in contact with Amiah and said that she had given birth to a baby girl not a boy. Amiah had reassured her that the baby boy would happen but not on the time frame that she expected. To this day, the young female customer had not had a baby boy, yet Amiah knew that one day it was destined to happen. It would be in a 'higher powers' timeline not the customers.

Returning from her flashbacks, back to present day, Amiah remembered her main focus at the Chi-Marcel mansion. The RBV mission. She had a meeting today with the Onai twins and they were to retry a group remote viewing, of the oval shaped planet which the Recathri alien came from. This was to see if there was anything on the alien planet which could help restore Brandon's visibility. They were to telepathically communicate with as many aliens on that planet as possible and repeat the same statement.

"We are human beings from Earth. An alien from your planet has made one of us invisible. We require the cure for invisibility. Talk to us anytime. We will be waiting. My name is Amiah Lily/Marcel Onai/Chima Onai."

Chima Onai had devised the statement on what to say to any alien that accepted a telepathic communication from one of them. He said that they should keep it short and sweet. Either the aliens understood English from planet Earth, or they didn't. He reminded them that the Recathri alien had managed to not only speak in English when it first met Amiah, but also had managed to understand the English that Amiah spoke.

As the three sat together on virtual hover chairs in the conference room at the Chi-Marcel mansion, a robot placed refreshments on the virtual table in front of them.

"Thank you." Amiah smiled at the robot.

"You are welcome, Miss Amiah Lily." replied the mechanical voice of the metallic robot.

"I love robots." Amiah said.

"They saved your son Brandon from the fire." Marcel replied knowingly.

"Yes." Amiah said proudly.

"We have a mix of robots here. We have the old-fashioned metallic style robots and the modern human style robots." Chima said.

"She can see that Chima." Marcel said.

The two men exchanged a brief look of annoyance with each other. It was only for a few seconds, but Amiah noticed it. She sensed a competitiveness between the twin men. She glanced away and then looked back at them. There was no time for anything other than the mission at hand. In Amiah's mind she often made mental notes about the Onai twins all the time. This 'irritation' she had once again sensed amongst the brothers, would go down in her mental notes as 'unprofessionalism'.

Amiah smiled at the twin brothers while thinking these thoughts. She had made sure that she was blocking both of them and checked to see if it was still working well. Amiah did not sense anyone intruding into her thoughts, so she decided they could proceed to the latest attempt for RBV.

Chima wondered if this time the telepathic communication with the Recathri alien planet and the aliens that lived there would work. It hadn't worked the many times that they had tried before. Why did Amiah believe that this time would be any different? he pondered. Still, he didn't want any doubts to hinder the progress that could be made, if any of them managed to connect mind to mind with the unknown aliens. Chima too had his blocking skills on.

Marcel hated the way his twin brother would make it so obvious that the two of them didn't always 'see eye to eye'. Here he was, Marcel Onai, joint leader of the best paranormal and psychically gifted all-male robotcyclist club in the universe, and his brother loved to challenge him. In Marcel's opinion, Chima loved to show off around him especially when a woman was around. Amiah Lily wasn't just any woman. Marcel quickly envisioned an image of Amiah Lily naked in his thoughts. The way he imagined Amiah's naked body to look like. Marcel also had his blocking skills on.

"Hey, do we need to block the aliens on this new planet, do you think?" Marcel said suddenly.

"No need." Chima answered.

"And why's that?" Marcel retorted back fast.

"We keep our thoughts purely on RBV mission so that if any alien reads our thoughts, they only read what we want them to know." Chima suggested.

"That makes sense Chima. We all think of nothing else except all matters that directly relate solely to the RBV mission. Restore Brandon's visibility." Amiah said confidently.

"Are we all ready to start?" Marcel spoke fast to distract from Amiah's praise of Chima.

"Let's do this." Chima replied.

"Ready." Amiah replied also.

The three leaders of the best paranormal and psychically gifted robotcyclist clubs on planet Earth, each closed their eyes and focused on the Recathri alien planet.

In their remote viewing, each saw different scenes from different parts of the alien planet. Amiah saw hundreds of tall tree shapes with silver spikes that dipped in and out of the trees that appeared to be breathing and speaking. Chima saw dark red flowing water that bubbled and boiled with steam coming out of various places. Marcel saw a large area of dry broken pale yellow sand, which had indentations of something walking on it. Each person tried to communicate with any alien lifeforms on this planet, using the statement pre-written by Chima.

The three sat in silence with their eyes firmly closed. Their hearts and minds focused on finding anyone to communicate with who could help with the RBV mission.

Ten minutes went by without a single successful telepathic communication with any alien lifeforms. Then, another twenty minutes went by without any contact. Soon, an hour and 15 minutes had gone by without any telepathic communication with any aliens whatsoever. Marcel reached his hand out to get hold of a virtual beer glass and swigged from it. It would soon be the end of their latest attempt at remote viewing the alien planet, for telepathic communication. They had all agreed that the 'remote viewing telepathic communication' session would last no longer than 2 hours. Marcel felt unusually drained from today's remote viewing session and wasn't sure what or who could be draining his energy. Suddenly, he found an answer.

Marcel sensed an unknown alien lifeform, the shape of an oval with silver spikes all over it racing around in his mind reading all the information about the RBV mission. Marcel felt no pain but just a sleepy tiredness that caused him to feel weak and lethargic. Apart from that, Marcel grinned with excitement. It was he, Marcel Onai, not his twin brother Chima Onai who had made the first successful contact with an unknown alien lifeform from the Recathri alien planet.

Amiah will be happy with me, not Chima. Marcel thought. He couldn't wait to get into Amiah's pants.

A laugh was heard inside Marcel's mind and Marcel blushed slightly. He instantly focused his thoughts back on the RBV mission and the statement that his brother had devised. He tried to connect mind to mind with the alien life form, which already was reading about RBV in his mind. To Marcel's surprise, he connected easily and quickly to the mind of the unknown alien. He began to repeat the statement that his twin brother Chima had come up with, but the alien stopped him and spoke to him in English telepathically.

"I have read the statement by your twin brother Chima Onai. The alien you call Recathri is what you would call in English on your planet, an escaped criminal. We will help you restore Brandon's visibility after you help us catch Recathri. Recathri's real name is eeejjjjeee." the alien with the silver spikes, explained to Marcel in Marcel's mind.

Marcel winced. The real name of the Recathri alien sounded like a very high-pitched squealing noise. There was no way he would be using the Recathri's real name anytime soon. In fact, he was certain that no singer on earth could reach that high frequency to be able to accurately say the real name of the Recathri alien.

"So what's the real name of your planet?" Marcel inquired of the alien.

"It's eeeeeeeieieiei..." the alien replied in the same high frequency tone.

"Stop, stop! I get it!" Marcel interrupted the alien's voice. "I won't be using your planet's real name either. For english speaking humans, we will use the name Recathri planet and the

Recathri alien. Yes, we need your help in finding the Recathri alien too. Is there any way we can have the cure first? Amiah Lily's son Brandon has been suffering with invisibility since the day of his birth and..."

The alien laughed inside Marcel's mind.

"What's so funny?" Marcel asked.

"Nothing." the alien replied.

Marcel paused for a moment before speaking again. He didn't want to lose his focus on the RBV mission but there was something strange about this alien, similar to the Recathri alien. Marcel decided to change tact a little to acquire further specifics.

"When can you come to Earth to help with the search for the Recathri alien?" Marcel asked.

"I do not want to come to Earth." the alien laughed again (in a very good imitation of a human laugh).

"So how will you conduct the search? From your planet?" inquired Marcel.

"I will telepathically communicate with you alone and guide you to capturing the Recathri alien. For this, you must allow me access to every part of your mind at all times. Not only in remote viewing but permanently. This is the only way." the alien suggested.

"Ok. You have my word that I will always allow telepathic communication from you and never block it. What can I call you?" Marcel asked.

"Anything you like." the alien replied.

Marcel thought for a moment.

"I'll call you... I don't know...erm...Blazon." Marcel said finally coming up with a name quickly. There was no significant meaning to the name. It was just the first name that Marcel thought of at the time.

"And you are Marcel Onai, correct?" Blazon confirmed.

"Yes. Listen Blazon, it's time for me to rejoin the others out of this remote viewing. I can hear the alarm going off in the background. See you on the other side." Marcel communicated telepathically with Blazon and opened his eyes.

When Marcel opened his eyes fully, he could see that both Chima and Amiah were staring at him from their virtual seats on either side of him. There was a visual timer displayed on the virtual alarm as it switched off. Just before the display disappeared, Marcel saw the time on the display. It showed 2 hours and 30 minutes. Marcel had been sitting in the remote viewing session with the alarm blaring for 30 minutes overtime.

"I swear I only heard the alarm go off like 2 minutes ago. That timer can't be right." Marcel explained wearily. He still felt tired from the whole experience of communicating with Blazon.

"The timer is right brother. Amiah and I have been watching you for 30 minutes. We couldn't wake you up as there was a spiky silver oval shape surrounding your entire body." Chima said.

"You look very weak Marcel. You don't have to tell us what happened yet. I think you should go and rest." Amiah observed thoughtfully.

"He's alright." Chima said.

"Look at his eyes." Amiah said.

The view of Chima and Amiah began to spin wildly in front of Marcel's eyes. Marcel felt like he was about to faint and the last words he heard before he did so, came from Amiah Lily.

"Marcel!" Amiah shouted out.

*****

Amiah and Chima stood watching over Marcel as he rubbed his eyes and sat up on the medical hover stretcher. Marcel jumped off the hover stretcher and blinked his eyes a few times. Next, he went back over to the virtual table in the virtual conference room and sat down like as if nothing had just happened. Realising that no-one was joining him straight away, Marcel turned in his seat to face Amiah and Chima.

"What? I'm fine." Marcel said with a hint of irritation in his voice.

Chima walked over to Marcel first.

"Brother, you just passed out in front of us. I think you should take the day off." Chima said taking a seat next to his brother.

Marcel laughed sarcastically.

Amiah walked over and sat in the seat next to Marcel. She turned to look at him and did a health scan of his body. Marcel was telling the truth. His vital signs and inside his body were in top condition. There was nothing at all physically wrong with him. Amiah didn't even detect signs of hunger or thirst, which she herself felt after the long remote viewing session.

"He is fine." Amiah confirmed. "I hope you don't mind but I just did a health scan over your entire body."

"Health scan?" Chima inquired curiously.

"Yes, it's similar to remote viewing, but I just look inside the human body and see if any abnormalities are clearly present, check his/her vital signs, etc. Then I intuitively receive information about that person's health. Marcel is in perfect 100 % health." Amiah explained.

"Bro, we were just about to take you out of here into the medical room!" Chima exclaimed. "But you're all good now."

"Listen to Amiah, Chima. She said it. Not me. 100 % health." Marcel grinned at Amiah first and then at his brother Chima. This was better than he expected. Not only did he feel ok, but Amiah Lily had also given him a free medical. Now, he wouldn't have to go for a medical check up and miss out on working on the RBV mission.

Marcel animatedly began to describe what happened in his recent remote viewing session of the Recathri planet. Marcel described everything he heard and saw. When he got to the part about the alien (he named Blazon) still having access to his mind at all times, Amiah stopped him mid-sentence.

"Wait, what? Repeat that last sentence for me." Amiah asked Marcel, her eyebrows raised questionably

"Blazon said that he would help me find the Recathri alien on planet Earth and would remain inside my mind to lead me in the right direction basically." Marcel replied. He detected the doubt in Amiah's voice and felt his guard go up.

"Are you telling me that this unknown alien from an

unknown planet in our solar system has access to your mind right now?" Amiah said. She couldn't believe what she was hearing. She at first thought that perhaps she didn't hear Marcel correctly.

Marcel could tell that Amiah didn't approve and changed his tone to try and calm her worries.

"Listen Amiah. Yes, I made a quick decision. I had to. I didn't know if this alien would take back his offer and then here we would all be, without any new leads whatsoever. Yes, I've taken a risk and I will take personal responsibility for everything that comes out of this. You have your intuitive sense about things I know, just like myself and Chima. My intuition tells me that this alien Blazon, being in my mind or having access to my mind or whatever you want to call it, is one of the few hopes we have left. Blazon directing me to find where the Recathri alien could be will help us complete the RBV mission. Brandon will get his visibility restored. I've done this for him." Marcel finished explaining. He calmly waited for Amiah and Chima to process everything he had just said.

Silence fell over the room for the next 3 minutes.

Amiah and Chima didn't speak a word at all during that time, but each were thinking that the risk Marcel had taken had all the elements for potential future danger.

Chima felt like yelling at his brother for being so irresponsible but held back to see what Amiah would say first. Maybe, Amiah would agree with Marcel simply because of the fact that Blazon could help locate the Recathri alien. Once the Recathri alien was found, then Blazon could talk to it via Marcel and Brandon could possibly receive a cure. Chima mulled over these thoughts in his head. On the one hand, he felt an unusual anger at the fact that his twin had put his life at an unknown risk and on the other hand… On the other hand, what if his brother's crazy agreement with the Blazon alien actually worked? What if this time his twin brother Marcel was right to take such a controversial risk? Chima pondered. He looked over at Amiah again as she began to speak in reply to Marcel.

"Marcel thank you." Amiah spoke with tears filling her eyes. She put her arm gently around Marcel's shoulder and looked at Marcel in his eyes.

Chima's mouth dropped open in surprise. He quickly regained his composure realising that Amiah was thinking of the good outcomes that could happen for her invisible son Brandon. Amiah did not appear to be thinking much about the unknown risk that there could be for his twin brother Marcel. His twin Marcel was now carrying around an unknown alien lifeform in his mind. Was nobody thinking of the millions of possible unknown risks that this could potentially cause? Chima wondered.

Aliens from other planets had to go through lengthy year long quarantines before they could visit planet Earth. Now, his dumb twin had let an alien inside his mind without the proper checks or any kind of quarantine, Chima worriedly mused. Chima eyed his twin and felt tears starting to fill his eyes just like Amiah's had. Chima's emotions were very different however, Chima felt fear for his twin brother's life.

"Thank you, thank you, thank you! Thank you for doing this to help my invisible son Brandon. I will never forget your kindness. The Amiah Riders and I will be indebted to you and your service for the RBV mission, in whichever way you, Chima and the Chi-Marcels choose. Robot bring me more refreshments!" Amiah said happily.

A robot member of staff laid down a virtual tray of refreshments on the virtual table in front of the three leaders of the separate robotcycle clubs. Amiah picked up two apples and bit into the first one in her left hand and then the second one in her right hand.

Marcel turned to face Chima and winked at his twin brother. Chima winked back. He couldn't let his brother see the emotion that had nearly come out of his eyes a while earlier. He remained composed and decided that the best thing was to just go along with this new change. Amiah Lily seemed ok with it, and she had highly intuitive skills.

Chima frowned. Chima knew his intuitive skills were exceptionally high also. So, why did he feel this strange fear for his twin's life? Chima shivered and reached to grab a few sandwiches from the virtual refreshments tray.

Maybe the Amiah Riders are used to taking risks with unknown aliens but the Chi-Marcels don't work that way, Chima thought.

"Marcel, do we tell the Chi-Marcels that you have this alien inside your head or no?" Chima inquired.

"Yes, we will tell them." Marcel replied drinking some water from a virtual glass.

Chima could be so dull, Marcel thought.

Marcel wasn't even thinking about the 'alien inside his head thing' anymore. His mind had moved onto other things. He sensed that Amiah Lily felt very close to him right now and he wanted to test her to see how far she would go. He couldn't do that in front of Chima. Chima would somehow get in the way, Marcel was sure.

How can I get rid of Chima, Marcel thought, so that Amiah and I are alone?

"We're both due on a training ride with the Chi-Marcels in half an hour, we can tell them afterwards." Chima said.

Marcel tilted his head to the side and narrowed his eyes briefly as if he had just heard something very puzzling.

"What's wrong?" Chima asked. "We better get over to meet the rest of the men soon before we're late. Doesn't look good bro, you know this already."

"Go on ahead of me Chima, I heard something from Blazon." Marcel said assuredly.

"What did he, I mean, what did it say?" Chima said, suddenly very curious about the new alien presence in his brother's mind.

"I'm not sure, it's not clear. I think I need to sit here and focus on deciphering his messages. Go on ahead without me. Apologise to the Chi-Marcels for my absence and explain everything that's happened. Will you do this for me brother?" Marcel asked.

"Yes of course. Tell me when you find out where the Recathri alien is hiding. I will bring the men over to provide help with anything you need." Chima replied.

Chima hoped that Amiah noticed the professional way he had just talked to his twin. Did Amiah Lily get turned on by professionalism? he wondered.

Chima picked up a handful of mints and waved bye to Amiah and Marcel. On his way out of the virtual conference room, Chima thought about the new robotcycle route that he and the Chi-Marcels were riding on soon. For the time being, Marcel, Blazon, Amiah and the Recathri alien would be far from his mind, as his deep passion for riding robotcycles took over.

Marcel had invented the small fib to get his twin out of the way so he could try and win over Amiah Lily's love.

"Hello Marcel. It is Blazon." a voice inside Marcel's mind spoke out loud. The voice of Blazon was neither male nor female. It just sounded like a neutral tone which did not definitely lean towards either the human male or human female voice recognition.

Marcel dropped his virtual glass in surprise, but as he was holding it close to the virtual table it did not break.

Amiah had heard the conversation between Marcel and Chima but did not want to interrupt any communication that Marcel was receiving. Therefore, Amiah waited patiently (inwardly excited) for Marcel to inform her where they would have to ride to, in order to find the Recathri alien.

Will this be the day that I finally see Brandon? Amiah thought. Her heart skipped a beat in anticipation of the good that could come out of this latest turn of events. Still, she remained quiet and patient, not wanting to intervene in the process.

Marcel put a finger to his mouth and looked at Amiah. He then shut his eyes and appeared to be in concentrating on whatever Blazon was saying to him. It was just his luck, to actually have the alien speak just a few moments after he had lied to his twin brother. Now, he would have to really put in the work towards RBV instead of trying to get into Amiah Lily's 'knickers' as planned.

What the hell does Blazon want? Marcel thought angrily.

"I assumed you would be happy to hear from me Marcel." Blazon said inside of Marcel's mind.

Marcel hesitated before communicating back to Blazon. So, Blazon could read his emotions. Well, this shouldn't surprise me, Marcel considered, after all the alien is residing in my head.

"Reading my emotions is not what you're here for Blazon." Marcel replied getting straight to the point. "Where have you located the Recathri alien on Earth?"

"The Recathri alien is upstairs with the invisible boy Brandon talking to him. I need you to go and..." Blazon began saying but Marcel interrupted him.

"Amiah's son Brandon!" Marcel shouted out loud. He took hold of Amiah's hand and pulled her up off her virtual seat. "It's Brandon! He's in danger!" he said.

Amiah let herself be led by the firm grip of Marcel's hand, out of the room. She quickly did a remote viewing of Brandon in a virtual playroom that the Chi-Marcels had designed for him. Brandon was standing on top of his mini-robotcycle and appeared to be talking with someone that Amiah could not see. She couldn't see any spirits around Brandon that he could be communicating with. Amiah sensed the urgency in Marcel's voice and ran along with Marcel to get to the playroom on the second floor. As they both entered the virtual lift at the same time, Amiah let go of Marcel's hand and asked him about what Blazon had said.

"What did Blazon say? Is the Recathri alien in there with Brandon?" Amiah demanded to know.

"Yes Amiah. We're here on the second floor. I'll try and see if Blazon is still there?" Marcel said.

Amiah was only half listening as she ran out of the virtual lift on the second floor and into the playroom nearby.

"Brandon!" Amiah called out.

As Amiah entered the playroom, she switched to a different

tact. She didn't want the Recathri alien to see her scared, so she chose to speak calmly to Brandon.

Brandon still engaged in conversation with the person only he could see. He didn't look behind to notice that his mother had entered the room and was watching him.

Amiah held herself back from running over to her son while Marcel stood next to her and communicated with Blazon.

"Does Blazon know what the Recathri is saying to my son?" Amiah asked.

"Blazon says that the Recathri is talking to Brandon about robotcycles." Marcel replied.

Amiah rolled her eyes. Now, it seemed like the Recathri alien was trying to make friends with her son.

But, why? Amiah thought.

"What does the Recathri alien know about robotcycles?" Amiah smirked.

"Blazon said that the Recathri…" Marcel began to speak but Amiah cut him off.

"Look, I don't care. I just want to know if Blazon can talk to this thing and find a cure for my son. What does Blazon say we should do?" Amiah said getting impatient. She could see her son Brandon at a distance appearing to laugh while talking to the Recathri alien, and this got on her nerves.

"Hold on." Marcel said with a look of concern on his face.

"What is it?" Amiah questioned anxiously.

Instead of answering Amiah, Marcel ran towards Brandon and held him back from being sucked into a bright red oval-shaped hole, which had suddenly appeared pulling little Brandon towards it.

"Mummy!" Brandon yelped.

Amiah ran over to try and help her invisible son, but suddenly a clear screen appeared which blocked her from getting closer. Amiah screamed out for Brandon from behind the screen.

Luckily, Marcel managed to pull Brandon away from the bright red oval-shaped hole, which had been sucking him in.

Marcel held Brandon in his arms and turned to bring him safely back to Amiah. The clear screen shattered and disappeared into nothing. Marcel reached Amiah who quickly took her son Brandon into her arms and hugged him tightly.

After hugging Brandon and talking to him for a while, Amiah turned to praise Marcel.

"Marcel you saved Brandon's life! Thank you and thank you Blazon." Amiah smiled happily at Marcel.

Marcel grinned back and winked at her.

EX-LOVERS

Two weeks later...

Amiah walked self-assuredly as she always did, into the Duneway high security virtual prison. The robot and paranormal security staff eyed her suspiciously as per usual. Amiah ignored them all. She had business to attend to. She wasn't here for the fun of it. Amiah also could see and sense the not-so-subtle hints of appreciation for her curvy, hot, sexy body. This morning Amiah had chosen to put on a sultry red slimline off the shoulder dress. This sensual provocative red dress left her smooth brown shoulders bare, and accentuated some of her best features.

Waiting for the security staff to read her mind and scan her body for weapons or anything else of interest, Amiah yawned loudly.

"Keeping you up, are we? Ms Lily." a security man (with psychic skills) asked Amiah.

"I just don't see why you have to check me 5 times before I get to see Landon. If there were anything wrong, shouldn't you have found this in the first initial search." Amiah snapped back at him.

Whether or not she was tired was none of their business. Amiah didn't have time for their sarcasm and vague insinuations. Amiah knew that she had been blocking everyone at Duneway high security virtual prison since she had left the Chi-Marcel mansion on her robotcycle. She hadn't detected any intrusions into her mind, so the security staff didn't know a thing. They were all one big bluff.

"Rules and regulations sweetheart, rules and regulations." a robot security guard answered Amiah.

Amiah held back laughter from escaping from her mouth. Someone had programmed an old-fashioned Essex accent into the security robot. The robot sounded ridiculous.

"This is the way it's always been Ms. Lily. You understand the concepts of procedure and protocol." one of the paranormal security guards replied.

Amiah laughed out loud. This was too much foolery. She couldn't help it. Amiah laughed so much that a robot security staff member handed her a bunch of tissues.

All the security team at the 5th checkpoint watched her coldly.

Amiah rolled her eyes.

"There's no procedural protocols for laughing is there?" Amiah said, her tone changing to one which displayed her real power and authority.

For a short moment after Amiah had spoken, the scene around her appeared 'frozen'. No-one moved around her. Amiah considered keeping them 'frozen' like this for the rest of the day but quickly changed her mind. The security staff had no idea what Amiah was confidently capable of. They were lucky that none of them were part of the RBV mission. Therefore, she had no use to paranormally interfere with any of them, unless it was either directly related to freeing Landon or RBV. Amiah soon commanded the scene around her to begin moving again. This was done by the power of Amiah's intention behind her strong paranormal focus on the action she desired.

However, it hadn't always worked so effectively. Sadly, when Amiah tried to use it to help her in a previous rescue attempt for Landon, this ability had fallen unexpectedly flat. This was a rare but possible occurrence with people who had psychic and paranormal powers. Even though a person has these skills, there would always be the chance that a higher power could override anything that was trying to be achieved.

It was a little bit like when people would use the old-fashioned saying that a natural disaster e.g. earthquake, tornado was an 'act of God.' Whenever a psychic or paranormal person's skills were strangely prevented, it was similar to an 'act of God' or an 'act of a higher power' or 'an act of the unknown.'. Amiah Lily had outstanding and frequent psychic and paranormal powers but there was always the 'act of a higher power' that could stop her if it/he/she so wished.

Amiah frowned at the thought of her many failed rescue attempts to free Landon. She wished with all her heart that a higher power would allow her to use her skills to rescue Landon successfully. Yet every time she tried, something would get in the way. Whether it was a God, higher power or something else unknown, Amiah and other psychic/paranormally skilled people did not know for certain. There were lots of guesses in the psychic/paranormal communities as to who was behind the rare times when even their gifts and abilities failed. Some people believed it was God intervening. Others believed it was a higher power with no name, who intervened. Still others believed that it was an unknown being, possibly an alien from another planet (not yet discovered) that intervened in the psychic and paranormal gifts of humans on Earth.

When the security staff started to move again from their previous frozen positions in time, they had no recollection of what had just happened. They continued to search Amiah using scanning light beams from the robots, and mind telepathy from the paranormal staff who remained seated on hover chairs. Now and again, the paranormal security staff would hover around Amiah and hover above her before returning to their corner of the room to talk amongst themselves. The security staff also made notes on virtual notepads.

Amiah waited for the fifth and final security check at Duneway high security virtual prison to be over. She felt an impatience growing within her as she continued to block the security staff from her real thoughts, whilst allowing them access to thoughts she wanted them to see.

"You're clear and free to visit prisoner...erm...Mr. Landon

Ross. You must not make physical contact with Mr. Landon Ross. You must not give him anything which could be deemed as dangerous under Duneway regulations section 5.9. You must not give him any food or drink. Please ask a member of staff if you are in any doubt of the rules of Duneway high security virtual prison. Have a good day." said a robot member of staff.

"Thank you." Amiah replied politely. Of course, she really wanted to say many other not so cordial things to the security team. Amiah held back, to keep her thoughts pleasant and acceptable just in case she was being mind-read still.

Amiah walked in-between two of the Duneway robot security staff, to be escorted to visit Landon. When she arrived at the room where she would be talking to Landon, it was full of other inmates also speaking to visitors. Amiah sat down on a virtual chair behind a virtual screen. Landon was seated on the other side of the virtual screen.

"Lot of people in here today." Amiah exclaimed.

"Yeah, we got some new men in here and these are all their visitors." Landon answered.

"They should have put us in another room." Amiah said loudly, to be heard above the noise in the visiting room.

Landon snorted.

"As if." he said.

"It was just a suggestion Landon." Amiah replied narrowing her eyes. She had just gone through five highly intrusive security checks from the Duneway security staff and Landon hadn't even noticed her outfit.

Landon and Amiah sat looking at each for a few minutes before either one of them spoke.

"You look different." Landon said in a bored tone.

Amiah was taken aback. Different? Is that all you can say? she thought.

"You've done something to your hair." Landon said, peering at her curiously.

"Landon. I put on the same sexy red dress that I wore on our first anniversary date. Don't you remember the night that you…"

Amiah stared incredulously at Landon. His memory seemed to be getting progressively worse the longer he was in there. Amiah sighed loudly.

The visiting room became quieter, and Amiah took this opportunity to explain the main reason why she was at Duneway visiting Landon. She wanted to tell him about how Marcel Onai had saved their son Brandon a few weeks ago. There had been a delay of weeks, before Amiah had got today's chance to talk to Landon about what happened. Landon had been in contact with a paranormal staff member who had tested positive for the highly infectious Frovid virus. Subsequently, Landon was put in an isolation cell to quarantine for two weeks and a half.

"Nah, I take it back. You look the same." Landon said sarcastically.

Amiah felt her heart begin to pound inside her chest. This was not how she had envisioned today's visit with Landon at all.

"I'm negative Amiah. I didn't have Frovid virus. They put me in the isolation room for nothing." Landon said, leaning forward to look at Amiah on the opposite side of the virtual clear screen.

"I know you don't have Frovid. This is why I knew it would be a good time to visit and tell you what happened. Marcel saved Brandon from being pulled into an unknown alien suction hole type of thing, that appeared in his playroom." Amiah said quickly before Landon could complain about anything else.

"What?" Landon said, his eyes widening. "Is Brandon ok? Why didn't you…oh..the quarantine thing."

"Yes, I couldn't get through to you telepathically and the staff here didn't accept my calls while you were quarantined." Amiah replied.

"Can they do that?" Landon asked.

"I don't know but that's what they did." Amiah replied.

"They can't do that, can they?" Landon said.

"It's their prison Landon but this isn't the point. Landon, I was so worried for our son, he… if it wasn't for Marcel saving him at the very last minute, Brandon would have been gone forever. This is something I just can't take Landon. I just can't…" Amiah said.

"Amiah it didn't happen." Landon said thoughtfully. "Tell Marcel, I owe him a favour from me."

Amiah was puzzled.

How could Landon return a favour for Marcel when Marcel could do much more than him as a free man? Did Landon forget that he was in a virtual prison for life? Amiah pondered. This wasn't some extended separation. Whatever Landon could come up with in jail (with his jail buddies) was nowhere near the power that the Onai twins yielded in the outside world, with all their freedom. Not to mention the exceptional paranormal and psychic abilities of the Onai twins and the Chi-Marcels. Amiah glanced around and checked that she was still blocking her real thoughts from the security staff, whilst at the same time allowing access to her fake thoughts. Everything was fine.

"Landon, Marcel doesn't want anything from you in return. He did it instinctively. He saw a way he could help, and he did it without me asking him to." Amiah said.

"So, you didn't return the favour? I find that hard to believe." Landon replied, leaning back again in his virtual chair and glaring at Amiah.

Amiah winced.

"What are you on about? You haven't even asked me what I'm going to do to monitor the frequency of unknown alien suction holes, while staying at the Chi-Marcel mansion." Amiah asked feeling annoyed.

Landon winced.

"Amiah, everyone knows that alien suction holes can appear anywhere and at any time. They are an 'act of God' or an 'act of a higher power.' There isn't much we can do about it." Landon said and shrugged his shoulders.

Amiah's mouth dropped open in surprise.

"Landon you act like you don't care! It doesn't matter if it's a random event or not, this sh*t can't ever f**king happen again! We're talking about our son Brandon here. Landon, hello!

Are you hearing me?" Amiah said much more loudly than she intended.

All the security staff supervising the visiting room, stared in the direction of Amiah Lily and Landon Ross.

Silence enveloped the visiting room for 60 seconds which seemed like eternity to both Amiah and Landon. Amiah worried how much of her real thoughts had overlapped into her fake ones. One of the psychic female security members of staff smiled at Amiah. Landon noticed it.

"You're attracting the girls now Amiah." Landon said and broke the silence of the room.

The female psychic security guard's smile dropped, and she barked out. "Visiting hours finish in 20 minutes." Then she turned to look in another direction, away from Amiah and Landon.

"Don't believe any of the staff here Amiah. Trust me, she's still listening just like the rest of them." Landon reminded Amiah, his voice softening.

"Landon, I didn't come here for you to tell me the obvious. This is about Brandon." Amiah explained again.

"What more do you want me to say Amiah? Huh? Brandon is alright now, isn't he?" Landon replied.

"Well, yes, yes he is." Amiah's mind raced. This was not turning out how she had expected at all. "Why are you angry with me Landon?"

Landon lifted his face upwards to look towards the ceiling of the visiting room and then lowered his face down to look at Amiah.

"Amiah. Amiah, if he's ok there is nothing to worry about. What more do you want me to do?" Landon replied, his face an expression of serenity and calm.

Amiah felt hurt at what she perceived as Landon's lack of interest, in the fact that their son had nearly died a few weeks prior. She sat opposite Landon speechless for a few minutes.

Landon didn't understand why Amiah was reacting the way she was. If something had seriously happened to hurt Brandon, then he could understand.

Brandon our son is fine, Amiah, Landon thought. He wondered if he should ask again, maybe he had missed something earlier. He rubbed his eyes with his left hand. He was still exhausted from all the stress and tests he had undergone during quarantine for the Frovid virus. He had been isolated from other humans, but robot staff came to see him daily to take blood or urine tests and perform lengthy medical scans. They had also woken him up at night to continue their testing regime. This prevented Landon from a good night's sleep for the entire two week quarantine period.

"Did Brandon get hurt in any way Amiah?" Landon asked Amiah, in a tired voice.

"No, but..." Amiah began to reply, before she noticed that Landon had stood up out of his virtual seat. "Where are you going Landon? I'm got more to tell you..."

"Amiah, I am exhausted. This is my first day out of the isolation cell, it's cramped in there and stinks of all the pee and poo samples they kept taking from me. Yes, even at night time..." Landon hesitated mid-speech as if remembering all that went on in his isolation cell. "Robot nurses, robot doctors and robot, and, and you are here dressed up like we're going somewhere together! You know as well as I do, that I'm in here for life. I'm in here for life Amiah. Get used to it."

After finishing what he had to say, Landon turned his back on Amiah and walked away from her to the exit door where he was joined by security to take him back to his prison cell.

Amiah didn't know what to say. She felt too stunned to speak after Landon's unexpected outburst. A short while later, Amiah finally found the words to say back in response to him.

"Fine! If that's what you want, I will!" Amiah said and got up to walk out of the visiting room via the visitors exit. She kept her thoughts as fake as possible so that the security team at Duneway wouldn't know the real reason behind her argument with Landon. Unfortunately, Amiah would always remember the real reason.

Landon no longer wanted her.

*****

Marcel watched Amiah ride into his garage at the Chi-Marcel mansion with a flirtatious smile forming on his lips. He had just been about to go out for a ride on his red robotcycle, when he heard the familiar sound of another robotcycle riding towards the front entrance. Marcel had intended his ride to be a leisurely ride, nothing business related. It was a ride out just for the fun of it. Marcel knew his twin brother Chima would not approve. Chima was busy inside the mansion, hard at work on the RBV mission. Marcel also, was supposed to be hard at work on the RBV mission but he had felt like going out for a ride and this is what he did.

Why is Amiah Lily here at the same time? Marcel thought. Is the leader of the Amiah Riders on break too?

Marcel sat calmly on his red robotcycle at the back of the virtual garage, and continued to watch Amiah on her black and gold robotcycle. Marcel saw Amiah get off her robotcycle and walk over to where the virtual fridge was. Amiah then grabbed some drinks and snacks from the virtual fridge, and placed them in a compartment which opened up at the back of her robotcycle. The compartment then robotically closed again.

It seemed to Marcel that Amiah was heading back out again on her robotcycle, and he wondered where she was off to now. He was aware that this morning was Amiah's visit, to see her ex-boyfriend Landon Ross at Duneway high security virtual prison.

Where is she off to now? Marcel thought. Well, if Amiah Lily can take a break from the RBV mission, then so can I, he concluded with a smile.

Amiah's thoughts raced fast. Even though she had ridden the long way home, she still hadn't managed to calm herself down after what just happened with Landon.

How can he put me through this stress? Amiah thought. He knows I'm already inundated with work on RBV and worry over the safety of Brandon.

This wasn't the Landon that she had fell in love with. This

wasn't Landon who had told her that he would always look after her and always love her. No. This was the Landon who had changed since that night he predicted his own downfall. Duneway virtual high security prison had just made Landon worse. In Amiah's opinion, Landon was more hardened, he was more cruel and selfish. The longer Landon was imprisoned, the more easier it felt to accept the title he had given her. Ex. She was Landon's ex. Landon was her ex. Maybe it was time she got used to the fact and moved on like he had just told her to, Amiah wondered sadly.

Amiah waited for tears to fill her eyes. She was thinking some very emotional, usually tear-jerking stuff so crying would most probably follow soon enough. Amiah took in a long, slow deep breath, held it inside for a while before slowly exhaling. She waited some more for the tears she expected to fill her eyes to enter. She waited some more.

Amiah tilted her face to the side. The expected tears at her racing sad thoughts, about finally accepting the end of her relationship with Landon, didn't form. Amiah blinked multiple times as is in disbelief that her eyes were not showing the emotion she had expected. Where were her tears for the lost love of Landon? Landon the love of her life. Landon her first real love, Amiah wondered. She blinked again twice. Both her eyes had perfectly clear vision. There were no tears brimming over the edges whatsoever.

Amiah set the destination on her robotcycle by speaking to it and rode off again out of the virtual exit doors of the Chi-Marcel garage. She didn't notice that a few minutes after she began riding away from the mansion, that Marcel Onai was following her on his red robotcycle.

Marcel Onai kept a safe distance away from Amiah on her black and gold robotcycle. He didn't want to make it blatantly obvious that he was following her. If it were too obvious then Amiah might change direction and return home, then there would be no chance to get some alone time with her.

A few times, at virtual traffic lights, Marcel had got a little bit too close to Amiah's bike, but luckily Amiah hadn't appeared to notice. At no time did Marcel question to himself, whether or not his actions were 'creepy'. He told himself that he just wanted to get to know her more. There was nothing wrong with that, surely, he concluded.

Marcel remembered the last time that he had been with a woman. It had been years ago. This was through no fault of his own. His first girlfriend, Freeda, had died in a horrific robotcycle accident and Marcel could not bring himself to date another woman again. That was until he saw Amiah Lily at one of his beaches...

Amiah Lily is every male robotcyclists dream woman. Probably every female robotcyclists dream woman too, Marcel thought.

Amiah had everything a man could ever want, in Marcel's current opinion. She was beautiful, sexy, talented, a gifted rider and possessed high paranormal and psychic abilities. What man or gay woman would not want to be with her? Marcel pondered.

Still, Marcel had not forgotten his anguish and the pain he experienced over his deceased girlfriend Freeda. He would never forget her glistening brunette hair, her gorgeous freckled tanned skin and her long legs which had wrapped around him every single night. Of course, he would never forget her, but even she would not want him to be alone for the rest of his life. They had never talked about the possibility of one of them dying and leaving the other. Marcel wished that they had this conversation. All he could think now, was that wherever Freeda was (in another dimension perhaps watching over him) that she would be happy with the new woman. The new woman Marcel Onai had set his sights on was Amiah Lily.

Marcel had spoken to Freeda numerous times in the spirit world, but he could never bring himself to talk about him finding a new girlfriend. He simply did not mention it to Freeda ever. It just didn't feel right. Sometimes, Marcel would imagine that the spirit of Freeda he saw in front of him or the tender words he heard by his ear at night, were coming from the real physically alive Freeda. Upon remembering that he was just communicating with the spirit form of Freeda, Marcel's grief and mourning had continued for years after the tragic accident. It wasn't enough for him to see his deceased girlfriend spirit or hear her voice around him. Marcel wanted more than that. He wanted her alive physically so he could make love to her while feeling her real living body close to his.

Making love with a spirit version of the woman he once knew was totally different. Marcel didn't care what anyone said. It was nothing like the real thing and only comforted Marcel in the moment. After Freeda went back to wherever spirit heaven, she was residing full time in, Marcel was alone again and his grief returned. Sometimes, his grief worsened the more he saw the spirit of his deceased girlfriend, as this would remind him over and over again that she was no longer alive.

Marcel's twin brother Chima told Marcel that he should just be grateful and appreciate the fact that he could still make love to a ghost of Freeda. This had caused a nasty fight between them, so Chima hadn't suggested this again since that time. Marcel's long period of grieving confused Chima and the other Chi-Marcels, who knew that Freeda's spirit regularly talked with Marcel. They wondered why Marcel was not trying to date other women, but instead talking with a ghost all the time.

Interestingly, since that night at the beach when Marcel had seen Amiah Lily, the ghost of Freeda had visited Marcel less and less. In fact, after the fire at Amiah Mansion, Marcel had not communicated with the spirit of Freeda at all. Marcel's mind was too consumed with his new love interest of Amiah Lily. Marcel would never forget Freeda, but maybe this was a sign from the universe for him to start again with someone new. Someone equally as beautiful as Freeda, someone gifted and talented and someone who loved riding robotcycles.

Someone like Amiah Lily, Marcel thought.

Marcel rode his red robotcycle around a sharp corner and into a driveway surrounded by trees and forestry.

Is she going to sit in the park? Marcel thought curiously.

What does this have to the do with any of the leads that I gave her for the RBV mission?

Marcel looked around at all the different tall trees and the variety of mixed flowers. He could see a sparkling blue lake in the distance with ducks on it. Marcel read the sign near the entry to the park. Grestons Forest – Privately owned.

So, why is she here? Marcel wondered.

Marcel followed behind Amiah at a larger distance than before, as they were the only two robotcycles amidst other vehicles, such as hover cars. The hover cars would overtake Marcel and Amiah's robotcycles when necessary. Marcel decided to speed up and catch up with Amiah's black and gold robotcycle. Amiah would soon figure out that he was there in Greston's forest with her. She was psychic after all. Marcel grinned at this thought. He had been blocking Amiah so it was unlikely that she would have intuitively guessed that Marcel was nearby. Marcel wanted to make Amiah aware of his presence for other reasons that were nothing to do with the RBV mission.

Marcel rode fast to catch up to Amiah's robotcycle. When he got up close next to her bike, he glanced over at her. Amiah looked back and then cut in front of him to ride into the forest. Amiah rode into the deep forestry area surrounded by tall pine trees and woodland wildflowers of bluebells, bramble and common dog violet. The common dog violet wildflowers had many bright orange butterflies on and around them. Some of the orange butterflies came over to the two people on their robotcycles. Marcel shook them off him, as he pulled to a stop next to Amiah's robotcycle.

Amiah got off her robotcycle and laughed at the sight of Marcel trying to shake off the orange-coloured butterflies from his shoulder and legs. It was the first time she had laughed since leaving Duneway virtual prison and she felt happy that Marcel was there to amuse her.

"Hey Marcel, are there new leads on the RBV mission? Has Blazon been talking with you again?" asked Amiah eagerly. She didn't seem bothered in the slightest about the fact that Marcel just so happened to be in the exact same forest as her, at the same time.

Marcel felt relieved that Amiah showed no sign that there was any problem whatsoever, with him being there with her. He relaxed a bit more and allowed the orange butterflies to settle on his arms and legs again.

"Your new look suits you." Amiah laughed again. Marcel looked silly. Nothing like the strong, gifted and talented leader of the Chi-Marcel riders.

Sensing this was his chance with Amiah, Marcel suddenly embraced Amiah and kissed her on the lips passionately. Amiah responded back with the same passion and tenderness. Marcel began to take his clothes off while at the same time kissing and undressing Amiah. Now, both of them were naked, Amiah straddled Marcel and began to make love with him. She made love with him the exact same way she used to with Landon. In her mind she tried to imagine it was Landon's dick she was riding and not Marcel's.

"Ohhhh! Yes baby give it to me." Marcel whispered in Amiah's ear.

"You want this. Take it." Amiah murmured into the black curly hair of Marcel Onai, as she lay on top of him gyrating slowly.

Marcel laughed deep and dirty.

After, she had made love with him, Amiah slowly began to massage Marcel's now limp dick until he became hard again. Marcel moaned in ecstasy saying the words "Ride me again honey."

"Come. Take me again. I want you so bad." Amiah said softly to Marcel.

"I know baby." Marcel replied sexily.

Marcel positioned his body on top of Amiah. Amiah moaned and gyrated her body in anticipation of Marcel's long, hard dick entering her again. Marcel's dick pointed at Amiah's lovebox and he whispered in her ear.

"I'm going to f*** you so... har... har... hard...I'm going to f***…Amiah baby, open up for me." Marcel frowned.

Amiah's lovebox had closed so tightly that Marcel could not penetrate her. Marcel kept on trying a few more times but Amiah's body refused to open up to him.

"I don't know why this has happened. We can try again later." Amiah said soothingly to Marcel, as she gently caressed his shoulders and kissed him on the lips.

Marcel cuddled Amiah in return and kissed her back roughly. Nothing was going to stop Marcel from making love to Amiah again. He had gotten too far to give up now. He held Amiah in his arms for a while before slowly laying her down again on her back. He used his feet to softly kick Amiah's ankles further apart, so her legs would open wide for him. Marcel again tried to make love with Amiah.

For the second time, Amiah's lovebox refused to open for Marcel's dick.

Suddenly out of nowhere, the sound of hysterical laughter permeated the air from somewhere in the distance away from the couple. Both Amiah and Marcel stopped trying to have sex and stared in the direction of the laughter. There was no-one else there.

"Did you hear that?" Amiah asked. She did a quick remote viewing scan of Grestons forest but did not see any other people in the nearby vicinity.

"Yes, I did. I've done a search of this area and there are no other humans around where we are." Marcel replied.

"Who or what was that?" Amiah asked curiously.

"I don't know Amiah. Who cares? Here, get on top of me again, maybe you'll relax a bit more and we can do it again." Marcel suggested humorously.

"Maybe *you* will relax a bit more!" Amiah laughed as she pushed Marcel onto his back and straddled him again like she had the first time.

On this occasion, the couple managed to make love even more intensely and lovingly, than during their initial sexual encounter.

DROP IT

It soon became plainly obvious to everyone living at the Chi-Marcel mansion, that Amiah Lily and Marcel Onai were seeing each other. Both Amiah and Marcel did not hide their growing intimacy and affection from the Amiah Riders or the Chi-Marcels. In their minds there was no reason to hide. Both were single and free to do whatever they wanted with whoever they wanted. It had taken the two of them long periods of time to move on from their respective past relationships but now finally they were both ready. Or at least they thought they were both ready…

Amiah had been going out with Marcel on romantic dates and making love with him for around 6 months before she started having vivid nightmares about Landon. They had been recurring dreams now for the past two weeks. Amiah was perplexed as to why Landon kept popping up in her dreams in a frightening way. She would wake up in a cold sweat and panicky. Marcel would just roll over and tell her to go back to sleep and that it was just a dream. Amiah knew from her experience that recurring vivid nightmares had significance. She debated this with Marcel one morning, as they both relaxed in his king size virtual bed together.

"This is day 15 of the same scary nightmare Marcel. I'm sure it means something. I have never been so sure of anything in my life." Amiah complained to Marcel who pretended to be asleep next to her.

Marcel didn't reply back, but shifted his position a little from laying on his front, to laying on his side to face Amiah.

"I know you can hear me Marcel. This is serious." Amiah said, poking Marcel sharply in his tummy to get his attention.

Marce's eyelids flew open showing his dark brown eyes underneath.

Amiah smiled at him.

"You told me that within a person they always know the answer to everything, Amiah. I don't see why you are worrying about it." Marcel said dismissively.

"Well, yes...but..." Amiah started to say quietly.

Marcel sat up and looked down at Amiah still laying on the bed naked looking up at him.

"You can't forget him can you?" Marcel said with a hint of irritation in his voice.

"What?" Amiah replied.

"It's you Amiah. You are doing this to yourself. You keep thinking about Landon and having bad dreams because you feel bad that's it's over between you and him. No-one needs to be a psychologist to work that at." Marcel said angrily.

"Alright, calm down. Why are you getting angry for?" Amiah replied. She sat up in bed to look at Marcel directly in his eyes. She wasn't scared of him. He could get angry as much as he liked.

Marcel looked away from Amiah's piercing stare and then looked back again.

"Tell me the nightmare one more time and I'll tell you what I think." Marcel said.

"You know what happens already." Amiah replied.

Marcel and Amiah eyed each other warily for a minute before Amiah spoke up again.

"I hear his voice whisper my name Amiah, then I see his body above me naked for a few seconds before it explodes in front of me and I feel...I feel all his blood splatter over my body as real as I'm touching your hand right now." Amiah paused and held Marcel's hand.

Marcel squeezed Amiah's hand gently. "Go on, let it out."

"Then after a while all his blood clears away from my body and I see multiple Landon's standing around me exploding one by one. It's... I see myself trying to stop it happening but I can't...

I can't stop him exploding around me...I try to hold him, I try to speak to him, I try to tell him to stop but nothing works. It goes on for what seems like a long time but is probably 10 minutes." Amiah explained.

"How do you know it's 10 minutes?" Marcel asked.

"I estimate it's about that." Amiah said shrugging her shoulders. "It happens just like it's real and makes me feel totally sick."

Marcel squeezed Amiah's hand again. "Amiah you can handle it. Yes, it is scary but it's only scary because you still have an attachment to Landon. If you let that attachment go completely and fully, I promise you these nightmares will stop. Trust me." Marcel said.

Amiah held her head down.

Marcel softly and slowly lifted Amiah's chin up and looked at her in her brown eyes.

"Remember that each time you have this dream, you know the outcome. What's the last part of the dream you see before you wake up." Marcel inquired.

"The last part is the last Landon I see explodes." Amiah answered.

"Yes and..." Marcel said. "Go on..."

"The last Landon explodes but nothing comes out of him, unlike the others. I just hear a bang and then there is nothing there. I wish all the explosions could be like that." Amiah laughed nervously.

"You need to let him go Amiah. The dreams won't end until you have done this, I'm telling you." Marcel said. "What about telling Landon about us? Have you done that yet?"

"I don't see any point in telling Landon about us. We don't know how long this is going to last?" Amiah said quickly.

"And there you have it!" Marcel exclaimed loudly.

"There you have...Marcel where are you going?" Amiah asked.

Marcel had let go of Amiah's hand and got up off his bed. He walked away from Amiah and into the shower room, closing the door behind him.

Amiah rolled her eyes. He was the one who had asked her to repeat what happened in the nightmare and now he couldn't take it.

Men, Amiah thought.

Amiah got off the bed also and went into a different shower room in the same bedroom. Both Amiah and Marcel didn't say another word to each other as they separately bathed and got dressed ready to start the day.

Later that morning, in the meeting room at the Chi-Marcel mansion, everyone working on the RBV mission grouped together. This also included a team of specialized robots that were to assist directly with anything related to the RBV mission. The robots were individually specialized in a variety of tasks which included strength skills, fighting skills, health skills, rescue skills, takedown skills amongst others. For example, if there were ever a situation where the risks would pose a probable threat to human life, then the robots would be used. Robots were very useful but had disadvantages and faults just like all other highly skilled technology.

Amiah led the meeting and stood at the front of a virtual hover stage, in front of the Amiah Riders and the Chi-Marcels seated on virtual seats in front of her. The Onai twins were seated also on virtual seats on the hover stage where Amiah stood.

"Ok everyone, let's start. First of all, thank you to everyone present in this room for agreeing to be part of the RBV mission. I can't express fully in words how impressed and grateful I am for all the hard work that has been undertaken in the past 8 months or so. I also would like to extend my gratitude to the Onai twins and the Chi-Marcels for welcoming us into their mansion at very short notice. I can easily speak on behalf of all the Amiah Riders that we feel like the Chi-Marcel mansion will always be our second home. This means you can expect us to visit every other day, even when the new Amiah Mansion is completed." Amiah said.

The audience which consisted of the Amiah Riders and the Chi-Marcels laughed happily. Marcel grinned at Amiah, while Chima appeared expressionless.

Once the laughter had subsided, Amiah spoke up again.

"I'd also like to say welcome and thank you to our newest robot members of the RBV mission who have been specially designed to perform individual highly skilled tasks. These will be utilised on an 'as and when necessary' basis." Amiah explained.

The robots in the virtual meeting room, stepped forward, clapped for a short while before stopping and resuming their earlier position. Their earlier position being one where they all stood at the outskirts of the virtual meeting room, ready and primed for action.

Amiah looked over at Chima and extended her right arm towards him in an introductory gesture.

"Now, I think Chima has some new leads in RBV that he would like to inform everyone of. Chima." Amiah said.

Chima stood up quickly and walked to the centre of the virtual grey hover stage. He began to talk in detail about areas where he or other Chi-Marcels had sensed the presence of the Recathri alien. He showed the audience locations on a huge display virtual screen behind him. He clarified the exact amount of time which had been spent following up every lead to do with finding the Recathri alien. He described what he considered to be the best way to move forward with other leads, towards a successful completion of RBV. He gave dates and times for a new schedule of paranormal work activities, to help restore Brandon's vision. After a lengthy speech, that lasted over an hour, Chima thanked the audience for their hard work and sat back down.

There was a short 20 minute break, while everyone in the room discussed what they had just heard and other new ways to find the Recathri alien. It was also widely discussed how they could manage to get the 'stubborn' alien to give them the cure for Brandon's invisibility. During this break, Amiah and the

Onai twins came down off the hover stage to chat with their robotcycle rider teams. Both leaders were impressed by all the new ideas and also the challenges which had been overcome to acquire new information for RBV.

As the break came to an end, Amiah breathed a sigh of relief as she walked back on the hover virtual stage. The grey hover virtual stage lowered itself to the ground as she stepped on it. It did this with everyone who was allowed access to be on it. Therefore, there was never a problem with a person not being able to get onto a hover virtual stage, irrespective of how high it was.

Amiah breathed a sigh of relief because she felt satisfied that one day her invisible son Brandon would get an effective cure for his invisibility issue. She had heard all the new ideas from the Onai twins, the Amiah Riders and the Chi-Marcels and they were all good ones. Amiah smiled to herself. She also felt very proud and privileged to be in a room with so many talented and gifted paranormal, psychic and highly skilled robotcyclists. She glanced quickly over at Marcel and felt her cheeks grow warm.

And I'm dating one of the best of them, Amiah thought, the joint leader of the Chi-Marcels, Marcel Onai.

Marcel also returned back to his virtual seat on the grey hover virtual stage. He pretended to not notice any glances or looks of affection from Amiah. In Marcel's mind, one of Amiah's issues was that she couldn't let things go that needed to be let go. Landon, and Amiah's obsession with 'curing' Brandon should both be let go, Marcel pondered. Although Marcel would never say this to Amiah Lily or anyone involved in the RBV mission, he often thought it.

Marcel had observed Brandon many times when around Amiah or himself. Brandon seemed fine to Marcel. Ok, no-one could see the little kid but apart from that he seemed a very happy child. Brandon had clothes to wear so he could be identified by his family and the riders at the mansion. Brandon also had virtual body suits he could wear outdoors in public. Marcel wondered if the problem was more that Amiah couldn't see him, rather than invisibility being harmful for Brandon…

Marcel continued to ponder this in his head while only half-listening to Amiah and Chima speak excitedly about new information to do with RBV. Of course, it was fun getting naked with Amiah Lily, talented leader of the all-female paranormal and psychic robotcyclist club, the Amiah Riders. Yet, it was also becoming a problem recently with her recurring nightmares about her ex Landon Ross. Once again, Marcel wondered if Amiah's refusal to let go of Landon, whether she admitted it or not, was just another selfish act. Similar, to Amiah's refusal to allow her son to live his entire life, as an invisible human being.

Marcel kept his own nightmares to himself. He didn't see any point in talking about it to Amiah.

I'm a man. That's just what we do, Marcel consoled himself in his own thoughts.

Marcel had never mentioned to Amiah that he had seen and heard the spirit of his dead ex-lover Freeda, in the same room when they were making love. Marcel hadn't told Amiah of the time when he had a nightmare of being inside Freeda's body at the same time she died and experiencing the same terror. He hadn't told Amiah anything that would worry her, so why did Amiah feel like it was ok to disturb his peace of mind? Marcel pondered.

Secretly, the best part of the RBV mission according to Marcel Onai was the takedown and redistribute of the Recathri alien and the planet where the alien came from. Restoring Brandon's visibility was the smallest element of this mission to Marcel. Sleeping with Amiah Lily was another small, albeit very fun part of the RBV mission.

"Marcel, Marcel?" Amiah said repeatedly.

Marcel quickly snapped out of his daydream and stood up from his virtual seat.

"Right, my turn to speak. Thank you, Amiah, Chima." Marcel spoke quickly, to cover up the delay in replying to his name being called. He had not heard Amiah call his name because his mind was elsewhere.

"I'll get straight down to business. I know most of you are thinking of going out riding right after we finish on your lunch break. While you are out riding always remember to keep in mind the RBV mission and follow up any leads you have. It is vital that we succeed in RBV as soon as possible. The longer Brandon is without visibility, the longer the Recathri alien is roaming illegally on our planet Earth... the longer we are all in danger. Overall, we are doing this for Amiah's little boy. We are here to help Brandon." Marcel said confidently.

Amiah smiled admiringly at Marcel and Marcel smiled bravely back at her.

"As all of you are aware, I have Blazon who talks to me in my head. If the Recathri alien is nearby, Blazon lets me know and he also warns me of other things to do with the RBV mission. I trust Blazon. He has helped me with some very important leads towards finding and communicating with the Recathri alien. Furthermore, Blazon helped save Brandon from the Recathri alien suction hole." Marcel explained.

"Marcel, you saved Brandon that day. It was mainly you." Amiah interrupted.

"Amiah just told me it was me, not Blazon." Marcel said winking at the audience.

Some of the audience consisting of the Chi-Marcels and the Amiah Riders laughed.

Amiah laughed too.

"Ok. It was both of you that saved Brandon." Amiah said.

"The main thing babe, is that Brandon was pulled back at the right time. He's alive, healthy and with us today." Marcel said looking at Amiah.

Amiah nodded and smiled at Marcel.

Marcel turned to face the audience again. Inwardly, he believed he was at an advantage. Marcel was at an advantage to take whatever he wanted from whoever he wanted it from.

*****

12:15am. The next day.

Marcel walked through his Chi-Marcel mansion which he jointly owned with his twin brother Chima Onai. He had deliberately kept busy all day to try and distract his mind from thinking about Amiah and her recurring nightmares. Now however, it was a quarter past midnight and he was tired from riding around all day on his red robotcycle. He had enjoyed every moment of the ride and wished he could have stayed out longer. Yet, Marcel also knew that he shouldn't be hiding or running away from any woman and her issues.

I'm Marcel Onai. A man, he thought.

Marcel waited for the security virtual doors to disappear to allow him entry into his bedroom. Immediately upon entering his room, he could see that Amiah was once again having one of her nightmares about her ex-lover Landon. He stood grumpily watching Amiah roll around on his king size virtual bed. He noticed the sweat all over her beautiful brown naked body and the look of fear on her face. This was too much for Marcel to take. He didn't sign up for this. He wanted to be with the beautiful, talented, psychically gifted robotcyclist. He wanted the woman that was powerful, in control and sexy in the bedroom to come back.

Marcel turned around and headed back out of his virtual bedroom. He would have to rethink this Amiah situation. He walked around his mansion deep in thought for half an hour. He decided to go out by the pool and relax outdoors for a little while. He used the downstairs guest room, got changed out of his riding gear and put on a dark blue open shirt with green & black shorts. Later on, (when he felt ready) he would go back upstairs to his bedroom and Amiah. Maybe in a few hours or so or more… he pondered.

Marcel stepped outside into his outdoors pool area. He felt the sides of his lips curve upwards into a small smile of pleasure. He could see some of the women from the Amiah Riders talking and laughing by different sides of the pool. He didn't know there was a party going on. No-one had told him. He hadn't heard any sounds of people talking until he had stepped outside. Marcel glanced quickly behind him.

Invisible sound barriers were up surrounding the entire outside pool area.

Why hadn't he sensed that earlier? Marcel wondered, shaking his head a little. If Amiah Lily was beginning to 'cloud over' his psychic abilities, then he definitely didn't want her.

Marcel took a deep breath in to relax and exhaled slowly. Happily, he could see that a handful of his Chi-Marcel riders were outside with some of the women. As beautiful, sexy and talented as most of the Amiah Riders were, they didn't have no power that could compare to Amiah Lily. Marcel looked away from the women and an image of Amiah appeared in his mind. He heard a voice next to his ear which sounded just like Amiah. Amiah's voice near his ear was calling out to him.

"Marcel, Marcel, Marcel..." the voice of Amiah said sexily by Marcel's left and right ears.

Marcel focused on blocking Amiah for a few minutes and then her voice stopped speaking by his ears. Marcel grinned.

I am the man. I control this shiz, Marcel thought.

"Marcel! Hey, come and join us. Where have you been riding?" one of the Chi-Marcel riders called Jason shouted out.

"All over!" Marcel shouted back.

"Jelitoonaa!" Derek, another Chi-Marcel rider shouted over at Marcel.

Marcel walked over to Derek and Jason who were talking with Jan (an Amiah Rider).

"Jan." Marcel smiled at Jan. "Are my men behaving themselves?"

Derek and Jason laughed.

"We were talking about RBV actually, I'm glad you're here. I wanted to ask you about..." Jan began to say, but was interrupted.

"Hey, there was no need to put the invisible sound barriers up everyone. Me and my brother Chima and Amiah Lily, we are not slavedrivers. Enjoy yourselves! When you're not working that is." Marcel added quickly.

Everyone around the pool laughed and smiled. It was a good, chilled out atmosphere. The Amiah Riders and the Chi-Marcels deserved a break now and again. They worked very hard on the RBV mission and other missions at the same time. Marcel didn't really need to point out about the invisible sound barriers. He only wanted to shut Jan up. Marcel instinctively knew that Jan wanted to talk about the RBV mission with him and Marcel wasn't in the mood.

Marcel walked away from Jan, Jason and Derek. He took off his dark blue open shirt and threw it on the floor. Then, he made his way to the other side of the pool. At the other end of the pool, Marcel stepped in a virtual clear lift which lifted him to the top of his 10 meter virtual green diving board. Marcel ran to the near edge of the virtual green diving board and did a reverse pike somersault dive into the clear blue water below.

As Marcel's hands hit the water below, he saw a quick image of Freeda (his deceased ex-girlfriend). Opening his eyes wide underwater, Marcel saw Freeda again in the water, glaring at him with strange eyes that Marcel could not interpret. Upon rising up over the surface of the water, Marcel took in a big gulp of air and blinked a few times.

Freeda, he thought.

Marcel began to swim up and down the length of the pool for the next 30 minutes. Slowly, he felt his mind clearing of his worries about Amiah and Freeda. As Marcel swam again to one side of the pool, he noticed a woman about to dive off his virtual green diving board. She was curvy and petite with long brunette hair. Marcel eyed her curiously. He assumed that all the Amiah Riders would be able to dive and perform somersaults off the edge of a virtual diving board. He casually waited to see what this Amiah Rider would do.

Marcel watched the Amiah Rider dive off the edge of his virtual green diving board, just as if she had been professionally trained. It was a perfect rendition of the exact same dive that he had performed around 40 minutes ago. The woman with the brunette hair had performed a reverse pike somersault dive just like he had. Marcel raised his hands above his head and clapped loudly. He grinned at the Amiah Rider. He didn't know her name. He checked her aura and found out her name was Petra.

Petra could see Marcel grinning at her and she grinned back briefly before looking away. Petra knew that Amiah seemed so much happier now that she was in a relationship with Marcel Onai. She knew all Amiah needed was to forget about Landon and find someone else. Petra was happy for her. There was no way she would do anything but smile at Marcel. With this thought, Petra turned away from Marcel and began to swim in the other direction. She was in the middle of trying to get another of the Chi-Marcel riders to join her and Louise, for another threesome. They had been grieving over Garcen for months now. It was probably time for them to get on with their lives also. Seeing Louise talking and flirting with a few of the Chi-Marcel riders, Petra got out of the pool to join them.

Marcel frowned as he saw Petra turn to swim in the other direction after she had smiled at him. He wasn't married yet. There was no reason he couldn't talk to her. Marcel began to swim in the direction of Petra but soon found there was something blocking his way. Marcel tried to swim against the invisible screen that blocked him from swimming after Petra from different angles. Nothing worked.

Marcel did not panic. He is experienced in all kinds of psychic and paranormal phenomena. Of course, sometimes he got annoyed by some things that happened but never scared. Amiah's recurring nightmares annoyed Marcel, but did not frighten him.

Marcel read the aura around the invisible screen and sensed that it had the aura of Freeda. Marcel quickly sent a message to Freeda in his mind. This didn't always work like other forms of telepathic communication. It seemed to Marcel oftentimes, that the dead were more likely to refuse communication than the living. Although, the dead were always listening and watching...

"Freeda, let me through." Marcel said impatiently using his spirit communication abilities.

Marcel again tried to push through the invisible screen in front of him. It would not budge. Marcel looked around at the other Chi-Marcels and Amiah Riders outside the pool. Luckily, nobody was watching him in the pool. This would be embarrassing for his Chi-Marcels to see their leader not able to get through this invisible screen. Marcel grew irritated.

"Freeda! Why?" Marcel said via his spirit communication skills.

There was no answer from Freeda and she did not appear to Marcel.

"Freeda. Alright, have it your way." Marcel said in his mind to Freeda's spirit.

Marcel turned away from swimming in the same direction as Petra and swam backstroke away from the invisible screen. When he reached the edge of the pool, he spoke again to Freeda's aura which he could still sense near him.

"Happy now?" Marcel said in his mind to Freeda.

Marcel heard laughter from above and below him in the sound of Freeda's voice. It was happy laughter and brought a smile to Marcel's face. This was the laugh he remembered so many times he had heard Freeda laugh, during their good times together. The memories made Marcel want to continue to talk to Freeda.

"I love you Freeda." Marcel said in his mind to Freeda.

Freeda didn't reply but the laughter gradually faded away into nothing.

Marcel sensed that Freeda's aura had left him and a tear came to his eye. He rubbed it away quickly and got up out of his pool to return back inside. He needed a woman in his arms to make him feel good again. Freeda was gone and Marcel's heart felt empty. Empty and cold.

Marcel left his outside pool area without saying anything to anyone. He went in the guest room again downstairs and showered, dried his skin and got into a new t-shirt and shorts. Then, he made his way upstairs via a virtual lift to get to his virtual bedroom.

Marcel confidently strolled into his bedroom. He sighed a big sigh of relief when he saw that Amiah Lily was asleep peacefully on his king size virtual bed. Marcel silently got into the bed next to her. He stared appreciatively up and down her beautiful body but did not touch her. He did not want to wake her up, only to have her give him yet another rendition of the recurring Landon nightmare. Marcel closed his eyes and exhausted from the day, soon fell fast asleep.

Amiah Lily's eyes flew wide open as soon as Marcel had gone into a deep sleep. She looked at the virtual clock at one side of the room in the shape of a red robotcycle. The time was 3:15am. Amiah sat up in bed suddenly feeling wide awake. She remembered having a nightmare about Landon, but she also remembered dreaming that Marcel was outside swimming and diving in the outside pool. Instinctively, Amiah remote viewed the recent past of the swimming pool area at the Chi-Marcel mansion.

Marcel could block her in many ways, but Amiah never told him the ways that he was unable to block her psychic and paranormal skills. Amiah had still been able to remote view any part of the Chi-Marcel mansion even when the Onai twins believed they were blocking her. She kept this to herself. She could view the past, present and future of any place in the Chi-Marcel mansion. She only had to 'tune in', to view it using her psychic/paranormal skills.

Amiah used her psychic ability now, to remote view the past of the outside pool area at the Chi-Marcel mansion. She watched with pride, how Marcel had performed a reverse pike somersault off his virtual diving board.

This is my man, Amiah thought.

Amiah felt her cheeks grow warm and her lovebox get instantly wet. She felt like she was falling for Marcel Onai. It was only the recurring dreams of Landon exploding so violently, that prevented her from fully embracing her new relationship.

Amiah continued to watch Marcel with love and pride. Then she saw one of her Amiah riders called Petra. Petra dived off the virtual diving board and did the same reverse pike somersault as Marcel. Amiah smiled with even more pride and love. Her Amiah Riders were equally as skilled as any Chi-Marcel. She loved them first before any man. Her love for her Amiah Riders was different to her romantic love for Marcel. Marcel was her lover. The Amiah Riders were her best friends. She loved them all.

Amiah was just about to switch off from viewing the past history of the outside pool area, when she noticed Marcel banging on something blocking his way, in the pool. She could see him pushing against something in front of him. Amiah knew enough about paranormal experiences to recognise quickly that there was something there. There was something that both she and Marcel could not see with their physical eyes. Amiah used her spiritual eyes and saw a woman standing in the pool beside Marcel with a pained expression on her face. The woman had glistening brunette hair and freckled tanned skin. This woman moved from Marcel's left and right side, above and behind him.

Amiah recalled a time when Marcel had told her about his deceased ex-girlfriend Freeda.

Is this woman in spirit, the ghost of Freeda, Marcel's deceased lover? Amiah thought.

She watched with interest and curiosity, as the spirit of Freeda started to float around in the air above Marcel laughing happily around him. She watched a smile appear on Marcel's face and she could see the look of pure love in his eyes.

Amiah continued to watch the scene via her past-history remote viewing skills. She watched carefully as all of a sudden, the look of love disappeared from Marcel's face. It was replaced with a single tear which Marcel rubbed away. Amiah gasped silently as she sensed Marcel's aura had changed.

Marcel's energy field had changed to one which was cold and empty.

HIDDEN PASSIONS

Chima Onai sorted through piles of virtual paperwork on the dark red virtual desk in front of him. He frowned at what he read on a single piece of virtual paper with glowing green writing on it. He instinctively tried to tear up the piece of paper, but it disappeared in his hands before he could do so. Chima slumped forward on his virtual desk and laid his head down on the surface. He was totally exhausted. He hadn't been sleeping well for the past 3 weeks, as a new lead about the Recathri alien, had been keeping him at work constantly.

Chima raised his head up from the surface of the virtual desk and then lowered it down again. He had tried very hard to find the Recathri alien to obtain a cure for Amiah's son, ever since the beginning of the RBV mission. Nothing had worked for a successful completion of the mission so far. Chima thought that this mission could potentially be one of the hardest and most challenging missions ever, for himself, Marcel and the Chi-Marcels. He couldn't remember another mission in the history of the Chi-Marcels, that had taken as long as the RBV mission to reach completion.

He admired the dedication and work of the Chi-Marcels. Payment for the RBV mission had never been discussed. Everyone was basically working for free to help cure Amiah Lily's son. Although, Chima had not seen his Chi-Marcels work harder and more consistently than they were currently doing for RBV. His brother Marcel on the other hand…

Chima again raised his head up from the glowing surface of his virtual desk and then lowered it down again. Chima thought about how his brother had been doing less and less work since he had started dating the leader of the Amiah Riders. All his twin brother wanted to do was hang around her, ride his robotcycle and pretend to be listening to Blazon's voice in his head. Chima lifted his head up slowly and re-checked the pile of virtual paperwork now scattered in different places on his virtual desk.

Something didn't add up.

Chima could see that Marcel had recorded down various leads towards finding the Recathri alien, but Chima intuitively sensed negative energy whenever he read about his brother's 'work'. Chima trusted his intuitive skills 100%. The only explanation for the negative energy he sensed when reading the notes that Marcel had made, about the work he had done for RBV was that…

Chima dropped the virtual papers in his hand and pushed back on his hover chair sharply. His hover chair hit the virtual wall behind him and disappeared. Chima fell down a short distance onto the floor below.

"Hover technology." Chima grumbled out loud to himself.

He got up off the floor and a new hover chair appeared next to him. Chima sat down on the new hover chair and it moved towards the virtual desk in front of him.

His twin brother Marcel couldn't have done as much work as he had recorded down on the club's records. The energy that arose out of those records was one of insincerity and untruths. Chima's eyes narrowed. So, here was his twin lying on the Chi-Marcel records. This would not look good to the rest of the club if they knew about it, he pondered, it would demoralise them and cause disagreement within their group.

Chima looked up from the virtual paperwork in front of him and at the virtual door at the far end of his study room. He looked around the room to the left and to the right. He was alone.

Chima closed his eyes and picked up a piece of virtual paper in front of him. He focused on the energy which emanated from the words.

"A-ha." Chima thought.

His previous assumptions had been confirmed. Marcel was falsifying club records and over-exaggerating the amount of work he did daily on the RBV mission. Chima discovered this by using his past remote viewing skills. Marcel wasn't at as many places on the hunt for the Recathri alien as he described. Chima counted only two accurate entries out of over a hundred.

Chima opened his eyes again. He felt stunned. He couldn't understand why his brother did not see the seriousness of the RBV mission. He was supposed to be in love with Amiah Lily. Chima's findings would surely hurt Amiah and his brother's new relationship.

If Amiah only knew... What can I do about this? Chima thought.

Chima rejected any idea in his mind about informing Amiah Lily, that there were a lot of untruths in the work that Marcel claimed he was undertaking for RBV. He also rejected the idea of confronting his twin at this time. Chima needed to see how far and for how long his brother Marcel would keep up his lies and deceit. For the sake of the Chi-Marcels, he would need more evidence than just his past remote viewing. To get the whole of the Chi-Marcel's robotcycle club to believe him, he would need them to see clearly for themselves. It couldn't just be his word against his brothers.

Chima remembered how happy Amiah had been talking with Marcel only a few days earlier. He had overheard Amiah say how proud she was of all the 'extra' work that Marcel had done for her invisible son Brandon. Chima knew all the gossip about the story of Landon, and how it had taken Amiah years to move on and find a new love.

Surely, this news about Marcel will devastate her, Chima thought sadly.

Chima felt his heart pound loudly in his chest. The last thing he wanted to do was hurt Amiah Lily. He took pleasure out of seeing her happy, smiling and laughing. He told himself that Amiah was happy with the efforts towards RBV, and her relationship with his twin was not the main reason she smiled.

Chima waited for his heart to return to beating normally again. He called a robot member of staff, standing in the corner of the room to bring him some water. When the robot returned with a virtual tray containing a clear virtual glass of water, Chima grabbed it. The robot turned around and walked back to it's original position in the corner of the room. Chima drank down all the water in one go and soon felt his heart beating at a more normal pace again.

Suddenly, an image appeared in front of Chima's face. It was an image of his twin brother Marcel. He could see Marcel waiting outside the virtual door of his virtual study room.

"Come in!" Chima said telepathically to his twin brother Marcel.

However, Chima continued to block his brother from reading his innermost private thoughts as he had learned to do since they were children.

Marcel entered the large virtual study room and saw his twin Chima seated on a hover chair behind his virtual dark red desk. He had heard Chima's voice telepathically in his mind but he sensed that his twin was blocking him to a very high degree.

"Wow. I can barely sense that you are related to me with all the blocks you have up in your mind!" Marcel exclaimed humorously.

Marcel was in good spirits. Amiah had been much happier with him, since he had made up a story about Blazon communicating with the Recathri to come closer to the Chi-Marcel mansion. He would tell Amiah as many stories about Blazon as he liked, while blocking her so that she wouldn't know most of them were not true.

"We're identical." Chima replied dryly.

The identical twins stared at each other blankly before Marcel broke the stare and sat down on a virtual hover chair.

"What brings you here?" Chima inquired curiously. There was no way that his brother Marcel was here to seriously work on the RBV mission, Chima pondered. Marcel must be here for some other reason.

"Can't I come and see how things are coming along with the club records?" Marcel answered back.

"Here they are. Take a look for yourself." Chima replied and stood up off his virtual hover chair.

"No, no, I don't need to see them. As long as one of us has checked them... it's fine." Marcel said vaguely.

Chima sat back down on his hover chair and felt a pang of sadness for his twin brother. Since Freeda had died in that horrific robotcycle accident all those years ago, Marcel was different. Marcel acted the same around the Chi-Marcels and anyone else he interacted with, but Chima could sense the changes in his twin. Freeda's untimely death had shocked his twin Marcel to his core. As the days, months and years went by without Freeda, Chima could feel the aura around Marcel changing. The changes were not good.

Chima picked up a virtual sheet of paper from his virtual desk and pretended to be reading something on it. He didn't want to have this conversation with his twin right now. The most important thing was to keep working on the RBV mission. The next important thing was to keep Amiah Lily hopeful and optimistic, that eventually one day, her son's visibility would be restored.

Marcel didn't say anything. It was clear to him that his twin brother was ignoring him, and Marcel thought he knew the reason why. His twin brother Chima was equally as psychically and paranormally skilled as he was. Marcel knew there was always a possibility that his brother would sense that some of his paperwork didn't add up. Chima could gain this knowledge from using his intuitive senses, such as past history remote viewing. Marcel smirked to himself as he saw his twin brother hold his head down studying a map on a virtual sheet of paper.

Marcel smirked because he didn't give a sh*t what Chima could sense about him. Chima was too soft to say anything. Chima put the club first, similar to Marcel but in different ways. His twin brother would not be able to understand that he also did everything for the Chi-Marcel robotcycle club. Chima believed too much in the goodness of others whereas Marcel believed he could see right through people, robots, aliens and anyone else who crossed his path. Right now, watching his twin studiously read the virtual paperwork in front of him, Marcel could see right through him too. Yes, his twin was blocking him from reading his mind, but the actions of his twin brother told Marcel all he needed to know. Chima knew something, and therefore was blocking Marcel to a very high level, so that Marcel could not easily read his mind.

Chima continued to ignore Marcel while pretending to re-read over all the virtual paperwork which he had previously read before. There wasn't anything new for him to read but he didn't want to talk to his brother. He was not only wary of what he might say but also what he might do. Every time, he thought of Amiah Lily and her feelings being hurt or heartbroken over his two-faced brother, it made Chima angry. However, he figured that this wasn't the time or place to show any kind of anger.

Chima took in a long, deep silent breath, and released it just as silently and slowly as he had inhaled. He didn't know how much longer he could sit there around his twin, knowing that Marcel was turning a very good collaboration with the Amiah Riders, into a potential emotional roller coaster and unprofessional disaster. Chima's thoughts raced in his mind, and he could feel his twin strongly trying to enter into his head to read his thoughts. Blocking Marcel was becoming more difficult the longer Chima's angry emotions raced in his mind. Chima decided the best thing for him to do next was to leave his virtual study room.

"Where are you going?" Marcel shouted after his brother who was already halfway to the virtual door.

"Out for a ride!" Chima yelled back.

Chima exited his study room, and stormed out of the Chi-Marcel mansion to get to the virtual garage where his red robotcycle awaited him. Seeing his red robotcycle calmed him a little. Chima got onto his robotcycle and his virtual helmet activated. Chima sped off out of the Chi-Marcel garage and away from his home.

He had to get away from his twin brother. The way he felt, he didn't know what he was capable of.

A HIGHER POWER

Landon Ross returned back to his virtual prison cell with five security robots around him. When he got inside his cell, he threw himself down on his bed and punched a single fist into his pillow. He had just finished talking to his ex-girlfriend Amiah Lily. Amiah had explained all the reasons why she had started dating Marcel Onai, yet her choice of a 'new boyfriend' uneased Landon. Landon sensed a negative energy around Marcel Onai and didn't think that Amiah had chosen the right man to move on with. Landon still wanted Amiah to be with someone and forget about him but Marcel Onai...

Of all the men she could have chosen...Landon thought, she chose the cocky, egotistical joint leader of the Chi-Marcel riders. Why?

Landon wasn't happy. He did not show this to Amiah during their conversation a while ago. Part of him was relieved that Amiah was no longer alone in the outside world and that she had found someone to be happy with. However, Landon believed that the choice of new boyfriend was not going to have a happy ending. He didn't tell this to Amiah. He didn't have to. Amiah had stronger intuitive gifts than him. Landon knew that Amiah would find out who the real Marcel Onai was in her own time. By then, sadly, Amiah's heart would probably be broken all over again.

It wasn't Landon's place to disturb Amiah's happiness in her new lover. More than anything in the universe Landon wanted Amiah to be happy. Landon prioritised Amiah's well-being and happiness so much that he had made her promise to move on and find a new man. No appeal would get him out of prison.

Landon was in a high security virtual prison for life. He could never be with Amiah Lily in the outside world ever again. Unless...

... unless he made a virtual prison break, he pondered.

His motivation for getting out of Duneway high security virtual prison was now even higher than ever before. Landon had to escape from Duneway.

Landon had to get Amiah away from Marcel Onai.

*****

Amiah rode back from Duneway high security virtual prison on her black and gold robotcycle. Tears filled her eyes thinking over her recent conversation with her ex-boyfriend Landon. She quickly blinked them away. It had been highly emotionally stirring for her to tell Landon that she had met someone and was in a relationship. Amiah wished she could have told Landon everything she was feeling but she couldn't bring herself to do it.

Amiah omitted telling Landon about her recurring nightmares about him. She omitted telling Landon that she had seen the spirit of Marcel's deceased girlfriend around him. She omitted telling Landon anything that would make him think she wasn't happy. Amiah knew the reason why Landon had suggested that she move on and find love with someone else. Landon had her best interests at heart. Landon was in prison for life. There was no chance of him ever being released from Duneway. Landon did not want her to be alone waiting for him for the rest of her life. Landon wanted her to be happy and Amiah knew this.

So, in return Amiah tried to tell Landon things that would make it seem like she was happy. In reality, she wasn't happy all of the time. She still had random arguments and disagreements with Marcel, but Amiah mostly tried to tell Landon good news about her life. She kept Landon informed of updates about the RBV mission, whilst simultaneously blocking the paranormal security guards. She had told Landon about the Blazon alien that still resided inside Marcel's mind also.

When Amiah had told Landon about the Blazon alien inside

Marcel's mind, Amiah had noticed a brief look of disgust that passed over Landon's face. Amiah had ignored it at the time. Now, while riding back to the Chi-Marcel mansion on her robotcycle, Amiah thought about it again. She wondered if Landon thought it was unhygienic in some way to allow an unknown alien lifeform access to parts of the human brain. This thought made Amiah Lily laugh to herself. Landon could be so funny at times.

She had so many good memories with Landon. It was sad that they would never be together again. One of the things that comforted Amiah was of course their 'jelitoonaa', talented invisible son they shared together, Brandon Ross. Another thing, were her sweet memories of sexy times between her and Landon which sometimes appeared in her visions. In addition, she knew Landon loved to see her happy even if it was not with him. Landon truly loved her.

Only a man who truly loves me would put my happiness before his own, Amiah thought.

Amiah heard a distinct soothing ringing tone around both her ears. This signalled that a new vision was about to start very shortly. Amiah found a place to safely park her black and gold robotcycle and waited for the vision to appear. The vision appeared in front of Amiah after a few minutes. Amiah watched closely and curiously to find out what her newest vision would reveal to her.

In Amiah's vision, Amiah saw a bluish-green mist which she at first thought could be related to the Recathri alien. As the bluish-green mist cleared however, Amiah saw three men from the paranormal security team at Duneway virtual prison. Then she heard a loud explosion, the three men disappeared and were replaced by more bluish-green mist again. In the background, just before the vision ended, Amiah was sure she could hear Landon's voice saying her name "Amiah.".

Amiah wondered if this was a sign for her not to give up on Landon. Could there be a way that a successful rescue attempt could be made? she pondered. Was this vision to give her hope to keep trying to free Landon? Amiah racked her brain as to what else she could possibly do to free Landon form Duneway high security virtual prison. There had to be a way.

Suddenly, another soothing ringing tone was heard near Amiah Lily's right ear.

A double vision, Amiah thought.

A double vision was when two visions appeared to Amiah, one after the other, leaving very little time in-between. Amiah once again waited in anticipation of what her newest vision would reveal to her.

In the second vision that Amiah saw in front of her, Amiah saw the deceased Chi-Marcel rider Garcen and her new lover Marcel Onai facing each other. Then, the two men began to laugh loudly together. Amiah checked the energy around both men as she watched them laughing in the vision. There was no background scenery. It was as if the two men were standing in the middle of nowhere. Amiah used her spiritual eyes to try and find out where both men were located but someone was blocking her. Amiah guessed that it was possible both men in the vision, had blocked her from finding out their location.

This second vision made no sense to Amiah. She read the energy around Garcen and the energy around Marcel. She sensed some good and some bad, but everyone had both good/bad energy around them at different times in their life. It was up to the person how they interpreted their negative energy and how quickly they could overcome it. Amiah wasn't frightened by either of the men. She only felt confused as to why she was being shown such an unexciting image of two men laughing together. The two men belonged to the same robotcycle club, the Chi-Marcels. Amiah was sure they had shared many humorous moments of laughter at different times.

Why am I being shown this now? Amiah wondered, it doesn't make any sense.

The second vison was also taking a longer time to end than the first vision Amiah had seen. There was the leader of the Chi-Marcels, Marcel Onai, and his deceased rider Garcen just laughing with each other. Amiah considered if this vision was sent by Chima Onai to torment her. It wasn't tormenting her in the slightest however, only she felt a little confused.

Chima Onai, Amiah thought.

Amiah's mind wandered off to the twin brother of her new lover Marcel Onai, as she contemplated Chima's possible involvement. Amiah wondered if Chima had sent this vision to her because he was jealous of his brother perhaps. Or, maybe it was the other way around. Maybe, Marcel had sent her this vision to stop her thinking about Landon, so she could keep her thoughts focused more on him.

Amiah frowned. This did not give any explanation why the deceased Chi-Marcel rider Garcen was in this vision also.

What does Garcen have to do with any of this? Amiah thought, I barely knew him.

Finally, after what seemed like a very long time to Amiah, her second vision ended. Amiah activated her virtual helmet and started to continue her journey back to the Chi-Marcel mansion. She had only been riding for 10 minutes before she heard yet another ringing tone by both her ears. Amiah quickly scanned her environment for another safe place for her to pull up and park her black and gold robotcycle. She soon found somewhere safe and again waited for her new vision to appear.

It was not unusual for Amiah to have multiple visions at any time for varying lengths. Amiah would usually stop riding her robotcycle and park to watch her visions. She could continue riding while the vision appeared in front of her, but it would be her own fault if she missed important information. There was a chance she would miss important information because she would have to pay attention to the road and other vehicles, while also viewing the vision. Sometimes, if information in a vision wasn't understood the first time, it would not be repeated again. Amiah didn't want to take that chance. Not with the RBV mission. Amiah knew she needed to pay attention to all the visions that wanted to show her something.

In Amiah's third vision, she heard the voices of human men

and human women talking in a language she did not recognise. Amiah sensed it was an alien language and connected it with the same energy as the Recathri alien. She could read the location more easily this time. The men and women were talking from a location on the home planet of the Recathri alien. They were talking in the Recathri language. Amiah tilted her chin upwards deep in thought as she listened for more information from the vision in front of her. She didn't understand one word they were saying in the Recathri language, and she again sensed that someone was blocking her from finding out more.

"Recathri. It's Amiah. I need to talk to you now." Amiah said telepathically in English towards the direction of the vision.

She could sense more strongly now, the Recathri alien presence emanating from the vision. She considered if the Recathri had sent her this vision for its own purposes. Gradually, the view became clearer, and Amiah could also see the appearances of the people talking in the Recathri alien's language. Amiah saw about 12 humans, male and female from the ages between 21 and 35. They were standing alone on a hot red surface which bubbled and boiled with the heat rising from it. The humans did not appear to feel the heat and carried on talking in a relaxed manner.

"Recathri! I know you're there. Talk to me. It's Amiah." Amiah pleaded telepathically again with the energy she sensed was related to the Recathri alien.

The Recathri alien (if it was present) did not answer Amiah either telepathically, vocally or in any other way. Amiah sighed out loud. She wished Marcel was there so Blazon could interpret the vision in front of her and communicate with the Recathri alien.

"Marcel, it's Amiah. Can you ride to Maromsaesc Street straight away? I've sensed Recathri energy coming from a vision. I think the Recathri alien is nearby. I want Blazon to be here to talk to Recathri. Hurry!" Amiah instructed Marcel telepathically.

Back at the Chi-Marcel mansion, Marcel Onai was just about

to bite into a grilled cheese and tomato pita sandwich, when he suddenly heard Amiah's voice in his mind. He waited for Amiah to stop talking in his mind, and then bit into the pita sandwich which he held in both hands. Marcel thought that Amiah had some 'nerve' bothering him while he was eating.

Marcel raised his eyebrows. There were so many reasons he could make up to pretend that he hadn't heard Amiah's telepathic communication. It was all too easy. Marcel reached for his virtual glass next to him and took a long swig of beer. Amiah would have to wait till he was good and ready.

At Maromsaesc Street, Amiah sat on her black and gold robotcycle parked up, watching the vision. The third vision continued to play out in front her. She waited for a reply, any reply from Marcel. Amiah looked behind her further down Maromsaesc Street in the direction of the Chi-Marcel mansion. There was no sign of Marcel's red robotcycle. She wondered if her telepathic communication had got lost somehow and not been received by her new lover. So, Amiah again tried to talk to Marcel via mind-to-mind communication. Mind-to-mind communication meaning telepathic communication.

"Marcel Onai. It's Amiah Lily. I think I've got a new lead on the RBV mission. Meet me at the north point of Maromsaesc Street." Amiah instructed for the second time to Marcel via telepathy.

At the Chi-Marcel mansion, Marcel remained seated in the virtual dining room eating. He had heard Amiah call him for a second time in his mind, but there would be no proof that he had received the message. Marcel picked up another grilled cheese and tomato pita sandwich and continued to enjoy eating and drinking.

Amiah can wait, Marcel mused.

Amiah felt confused and a little angry. Marcel wasn't making a very good impression with her. Here she was in need of his help and assistance, and he wasn't even answering her calls. Soon, Amiah stopped that train of thought. It was certainly possible that Marcel did not in fact even receive her communication.

It was possible that the message got lost somewhere in the spiritual realm for higher or unknown purposes. As powerful and psychically/paranormally skilled as Amiah Lily was, she knew there was always a 'higher power' out there with even more control. This 'higher power' had exceedingly more control, authority and power.

Amiah giggled to herself as she considered talking to this 'higher power' to bring Marcel to her. As the short laughter exited her mouth, Amiah heard a voice which seemed to come from the sky above her.

"You see." said a male deep voice coming from the sky.

The area of Maromsaesc Street, where Amiah had parked her robotcycle, was empty. There were some hover vehicles moving along the virtual roads but there were no people anywhere.

Was that an alien imitating a human male's deep voice I just heard? Amiah wondered.

Next, Amiah heard a loud rumbling noise as a long crack cut across the surface where the 12 men and women stood around talking in her vision. It appeared to Amiah like an earthquake was happening in the vision. She worried for the safety of the unknown people in the vision but before she could see what occurred next, the third vision abruptly ended.

Amiah sensed that the Recathri alien energy was also gone along with the vision. She felt angry that Marcel had not been with her to help her connect with the Recathri alien. Why didn't Marcel hear her calling him twice? Had something happened to him while she was away? Amiah pondered and sighed.

She was just about to continue her journey to the Chi-Marcel mansion, when she sensed the reappearance of the Recathri alien again.

Without thinking about her next decision more than twice, Amiah chose to use another method of psychic interaction with Marcel called telekinesis. She focused on hitting various parts of Marcel Onai's body to attract his attention. It worked. Marcel quickly telepathically spoke back to Amiah and said the words: -

"Amiah! Stop it!"

Now that Amiah had Marcel's full attention, she again told him that she could sense the Recathri alien presence and wanted him to come immediately to Maromsaesc Street. Marcel said that he was 'on his way' so Amiah waited for him to turn up. In the meantime, Amiah spoke to her Amiah Riders and informed them also to come to the north point of Maromsaesc Street. She required all the 'back up' she could get. It was time that the Recathri alien was caught and brought to justice. It was time that little Brandon could be seen by all the people who loved him.

It took only 10 minutes before an impressive sight of the Amiah Riders, the Onai twins and the Chi-Marcel riders all turned up at Maromsaesc Street. They surrounded Amiah on their robotcycles as everyone listened to Amiah call out to the Recathri alien to give itself up.

Marcel heard Blazon talk to him in his mind. Blazon instructed Marcel to stand next to Amiah and call on the Recathri alien. Marcel did so and then it all happened very fast.

A large virtual silver cage appeared, containing a huge glowing green worm like creature with all different lengths of silver spikes coming out from every part of its body. Oval-shaped white eyes and an oval-shaped purple mouth appeared and disappeared randomly on different parts of the glowing green worm's body too.

Everyone watching erupted in shouts of excitement and happiness.

The Recathri alien had finally been caught.

Now, how long would it take for the Recathri to give the cure for invisibility to Amiah for her son Brandon? This was the next question on everyone's minds after the exuberant shouts had quietened down.

"We got it!" Jan said to Amiah. She rushed over to Amiah and embraced her.

As soon as Jan touched Amiah, Amiah had a sudden quick vision of Jan making love with Marcel. Amiah stood back from Jan's embrace. She couldn't believe what she had seen so clearly in her vision, but she trusted it. She stared at Jan coldly.

"You… you slept with Marcel?" Amiah said in disbelief.

Jan blushed and held her head down.

"I…Amiah…I'm so sorry. It…" Jan answered in a quiet voice.

Marcel didn't say anything. In a way he was pleased that Amiah had found out, after she had selfishly used her paranormal powers to beat him into coming to Maromsaesc Street. For Marcel, the novelty of being with Amiah Lily had started to wane when Amiah began having her recurring nightmares about Landon. Amiah had become more trouble than she was worth, in Marcel's opinion. Jan had been giving Marcel the adoration, respect and fun that Marcel knew he deserved.

There was silence around all the club members and leaders both male and female. The only noise came from the Recathri alien in the virtual cage.

Amiah had another vision of her invisible son Brandon and remembered what was most important to her.

If Marcel wants to go, he can go, Amiah thought.

She had more important things to attend to and she could not wait to see Brandon after years of not being able to. She thought of Landon and how happy he would be once Brandon was finally visible. With these happy thoughts filling Amiah's mind, Amiah addressed everyone.

"Can someone go back to the Chi-Marcel mansion and bring Brandon here?" Amiah shouted out to everyone listening.

"I'll do it." Jan suggested.

Amiah glared at her.

"I'll get him." Chima offered.

Amiah smiled at Chima kindly. Chima smiled back and rode back down Maromsaesc Street to bring Brandon to Amiah.

After 10 minutes, Chima rode up on his red robotcycle with Brandon sitting in front of him. Brandon was not wearing his virtual bodysuit as he normally did in public. Brandon was invisible to everyone, but his clothes and shoes could be seen.

"Marcel. Ask Blazon to tell the Recathri to cure my son." Amiah ordered Marcel.

"Ok." Marcel answered.

Marcel felt bored of this whole scene already, and desired (nearly as much as Amiah) for Brandon to be cured so he could get to the real part of RBV. The best part of the RBV mission, (according to Marcel Onai) was the takedown part of the Recathri alien's home planet. Blazon and Amiah did not have a clue as to Marcel's main priority and focus.

The Recathri alien in its worm like form with spikes, began fighting with something that none of the humans watching could see. All they could see was the Recathri attacking and retreating back into the corner of its virtual silver cage. The Recathri alien seemed to be losing and was being thrown about mercilessly. The fight between the Recathri and the invisible thing also present inside the virtual cage, lasted a total of 10 minutes. Then the large silver virtual cage and everything inside it disappeared. Thunder and lightning came from the sky but there was no rain. The lighting hit the ground 3 times in the spot where the virtual cage once stood.

"Mummy!" Brandon shouted out.

Brandon got off Chima's red robotcycle and ran over to Amiah.

Amiah turned around to see her son Brandon for the first time ever. To her elated delight, Brandon was fully visible to her and everyone around them. Amiah tenderly embraced Brandon and ran her hands through his hair and over the features on his face. Tears of joy filled Amiah's brown eyes and she grinned with love, happiness and relief. Brandon had her brown eyes and her nose shape. His smile and hair were like Landon's. Brandon was also the same beautiful brown skin colour as her. Brandon was perfect to Amiah in every way. She cried with great relief and happiness.

"Brandon, I love you! I'm so happy I can see you!" Amiah exclaimed joyfully.

All the robotcycle riders and the Onai twins began to shout exuberantly and victoriously. The RBV mission had finally been completed for most of them.

*****

Later on that evening at the Chi-Marcel mansion...

Amiah ended the virtual video call with Landon as Brandon waved and smiled goodbye to his father. She would bring Brandon to Duneway as soon as it was Landon's next visiting day. She didn't tell Landon what she had found out about Marcel. It wasn't the right time to talk about it with Brandon there listening.

"Amiah we have jelitoonaa news!" Saraina exclaimed excitedly.

"The new Amiah Mansion is ready! Wait till you see it. It's a million times better than the old version." Melissa explained.

Melissa showed Amiah virtual images of the new improved virtual Amiah Mansion. Amiah grinned again. Melissa and Saraina were right. The new Amiah Mansion is stunningly even more impressively beautiful and exquisitely designed (internally and externally) than the previous mansion. Amiah again felt a strong pride and deep admiration for the talents and abilities of her Amiah Riders.

Amiah stood up and hugged Melissa and Saraina. Brandon also got off his virtual seat and hugged the three women.

Chima Onai entered the virtual study room.

"Amiah can I speak to you for a minute. It's ok, if you're busy I'll..." Chima said

Melissa and Saraina exchanged knowing glances and winked at each other. Amiah noticed and smiled at them. It was like as if they could read her mind at times.

"Brandon, it's nearly bedtime. Do you know what? I think if we hurry, we can still get some ice-cream in the virtual dining room before you go to sleep. Would you like that?" Melissa suggested to Brandon.

"Vanilla ice-cream?" Brandon inquired.

"Yes, vanilla." Saraina replied.

"Yes! Mummy can I go now?" Brandon asked Amiah pleadingly.

"Well..." Amiah paused teasingly. "Of course you can son.

Mummy will come and meet you upstairs in a little while."

"Yeah! Ice-cream!" Brandon sang out happily as he walked out of the virtual study room with Saraina and Melissa holding his hands.

Amiah was now alone with Chima. She waited expectantly for him to speak first.

Instead of speaking, Chima took Amiah softly in his arms and kissed her lovingly on the lips. Amiah responded with equal enthusiasm, and they kissed intensely while gently caressing each other. Gradually, their kisses and caresses became more passionate and Chima lifted Amiah up to sit on his waist. Amiah laughed happily as Chima twirled around in a circle whilst still carrying Amiah.

Chima laughed along with her.

Chima Onai, Amiah thought excitedly.

This time, Amiah felt deep within her soul that her new love with Chima would last a lifetime. It was a definite unquestionable strong sense that could not be denied. A higher power had brought them together.

As Amiah laughed and kissed Chima, she thanked the higher power in her mind that so many good things were happening all at once to her.

Amiah heard a voice next to her left ear, which said the single word "God" in a quiet female voice.

Amiah smiled and spoke telepathically to anyone out there who could hear her in the universe...

"Thanks God." she said.

CONNECT WITH THE AUTHOR

You can connect with the author Wenda S Parsons on the following social media pages: -

Instagram: **wendasparsons**

Twitter: **@ParsonsWenda**
Facebook: **Wenda Parsons/Wenda S Parsons**
Linked In: **Wenda S Parsons**
Tik Tok: **Wenda S Parsons**

OTHER BOOKS BY WENDA S PARSONS

THE UNI OF MAROMSAESC – A Paranormal Futuristic Fiction novel.

Available on Amazon.